SKYLINE

SKYLINE

David Scott Milton

G. P. Putnam's Sons
NEW YORK

For my father, my brother, the memory of my mother,
and Sheila, my patient, loving wife.

Acknowledgments

*I wish to thank Michael Gruskoff for his belief, ideas, and boundless enthusiasm.
Without him the book never would have been written.*
Sarah Ann Fox provided a keen critical eye. Her suggestions were invaluable.
Stella Gardiner performed much fine and detailed research.
*Nancy Moon located an obscure volume on Benny Leonard which had become an
obsession with me.*
Christine Schillig gave inestimable help in shaping and clarifying the work.
*My editor, Phyllis Grann, showed me what was lean in the book, what fat, and
how to turn it all into muscle. I am enormously grateful.*

DSM
January 1982

The author would like to thank Warner Bros. Inc. for permission to reprint the lyric from "Will
You Love Me in December as You Did in May" by James Walker and Ernest Ball, © 1905 (Re-
newed) Warner Bros. Inc. All rights reserved.

Library of Congress Cataloging in Publication Data

Milton, David Scott, date.
  Skyline.

  I. Title.
PS3563.1448S57   1983   813'.54   82-5209
ISBN 0-399-12599-X   AACR2

Printed in the United States of America.

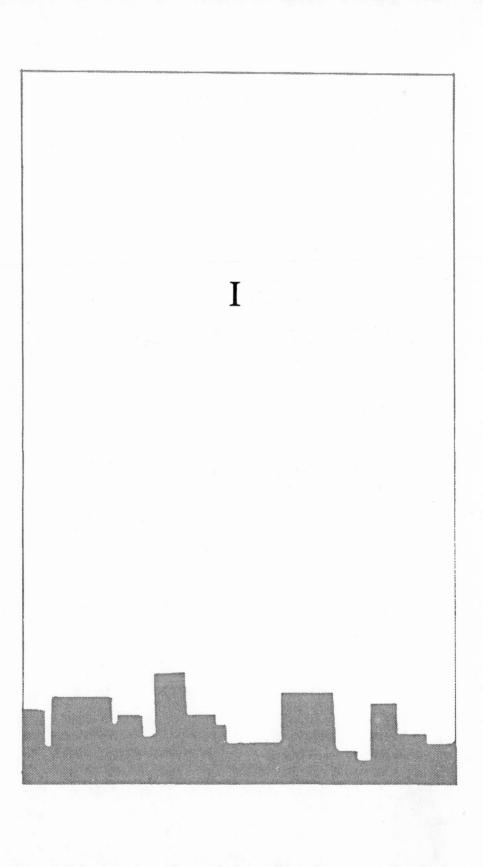

I

1

At dusk Mike Roth, leader of the Ludlow Street Nobles, walked his gang the distance between his neighborhood on the Lower East Side to South Street and the Brooklyn Bridge. The night was muggy. A haze hung over the East River.

Mike Roth was nervous. His hands were sweating. He could feel his heart pounding in his chest, and it seemed to him louder than his footsteps on the cobblestone street, so loud he was sure everyone could hear it.

There was to be a fight, one-on-one, between Mike Roth and a kid by the name of McGrath. Mike Roth was fifteen, small, dark. McGrath was a year older, the leader of the Young Dusters, an Irish gang over in Greenwich Village. He was bigger than Mike Roth. He had a reputation for being very tough.

Earlier, there had been name-calling and shoving between the two gangs on Hudson Street and it had been decided that the two leaders, Roth and McGrath, would settle it between them.

They had agreed to meet that night at the Fulton Street docks.

Damn, Mike Roth was afraid. It was always like this before a street fight, this corrosive, terrible fear. Damn!

The Young Dusters laughed and joked as they moved down Lower Broadway heading for Fulton Street. Tony McGrath, though, did not laugh. He was annoyed. How had he been roped into this fight?

He had worked all night loading produce in the Gansevoort Market. After, he had gone to McMahon's speakeasy on Clarkson Street to do some cement work: Prohibition had come in the first of the year and the owner, John McMahon, was turning the place into a fortress, adding concrete walls, putting up steel doors.

It had been noon when he finally got to bed, and then Jack Foster had awakened him with news that the Yids were looking for trouble on Hudson Street.

Why had he listened to him? He was the bastard son of a Bowery whore, and not even a Duster. He was always stirring up trouble. He had come over the roof and down a drainpipe and into Tony's bedroom to awaken him. That was Jack Foster's way. Thin, blond, a year younger than Tony, with a pretty face marred by bad complexion and rotting teeth, he was like a rat, scurrying through Lower Manhattan, always pitting people against each other.

And so now Tony would be fighting this Jewish kid called Roth.

The Young Dusters were nearing the Fulton Street docks. Tony began to sing: *"My Name Is MacNamara, I'm the Leader of the Band."* The rest of the gang joined in. He told himself he was not afraid. This kid Roth looked too smart to be a fighter. No, he wasn't afraid. But his hands were perspiring, and that made him angry.

The Nobles came to the Fulton Fish Market in the shadow of the Brooklyn Bridge. The market was dark now, but the streets stank with the residue of the day's use. The only sign of activity was across South Street at Sweet's Restaurant, where cabs filled with uptowners came and went.

Mike Roth's mouth was dry. He was perspiring, and it wasn't only the evening's heat that was the cause. His fear shamed him and the fight would be as much with his own fear as with the Irish kid from the Village.

The dock area was deserted, and secretly Mike prayed that the Dusters wouldn't show up.

The Ludlow Street Nobles gathered at the base of one of the immense granite bridge supports. "How's your breathing, Mikey?" asked Nig Kottler, one of the Nobles.

"Good. I feel good." He did not feel good. He felt afraid. What was he fighting for? How had he been forced into it?

A younger Jewish kid from the neighborhood had been beaten up, but no one had seen the kid, no one knew his name: only Jack Foster, the *mumser* and a *goy*. Foster had come to them early in the day to say the Young Dusters wanted their asses. Foster was always trouble, and still they had gone along with him.

It had been hot and everyone had been feeling edgy. A good fight would clear the air. Only Mike had his doubts.

"Here they come!" Crazy Saltz yelled. Down the center of South Street came Tony McGrath and the Young Dusters. They moved along the fish market beneath the bridge, whistling and singing as they came.

"Warm up, Mikey," Yoodie Greizman said. "My cousin Zummy done some boxing. He says you got to get your muscles warm."

Fear stirred in Mike's stomach. He began to dance around, trying to get loose.

The Young Dusters paused before the Nobles. Mike Roth danced and shadowboxed. "A regular Benny Leonard," one of the Dusters said derisively. Tony McGrath smiled. *"Oh, my name is MacNamara, I'm the leader of the band,"* he sang.

Tony took off his jersey. He was larger than Mike, and his body was thickly muscled. Feeling absurdly inadequate, Mike took off his shirt also. His ribs and collarbone jutted prominently from his thin body.

Yoodie Greizman spoke with the Dusters. "Just the two of them, fair fight. They fight until one of them calls quits or drops. Just fists. No biting, no kicking, no saps, no brass knucks."

"We fight fair as the other guy," said one of the Dusters.

"I have no quarrel with you," Tony said to Mike. "I don't know how this hey-rube come up."

"I got no quarrel with you, neither," said Mike.

"The sheenie's yellow-bellied," one of the Dusters said.

"Who you calling a sheenie, pig-faced mick," Crazy Saltz screamed, ready to tangle.

"Mockie bastards!"

"You hear that? You got to fight 'im, Mikey," Nig Kottler yelled out.

"I don't want this fight, neither," said Tony. "But we got to do it now."

"C'mon, then. Let's go!"

The two gangs headed toward the water. Empty packing cases, reeking of fish, were stacked at the water's edge, and Mike and Tony moved to an area between the cases. Lights from the bridge cast a yellowish glow over the area.

Mike Roth turned to face McGrath. McGrath hit him, a hard, cracking punch which brought tears to his eyes. Before he could get off a punch of his own, a barrage of blows drove him against a packing case. He felt blood spurt from his nose, and the ground tilted at a crazy angle underneath his feet.

He could hear Nig Kottler's hoarse voice screaming: "Fight 'im, Mikey! Fight 'im!"

He lowered his head and dived toward McGrath. McGrath continued to slam at him, and his fists were hard as stones. Slashes of red streaked his vision and he tried to grab McGrath. This is one tough punk, Mike thought, fighting to hang on. Another punch cracked his head; he felt as though he had been hit by a baseball bat. He suddenly realized he was on his knees.

He could see McGrath's brogans dancing in his view. "Kick the sheenie, Tony! Kick 'im!"

"Get up, Mikey! Fight 'im!"

"You had enough?" McGrath said, poised above him.

Mike shook his head.

McGrath backed up and permitted him to get to his feet.

"Hit 'im, Mikey! Hit 'im!" It was Nig Kottler screaming, his voice desperate. Mike burned with shame. McGrath had wrecked him, bloodied his nose, before he could even get in a single lick.

He circled around McGrath, struggling to clear his head. His face was numb. McGrath was blurred in his vision. He couldn't seem to get enough breath. He felt as though he was about to throw up.

McGrath watched him, his gaze dark and serious, muscles of his neck and shoulders tense, right hand cocked ready to punch.

Mike tried to go in, but before he could wing off a blow, McGrath's right whacked him. He caught the punch on the forehead, and blotches of red danced in his vision again. McGrath followed up with a flurry of blows, but Mike moved away, eluding them. He circled back out of McGrath's range until the red streaks faded.

"Come on, you yellow sheenie, fight!" a Duster yelled.

"Fight 'im, Mikey! C'mon, fight!"

Mike stopped short, pivoted. He ducked low and ripped a barrage of blows to McGrath's stomach. The Irish kid grunted and tried to back off. Mike brought his hands up and landed two hard punches to McGrath's head.

McGrath blinked and tried to shake the blows off, and came back in swinging. Mike moved back out of range again.

McGrath was breathing hard now and he looked annoyed, and Mike felt better. He knew he had hurt him. He was beginning to get the feel of the fight.

McGrath charged in, punching wildly, and Mike continued to move back, keeping his fists in McGrath's face.

McGrath stumbled off balance and Mikey charged him and pounded in two good shots to the stomach. McGrath tried to push him off, but Mike winged a punch to the mouth. Tony backed up and Mike continued after him. He pressed McGrath against a packing case and slammed his head with good, solid cracking punches. His head went from side to side and he looked surprised and there was a hint of fear in his eyes.

Mike's arms burned with fatigue. He continued to punch out. He was soaked with perspiration, and on the rim of his vision he could see blood on his belly. He assumed it was his own, but he couldn't be sure.

He felt as if he could not punch anymore. He could not get enough air. He felt like he would fall from lack of air and the terrible burning in his muscles, and still he continued to punch out at McGrath. Some found their mark; as many missed. A few slammed off the packing case, and his knuckles were smeared with blood.

McGrath lunged off the crates and leaned on him. He was bleeding. Blood streamed from his mouth as he grappled with Mike.

Mike slipped on the greasy dock and went down, and McGrath fell on top of him. They rolled around on the oily planking, the stench of fish guts sour in their noses and mouths, and they kept punching and clawing at each other.

Tony tried to get up, but Mike wouldn't let him go. He punched out, and McGrath fell backward, sprawling.

"Get up, Tony! Get up!"

"You got 'im, Mikey!"

Tony tried to rise once again. He pushed himself at Mike, and Mike banged his head over and over with hard, desperate punches. McGrath grabbed a hold on his belt buckle with one hand; with the other he grabbed Mike around the neck and hung on.

Gasping for breath, both of them clawed at each other on the dock planking, slapped ineffectual punches, kicked.

A siren wailed in the distance, came closer. Angry, ashamed, Tony punched out wildly.

He had no strength left in his arms, and still he continued to punch away. He got in one or two blows but couldn't be sure if they had done any damage. He could see the streetlamp on the bridge above, and it bobbed in his gaze and the bridge seemed to be spinning around and the dock planking beneath him was spinning and he felt sick to his stomach. Fists were cracking against his skull, but he couldn't feel them. He was all numbness and fatigue, and he just hung on.

They were on their feet again. They came together and then fell to the dock once more, thrashing at each other, dripping blood, fish mess, sweat.

McGrath prayed to get in one more punch, but he couldn't lift his arms. Mike struggled to rise. He couldn't make it. He went forward on his knees, still slapping blows at McGrath.

Now the siren was very loud, and suddenly the area at the water's edge was flooded with light from the headlamps of a police car. Two policemen moved between the packing crates. They watched, amused, as McGrath and Roth continued to slap at each other, moving with agonizing slowness, slipping on the greasy planks. "Come on, Tony, come on!" one of the cops said, an Irishman from the West Village.

McGrath threw himself toward Roth, swinging, missed him, and went down on the dock and could not rise. He lay facedown. He tried to roll over but couldn't make it.

The cops were smiling. "What kind of mick are you, Tony?" the Irish cop said. McGrath tried to speak but couldn't. Mike sat on the dock and gagged; nothing came up. "I never thought I'd see the day," the Irish cop said.

"This kid is tough," McGrath said at last, barely getting the words out.

Using a packing case for support, Mike managed to get to his feet. He picked up his shirt and began to wipe away the blood from his face and chest.

"You're tough, Mike," Tony said.

"You're tough yourself."

"What started it?" the second cop said.

"They beat up one of our boys," said Mike.

"We never did," Tony said.

"Jack Foster said—"

"Jack Foster, that weasel," the Irish cop said. "You should have more sense than to listen to that whoreson runt."

They heard laughter from above. Jack Foster sat on a thin bridge span. He had been watching the whole time. He kicked his legs out in the air and howled with shrill laughter. Then he clambered up to the roadway level, dropped his pants, and flashed his ass at the kids below before fleeing into the night.

2

"What happened, Mikey?"

"Nothing."

"You been fighting again?"

Mike entered the kitchen to his apartment. Florence, his mother, was giving his sister a bath. The tub was in the kitchen.

"You're red and black all over, Mikey," his sister said. "You look like a beet." Ruthie was nine years old, frail and dark, a sickly child. She smiled. Her smile had a forlorn quality, a sadness to it.

Mike had been in bed all day. He wanted to get up, but had been unable to make it. His body was a mass of pain and bruises.

Florence Roth shook her head, tutted. "When your father sees you, Mikey. When he sees you." A thin woman in her forties, she looked much older. Despite having come to the United States as a young woman, she still spoke with a heavy accent.

Mike took up a large drawing pad and some pencils from a cupboard next to the tub. He started for the door. "Not too late, Mikey," his mother said. "We'll be eating soon."

The sun was setting, but the city continued to steam. Mike left the apartment and took the steps of the tenement slowly to the roof. The pain was terrible in his legs, his back, his arms. Jesus, that McGrath, Mike was thinking. What a beating!

He wondered if Tony was also suffering, and decided he must be. Mike had gotten in some beautiful licks.

He considered what his father would do when he saw him. Charlie Roth didn't object to his fighting: he did his share of it himself. He did object to his son losing, though, and Mike was sure he didn't look like a winner. The toughest part of losing a fight was the threat of a beating from his father afterward.

He moved to the roof of the building. When the heat, the press of people in the streets, the closeness in his apartment, became too much to bear, he would make his way to the rooftop. He would sit there for hours, sketching in his pad, feeding the pigeons, doing his Eugene Sandow strongman exercises.

He sketched the skyline, bridges, elevated trains, trolley cars. It was the only time he was truly at peace with himself and the world around him.

Yiddle November, a local tough guy who ran a gambling house over on Allen Street, was on the roof tending to his pigeons. Mike's brother, Harry, and several friends were with him.

Harry was dark and stocky, a few years older than Mike. He hung out with a crowd of neighborhood tough guys. They wore precisely pressed trousers hiked up, colorful suspenders, high collars open at the neck, derbies.

Yiddle was a large, sad-looking man who seemed to become human only when he was with his birds. Often Mike would see him on the roof, and he talked about his pigeons, their loyalty, their uncanny ability to always find their coop.

He stood at the edge of the roof now, whistling the pigeons back to the coop. They flapped and wheeled in the sky, then dived down to the roost.

In the west the sky was a muddy salmon color where the sun had just disappeared. The air was thick and gritty, and so heavy it was like trying to breathe syrup.

Below was Seward Park. Beyond, the lights of the Williamsburg Bridge spanning the East River could be seen through the evening's haze.

As Yiddle handled his pigeons with his great ham paws, holding them with solemn delicacy, examining their legs and the undersides of their wings before placing them in the coop, Harry and his three friends watched without talking.

Mike looked on from a distance. He knew better than to come around Harry when he was with his gang. Harry saw him and waved him over to the group. "Yiddle, this is my kid brother, Mikey."

"I know Mikey," the old-time gambler said. "I see him up here doing his drawings. You ever draw my pigeons, kid?"

"Naw."

"He likes to draw buildings mostly," said Harry.

One of Harry's friends laughed quietly. His name was Ben and he was only a year older than Mike, but he hung out with the big boys. He had a reputation for cunning and viciousness, and even Harry was a little afraid of him. "You know Benny Siegel, don't you, Mike?"

"Yes."

"And Little Farvel and Shadows . . . ?"

Mike Roth nodded at his brother's friends; they hardly looked at him.

Mike felt uneasy for his brother. Farvel Kovalick, Shadows Kravitz, and Benny Siegel were known as *shtarkers,* tough guys who earned their flashy clothes, ornate rings, and stickpins by shaking down neighborhood shopkeepers and peddlers. Harry, essentially a coward, thought he gained status by running errands for them. They kept him around for laughs.

"Mikey leads the Ludlow Nobles," Harry said. "You hear about what happened yesterday?"

"I heard something about it," said Yiddle.

"Mikey and the Nobles went right up Hudson Street and challenged the Young Dusters. He fought this guy McGrath down by the docks last night."

Ben smiled. He was a dazzlingly handsome kid with large, bright blue, feminine eyes. There was something not right in his smile, something un-connected to what he was smiling about. "Looks like you took some lumps."

"I gave some, too."

"I heard all about it," Ben said. "Jackie Foster told me."

"That *mumser*," Louie Kravitz said.

"The Young Dusters, what are they?" Yiddle November said. "They suck hind titty. The old Hudson Dusters, they were rough ass. Monk Eastman would clean up on them, though. Monk and I would clean up on them. Ask anybody."

"Monk's out of prison," Harry said.

Ben laughed. "He should have stayed there."

"Don't mess with Monk," said Yiddle.

"Is that right," Ben said.

"He'll teach you. He'll teach you good."

"I can't wait. I want to be teached."

"Yeah, he'll teach you, all right," Yiddle November said. He started across the rooftop, moving with a heavy lumbering gait. "C'mon, you guys'll come with me. You'll watch some *stuss* over at my place." *Stuss* was a Yiddish gambling game popular on the Lower East Side.

"Not you, Mikey," Harry said.

"I'm almost as old as Ben here."

"But Ben got more *tsechel*," Little Farvel said. "He would have hit this McGrath with a baseball bat."

"With a thirty-eight," Shadows Kravitz said.

"Hey, leave the kid alone," Harry said.

"Watch your mouth," said Ben, suddenly turning on Harry. "You talk with a big mouth to your mother or father, not to my friends."

"You want to start something with my brother?" Mike said.

"Mikey, stay out of it," Harry said, nervous.

Ben glared at Mike, who did not look away. "If I start with you, Mikey, you won't just have puffed eyes."

"Anytime," Mike said.

"He doesn't mean that, Ben," Harry said.

"I like Mikey," Ben said, suddenly smiling. It was a dazzling smile. "He has balls. You ought to borrow a few from him, Harry."

Yiddle was at the door leading from the roof. "Come on, don't act like a bunch of kids. Mikey, go down and help your mother. Be a good son to your mother, Mikey. Tell her Yiddle November said you should be a good son." He peeled off a bill from a roll in his pocket. "Harry, run off and get us some cold cuts. I like cold cuts when I'm playing *stuss*." The old-time racketeer left the roof, followed by Harry and his friends.

Mike sat for a while sketching. The skyline to the east was dark now, and he drew the silhouette of buildings, bridges, smokestacks, and felt a sense of peace in the sharp outline, the precision of the work.

"Mi-key! Mi-key!" It was his mother calling. Her voice sounded to him from the fire escape below, through the din of family arguments, the creak and clop of horse-drawn carts, a knife sharpener's harangue.

"Get your father from downstairs," Florence said when he returned to the apartment. "Dinner's almost ready." A large pot of cornmeal mush, *mama-liga,* bubbled on the wood stove.

Mike hurried down the tenement stairs to the basement.

Charlie Roth, a carpenter, was hunched over his workbench. He did not acknowledge Mike when he entered.

Mike stood at a distance and waited.

His father was a large, powerfully built man with a thick black mustache and perpetually scowling expression. He surveyed his work. Then, muttering to himself, he went back to it, scraping angrily at a section of wood.

He was not a happy man. Orphaned at an early age, he had come to America from a small town in Rumania expecting much. He had not gained it.

In exchange for doing repairs in the building, the landlord had given him the basement area for his workbench. He had no steady job and was forced to pick up work wherever he could. Lately he had been working as a roofer.

He had a violent temper and was known among the greenhorns on the Lower East Side as Charlie the Meshuggener—a gambler, a drinker, a brawler. He was extraordinarily powerful—in his youth he had been a blacksmith, then a circus strongman—and would never back off from a fight. With all his faults he was fiercely honest and had nothing but contempt for the gangsters and ward heelers who dominated the life of the immigrants on the Lower East Side.

His cellar workshop was his sanctuary, a chaotic jumble of materials: pieces of board, kegs of nails, tools of all sizes and shapes. In one corner he had built a shed; inside was a large metal tub. In the tub he made his own wine, and the whole area reeked of fermenting grapes.

A single bare light bulb burned from the ceiling.

"Dinner is ready," Mike said.

Charlie Roth did not look at his son. He continued to work with a scraper to bevel the edge of a shelf; he was building a cabinet from an armoire he had found abandoned on the street.

He stepped back to study his work again. "It's good. Good," he muttered. "But who cares? No one cares about nothing. They just want to keep Charlie Roth down. I spit on them, *goniffs,* chiselers."

He moved to an enamel washbasin and scrubbed his hands. He scrubbed for a long time, using the most abrasive soap on the market; nothing seemed to get at the tar and pitch embedded in his skin. The materials of the roofer's trade were a constant rebuke to him. He hated the griminess of his hands, but he could not get them clean. When he dressed to go out in the evenings, he always wore gloves.

He looked directly at Mike now. He scowled. "You had a fight?"

"Yes."

"You look like that, you didn't win."

"He looks worse."

His father cocked his hand as though he would slap out at Mike. Mike flinched. His father waved in disgust and moved out of the basement. Mike followed, burning with anger and shame.

In the kitchen upstairs, Mike's mother had set the table. Dinner was Rumanian *mamaliga* served with goat's cheese. They had it most evenings; it was cheap and filling. When times were good, they would have it with stuffed cabbage or *carnaltze,* ground beef heavily seasoned with garlic. Times were not good these days.

"Where's Harry?" Charlie said.

"He went to see a man about a job," said Mike's mother.

"Sees! This and that he's always seeing. A paycheck he never sees. He wants to work, he should work with me on the roofs."

"He wants a different kind of job," Florence said.

"Sure. He wants the kind of job where he has a half-dozen *kurvas* working for him."

"I wanted him to stay in school—"

"You, little one, eat."

Ruthie was dabbling in the creamy yellow mush on her plate. "I'm not hungry," she said.

"She's not feeling well," Florence said.

"What's the matter, little one?"

"I don't know. I'm just not hungry."

Charlie put one arm around his daughter and lifted her fork to her mouth. She nibbled at the cornmeal without interest.

"Eat it, eat it," Charlie said impatiently.

"Papa, let her alone," said Mike.

"Butt out, you hear me? I want you to start eating!" he yelled at Ruth.

The child began to cry softly. "Enough!" Charlie yelled. They went through the rest of the meal in silence. Ruth continued to dabble with her food.

Charlie downed two glasses of sweet Rumanian wine. He sighed and muttered to himself. "They want to keep me down. All of them."

"Who wants to keep you down?" Mike said, still furious at his father for having raised his hand to him earlier, for having yelled at Ruth.

"Butt out, mister."

"You're always saying they want to keep you down. Who?"

"You and your brother know. You see them all over this place. *Vantzes.* Gangsters. Pimps. I heard about a place in South Dakota—nothing but Jews, but good farm people. I know farmwork. They'd welcome me with open arms. Not like these *vantzes* down here. If I could just get a piece of land, I'd show them. I'd show everyone."

"Why don't you go there, then? Go to South Dakota," Mike said.

"Mikey," his mother said.

Charlie set down his fork and glared at Mike. The muscles in his forearm stood out in thick cords. "One word," he said quietly.

"You're always talking about a farm someplace, South Dakota. Go there."

Charlie slapped Mike hard across the face. Mike stared down at his food. He could feel tears coming to his eyes, but he blinked them away. He would not give his father the satisfaction of seeing him cry.

"Charlie," his mother said.

Charlie stood up. He flung his plate against the rear wall of the kitchen. The plate shattered. He kicked his chair over. "I'm not killing myself with work to get back talk from a punk!"

"Charlie, Charlie . . ."

"He's a punk with no respect. Him and his brother. This is Mr. Punk here, and the other one Mr. Pimp."

"Okay, Charlie." Mike's mother got up and began to pick up the shards of broken dish. Ruth had begun to cry again; she pursed her lips and fought not to show it. Her whole body shook with sobs.

Florence gathered Ruth to her and attempted to quiet her. Charlie left the kitchen. Florence looked over at Mike and shook her head. "Why start with him?" she said. "He's an unhappy man. Why start?"

Mike said nothing.

Charlie returned to the room. He had changed into a dark, rumpled suit. He picked up a pair of black leather gloves and a derby from a shelf next to the door. He donned the gloves and hat.

Without a word he moved out of the apartment and down the stairs to the street below.

Florence held her daughter. Mike went to the kitchen window. He could see his father hurrying off toward the West Side.

The night air was very still. No breeze blew.

After dinner Rose Ann McGrath, Tony's thirteen-year-old sister, sat with her young brothers in the living room of their railroad flat on Hudson Street and began a story for them. The boys—Emmett, eleven years old, James nine, and William seven—huddled on the couch.

Rose Ann, a shy girl with a melancholic expression, had long red hair and a quiet voice and a way of telling a story that made the flesh crawl. It was as though she really had seen all the terrible things she spoke about. She told fantastic tales of witches and murder, and the boys scrunched down, anticipating the fright she would give them.

Rose Ann's best friend, Theresa McMahon, the daughter of John McMahon, the speakeasy owner, was there also, watching with a serious gaze behind her thick spectacles. She and Rose Ann were inseparable, and both so introverted that Tony often wondered what on earth they ever had to say to each other.

"One day this very beautiful girl was found murdered," Rose Ann said in a hushed voice. "She was buried, and as she lay under the earth in a coffin, her eyes suddenly opened . . ."

The boys scrunched down lower in their seats. Theresa popped her chewing gum.

Bess McGrath, hefty, with a round, rouged face, bustled into the living room. "Rosie, such stories! You'll be giving the little ones nightmares."

"No, Ma. We like it," Emmett said, not very convincingly.

"Yeah, yeah," the other two boys said.

"Tell them stories of the old legends," Bess said.

"I tell true stories," Rose Ann said.

"Rosie!" Bessie huffed. "I'm telling you, Theresa, the thoughts in that girl's head . . ."

Rose Ann grew silent. She twisted the ends of her long red hair between her fingers and stared out the window.

The younger brothers, all fair with light skin and eyes and red hair like their sister, looked disappointed.

Tony entered from the kitchen, carrying a large carton. "Theresa," Bess said, "if you see your father before I do, tell him the rest of the leaflets will be ready on Monday." She and Tony had been packing leaflets for the political organization, the United Irish Club.

Bess adjusted a small flowered hat on her head in front of a clothes-rack mirror. "Rosie, tell the little ones the story of Dierdre and how she fled from King Conchobar—"

"Let her tell her own stories, Ma," Tony said, hoisting the carton onto his shoulder as he and his mother prepared to leave. "She tells good stories."

"There's blood and gore enough in the world without telling tales about it. And be sure the boys get to bed early. Tomorrow after church we'll all be on leaflet duty. The Hall needs every one of us."

After Bess and Tony left, Rose Ann continued her story, but something was missing from it now. She fought tears. Theresa came to her and smoothed down her hair and told her how beautiful her stories were. But something was missing.

On the street, Bess said, "It troubles me, the things she dreams up. Her father and his drunken carryings-on has filled her head with so many bloody thoughts of war and killing. She's seen too much with that man."

"She just has soft feelings," Tony McGrath said. "Her feelings get hurt so easy."

"I can't always be worrying about her feelings. I have work to do in the world."

They passed a young girl playing with a rubber ball against a stoop. Thin and bony, she nevertheless had a pretty, though tomboyish face. "Laura dear," said Bess. "The girls are upstairs. Why don't you play with them?"

"I don't want to play with them. They never like to do things I like."

"Such as?"

"Play dress-up and things."

"Well, they're not playing dress-up with my hats and makeup. You girls are too young for that."

The girl shrugged and went back to her game. As they continued down the block, Tony noticed the girl staring after him.

"That's Jerry Maddox's daughter," Bess said. "Poor soul." Jerry Maddox was a dockworker who had recently been killed in a waterfront accident. "The Club is trying to provide for them but the mother drinks it all up. Do you see how scrawny the little thing is?"

Through the winding cobblestone streets of the West Village, Tony and his mother walked. They moved past Christopher and Barrow, Morton and Leroy.

On this broiling summer evening the whole neighborhood seemed to be outside, sitting on the tenement stoops, lolling on the sidewalks, fanning themselves on the fire escapes—scruffy, half-naked kids, thick-muscled men in undershirts, dowdy women in cotton dresses. Someone had opened a fire hydrant and the kids were splashing about under sprays of water.

Tony, who had a naturally exuberant manner, was subdued this evening. He was painfully aware of the bruises he wore on his face, ashamed. The punches he had taken from the Jewish kid the night before were badges of defeat. Everyone would see them. The Young Dusters had all claimed he had gotten the better of the fight, but he knew otherwise. At best, it had been a standoff, and to Tony that was the same as losing.

"Bess, they canned Tinker Moran over at the paving works!" a woman called down from a fire escape.

"I'm going to the Boss right now," Bess yelled back. Bess McGrath was a Tammany district captain; on her walks through the neighborhood she was a constant target for complaints and solicitations. She knew everyone, mediated their concerns. "The Boss'll do what's right for Tinker, Mary, don't you worry now."

At the corner of Hudson and St. Luke's Place an elderly woman approached Bess. "My Eddie can't even lift himself from the bed no more." She spoke with a thick Irish accent; she had tears in her eyes. "Could you talk to Beau James?"

Beau James—James J. Walker, a state senator, and Tammany's golden boy—was one of their own, born and raised in the neighborhood. He lived with his wife, Allie, just down the block on St. Luke's Place.

"I'll talk to Beau myself," Bess said.

A man on a stoop called out to her: "When you see the Man in the Derby, tell 'im I says it's a crying shame what the party done in San Francisco. They didn't even treat the Man in the Derby like a white man."

"We lost it, but we'll win another day," Bess said. "We got to get ready for the big fight in November."

A few days earlier, at the Democratic national convention in San Francisco, Al Smith, the Man in the Derby, had been squeezed out of the party's nomination for President; he would stand for reelection as governor of New York in the fall.

"The saints in heaven bless you, Bess!"

"And you, Bucky!"

She and Tony continued on to Clarkson Street, where they entered a red-brick building, the Edward L. Ahearn United Irish Club of the Fourth New York Assembly District. Across an alleyway was John McMahon's speak-easy, and there was constant coming and going between the two buildings.

On the main floor of the United Irish Club a flock of ruddy-faced old gaffers sat playing cards. The floor was black-and-white tile. A globe lamp hung from the ceiling, and there were green-shaded lights directly over the tables.

The room was thick with cigar smoke. A brass spittoon rested in one corner. The walls behind the spittoon were stained with tobacco juice. Prominently displayed were two large photos of Governor Alfred Emanuel Smith and State Senator James J. Walker.

"Women in the clubhouse. What's the world coming to, I ask?" a card player said as Bess and Tony moved into the room. The man winked at the other card players. "Oh, excuse me, Bessie. I didn't see you there."

"Has my Paddy been by?"

"He's in Johnny's speak, trying to forget the ups and downs of the day." The card players all laughed. Tony's father, Paddy McGrath, worked at City Hall as an elevator operator.

Tony followed his mother up the stairs to the second floor, where a group of women sat around a table sorting leaflets. Tony set the carton down in the middle of the table. "Well, look at this," one of the women said. "Look what the sheenie done to you, Tony!"

Tony blushed.

"Would you ever believe it?" the woman went on. "A sheenie would do that kind of damage?"

"Did he hit you with his beak nose, Tony?" one of the other women said.

"I don't like that talk," said Bessie. "I don't like that talk at all."

"We're just joshing the boy."

"I don't care about that. I won't have that hate talk about sheenies and that sort of guff. I hear it everywhere I go and I don't like it and I'll hear no more of it around here."

She spoke with a tone of authority, and the other women paid heed to it; she was their captain, and in a Tammany Club, everyone knew his place.

"Now we have to start pushing, and we have to start pushing hard, and we'll need all the good people we can get on our side—Jews, coloreds, Italians, and everyone. The Man in the Derby has had a sore disappointment and we're not going to let him down. We start working for him tomorrow and we don't ease up until after election day. So no more of this talk about sheenies!" She shook a stubby finger at the women. "And before you start riding my Tony like you done, I suggest you get a peek at the other guy. I hear he looks like McGillicuddy's pig after the sausage was made!"

The women laughed, and Bess tousled Tony's hair and led him downstairs.

In the card room there was a hullabaloo. A thin, sad-looking man was doing a palsied dance in the center of the card room while the men sang and clapped. "Look who's here, Bessie, look who's here! It's the chief executive officer of the city's elevators!" one man called out, his face red with laughing.

The dancing man was Paddy McGrath. He made a small bow to Bess and continued dancing between the tables, moving with a herky-jerk tremor. He had been gassed in the Great War; the poison had paralyzed half his face, one arm, and his side. He drank because it eased his pain.

"Come on, Paddy," said Bess. "This ain't Mr. Albee's circuit."

Paddy snapped his fingers at his wife and winked. He limped around in a circle. In a tremulous voice he began to sing: " 'Oh, Genevieve, my Genevieve, the days may come, the days may go . . .' "

The men at the tables laughed and applauded. Paddy smiled and bowed to each table. "Come on, light o' my life," Bess said, "we're going home."

"I used to sing that with Jim Walker, you know. Over at Brotty's Liquor House opposite Flannery's on Hudson," Paddy said, ignoring his wife. "It was Old Bill, his father's, favorite song. Oh, Jim and me had some times. Jim Talker, I always called him. He could talk the ears off a brass monkey even as a kid."

"What about the time you and Jim stole the junk man's horse and rode it into McGurk's on the Bowery?" one of the card players said.

Paddy McGrath laughed until tears came to his eyes. "McGurk's old place! Suicide Hall, they called it, so many chippies was drinking poison!" Paddy laughed and wheezed. "You know what old McGurk used to say?"

"What's that, Paddy?" one of the card players said, as though on cue, They had all heard the story many times before.

" 'I never pushed a girl downhill any more'n I ever refused a halping hand to one trying to climb up!' " Paddy said with a thick affected brogue. He wheezed with laughter. "Suicide Hall! Oh, the Bowery was some apples in them days!"

"Sure it was," one of the card players said.

Paddy began to sing: " 'Oh, the Bowery, the Bowery / They say such things and they do strange things / On the Bowery, I'll never go there anymore!' "

The men all joined in, and soon the room rocked with song.

"Are you coming, Paddy?" said Bess, a note of impatience in her voice.

"Leave him be, Bessie, the man must relax. The Hall made sure they fitted him with a tough job, riding the ups and downs with the likes of Mayor Red Mike Hylan—"

"Go on ahead, Bessie, I'll be home soon," Paddy said. He spotted his son. "Who is that? Tony with you? Come over here, Tony." Tony moved to his father. The man smelled of perspiration and booze, and it turned his stomach.

He remembered when his father had gone off to war, tall and strong, dazzling in his khaki uniform. He had returned an old, broken man.

Paddy hugged his son to him, pawed his hair, planted a kiss on his forehead. "You fought someone last night, they was telling me."

"He fought some mockie," one of the card players said.

"You fought with heart, they was telling me."

"And his face too," another of the card players said. "You should have teached him how to hold his mitts up."

"I teached him. Don't you worry about it," Paddy said heatedly.

"Come on, Tony," Bess said. "Your sister and brothers are waiting." Tony moved to his mother. "Paddy, please, home before dawn!"

"Home before dawn," Paddy McGrath said, crossing his heart. *" 'East Side, West Side, all around the town / The tots sing ring rosie, London Bridge is falling down,' "* he sang in a faltering tenor voice. *" 'Boys and girls together / Me and Mamie O'Rourke / Tripped the light fantastic / On the sidewalks of New York.' "*

He winked, snapped his fingers, and did his awkward, cripple's dance around the room.

Paddy McGrath left the United Irish Club, but instead of going home, he walked east, moving crosstown. He passed Seventh Avenue and cursed aloud. The newly widened avenue was an ugly gash through the heart of the old neighborhood. Cars sped through the wide thoroughfare, causing people to scatter in their path. Half-demolished buildings gaped on either side of the street.

And now there was talk of renovating Sixth Avenue also. And of building a tunnel to Jersey down by Grand Street. Would it never end, this destruction of the old neighborhood?

Paddy McGrath stopped in the middle of the avenue and shook his fist at the oncoming traffic. The outrage performed on Seventh Avenue was symbolic of the outrage done to Paddy McGrath's life. He had marched off to war from a world safe, contained—a neighborhood where everyone knew everyone else, where everyone cared for everyone else. The war had changed all that, shattered Paddy's life and shattered his neighborhood too.

Nothing was the same anymore. Women had invaded the United Irish Club. They kept to the second floor, but nevertheless—women in a political club! And they had just won the vote. Only last week the Tennessee legislature had become the thirty-sixth state to ratify the nineteenth amendment.

Eight months earlier, the Volstead Act had outlawed the sale of liquor. Booze was illegal, woman had the vote. What was the world coming to?

Muttering to himself, Paddy walked on through the quiet of Washington Square, through the Negro area south of the park, to the Bowery. Bums, Chinamen, painted whores, dark-skinned Italians, bearded Jews, greenhorn women in babushkas, twill-clad workingmen thronged the avenue, wove through the great iron El stanchions.

Past saloons shuttered by the new prohibition law, pawn shops, cut-rate dry-goods stores, all-night diners, soup kitchens, religious missions, bawdy theaters, Paddy McGrath made his way.

He entered a tenement, climbed flights of piss-stained stairs.

On the top floor he found the haven he was seeking: a railroad flat done in red flocking, lights low, Caruso singing "M'appari" over a gramophone.

A girl in her late teens sat in a soiled slip at a table in the kitchen. "Hello, Paddy," she said, hardly looking at him. She spoke with an accent, Polish or Russian. "Katie's busy with a trick. You want to wait?"

" 'The Bowery, the Bowery—Folks who are on to the city, they say / Better by far that I took Broadway,' " Paddy sang, winking and snapping his fingers, attempting an awkward jig.

There was a sound of a toilet flushing in the rear of the house, then Kate Foster came down the long hallway. She was a woman in her thirties, almost pretty. She had faded blond hair and tired blue eyes. She wore a red silk robe over panties and bra. "Paddy McGrath, you old scoundrel," Kate said, "making all that noise."

A man had followed Kate from the back of the apartment. He had on a derby and was adjusting a pair of leather gloves on his hands. "You know Charlie Roth, don't you, Paddy?" Kate said.

"Sure, I know Charlie."

Charlie Roth didn't look pleased. He took a cigar out of his jacket pocket and patted his pockets for a match. Kate lit the cigar for him with a kitchen match.

"Charlie's a good-time Charlie and I'm a good-time Paddy. Charlie and I go way back, ain't that right, Charlie?"

Charlie eyed Paddy warily, uncomfortably. "I wouldn't say I know you," he said. "We've met in passing."

"You was sticking it in when I was pulling it out," Paddy said, laughing loudly.

Charlie looked away. He tipped his derby to Kate, then left.

"The nerve of that guy, high-hatting me like that," Paddy said. "Wait till he wants something down at City Hall. Just wait."

"He can ring for the elevator all he wants, you'll keep him standing all day, won't you, Paddy?" Kate said.

"And worse, mark my word. And worse."

Kate took Paddy back to her room. There were white curtains on the windows and a flowered bedspread. There was a porcelain Madonna with Child on the bureau.

Paddy sat on the edge of the bed while Kate took off her robe and under-clothes. Her body was thin but well formed.

Someone was at the window peering in from the fire escape. "Get out of there!" she screamed. "Goddammit, Jackie, get!" She rushed to the open window, swinging her bra like a whip.

Jackie Foster, his face a pinched, angry mask, scurried up the fire escape to the roof. "I'll kill you, you little son of a bitch!" she screamed.

"He's such a pest," she said, returning to the bed.

"Who did you get him by? Was it me?"

"Either you or some millionaire I ran into," she said. She moved her hand between his legs and began to massage him.

"I just want to talk," Paddy said.

She lit a cigarette and leaned back on the bed.

"Did I ever tell you about the time Jim Walker and me got into a fight in the cemetery behind St. Joseph's?"

"I don't think you did, Paddy."

"You see, I had this red-white-and-blue spinning top. My father had made it for me, and one day I was in front of the school . . ."

As Paddy spoke, Kate gazed at the window. Her son was back on the fire escape, staring in with wide, ghostlike eyes. She had no strength to keep chasing him. She looked away, back to Paddy. What did the kid want from her, anyway?

3

Mike Roth gazed from his tenement rooftop out over the city. Everything seemed gray—the sky, the buildings, the streets. A freezing wind blew in off the river. It looked as though it might snow.

He had brought his sketch pad with him but did not use it. The city seemed ugly to him this night. He tried to conjure up a better, more beautiful place—grass and trees, pools of water, parks. Within him he felt a terrible ache for something clean and open and pure. If only the gray tenements could be pulled down! People would cease to scream at each other. They would treat each other with dignity. He dreamed of a great garden that would stretch through the Lower East Side; everything would be green and light and people's hearts would sing.

The gloom of late autumn had settled within him. The apartment downstairs was freezing. The only heat came from the kitchen stove. It was almost as cold down there as it was on the roof.

His sister, Ruth, had not been well—a lingering cold with fever had grown worse. She hadn't been to school for weeks. She lay in the large bed in the back room, sleeping between Charlie and Florence at night. She had grown very thin and quiet. Her dark eyes seemed wider and sadder than ever, and it broke Mike's heart. He could do nothing for her.

Night sneaked into the city: a black cat, Mike thought. A sprinkling of lights winked on and he felt relieved. He hated the gloom of a wintry day dying. Darkness was magical and merciful, transforming everything. Bridges became jeweled links; lights twinkled on the harbor and on boats plying the river, diamonds on velvet. Gray concrete vanished as completely as any prop behind a magician's cape. The hell of tenement poverty, meanness, despair, seemed unimaginable in the rich darkness of night.

A movement in the corner of his eye startled him. It was his brother, come so silently to the roof he had not heard him. In his dark overcoat and fedora hat he looked older than his eighteen years, a stranger.

In September Harry had moved out of the apartment to a rented room on Essex Street. He had no regular job but ran with the neighborhood tough guys, operating games of street dice. Charlie had come upon him one day setting up craps behind the Rutgers Square Settlement House. Charlie kicked him from one end of the yard to the other. After that Harry had stopped coming around the house. From time to time he would slip Mike some money to give to their mother.

"What's good, kid?" Harry said, approaching.

"Things are the same. Ruthie's not doing so well."

"What does the doctor say?"

"The old one, Rosen, says it's a cold—feed her broth and use a croup kettle. The young guy says he doesn't know what it is, maybe she should go to the hospital."

Harry remained quiet for a while. He stared out into the night. "I got a problem. I owe some guys some money. We were *shiessen* craps, you know, and it didn't work out. What I was thinking, Mikey, you fight good. Militinu has that speak over on Rivington and Benny and Meyer protect it for him. They been running fights there. I could get you a fight. You make five dollars, I bet it just right, and we got action."

"No, Harry. I'm not going to do that."

"Why not?"

"I fight to protect what's mine. I don't fight to hurt someone for money."

"I'm in a bad jam, kid. You got to do it for me."

"You had no right getting into a mess like that!" Mike was yelling now, and he hated himself for it and he hated Harry for putting him in this position.

"All right, I'll let them beat my head open, then! I'll tell 'em, here I am, crack it open, my brother won't help me! If you can't help me, Mikey, who will?"

Mike stared out over the city and thought: He's my brother. "All right," he said.

Sammy Militinu's speakeasy, Pearl of Rumania, was in the basement of a tenement on Rivington Street. It was a wide, low room with oilcloth-covered tables. On the walls were paintings of fleshy nude women. In one corner was a yellow canary in a cage.

The place was filled with garment workers, cab drivers, pimps, gamblers, gangsters. The working people wore sweat-stained shirts, heavy twill trousers, caps, boots. The gangsters and pimps who lived off them wore sleek sharkskins, camel hair, pinstripes. There were a few women in the place, mostly whores.

In the center of the basement room a roped platform had been constructed for boxing.

Harry led his brother through the lively, odorous crowd to a storage room behind the kitchen. On a bench was a carton filled with boxing trunks and mismatched gym shoes. "I don't want to wear these," said Mike.

"Wear 'em. They look professional. This is a business, and looks count. You win this one, we'll buy you your own."

His opponent, a fat greenhorn from the neighborhood, named Mushy, was standing next to the kitchen. His trunks did not fit him; they barely came up over his sloppy belly. He outweighed Mike by thirty pounds. He was a strong kid but not very bright.

He stood alone, embarrassed, grinning stupidly. Harry whispered to Mike, "I'm gonna bet you knock him out. That's the only way we'll get any action."

"I don't want to hurt this kid."

"He's a *chaye,* an animal. How can you hurt him? I'd offer him a few bucks to go down, but he doesn't speak English. Even his Yiddish is like nothing I've heard."

Harry left the storage room and Mike got into the trunks. He couldn't find shoes that fit, and settled for a pair that were a size tight.

Mushy grinned at him and waved. Mike waved back. He moved through the kitchen and stood against the rear wall of the speakeasy and watched a fight in progress.

Two kids whom Mike had never seen before were slamming each other all over the ring. Both had blood smeared across their faces and on their chests.

Mike spotted Harry with Ben Siegel, Little Farvel, and a greenhorn kid whose real name was Meyer Suchowljansky. They called him Johnny Eggs or Little Meyer. He was barely five-foot-five, but tough as anybody in the neighborhood. Sitting next to him was his brother Jake, whom everyone called the Hunchback. He towered over his brother, but in order not to embarrass him, walked bent over as though carrying a sack across his shoulders.

Siegel and Johnny Eggs monopolized the crap games in the area; Harry worked for them. They sat at a table, while he was on a stool to one side. Harry laughed and nodded, trying to get into the conversation. Everyone ignored him.

In the ring one of the fighters in desperation hurled himself headlong at the other boy and cracked him flush in the mouth with his skull. He grabbed the kid and pushed him back through the ropes and slammed him over and over again.

At the end of the round the kid against the ropes was a bloody mess.

Mike and Mushy were brought into the ring. Someone pulled a pair of boxing gloves on Mike—the same ones used in the previous fight. The insides were soaked with perspiration. It was the first time Mike had ever had boxing gloves on, and though they were only four-ouncers, they felt like pillows. He didn't like the feel at all.

A red-faced man blew a whistle, and the fight was on.

Mushy remained standing in his corner, grinning at the crowd. He looked silly and pathetic, and Mike waved to him to come and fight. He lumbered toward Mike, still grinning, eyes wide and foolish, as though he were a spectator at his own bout. He slapped out at Mike with his gloved hand. Mike ducked to one side and hit Mushy in the stomach.

Mushy expelled air, a hurt expression on his face. Mike moved toward him and hit him a couple of times lightly. He hated the feel of the gloves on his hands.

Mushy pushed him away, then lunged at him, swinging wildly. Mike saw the punch start, a lazy, looping haymaker. He ducked to avoid it, without concern. It came down on top of his head, and suddenly Mike found himself sitting on the floor.

He felt as though he had been hit by a brick. Spots of color danced in his vision. What were Mushy's fists made of? He had never been hit so hard, not even by Tony McGrath.

The man who had blown the whistle to start the fight was above him counting. He heard the man call out five, six, seven. With a shock he realized the crowd was jeering him. He heard his brother screaming.

Harry had climbed up on the apron of the ring. His face was contorted, terrible. Tears in his eyes, he shrieked, "It's my ass, Mikey! It's my ass! Get up!"

"Eight, nine . . ."

Mike leaped to his feet. Mushy hit him again. Again he found himself sitting in the middle of the ring.

"Mikey, please, please, please. Don't do this to me, Mike!" Harry blubbered.

Mike grabbed the bottom strand of the ropes and pulled himself up. Mushy was right on top of him. Punches winged in from every angle. Mushy's sweat sprayed all over, and the odor of him was nearly as devastating as his fists.

Mike wrapped his arms around the greenhorn's midsection and hung on. Mushy's trunks, an ill-fit to begin with, slipped down below his waist. He tried to grab them, but they fell, exposing his rubbery behind. The spectator's howled.

Mike could see panic in Mushy's face. Profoundly embarrassed, he tried to pull his trunks up. Mike hit him, but the punch appeared to have no effect. Mushy pushed him off and struggled to get his trunks up.

In a rush of anger and frustration, Mike tore off his boxing gloves and went at Mushy with his bare fists. Mushy gave up on the trunks and tried to cover his face.

The referee struggled to pull Mike away, but Mike kept going.

By this time Mushy's trunks had slipped around his knees, and he stumbled awkwardly about the ring, trying to escape.

The crowd roared with laughter, while poor Mushy suffered a nightmare of embarrassment.

Mike cracked in three terrific belts, and Mushy toppled over in a heap.

The referee wrestled Mike to the canvas. Harry jumped into the ring, held the referee around the neck and tried to throttle him.

Mushy was out cold. A heavyset workingman, struggling to revive him, bellowed a stream of Yiddish epithets in his ear. Finally he was brought around. He sat dazed in the center of the ring. Someone pulled off his gloves. Pennies showered the canvas: greenhorn Mushy, desperate Mushy, had concealed a roll of coins in each glove.

Violent argument erupted. Harry stormed about the ring, bawling, shouting, threatening. In the end, talmudic reason held sway: since Mushy had committed the first sin, Mike's infraction was forgiven. He was awarded the fight by a knockout.

There was a rhubarb near the kitchen. It was Charlie Roth, angry and drunk. He had grabbed Harry by the lapels and was slapping him about the head. "You done this to him. You make him fight for money! What kind of man fights for money?"

Harry cowered under the blows. Ben Siegel, Johnny Eggs, and Little Farvel laughed. Harry looked as though he would weep. Sammy Militinu pulled Charlie away and gave him a table of his own and a bottle of Rumanian wine.

Mike finished dressing, collected his five dollars, and joined his father at the table. "Your brother is a *vantz,* hanging out with those pimps," Charlie said, waving the wine bottle in front of him. "I could tear you all apart—you, your brother, those pimps and chiselers!" He squeezed his hands tight around the wine bottle and brooded.

A man joined them at the table. He was in his mid-thirties, with the battered face of an ex-pug. He gazed at Mike over a thick cigar clamped between his teeth. Mike realized he had a glass eye.

"The kid did good," the man with the glass eye said to Charlie. "Who is he, your boy?" Charlie didn't answer. "My names Kotovsky. I got some boxers down by the settlement house, Rutgers Settlement House. I teach 'em. I fought with Benny Leonard, Leach Cross. A hundred and seventy-five pro fights. I went by the name of Battling Wilson."

"What do you want with my son?"

"I'd like to teach him, you know? Make a pro out of him."

"So's he can have one eye like you?" Charlie said.

"That was an accident. I was got with a good thumb. It happens sometimes."

At the door Ben Siegel, Little Farvel, Johnny Eggs, and Jake the Hunchback were preparing to leave. Harry waved Mike to him. He peeled off a five-dollar bill from a roll in his hands. "Here. Thanks for helping me out, Mikey."

"Hey, Mikey, you're one tough kid," Ben said. "Why don't you come work for Johnny Eggs and me?"

"He got too much heart," Johnny said. He had a flat, solemn, monkeylike face and spoke with an accent.

"What's the matter with heart?" Harry said.

"If you like children, flowers, old ladies—it's a good thing. For our business, it's not so good. For our business, it's better you should have no heart. Like Benny here."

Ben scowled.

"Ben has heart where his brain should be, and brain where his heart should be," Little Farvel Kovalick said. "He's a bug."

"Benny's all right. Benny's the best," Johnny Eggs said. "He does what he has to do."

Bugsy Siegel smiled.

4

At the Edward W. Ahearn United Irish Club a pall lasting for weeks had settled over everyone.

In the November election things had not gone well for the Democrats. Warren G. Harding had trounced Cox in the presidential battle and Al Smith, seeking reelection as governor of the state of New York, had been beaten also.

During the campaign Al Smith had come walking through the neighborhood, a short, sad-faced man with a large cigar and derby hat. He spotted Paddy. In front of everyone—Boss Ahearn, Jimmy Walker, Tammany Chief Charles Francis Murphy—he called out, "How's things, Paddy McGrath?"

"Just fine, Al!"

"Harvey Duff!" Al Smith yelled.

"Corry Kinchella!" Paddy yelled back.

Al Smith laughed. He addressed his entourage: "Harvey Duff and Corry Kinchella—they were characters in *The Shaughraun*. Paddy and I acted it together at the old St. James Dramatic Society. Sober or drunk, Paddy McGrath was as fine a ham as ever trod the boards. Better even than Jim Walker!" This had brought laughter and applause from the crowd, and Jim Walker had tipped his hat to Paddy, who beamed as the group moved off down the street.

Later Al Smith had met with Bess at the United Irish Club. "What can we do for the ladies, Bess?" he asked.

"We have to do for them what we do for everyone. Give them hope in this world, a chicken in the pot, warm clothes for the kids in wintertime."

"We're in a tough fight, Bess. Will you help me out?"

"I'll crawl on my knees through the neighborhood, Governor."

Al Smith had smiled and hugged her and planted a kiss on the side of her face. "We're from the same stock, you and me. Good, hardworking people."

"That we are, Al. God bless you."

And now Al Smith had been defeated. Bess McGrath, who had worked with prodigious energy and dedication for him, took to her bed sick after the election. Paddy drank more heavily than usual.

Tony McGrath had dropped out of school. Johnny McMahon had persuaded him to take up prizefighting as a profession. Several evenings a week he would appear in the ring at one of the speaks or at neighborhood fight clubs like the Dry Dock, the Villagers A.C., the Fairmont, and the Sharkey.

McMahon began to hatch plans for Tony's career. Tony had knocked out everyone who had entered the ring with him, and it was generally agreed he needed tougher competition.

A brawler named Rafferty, terror of the West Side docks, was picked to go up against Tony at McMahon's speak. Though his ring experience was limited, in a street fight he had no match. He was older and bigger than McGrath and was sure to draw a crowd.

The week before the fight, a tremendous excitement swept through the West Village. Everyone chose up sides. The dockworkers, truck drivers, construction men, went for Rafferty; the old pols, the hangers-on at the United Irish Club and McMahon's, went for Tony McGrath.

The night of the fight, a snowy Friday, McMahon's was packed. The crowd was jammed against the back wall, sitting on the tables, standing on chairs. They had had several hours to bet and drink and argue, and everyone was feisty with alcohol and wild for action.

Rafferty looked formidable. He outweighed Tony by thirty pounds, had shoulders like cantaloupes, was missing front teeth, had a face gashed with scars. His stomach was massive, a solid barrel girth, not fat. He stood at the ring's edge drinking beer from a pitcher and joking with his supporters.

Jim Walker and Boss Ahearn occupied a large table just below the ring, which filled the center of the bar area. Walker's table was crammed with spiffy folk; a pretty young lady hung on Walker's arm.

Tony was dismayed at the public display Beau James was putting on. Everyone knew he kept a mistress—Vonnie Shelton, a chorus girl. It was one thing for a state senator to appear in a speakeasy—all the politicians did it—but quite another to flaunt his chippy there. Walker's wife, Allie, a dumpy, round-faced woman, was popular in the neighborhood; their house on St. Luke's Place was a favorite gathering place for the local ladies. Walker was really rubbing it in, appearing among friends and neighbors with his mistress.

Still, he was Jim Walker, one of their own, the darling of Greenwich Village. He could do no wrong.

Johnny McMahon called over the edge of the ring to Jim Walker's table, "Hey, Talker, come up here. Referee this thing!"

Everyone in the place laughed and applauded, and Jim Walker rose and entered the ring. "We've been through a tough time, folks. A great man and dear friend, Alfred Emanuel Smith, has taken a shellacking, but if you think he's down and out, you got another think coming!" The speakeasy rocked with cheers. Jim Walker waved Rafferty and Tony to the center of the ring. "Boys, let's see a good clean fight. We're all friends and neighbors here and we like to see you mix it up, but not in hate. In a mean fight between Irishmen, only the landlord's the winner! Okay, fellows, let's see you do your best."

Rafferty took a deep swallow of beer, sloshed it around in his mouth, and spit it in one corner of the ring. He did not look at Tony. Ernie, the bartender, clanged a large brass fire bell, and Rafferty and Tony went at it.

Rafferty had a great gleaming jaw; it stood out beneath the overhead light as though carved out of rock. Tony sighted it and went right for it.

He threw a wide, arcing overhead punch and caught Rafferty coming in. Thee was a loud popping sound as McGrath's fist blasted the hinge of his jaw. Rafferty went to one side and crashed to the canvas. He rolled over on his back; the crowd looked on in stunned silence.

The dockworker's jaw was ridiculously askew. He did not move. One punch had been thrown in the fight, and the terror of the West Side docks had been flattened cold.

Jim Walker stared down at the man. He did not bother to count. He looked out at the crowd and smiled a puckish grin. "Is there a doctor in the house? We got a man here terrible sick."

The crowd howled.

Later, after Tony had changed into his street clothes, Johnny McMahon brought him over to Walker's table. "What do you think, Bill-O?" he said to a handsome, husky fellow at the table. "Is he ready for the big time?"

"I'd like to see him at Boyle's Thirty Acres, but first he needs seasoning," Bill-O said. He had a light Irish lilt to his voice.

Boss Ahearn joined the table. He was a large red-faced man with a great shock of white hair. "Lad, you're a hunk of the old sod—John L. Sullivan, Gentleman Jim, Terrible Terry McGovern. They were Irishmen all, and good Catholics who would cross themselves before they entered the ring."

Flushed with victory, Tony grabbed up a mug of beer. He tilted his head back and drank deep. "It's a good feeling, ain't it, lad?" Boss Ahearn said.

"God help me, I loved the sound of that ape's jaw snapping," he answered.

"Bill-O here would like to promote the lad," Walker said. "You know Bill-O, don't you, Boss? He's in the legal department with the police."

"What's the name again?" Boss Ahearn said, craning forward.

"Bill O'Dwyer," the husky fellow said.

"He gave me advice on that bill to legalize boxing in the state," said Walker.

"And aren't you ashamed to be bringing a member of the force to a speakeasy to watch an unlicensed prizefight?" Boss Ahearn said, his eyes merry with laughter.

"Where was the prizefight?" Walker said. "I saw a swimming match where some poor lad took a high dive into a pool with no water and broke his jaw."

"Bill-O, why don't you pay a visit with Jim here to see Silent Charlie Murphy over at the Hall on Fourteenth Street?" said Boss Ahearn. "We have to get you out of the legal department and into where the money is! And as for this young man"—turning to Tony—"we must keep an eye on him. After all, he's Bessie McGrath's boy."

"We certainly shall keep an eye on him," Walker said. "And cover our jaws up while we're at it!"

Everybody laughed. "Keep him in mind, Bill-O," said Boss Ahearn.

"I surely will, sir."

"The men of the Hall must look to their own."

James Walker stood, took the hand of the young lady with him and brought it to his heart. He began to sing in a ragged baritone: " 'Will you love me in December as you do in May / Will you love me in the good old-fashioned way? / When my hair has all turned gray / Will you kiss me then and say / That you love me in December as you do in May?' "

The crowd clapped and whistled as he brought the lady to her feet. He turned with her and danced her to the door, then tipped his derby to the crowd before exiting out into the snowy night.

5

Mike Roth's sister, Ruth, did not get well. She became thinner, quieter. In February old Dr. Rosen agreed with young Dr. Krochmal and they took her to the hospital. In March, a week before Mike's fifteenth birthday, she died.

Mike had come to the hospital after school and was sitting with her. He had brought his sketchbook with him and was trying to get her interested in the drawings. Instead, she stared, directly at Mike, into his eyes.

All about him in the gloomy ward youngsters coughed and cried and slept. He did not see a nurse, and when he turned back to his sister, she did not move. She stared at him with great, dark, empty eyes. There had been a feverish burning in her gaze the past week, and now it was gone.

He realized she was dead. He sat on the bed with her, gathered her in his arms, and rocked her for a long time.

At the funeral, as the pathetically small casket was lowered into the frozen ground, Florence tried to leap into the grave. "Don't take my baby! Don't take my baby!" she shrieked over and over. "Don't take my baby!"

And so it was that Mike Roth lost his sister.

While the family sat *shiva,* people from all over the neighborhood would stop by with platters of food, cold cuts and chopped liver, herring, smoked fish.

Ben Siegel, Johnny Eggs, Jake the Hunchback, and a kid they called the Judge, Lepke Buchalter, arrived with an enormous basket filled with fruits and candies. After they had paid their respects, someone discovered a hundred-dollar bill in among the items in the basket.

Tammany chief Charles Francis Murphy sent over a huge corned beef with ward boss Kravitz.

Charlie Roth consumed large amounts of Rumanian wine and grew belligerent. "Why do they bring us all of this? What does it mean? Why all this for the daughter of Charlie Roth?"

"You have good friends, Charlie," said Kravitz, a short, sweaty man.

"They're his friends," he said, pointing an accusing finger at Harry. "Gangsters. Pimps. They're the only people who have money for this!"

The older folk, neighbors and friends, workmen in thick, rough outfits, women with shawls and heavy sweaters, stirred uneasily. Charlie the Meshuggener was starting up again.

Charlie Roth looked over at his wife. She had not talked since the funeral. She wept silently night and day. She stared at a photograph of Ruth on a pony, taken by a street photographer just outside the tenement house. She kissed the photograph and hugged it to her breast and rocked and moaned.

Charlie went to her and held her close to him. "What does it matter? What does it matter?"

In the weeks following his sister's death Mike Roth began to visit the settlement house on Rutgers Square. He would train in the wide, drafty gym; in the evenings he sat in on sketching classes held in the basement.

Harry, his brother, tried to get him to continue boxing around town. Moe Kotovsky, the one-eyed coach at the settlement house, prevailed on him to stay away from the speaks and clubs for a while. "Mikey, this is a science, an art," he told him. "You got a good brain and you got all the other attributes to make a really fine fighter. Learn everything there is first. Then you'll go back out into that jungle."

Kotovsky had grown up in the neighborhood with Benny Leonard. He had a first-rate career until he lost his left eye in a fight with Battling Levinsky. His attitude toward fighting was that of a sculptor: you molded your body and you molded your craft. Fighting was something you carved out of life, whittling away at it, shaping it.

He would work with Mike hour after hour on basic combinations, jab and hook, jab and cross, counter, counter. Feints, dodges, small rhythmic hitches. He would stand on a handkerchief and let Mike throw punches at him, and though he had only one eye he would duck them all and never move off the small white square.

He would work Mike on the light and heavy bags, then shadowbox side by side with him. Toward the end of the day Kotovsky would take out the battered gloves from a metal locker and put Mike in the ring with one or another of the kids who trained at the settlement house.

Once in a while there would be an amateur tournament at a ballroom or settlement house around the city. Kotovsky entered the fighters from Rutgers Square. They gained a reputation for being hard, tricky fighters— brainy Jewboys who outthought you as much as outfought you. And Mike Roth was considered the best of the Rutgers Square bunch.

In the late spring when school let out, Mike landed a job in the Fulton Fish Market, through ward boss Kravitz. For ten dollars a week he worked from four in the morning to four in the afternoon unloading fish from the boats that sailed through Buttermilk Channel to the East River and the docks of the market. The fish were packed into barrels with shaved ice, and the barrels distributed along the market.

In the morning he ran the distance to the market and back home again in the evening. He would have a package of fish with him—a bonus of the job—which he left with his mother and then hurried over to the settlement house to work out and shower and get the fish smell off him.

He fought in several amateur tournaments in the early summer and wrecked whomever he came up against. Hoisting heavy barrels all day had added strength to his arms and shoulders, power to his punches.

He had grown and was putting on weight. He was no longer able to fight in the lightweight class, and Kotovsky moved him up to welterweight.

One Friday evening toward the end of July he was given the opportunity to put in overtime at the fish market. Because of the Jewish Sabbath, the settlement house closed early; he couldn't work out, so he accepted the overtime. He labored until nearly seven o'clock scrubbing out an enormous icehouse where leftover fish was kept for the next day and sold at a discount.

The day had been hot, but the evening brought coolness with it; a light breeze blew in off Upper New York Bay. Mike climbed an iron stairway to the Brooklyn Bridge.

He stood on the bridge and watched the boats as they glided through the narrows into the bay. Lights winked on in Brooklyn. Gulls wheeled and dived above the bay. A large ferryboat plowed through the churning waters between the Battery and Staten Island. The water under the bridge went from blue to gray to black as dusk moved in from the Hudson.

Mike Roth opened his sketchpad and with sharp, precise lines drew a city in silhouette—bridges, buildings, docks—a city purged of ugliness.

He envied the purity a person could achieve in a drawing. Mike was not a grown man, yet the desire within him to rid his world of squalor, meanness, and pain was enormous. He yearned to lose himself in some governing ideal, to be as pure and clean as the strokes limned on his drawing pad.

A flutter of movement caught his gaze. A girl had come up onto the bridge. She stood at the railing, just beyond the stairway. She was young, not quite Mike's age.

She looked over at him but seemed to be staring past him. She was the loveliest woman Mike had ever seen, with long red hair, very light eyes, pale skin. In the light of dusk she seemed not of this world. Mist had gathered on the bay, and it was as though she had floated in on the mist.

She stood watching Mike. He smiled at her. She smiled back, a dreamy, delicate smile.

He moved along the walkway to her. "Hello."

She did not answer.

"The city's nice from here."

"Yes, it's lovely." She had a quiet voice. She continued to stare at him.

"Do you come here very often?" She nodded. "Where do you live?"

"Over there," she said, pointing toward the West Side. She took the sketchpad from his hand and studied the drawing he had been working on. "That's the city."

"Yes."

"Oh, it's so beautiful!"

Her soft, throaty voice stirred Mike. A dizzying weakness moved within him. He had never seen a girl so lovely, and the idea occurred to him that perhaps she wasn't real. No human could be this exquisite!

"I have to get home," she said, handing him back his sketchpad.

She started down the stairway. "Wait!" Mike called out to her. She turned. "Do you come here very often?"

"Yes."

"Tomorrow evening?"

"I don't know."

"Please," he said.

She started to answer, but the words did not come. He moved toward her. He reached into his shopping bag and brought out a newspaper-wrapped package. "I work in the market. This is for you." He suddenly felt stupid, awkward: a package of fish as a present!

She smiled, a secretive, quiet smile. "Thank you," she said.

"My name is Mike. What's yours?"

"Rose Ann," the young girl said, then hurried off down the stairway.

He stood on the bridge, transfixed. Had she been real? Was he dreaming?

He gazed down onto South Street. He could not see her. Where had she disappeared to? Then he saw a flash of red hair and the girl's dancing figure moving west along the dock.

Mike leaned on the bridge railing. The damp evening air slapped at his face. Eddies of whitecapped water swirled against the dock below. "Yow!" he shouted. "Yoweeee!" He broke into a fast, skip-rope, prizefighter's dance, throwing punches in the air.

A couple out for an evening stroll on the bridge turned to stare at him. He ignored them. He danced and shadowboxed in a rapid circle, then took off at a run down the stairs to the street below.

He raced full speed all the way back to Ludlow Street, his heart wild with emotion. Mike Roth was in love.

6

"Talk to your sister," Bess McGrath said to Tony in the kitchen of the apartment as she fussed over her lipstick in front of the mirror above the kitchen sink. "She's supposed to stay with the kids, and I come home and she's not here. So much work to be done at the club! I can't be here and there at the same time."

"I'll talk to her."

"So much to be done. Your father and everything, he just gets worse. I don't know. I just don't know."

She was tired, desperately tired. The United Irish Club, with its feckless, opportunistic pols, drained her. Someone had to do the work. There were minor skirmishes to be fought and great political battles on the horizon, and everything drifted. The men drank, joked, played cards; the women gossiped, fussed with their hair, dabbed their faces with powder, sneaked cigarettes. Who would hold it all together? Who would win the war for the Democrats, for Alfred Emanuel Smith? Who would struggle for the plight of the poor working people of the ward? She realized she had been neglecting her home, neglecting her family, but what could be done?

Paddy was almost never in the house these days. He spent more and more time on the Bowery. It concerned Bess, but what could she do? The man was fragile, the man was sick. She prayed that nothing would happen to him or Rose Ann or any of them. Yet, there was a job to be done. The United Irish Club must be served.

Jackie Foster told Tony he found Paddy wandering drunk on the East

Side at all hours of the night. "I look out for him, you know me," he said, flashing his sly, simpering grin.

Foster was rising in the world, making a reputation for himself as a strong-arm punk in the protection rackets operated by Lansky, Buchalter, and Siegel.

He was vicious and cunning; he enjoyed hurting people who couldn't fight back. Tony despised him, but he could not shake him. Wherever he turned, Jackie appeared. "Don't worry, Tony, I'll make sure nothing happens to Paddy. We're blood, Tony, we're blood."

And he would be off on his obsession, insisting a miraculous egg of his mother had been impregnated by all the world's heroes. He and Tony were brothers. "I feel the blood between us. We even look alike. I feel love for you, Tony."

He claimed an army of great men as blood of his blood: Babe Ruth, General Pershing, Arnold Rothstein, President Harding. And who could dispute him with finality? His mother was a whore. She had slept with thousands.

It was madness, of course, but Jack Foster had adopted it as his religion: he was brother to Tony McGrath and all the great men of the world.

"Please, Tony, you'll talk to Rose Ann?" his mother said, adjusting her flowered hat. "It troubles me, Tony. You know when Paddy was away at the war she cried every night. I would have to hold her in my arms and she would tremble like a leaf. And he came back like he did, with all his drunken carryings-on, his nightmares and wild rambling talk of death in the war. She's not like you and the boys. She's not like me. She's fragile, you know, a flower."

"I'll see to her," Tony said.

After Bess left, Tony prepared to go to work at the Gansevoort Market. He looked in on his sister.

"Rosie?"

She opened her eyes and stared at Tony with a clear and direct look, as though she hadn't been asleep at all.

"Where have you been to at night when I'm at work?"

She didn't answer.

"You can't leave the kids like that."

"I stay with them."

"Mama says she comes home and you're not here."

"I am here," Rose Ann said in a hushed voice.

"Do you spend time with Theresa? Is that it?"

She didn't answer for a long while. "What's the matter?"

"Do you think I'll go to hell?" she said.

"Why?"

"Papa always says I'll go to hell."

"He's drunk."

"He frightens me. Sometimes I have dreams."

"What kind of dreams?"

She shook her head. She would not tell him.

In the morning, after he finished at the market, instead of going directly to the gym at the Greenwich Village Settlement House, Tony came home. His brothers were there, playing pick-up-sticks on the living-room floor. "Where's Rosie?" he asked.

"She went for a walk," Emmett said.

"She's out every night," said Jim.

"Where does she go?" The brothers didn't answer. "Doesn't she say?"

"I think she has a boyfriend," Willy said.

"Who?"

The brothers looked uncomfortable but said nothing.

After work on the night following his meeting with Rose Ann, Mike Roth hurried to the walkway on the Brooklyn Bridge. He waited, but she did not appear.

He searched the walkway on the bridge from Manhattan to the Brooklyn side. An occasional woman came by and Mike would pray that it was Rose Ann. It never was.

The pain of his loss was terrible inside, wrenching.

Past midnight, exhausted, he left the bridge. He walked down through the streetcar-terminal arcade, past shuttered news and hot-dog stands, and came out into the night. The air was thick and humid. He walked down Frankfort Street to Dover and then turned onto South Street.

And then he saw her seated on a bench at the river's edge.

Rose Ann turned to him and did not look at all surprised.

"Hello," Mike said to her.

"Hello." She stared at him, vaguely quizzical, as though she didn't quite know who he was.

"How have you been?" he said.

"Oh, I'm fine."

"You know, you shouldn't be out here so late. It's dangerous."

"I'm not afraid," she said. "I just have to get out on these warm nights. You almost can't breathe in our house."

She continued to stare at him, and he felt foolish and uncomfortable. "Do you mind if I sit?" She smiled but didn't answer.

He sat on the bench next to her. He had gone over and over in his mind what he would tell her when he saw her, and now he could think of nothing to say. He stared at her, fixed her in his mind, studied the delicate curve of her neck, the smoothness of her skin. She had a small birthmark on one cheek; he tried to freeze it in his memory.

"I'm happy you're here," he said at last, the sound of his voice hoarse and unnatural to him.

"I have a lot of responsibility. I have younger brothers to take care of."

"Did you like the fish I gave you? I mean, did your family like it?"

She looked at him, puzzled. "Oh, the fish. Yes, thank you. It was delicious."

Neither of them spoke for a long time. The water of the East River lapped at the pier's edge. A large boat moved from the far end of the bay toward Buttermilk Channel. Its lights glowed through the mist, a phantom garland. Mike felt her body rest against his ever so lightly. He put his arm behind her on the back of the bench.

His mind was racing: what do I do now? Should I touch her? Do I dare try to kiss her?

She turned and looked into his face. There was something pained in her gaze, a sadness there.

And then he was kissing her. She had moved miraculously into his arms and was twisting against him, her mouth hot against his. He could feel her trembling under his hands. She moaned softly and he kissed her neck and her ears, and she dug her fingers into his back.

She was a flower, indescribably delicate. The smell of her was sweet, the touch of her like rose petals. He was dizzy with the fragrance of her, the feel of her.

He had never been with a woman. He had met whores and he knew what you did with them, but had never experienced it. He felt there was something pure and holy about a woman, and he could do nothing with them without love. And he loved Rose Ann, beautiful apparition!

He moved his hand down to touch her breast, did it awkwardly.

She got up quickly, her face flushed. "No. I'm a good Catholic girl. I don't behave that way." She started to move away from him.

He hurried after her. "I'm sorry. I didn't mean anything by it. I like you so much. Don't walk away from me like this."

"The sisters at St. Veronica's wouldn't approve."

"I'm sorry. Forgive me."

She permitted him to walk her through the Battery to Greenwich Street, and up Greenwich to West Broadway.

At Hudson she stopped. She would let him go no farther.

"I have to see you again. Please."

"I'll be on the bridge tomorrow night."

"Promise?"

"I promise."

He leaned forward to kiss her once more, but she hurried off before he could touch her.

When he arrived home he found his mother sitting in the kitchen. She looked drawn, gray with grief. Since the death of Ruth she rarely slept. She would sit at the kitchen table toying with a cup of cold tea, staring at the picture of Ruthie on the pony.

"Ma, come to bed," said Mike. "Try to sleep."

"No. No. I close my eyes and see her face, that sweet little face. How can

I sleep, Mikey, with that sweet little face staring at me?" She sighed, gazed into her teacup.

Mike walked down the hall to the rear of the apartment. In his room he thought of Rose Ann, the wondrous fragrance of her, the delicate feel of her as she trembled under his touch. Extraordinary creature!

He climbed out onto the fire escape, followed the ladder up to the roof.

The city spread all about him, a dizzying carpet of lights. The bridges to the east arched in bold magnificence and he felt as though he were reaching with them—where? To what? The spans of granite and iron, in their wondrous stretch, promised a world of possibility. He was soaring with them into the future, overleaping all that was ugly and miserable—his tenement existence, poverty, ignorance, brutality.

All would be transformed one day, all would be clean and pure, marble and steel.

He would hold Rose Ann in his arms and dance with her across the Brooklyn Bridge as though it were a rainbow!

He did a boxer's skip motion in a circle, feinted, countered, executed a dazzling combination.

He stopped.

Someone was sitting at the far end of the roof on the parapet, watching him.

"You look good," Yiddle November said in a soft, tired voice.

"Just trying to get the rust out," Mike said, embarrassed.

"I hear you box good."

"I'm trying to learn."

Yiddle November's face was gray in the moonlight; his large body sagged as though under a great weight. "Learn what you can, kid. Keep your nose clean." Behind him in the pigeon hut his birds made a soft, cooing sound.

"Everything's changed these days," Yiddle said so softly Mike barely heard him. "They have no respect these days. They killed Monk, you know."

"Yes."

Monk Eastman, one of the old tough Lower East Side gangsters, had been in eclipse for some time. He had left prison, fought in the Great War, turned legitimate. Some months back he had been gunned down in front of the Blue Bird Café on Fourteenth Street. "Why kill Monk?" Yiddle asked. "Why? Those kids have no respect." He shrugged. "I remember in the old days Monk Eastman would walk down Essex Street and even Dry Dollar Tim Sullivan himself would quake in his boots. But what does it mean to Benny Siegel, Suchowljansky, the *mumser* Foster? Stay clear of them, Mikey, and tell your brother. This is Yiddle November talking, you hear?"

"I'll tell him."

"What do they care, what do they know?" Yiddle said. He stood and peered into his pigeon coop. "There, there," he whispered into the coop. "Everything's going to be all right."

Then he lumbered across the roof and down into the stairway.

* * *

The next night Rose Ann showed up for her meeting with Mike on the bridge. They strolled hand in hand along the walkway beneath the granite arches to the Brooklyn side. On Sands Street they stopped at a candy store and Mike bought Rose Ann an egg cream.

They talked and Rose Ann watched him with great wide eyes as though he were saying the most interesting things in the world. She didn't say much, and to Mike this was part of the attraction she held for him. There was mystery to her, and depth, and Mike was dazzled by the beauty of her.

He told her about his dreams. He would change the Lower East Side, rid it of squalor and poverty, rebuild it as one immense park with ball fields, playgrounds, swimming pools. He would take all the young children and make sure they had enough food and sunlight and warm clothing. No child would ever get sick and die.

"I have bad dreams," she said softly.

"What kind?"

"People kill me."

"Who?"

"Men. Horrible and twisted men."

Mike was confused. "Why would they do that?"

"Because I'm Deirdre. She was a princess. At her birth it was prophesied she would have an unhappy life. That's the way I am. Deirdre was hidden away so she could never look on men. She was to be the bride of Conchobar, King of Ulster. One day she spied another man and fell in love with him . . ." Her voice was breathy, her eyes bright with excitement. "She ran off with him and his brothers to England. King Conchobar lured them back. He killed all but Deirdre. Deirdre died weeping over their graves. She caused her lover's death. I have been bad and deserve to die."

"That's foolish. You don't deserve anything of the sort."

She shook her head. "Sometimes I have so many different thoughts in my mind. They just get all jumbled up."

"That happens to me too. My father has a hot temper and we get into arguments and I feel like my head is going to burst."

On the way back to Manhattan, in the center of the Brooklyn Bridge, Mike took her in his arms and kissed her. She grabbed on to him, trembling. Then she pulled away.

He walked her to Hudson Street. She insisted they part there. She told him she would see him again on the bridge, but she would not tell him when.

They met several more times after that. Gradually a pattern was established. They would meet on the bridge at night, usually on weekends. They would stroll to Brooklyn to the candy store on Sands Street. He would walk her back to Hudson Street. She would not let him walk her farther, nor would she tell him anything about herself, her last name, or where she lived.

The mystery of her excited him. He dreamed up fanciful backgrounds for her: she was an heiress of great wealth, an actress from uptown, an Irish princess. He told her about this and she laughed and then got very serious and would reveal nothing about herself to him.

He found himself confused and troubled by her. At times they related to each other as though they were great, good friends. Her shyness would vanish and they would laugh and talk about silly teenage things. She told him about a girlfriend named Theresa who had a crush on a boy who wanted to become a priest. Theresa was not very pretty and she could not tell the boy how much she liked him. She talked about how she and Theresa practiced dancing together, how they were both interested in needlepoint, how Theresa had won a prize for spelling at school.

At other times she would come to him greatly upset. She could barely talk.

Mike continued to work out at the gym. Those nights when he was not with Rose Ann he would go to the Rutgers Square Settlement House and concentrate on his boxing, pushing himself until he was ready to drop. The presence of Rose Ann remained with him and the turmoil he felt about her was channeled into his workouts. It was the only physical release he felt in boxing that gave him any measure of contentment.

That summer he had a few more amateur fights. He tried to get Rose Ann to come to them, but she would not.

One night as they strolled the bridge he told her he was Jewish. She seemed totally unconcerned. "I knew it," she said.

"Does that make any difference? That I'm Jewish?"

"Difference? In what way?"

"I love you," he said quietly.

She put her fingers to his mouth. "Shhh, don't say that."

"Why not? I love you so much, so very, very much. I can't think of anything else but you. Even when I'm boxing, I think of you."

She laughed a quiet shy laugh and pressed in against him. He was aware of the warmth, the tenderness of her body against him, of the myriad lights speckling the far shore, the ocean breeze, a clatter of passing elevated trains, the low moan of boat horns.

And he realized she was weeping. "What's the matter?"

"You shouldn't have said that," she whispered.

"How do you feel about me?" he asked

She did not speak for a very long time. Then she said, "I like you too much."

Mike Roth knew so little about Rose Ann. He had kissed her and that was all. Yet increasingly he found himself imagining her as his wife. Foolish!

He knew they were just kids, but he couldn't get the thought out of his mind. He wanted to bring it up to her but was too shy.

"Do you ever do things you know are wrong and you can't stop yourself?" Rose Ann said to him one night as they strolled along South Street just below the Brooklyn Bridge. She spoke in hushed tones. She had been quiet all evening, pensive.

"I argue with my father when he's drunk," said Mike. "I shouldn't, but I do, and I feel bad after."

"Oh, I mean things worse than that. It's like we have another person inside us. We're two people. Do you believe in the devil?"

"No."

"He's real—I know he is. The nuns told me about him. And I found out. He's real."

"How did you find out?"

"He comes to me," she said. Then she laughed. She stared out at the water and did not talk for a long time.

"I want to marry you someday," he said.

"Really?" Her voice sounded detached. "That would be sweet." She began to laugh again, and Mike felt embarrassed.

"You're making fun of me."

"Oh, no. No." Then she whispered, "I'm Deirdre." And her eyes were bright and the expression in them was strange, and it seemed that she was not really with him.

One day in early fall after Mike had started school, his brother, Harry, and Jackie Foster approached him outside the settlement house.

A year ago Jackie had been a punk kid, a stray dog hanging around for acceptance. Now he wore sleek, expensive suits. He walked the streets wire-tense, as though he owned them.

In the old days Harry would have hesitated to be seen with him, a weasel. Now he treated him with the same deference bordering on awe he showed for Ben Siegel and Johnny Eggs. Jack Foster had found his place in the world.

Mike turned from Foster. "What are you doing hanging with him?" Mike said to his brother.

Harry grew uneasy. "Jackie's an old friend."

"He treats you like dirt. They all do," Mike said. Harry's handsome face paled; he looked suddenly very small and lost, like a kid who's been left out of a stickball game. Mike felt bad for what he had said. "They're not for you, Harry."

"You shouldn't talk mean about me, Mikey," Jack said. "We used to be friends."

"We were never friends."

"If you say so," Jackie said, starting at Mike with his narrow eyes. "Don't you think Mike and I look like each other, Harry? Don't you see the resemblance?"

"My ass and your face," Mike said, and left them outside the settlement house. He went through his workout, showered, dressed. On the street, Jack Foster was waiting for him alone.

"Let me talk to you, Mikey."

They walked along Rutgers Street toward the East River. "I care for you, Mike. I know you don't like me much. You call me *mumser* and like that. I still care for you."

They came to the park at the river's edge. "I'm a good friend of yours. You'll never know how good. We're brothers, Mike." He laughed a breathy, foolish laugh. "I'm going to show you how good a friend I am."

"I have to get home."

"A minute," Jack said. "You've been seeing a girl—"

"How do you know?"

"I know a lot of things."

Of course Jack would know about him and Rose Ann. That was his way, haunting rooftops, bridge spans, subway tunnels, a gray city rat, spying out everything.

"Do you know who this girl is? This girl is the sister of Tony McGrath."

Mike heard him and knew now: that was it! Tony McGrath's sister! That was why she was so secretive about her family: she would have known about the rivalry between the Nobles and Dusters, the fight he had had with her brother.

The sister of Tony McGrath involved with a Lower East Side Jew—McGrath, the family, the Dusters, all would have been disgraced.

Now he understood why she had been so troubled at times when she met him.

"There's something else," Jackie said. "Come with me."

Jack took Mike by trolley across Canal Street. They got off on West Street adjoining the Hudson River dock area.

The street was jammed with waterfront toughs, Spanish and Portuguese sailors, longshoremen, laborers, trucks, horse-drawn carts, automobiles. Speakeasies flourished; every other building held a pawn shop.

Jack led Mike to a darkened warehouse at the farthest end of the dock area. Why is he bringing me here? Mike thought, suddenly nervous. There were rumors Jack Foster had killed people. Is he looking to do me in because I insulted him earlier?

They climbed a ladder at the end of the warehouse and crawled to the edge of a loading platform overlooking a darkened area of the docks. Jackie suddenly reached behind Mike, grabbed him by the neck, and forced his head forward.

He struggled under Foster's grip, but he could not break it; Jackie's hand tightened and pressed Mike's head forward, toward the edge. "Mikey, you're my brother. Look, look!"

The dock below was dark, but a spill of light from the street carried into one corner. There was a group of people sitting on the dock floor—a half-dozen longshoremen, sailors. Several had their shirts off.

In a corner of the area a girl lay nude with her legs spread. A man rolled off her and another of the men got up and crossed to her and moved on top of her.

She moaned and wrapped her legs around the man. He pushed hard into her and she continued to moan. Her eyes were closed and she faced toward the loading platform.

It appeared as though she were in great pain.

The moon was out, and moonlight washed her pale face. Her long red hair was spread out on the dock floor.

It was Rose Ann McGrath.

7

On Friday night Mike was to meet Rose Ann on the Brooklyn Bridge, but he could not bring himself to go. He was crazed and did not trust himself. He did not know what he would say, what he would do.

He slept badly, had no appetite for food. The image of her lying with the men on the West Side dock festered in his mind, brutal, ugly, obscene. He could not erase it from his memory.

He poured his pain and confusion into his fighting, ripping at the heavy and light bags, pounding his sparring partners mercilessly.

The world had become a terrible place for him.

Later, he walked east down to the river, moving toward the Brooklyn Bridge. It was a cold, early-autumn night. The wind cut in off the water, chilling him. He huddled in his wool jacket and hurried on against the wind and cold.

The bridge arched in the night, an immense, grand magnet, pulling him to it. .

In his head he saw Rose Ann on the dock with the men. The pain he felt inside was terrible, choking.

The bridge walkway was quiet. An occasional couple strolled by. He stopped midway across and stared down into the water. He felt lost, lost, desolate inside.

Someone was watching him. He turned. Rose Ann stood leaning against the thick trunk of one of the bridge's suspension cables. She was clad in a thin cotton dress. She looked pale and wasted in the gray light of the bridge, a spider in a steel web.

"I waited all night on Friday. You never came. What happened?" She asked the question hesitantly; her voice was small.

He could not speak for a long time. Her long red hair, tossed by the wind, twined her neck and face, strands of a spider's web. Her face was streaked with tears, but she was not crying. She is a spider, Mike thought. "I loved you," he said.

"And you don't anymore?" She asked the question hesitantly, afraid of the answer.

"You were with some men on a dock the other night. I saw it."

She stared at him with sad, pained eyes. Her voice was so soft it was almost lost in the wind. "I don't know what you're talking about."

"Liar! It was you! They were on top of you! You're a whore, that's what you are. You're a whore!"

She began to cry; the sound was muted. She trembled. "You told me you wanted to marry me." Her voice was small, small, almost a moan.

"I loved you. Now you disgust me."

"It wasn't me. It wasn't."

She moved toward him. He pulled away. "Don't touch me!"

"No," she whimpered. "Please. No."

He held his fist as though to punch out at her. She stopped. She opened her mouth to scream, but no sound came. She turned and ran from him.

He watched her figure receding along the walkway, hurrying toward the Manhattan shore. She grew small in the immense weave of the bridge; then she was gone.

He felt a stab of pity within him and smothered it. He would not feel pity for a whore. No.

A man must be tough to exist, he told himself. He was no longer a child.

Moving through the neighborhood, Tony McGrath spotted Theresa McMahon coming out of the corner store with a bag of groceries. He hurried to her and took the bag of groceries and they walked along Hudson Street. "I'm worried about Rosie," he said. "She's been going out of the house in the middle of the night. Sometimes she's gone until morning. What is it?"

"I think maybe she has a boyfriend."

"Who?"

"She won't tell me."

"Is he from the neighborhood?"

"I don't know."

At home he tried to talk to Rose Ann about it. She wouldn't answer him. She sat by the front window and stared out and remained silent.

When he returned in the morning from work at the market he found her still sitting by the same window, staring out. She looked thin, terribly pale. "What's the trouble, Rosie?"

She just shook her head. She did not look at him.

"Rosie, what is it?"

She wouldn't answer, and he knew that something was desperately wrong, but he was helpless to do anything about it.

He spoke to Bessie about it and she did not go to the United Irish Club that day. She stayed with Rose Ann.

Rose Ann's eyes were vacant. She sat staring out the front window. "Child, what is it? What's the matter with you? Has someone done something to you?"

Rose Ann did not speak. Bess put her arm around her daughter and sat with her at the window. "Things have not been easy with you, Rosie. I know that. Your father's not well, the war, the drink, and I'm not always here. But you know how much we love you, little darling. Please tell me what's troubling you."

Rose Ann did not answer. She got up and wandered into a back room. Bessie watched pained and bewildered as her daughter walked from room to room. "What are you looking for, Rosie?"

She remained silent.

In the late afternoon after his workout at the gym, Tony returned home. "I don't know what to do," Bessie said. "Something's happened to her. I just don't know what to do."

Tony sat his sister down on the living-room couch. "Rosie, please tell me—what happened? Theresa said she thought you had a boyfriend. Is that it?"

"I am full of sin," she said. "The sign of the Beast is on me. He holds me as a slave. I am the beloved of the Beast!"

She moaned and began to tear at her clothes. She dug her fingernails into her skin and ripped her flesh. "Beloved of the Beast!" she shrieked.

Tony quieted her and she huddled against him on the couch and would not utter another sound.

At the United Irish Club the women who worked with Bess noticed a change had come over her. She continued to push as hard as she had ever done to keep them all on their toes, but there was no joy or humor in her anymore. One night over tea she confided in several of the women. "Something's happened to my child Rosie. I'm at my wit's end. We have to keep a watch on her all the time. She wanders off. We find her late at night down by the dockside. She looks a terrible mess. I think she's lost her mind," Bess said, and it was terrible to have uttered it.

"What will you do with her?"

"I don't know. I don't know. What do you do with a person like that? I never stop praying. I pray for her and I pray for my Paddy and my heart is just so heavy. What else can I do?"

None of the women had an answer for her, and they found it disquieting that the woman who was so powerful in their political club should be so helpless in dealing with her own daughter.

For his part, Tony decided that some injustice had been done to his sister. He visited Theresa again and pumped her for information about a boyfriend. He learned little but came away convinced that, yes, she had been involved with a boy. But who? And what had he done? Tony resolved to find out.

"What do you think, Bessie?" Boss Ahearn said one night in the United Irish Club. "Is Tony ready for the big time?"

Boss Ahearn, John McMahon, and Bill O'Dwyer were planning long-range strategy for Tony's career. Bess and Theresa McMahon sat at a table nearby, working with a list of all the families in the ward, sorting and folding political leaflets.

"He's eating regular and sleeping good," Bessie said.

"But is he looking mean? Does he snap and bark at everybody?" asked the Boss.

"He's mean enough, Boss," Bessie said.

"You got to be mean in this world," said Boss Ahearn. "You got to know whose arm to twist, and how hard."

"I always felt you could catch more flies with sugar than vinegar," Bill O'Dwyer said.

"Bill-O has his point there, Boss," added McMahon.

"He hasn't been in the game long enough," Boss Ahearn said. "What do you think, Bessie? Does Bill-O have the stuff for the political life?"

"He's handsome enough, but he's too nice. He should have become a priest."

"My mother always told me that," said Bill-O. McMahon had brought him in to work on the management of Tony's career. In addition to his job with the police force, Bill-O had been promoting Irish soccer in America. He had good contacts with Irish sportsmen in New York, New Jersey, and Pennsylvania. They would do business with him if he approached them with a first-rate prizefighter, particularly an Irish kid.

Bill-O had been a cop over in Brooklyn for almost five years. He was eager to get out of police work. A terrible thing had occurred recently: a man had attacked him with a knife and he had been forced to kill the man. He had changed after that. He was still polite, friendly, smiling, but there was an underlying seriousness in him now, a watchfulness. He wanted desperately off the force, and Boss Ahearn and Tammany seemed the key to a different future for him.

"If this thing with Tony works out, Bill-O," McMahon said, "you won't need the priesthood or the Hall or nothing."

"Blasphemy!" Boss Ahearn said, a twinkle in his eye. "I don't mind what you say about the Church, but the Hall is sacred ground here. Now, how is Tony's bathroom habits, Bess? We want him regular for fighting."

"Posh," Bessie said with a wave of her hand, while Theresa, embarrassed, stared down at the table. "I gave up checking that when he got out of diapers, Boss."

"These things is important," Boss said. "A fighter got to be regular, you know. There are things in this life of grave importance. The clerk at the license bureau gets his fiver. The cop on the beat gets his too."

"Amen to that, Boss," McMahon said.

"Do they take care of you over in Brooklyn, Bill?" Boss Ahearn asked.

"I never take it."

"He won't sell cheap, Boss," said McMahon.

"That's the boy, Bill-O," Bess said. "That's the boy."

"Wait a second, Bess," said Ahearn. "He didn't say he wouldn't sell. He just said he won't sell cheap."

"His mother wanted him to be a priest. Give the lad credit for moral fiber," Bess McGrath said.

When Tony McGrath wasn't training or working at the Gansevoort Market he prowled the West Side, trying to find out what had happened to bring his sister to madness.

He sensed a certain discomfort among the men who worked on the docks whenever he broached the subject, but no one would tell him anything.

Crossing West Street one evening, he heard someone call his name. He turned to see Jack Foster hurrying through traffic toward him. "I know something about your sister," he said when he reached him. He looked troubled; he spoke with a sincerity so feigned it caused Tony's skin to crawl. "I know all about it. I couldn't bring myself to tell you—"

"What do you know?"

"She's been coming down to the docks here."

McGrath stopped in the middle of the street. Jack backed away from him. Traffic sped around them.

"What do you mean, she's coming down to the docks?"

"I shouldn't have said nothing," Jack said.

"Why is she coming down to the docks?"

"You know, girls sometimes come down to the docks."

"Did you ever touch my sister?"

"It was that kike done it, Mikey Roth. He got her to put out for him, then he threw her over. I'd see them walking down by the bridge by Fulton Street. He was working at the fish market then."

McGrath remembered: last summer Rose Ann would come home in the late evenings with packages of fish for the family. She said a man at the market had given them to her, a friend of Paddy's.

"So when Mikey wouldn't have no more to do with her, she started coming by the West Side docks and these men down here, you know the way they are—"

Tony hit Foster. It was a short, chopping blow just below the ribs. Jack sank to his knees at curbside. He began to gag. "It was the kike done it, Tony. The kike." His face was contorted with pain, but behind it, it seemed as though he was smiling.

Tony left him at the curb and ran the distance back to his apartment.

Rose Ann was seated next to the window. The kids were in the room with her.

He took her face in his hands and turned her to him. "What did Mike Roth do to you?" he demanded. "What did he do?"

She didn't answer.

"What!"

Her voice was barely audible. "He said he wanted to marry me," Rose Ann said.

"Are you a virgin? Rose? Are you a virgin?"

She would not speak.

Later, when Bess came home, she and Tony took Rose Ann to a doctor on Perry Street. He was balding, with a brush mustache. He sucked a sweet-smelling lozenge which he rolled between his lips and teeth.

He examined Rose Ann. After, he looked uncomfortable. He shifted the lozenge around in his mouth. "A girl can lose her viginity in a number of ways," he said. "Horseback riding, bicycle—"

"She doesn't ride horses or a bicycle," Tony said.

"Yes, well . . ."

"Is she a virgin?" he yelled.

"Tony, Tony," Bess said. Rose Ann sat staring at the wall.

"Technically—"

"Don't tell me technically. Is she a virgin?"

"No. No, she's not."

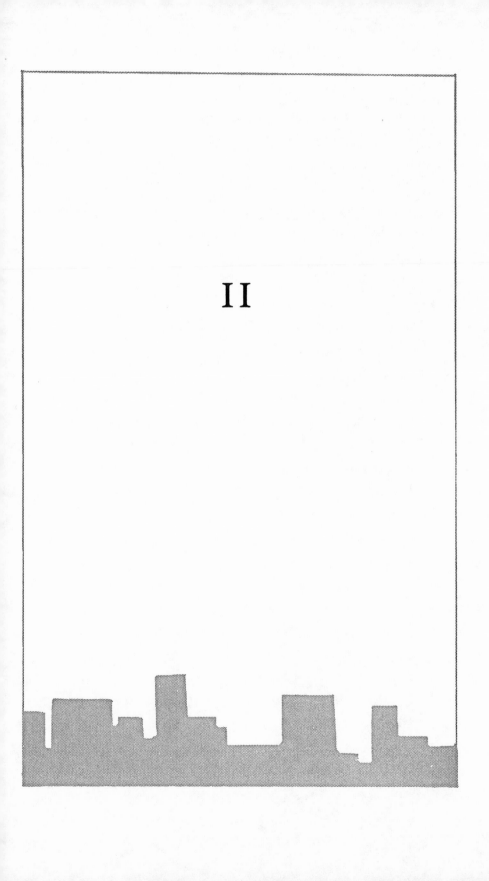

II

8

Before the Great War, Kid Noonen had been a top-ranked lightweight. He had fought Leach Cross, Battling Hurley, and Frankie Madden and acquitted himself well. He had gone off to war and had become a hero. Back home after the armistice he became "Soldier" Noonen and attempted to pick up where he had left off. His career was going well until he ran into Lew Tendler of Philadelphia. Tendler had knocked him senseless in the first round, and from there on it was a slide downward. He gained weight. He moved into the welterweight class, then middleweight. What he gained in pounds he lost in prowess, so that by the year 1924 he was a light heavyweight and fighting preliminaries.

Johnny McMahon hired him to work with Tony McGrath. He had lost the edge of his ability, but there were few fighters around with his canniness.

"The cabbage, Tony, use the cabbage!" Soldier Noonen called out now as he slipped punches and came in with a hard combination to McGrath's midsection. He and McGrath were sparring at the gym in Greenwich Settlement House on Jones Street.

Tony had a job now over on the West Street docks—Bill O'Dwyer, who had been a dockworker before becoming a cop, had secured it for him. He would labor there in the mornings; every afternoon he trained with Soldier Noonen.

In the beginning Noonen had used Tony as a punching bag, and Tony discovered that the worst pro was capable of humiliating the best amateur. Noonen knew every vicious trick in the trade—thumbing, heeling, hitting on the break, rabbit and kidney punches—and he was not averse to employing them in the gym.

They went at it day after day, week after week. After two months Tony wanted to chuck the whole thing. The Soldier was too rugged. Boxing had been fun for him at one time; now it was a form of torture. But he stuck with it. The mean streak in Soldier had angered him and filled him with determination.

It took him nearly six more months before he started to get to Noonen. Even then he wasn't certain it was his ability or a general decline in the Soldier's prowess.

At about this time Johnny McMahon and Bill-O began to get him fights: smokers at Knights of Columbus Council Hall on Twenty-third Street, the Presentation Catholic Young Men's Club in Brooklyn, the Sharkey Athletic Club, and the Avonia Athletic Club.

These fights were usually for a few bucks and a sandwich and a glass of ginger ale. After training with Soldier Noonen, he found that the guys he went up against were pushovers.

Soon McMahon and Bill-O had him fighting tougher boys in preliminaries at the Bayonne A.A., the Jersey City Armory, and the Pioneer Athletic Club, where the purses might be as much as two hundred dollars.

He had developed into a solid middleweight and he was still growing. He had one ambition: to fight in Madison Square Garden at Fourth Avenue and Twenty-sixth Street. There were rumors that the New York Life Insurance Company, which owned the Garden, would be tearing it down. To fight in the same arena that had seen the Irish heroes of an earlier day—Bob Fitzsimmons, Kid McCoy, the great John L. Sullivan, and Gentleman Jim Corbett—was Tony's passionate dream.

Bill and McMahon were working on it, but McGrath's ability had become a stumbling block to his advancement: none of the good middleweights wanted any part of him.

"Watch it, watch it," Soldier Noonen yelled, feinting one way, darting another. He grabbed Tony and held, punched, and backpedaled. Tony was on top of him, whacking a furious chop to the side of the head. Noonen's knees buckled and he waved McGrath off. "That's it for today," the Soldier said.

They left the gym and walked over to McMahon's speakeasy. It was a crisp fall day and McGrath felt good. He had just turned eighteen. He was hitting his stride. He had a sense within him that no one could beat him—not even the kid from the Lower East Side, Mike Roth.

In the past couple of years, since he turned pro, he had thought very often about Mike Roth. An echo of his battle with Roth stayed with him. Jesus, the kid had been tough! There were days when he felt no one could whip him in the ring. Yet often at night just before he dropped off to sleep the fight at the docks would come to him in vivid detail; he would go through it blow by blow.

What had beome of Roth? He had fought in a few amateur tournaments and whipped everyone he went up against. Knowledgeable people said he would turn pro; everyone was watching him. Later, he just faded. Tony heard he broke his hand and lost interest in prizefighting. In this year, 1924, no one spoke of him at all. But Tony McGrath remembered.

Tony had given up concerning himself with what happened between Roth and his sister. Since that time Rose Ann had become increasingly more withdrawn, sadder, and he recognized that her involvement with Roth had been only a catalyst to her breakdown; had it not been him, it would have been someone else.

Sometimes late at night he would sit with Rose Ann and attempt to get through to her, to penetrate the shell of madness in which she lived. His efforts were futile and he would feel a profound sense of injustice. Why? Why her?

Bess had the most difficult time of it. She could not spend more than a few minutes with Rose Ann, barely could bring herself to talk to her. She would become choked with emotion, feel herself losing control, and hurry from the house to busy herself with her political work at the United Irish Club, seeking to find for others a simple justice in the world to replace that which she sensed could never be restored: her daughter's sanity.

Rose Ann stayed in the house now most of the time. She played with dolls like a little girl. The younger brothers watched out for her.

Emmett was fifteen years old, a tall, handsome kid who recently had left school and was working with John McMahon's construction business.

Greenwich Village was changing. There was a building boom; the old houses were coming down and large apartment houses were replacing them. McMahon had taken his profits from the speakeasy and put them into real estate and construction. And he dreamed of owning a future boxing champion.

"Hey, Champ, what'll you have?" Ernie, the bartender at McMahon's, called out as Tony and Soldier Noonen entered.

"Milk," McMahon said. He was seated at a table with Boss Ahearn and Bill-O. It was early evening and the speak was almost empty.

"Give me a beer," Tony said, approaching the table.

"You want to fight in the Garden with a beer belly on you?" McMahon said.

"What do you mean, Garden?"

"We got you in there, Tony," said Bill-O. "Six rounds, three weeks from Friday."

"The Garden?"

"By the holy saints!" McMahon said, grinning.

"The Garden!" Tony hugged Bill-O around the shoulders. "The damn Garden!" He danced around throwing punches in the air.

"Thank the Boss here," said Bill-O.

Soldier Noonen approached the table. "Did you hear, Soldier?" Boss Ahearn said. "We got the Garden for the kid, you old bag of cauliflower."

"Cauliflower is it!" Soldier Noonen said, faking as though to square off with the Boss.

"Don't mess with me, Soldier, I'll kick you in the family jewels. That's the only way I play the game."

"Yes, sir!" the Soldier said, snapping to attention and saluting.

"Give us champagne, Ernie!" Boss Ahearn called to the bartender.

"I got some guinea wine I can piss in. That's the best I can do, Boss."

"We got to celebrate here, do you see what I mean?" Boss said. "There's great good news. Tony's got the Garden and Bill-O here passed his bar exam."

"That's lovely Bill, lovely," Tony said, greatly pleased, although he was only dimly aware of the significance of Bill-O's accomplishment.

"He'll be leaving the force and I want to get him together with Alderman Joyce over in Brooklyn," said the Boss. "There are great things to be done in Brooklyn." Bill-O looked uncomfortable.

Ernie brought a gallon jug of red wine to the table.

"The Talker was by the other day," McMahon said. "And your mother, Bess, really let him have it. 'Talker,' she says, 'when are you going to get off the pot?' 'What do you mean, Bessie?' the Talker says. 'We wants you for mayor, all your friends do,' Bessie says. 'But you got Red Mike Hylan. What am I going to do about Red Mike?' 'Speak with Alfred E.,' she says. 'He'll tell you what to do with Red Mike.'"

"She's right about that," Bill-O said. "Alfred E.'ll call that tune there."

"No doubt in my mind the Hall is going to back Jim Talker," Boss Ahearn said.

Bill-O replied, "McCooey over in Brooklyn isn't going to like that."

"The Man in the Derby will call the shot eventually," said McMahon. The Man in the Derby was Al Smith, who two years before had regained the governorship of the state in a landslide election.

"The Man in the Derby never did like Red Mike," Boss Ahearn insisted. "Red Mike is nothing but a Hearst man, and everybody knows it. Hearst calls the tune and Hylan and McCooey dance to it. That's why we'd like to see you become active over in Brooklyn, Bill-O."

"Bill-O's a poet," McMahon said. "He doesn't have the stomach for the political life."

"Poets do very well with the Hall. Al Smith is a poet, Jimmy Talker's a poet, and I agree, Bill-O's a poet. The city needs poets. Our people like a man who's given to singing and dancing, tripping the light fantastic like Mr. James J. Talker—"

"—given to the ladies," McMahon said with a twinkle.

Boss Ahearn leaned back in his chair and chomped meditatively on his cigar. "That's his problem, running around with that damn chorus girl where everyone can see him. You know, the governor looks down on that sort of thing. He's a family man, and unless Talker becomes a little more discreet, well, who knows, Mike's still not out of the ball game.

"The Talker's a special sort," McMahon said. "The Talker's one of a kind, he is."

Boss Ahearn stood. "Well, I got to be getting home. The battleax is waiting with the rolling pin." He extended his mitt to Tony and left. At the door he turned. "See that material gets over to the typist, Johnny."

"Sure thing, Boss."

After the Boss departed, Bill-O got up and prepared to leave. "Come walk me to the subway, Tony."

"Tony, you know where the Maddoxes live over on Bedford?" John McMahon asked.

"I know where they live."

"Drop this over," said McMahon. "The oldest girl's been doing work for the Boss, and the Boss's friends help out the family." He handed Tony a large folder filled with papers.

"And don't linger, Tony," said Ernie. "The girl's a looker, and a guy in training shouldn't tempt himself."

"Laura? The one with all the freckles, went to St. Veronica's with my sister? She's a puppy dog."

"If she's a puppy dog, show me the kennel," replied Ernie.

On the way to the subway, Bill-O was quiet. "The men of the Hall are magic," he said at last, as though talking to himself. "Boss Ahearn, Mr. McCooey over in Brooklyn. All kind, good people, family people. And they end up owning you. They own you by their kindness. That's a sort of magic."

"I don't understand."

"They want to do favors for me."

"What's wrong with that?"

"If I let them, I'll have to pay them back someday."

"You mean my fight in Madison Square?"

"That's the least of it, lad. That's the least of it."

Tony watched as Bill-O moved down the stairs to the subway, and he realized how much he cared for the man: he was honest, strong, yet with a loneliness about him, a shyness—poetic, as Johnny McMahon said.

The Maddox family lived on the top floor in a cold-water flat tenement. There were seven kids in the family and their longshoreman father had been killed in an accident at the docks. They were desperately poor.

The door was opened by a strange woman, tall and beautiful.

"Is Laura here?" Tony asked. "I have something for her."

The woman smiled but did not answer.

"This is the Maddox house, isn't it?"

"Last time I checked, it was," she said, and then began to laugh. "Hello, Tony."

There was a sudden shock of recognition: it was Laura Maddox! He remembered her as a funny-faced gangly kid, all freckles. Although not yet eighteen years old, she was now a cool, strikingly attractive lady.

Her clothes were out of keeping with the tenement surroundings; she looked as if she had just come from an uptown bash. She had on a tight black dress, gold high-heeled shoes, and her blond hair was marcelled in the current flapper style.

Tony felt foolish, as though he were the kid and she the adult. "Johnny McMahon sent this over," he said, handing her the folder.

"Oh, yes. Well, come in!"

"I have to be getting along."

"For one minute, Tony."

He moved into the apartment. It teemed with disorder—bathtub in the kitchen, kids' clothing hanging all over, paint peeling from the ceiling.

A thin gray-haired woman sat at the kitchen table in a torn housedress. There was a jar of bootleg whiskey in front of her. Through the arch leading into the living room Tony could see the forms of sleeping children scattered about on mattresses on the floor. "Ma, you remember Tony McGrath, don't you?"

The woman looked up. "Bess McGrath's boy? Ah, your mother, she's a saint, lad. Heaven only knows when my Jerry was taken from me what that woman done for us! God bless her, God bless her, God bless that woman!"

"Let's go in the back," Laura said to Tony. "My mother starts her 'God blesses' we could be here all night."

She led Tony down a long hallway to the rear of the apartment.

Her room was neat, well-furnished, and done in pastel colors—a curious contrast to the rest of the place. On the wall were pictures cut from magazines and framed—Ramon Novarro, Valentino, John Gilbert, Clara Bow, Renee Adoree. A large ornate plaster cast of Jesus on the Cross hung above the bed.

"This is swell here," said Tony, ill-at-ease.

"Thank you." She sat on the edge of the bed. "Sit down."

Tony sat on a delicate pink-upholstered chair in one corner of the room. "I've been following your career," Laura said. "You've become quite the neighborhood hero."

Her manner of speaking seemed forced, almost British, with an edge of street toughness.

There was a gold evening purse on the nightstand and she removed a cigarette from it and lit up. "I don't suppose you want one?"

"I'm in training."

"Of course." She inhaled deeply and blew smoke out through her nose. "How's Rosie?"

"She has some all-right days. Not many."

"She was always such a sweet, good girl. It's a sad thing, Tony. I would hear these stories about her, you know, with men and everything, and I just couldn't fit it with what I knew about her. She was always so innocent."

"It's a mystery," said Tony, not wishing to discuss it. "When was the last time I saw you?"

She laughed and there was a girlish lilt to it that thrilled him. "I don't know when you last saw me. I used to see you all the time."

"Have you seen me fight?"

"No, though about five years ago I saw you with the Young Dusters and there was a big hey-rube over on Hudson with some sheen—Jewish fellows from the East Side."

"That's right."

"And then one day I was playing on the stoop in front of your house and you and Bess came by."

"You have a good memory."

"For certain things."

There was an uncomfortable silence. She was staring at Tony and he felt awkward. "Three weeks from now I'll be fighting in Madison Square Garden," he blurted out, feeling clumsy as he did it.

"Oh, that's marvelous."

"What do you do now? Are you in school?" Again, he felt foolish. Of course she wasn't in school; she was obviously out in the world.

"I work for the Hall, sort of."

"A political job?"

"Yes. I work for a positively brilliant man who is a confidant of the governor of the state, Mr. Al Smith."

"That must be very interesting."

"It's very exciting. I'm quite lucky." She leaned back on the bed, hiking her dress up high on her leg; he could see the flesh above her knees. The cigarette dangled from her lip and she gazed at Tony with half-shut eyes while smoke curled toward the ceiling; it was a pose he recognized from a hundred vamp-girl films. "I was in secretary school. Your mother came over to see if there was anything she could do for us and then sent me to see Mr. Ahearn. He knew I was studying to be a secretary so he sent me over to Mr. Jason Karl, who is a very, very exceptional man of great prestige. He works for the Parks and Roads Commission of the state."

"I see."

"Yes." She stubbed out her cigarette in an ashtray beside the bed. She continued to stare at Tony. "Do you like the way I look?"

"You look good."

"I go to class once a week at this beauty school. They teach you how to put on makeup and how to walk." She got up and strolled the length of the room, standing very tall with her shoulders held back. "It's very uncomfortable until you get used to it," she said, slumping back into her former posture. "And they teach you how to talk: *'I am the very model of a modern major general,'*" she recited rapidly in a clipped British voice.

"That sounds good," he said, not believing it.

"I want to be beautiful."

"You are beautiful."

"Come here, Tony, kiss me." He hesitated. "Well, come *on,*" she said impatiently.

He moved to her. His heart was racing wildly and he could feel perspiration forming on the palms of his hands. "What about your mother?"

Laura Maddox stretched her leg out and kicked the door to the room shut. "She's drunk as a loon as usual. She never gives me lip about anything I do. She better not. I'm supporting this family."

She opened her arms. Tony leaned forward and kissed her. She threw her arms around him and held him tightly. They kissed for a long time. Tony stretched out on the bed next to her. She pressed her body tight against his. He could feel the heat of her sex burning against him.

He heard a sound in the hallway, a floorboard creak, footsteps. He froze. Then he heard a door close. "She'll be out like a light," Laura said. "The building could fall down and she wouldn't hear it."

He slid his hand under her dress. The skin of her legs was velvet. She spread her legs and he felt the silk of her panties and then his fingers moved about the edge and he could feel a curl of hair.

She sat up quickly. "No. Not like this."

"What?"

"I want it to be right between us." She lit a cigarette. "Everyone thinks I'm so fast. Well, I'm not. When I go to bed with a man I want it to be for love." She stared at him. "I could love you." She smiled at him and she looked beautiful beyond imagining.

"I've had a crush on you since I was eight years old, when I used to stop by your house to play with Rose Ann and Theresa McMahon. I've always thought I could love you." She grew thoughtful, almost sad. "Could you love me, too?"

"Yes," Tony answered, and to his amazement he realized he meant it: he was already in love with her.

9

The three weeks before Tony McGrath's Madison Square Garden appearance went by for him as though in a dream. He struggled to keep his attention on the fight. All he could think of was Laura Maddox.

He tried not to see her. He explained he had to keep his concentration on the fight. Nevertheless he would come to her after his training and they would lie on her bed fully clothed and kiss and press their bodies tightly together. He would be swept up in passion then catch himself. He would stand up quickly and pace the room. He would shadowbox in front of the mirror while Laura laughed at his discomfort.

One night he took her out to dinner at Mock's on Hudson Street. Laura insisted on paying. Tony argued with her, but she explained that her boss, Mr. Karl, had given her a bonus for work she had done at home. If she gave it to her mother, she'd only drink it up.

After dinner they walked over to Washington Square Park. They sat on the edge of the fountain and watched the swells who inhabited the north side of the square, women in gowns and furs with men in tuxedos and top hats on their evening strolls.

It was late fall and very cold, and they huddled together and he kissed her softly, gently, a man very much in love.

He told her he loved her.

"I love you, too, Tony."

"I want you so bad." He slipped his hand under her coat and began to move it over her breast. Her breathing quickened.

"Oh, yes. I want you, too. But it has to be special."

"After the fight. I have to save myself. Boss Ahearn says that's how the Great John L. lost to Gentleman Jim, fooling around before their match."

She promised to come to the locker room when the fight was over. They would take a hotel room together that very night, one of the grand places on Fifth Avenue. She would pay for it.

He wanted to buy her a ticket for the bout but she would not hear of it. "The Tammany people will all be there. Mr. Karl insists on taking me."

He grew quiet.

"What's the matter?"

He didn't answer.

"You're jealous!"

"Yes."

She laughed, and her laugh was like music to him. "Oh, Tony, he's an old man. He must be nearly forty. His wife is dead and he's lonely. And he likes me with him because he gets ideas and he needs someone to take notes. He's an engineer and he's always dreaming up designs for buildings and roads and bridges and things like that, things for the state."

They kissed and her lips were soft as rose petals.

On the way to the Garden the day of the fight in McMahon's Hudson roadster with Johnny, Bill-O, and Soldier Noonen, he gloried in his fortune. He couldn't remember when he had been so happy. How extraordinary his life had become! Laura Maddox loved him. They would be together after the fight. In a short while he would be boxing in Madison Square Garden!

All the neighborhood folk would be in attendance—his friends and family, Tammany big shots, show-business celebrities, great athletes. Al Jolson would be there, and Babe Ruth and George M. Cohan! And Laura Maddox, beautiful beyond imagining, an apparition! And she was his, his love. He was drunk with love of her, dizzy with anticipation of her.

There were two headline bouts that night, featherweights in an elimination tourney to see who would get a chance at a title fight, Kid Kaplan against Bobby Garcia, then Danny Kramer and Mike Dundee. Tony McGrath was in the last preliminary.

His opponent was a journeyman fighter by the name of Ace Hepner, also known as the Dakota Wildcat. The Wildcat with his scarred face and battered nose appeared fierce, but turned out to be a pussycat who dived for the canvas at the first solid punch Tony landed. Despite the crowd's jeers, he would not get up, and Tony was awarded a knockout in the first round.

After he dressed he waited in the locker room for Laura, but she didn't show up. His brothers came back with Paddy and they had all been drinking, even Willy, the youngest. Paddy could barely stand and Tony instructed Emmett, who was the most sober, to take everyone home in a cab after the main events.

Bill-O and Johnny McMahon had returned to the arena to see Kid Kaplan mix it up with Bobby Garcia. Tony waited for a while in the locker room, then went back to the rear of the Garden. He searched for Laura in the crowd but could not see her. Jason Karl and Laura were nowhere around.

After the Garcia-Kaplan fight, Bill-O joined Tony. He had his overcoat on. "Where are you off to?" Tony asked.

"I'll be going back to Brooklyn. My wife will be waiting up for me."

"I'll walk you to the subway. I want to get some air."

At the subway entrance Bill-O said, "What's the matter, lad?"

"I just feel empty, is all. My first fight at the Garden, I thought it would be a bigger deal. It was just a fight." He could not tell him about Laura, the disappointment of her not showing up after the fight.

"That's the way it goes. You got one of your dreams tonight and they're like dust: you touch them and they just crumble. But you have many more coming." He shook hands with Tony. "I'll try to get over to the gym during the week," he said, then hurried down into the subway station.

Tony started back toward the Garden. A crowd was coming out; the last main event was over.

McMahon's Hudson pulled up to the curb. Inside were Johnny, Boss Ahearn, and a small elflike man whom Tony had never seen before. Tony slid into the backseat with the man. "This is Frank Matthews, Tony," McMahon said. "He used to manage Kid McCoy."

"The *Real* McCoy," Matthews said. He was a man in his sixties, but he had the face and smile of a kid. "You looked good out there tonight, Tony."

"But can we make him a champion?" Boss Ahearn asked.

"I think we can," answered Matthews.

Johnny was steering the car toward the Lower East Side. "Drop me home," Tony said.

"Like hell," said Boss Ahearn. "We're celebrating, boyo!"

Tony protested, but McMahon wouldn't hear of it. Benny Leonard's brother had opened a new speak. The top operators in the fight game gathered at the place. "There's deals to be made there, Tony," McMahon said. "We want everybody to see your face. Publicity's important in this game."

"Hard work'll make a man successful," Boss added, "but it's publicity that puts the cap on it. There's guys couldn't get a shot at an eight-rounder, became champs when they had the right newspaperman pushing them."

Benny Leonard's brother's place was called the Ringside and the dance floor was designed to resemble a boxing ring. The club was crammed with fight people, racket boys, politicians, high-class notch girls.

They were given a table right next to the dance floor, and people kept coming up to it, conferring with Matthews, congratulating Tony. The music was loud, the bootleg booze rotten.

Tony thought about Laura. What had happened to her? Why hadn't she joined him after the fight? He was angry and depressed and his win that night was like ashes in his mouth.

"Kid McCoy's real name is Norman Selby," Matthews was saying, "and he's one of the meanest, trickiest men I ever come upon. His favorite joke is, he comes into a gym and offers some kid a boxing lesson for five dollars. The kid shells out the fin spot—after all, this is the Real McCoy! 'Who's that with you?' McCoy says, and when the kid looks back, he cold-cocks him. 'Lesson number one,' he says. 'Never turn your head on your opponent.' "

"Frank'll be coming aboard with us," McMahon said to Tony. "He'll be managing with us."

"Does Bill-O know this?"

"Bill-O's a nice fellow," said Boss Ahearn, "but he isn't acquainted with all the ropes yet, get what I mean?"

"We'll teach him the ropes," Matthews answered.

There was a stir at the rear of the club and a large party entered. The band began to play "Will You Love Me in December As You Do in May?" and Tony realized James J. Walker had arrived. In his group was Laura Maddox with Jason Karl.

The crowd cheered and applauded and he waved as he made his way toward the dance floor. Two waiters moved a table to where Tony's group was sitting, and Jimmy Walker and his party joined them.

There was too much noise and confusion for introductions; everybody just nodded and waved around the table. In addition to Laura and Karl, there were three other couples in the party. The men appeared to be business people, the women showgirls or hookers. Jim Walker, who was without a woman this night, sat next to Tony.

More drinks were brought to the table, and Walker lifted his glass: "To one of our good tough Village boys, the pride of Hudson Street, Irish Tony McGrath!"

Everyone laughed and toasted Tony, and he should have felt proud, but he was upset and his mind was racing: Laura had seemed surprised to see him when she entered the club. Even now she had not looked at him directly. Why? What was going through her mind?

She made no sign that she even knew him. He wanted to speak to her, but she was at the far end of the table.

"Where's Vonnie?" Boss Ahearn asked, leaning across Tony.

"Have to keep her out of sight," answered Jimmy Walker. "We're trying to win Algie over."

"He'll go along," Boss Ahearn said. "There's no one smarter than Algie Smith, and he has to realize Red Mike's a stone around our neck. And Red Mike's tied to Hearst, and Algie hates W.R. with a passion I've rarely seen."

"To Algie, Hearst's name stinks all over the city. He's never forgiven him for that milk thing," Walker said, referring to a charge Hearst had made in his papers against Al Smith. "W.R. made himself an enemy for life when he accused Algie of taking the milk out of babies' mouths."

The master of ceremonies announced Miss Bee Bee Palmer, and a woman in an impossibly tight silver flapper dress dripping with beads and frills launched into a demonstration of the shimmy dance. She shimmied and shook as though her body was agitated by an egg beater, and the crowd whistled and squealed.

When her act was over the master of ceremonies announced: "I have the great pleasure, ladies and gentlemen, of introducing you to a young man who's one of the best prospects to come down the pike in a long time. Tonight at Madison Square Garden he was a preliminary fighter, but I'm sure you'll be seeing him soon in main events. I'm referring to the Irish Belter, Tim McGraw!"

He waved in Tony's direction and Johnny McMahon stood up and bawled out loudly: "McGrath! Irish Tony McGrath!"

"That's what I said," the master of ceremonies shot back, "only I said it with a Yiddish accent!"

Everyone laughed and the band broke into a few bars of "When Irish Eyes Are Smiling," and Tony rose and took an awkward bow.

"And also sitting over there in the Shamrock section"—laughter and a few hoots—"I have the great honor of introducing to you my very dear friend, a friend of the prizefight game, a friend to Jew and Irishman alike, the very colorful James J. Walker, the next mayor of the city of New York!"

Beau James stood and the band played a few bars of "Will You Love Me in December As You Do in May?" "I accept the nomination," he said, to laughter. "My friend Georgie up there has been *nudging* about this for some time now. I honestly prefer to remain in the state Senate, but if the call came, I might be persuaded to accept it. And I'll tell you why. I love New York. I love New York more than anything in the whole wide world!"

The crowd broke out in wild cheers. Walker sat down. McMahon and Boss Ahearn reached over and shook his hand. Tony shook his hand also, and to his surprise found it cold and clammy. Despite his apparent ease and good humor, Jim Walker was nervous, and Tony found this bewildering.

Laura was up now, moving toward the ladies' lounge. Jason Karl appeared lost in thought. He doodled on a small notepad on the table in front of him. Tony got up and followed after Laura.

He waited in an alcove between the rest rooms. Laura Maddox came out. She smiled, but it was thin and tense. "I'm sorry, Tony. Something came up with Mr. Karl and I had to go with him for a short while."

"How about now?"

"I can't do that. I have things to go over with Mr. Karl."

Tony felt his stomach grow very tight. "What things?"

"Business."

"At this hour?"

"Don't be like that, Tony. There are important political matters going on right now between Mr. Walker and Governor Smith, and Jason is in the middle of it all." She pressed his hand but she kept glancing over at the table where Jason Karl sat. "I want things to be right with us. We'll be together very soon. I promise you."

"Do you love me?" Tony said, feeling stupid as he asked.

"Yes." She leaned close to him and kissed him on the cheek. "I love you very much."

She returned to the table. Tony waited a minute, then followed after her, confused. He felt as though he was out of his league, playing a game the rules of which he was only dimly aware.

Someone grabbed his arm before he could reach his table. It was Jackie Foster. "Tony, say hello to my friends." He indicated three slick, heavy-lidded East Side tough guys at the table with him. "Ben Siegel, Johnny Eggs, Lepke Buchalter—this is Tony McGrath." The men were engaged in serious discussion and barely acknowledged Tony. Jackie pulled Tony down to him and said in a voice only he could hear, "These are big men, these mockies. I know which side the bread is buttered on." He patted Tony's cheek. "How's Rosie doing?"

Tony pulled away. "What business is it of yours?" he said angrily.

Siegel looked over at him. "You got a loud voice. Take a walk before I rip your tongue out."

"Tony's all right, Ben," Jack Foster said. "Him and I are like brothers. Isn't that right, Tony?" He laughed his curious nasal laugh.

Tony was staring at Siegel. "I told you to take a walk," Siegel repeated.

Buchalter said something in Yiddish to Siegel, who smiled and shrugged. He looked up at Tony with an utterly benign, open expression—a small, friendly boy. "Lep tells me I'm being rude. I apologize."

Tony moved off. When he reached the table, he discovered that Laura and Jason Karl had left.

10

In January of the new year Yiddle November was gunned down in the early dawn as he closed up his gambling club on Allen Street.

His funeral was a grandiose event. Limousines stretched along Ludlow Street, north, well past Rivington. A number of veteran hackney drivers also brought out their horses and carriages for the occasion. The weeping and wailing in the street were spectacular.

Mike Roth stood on the sidewalk as the old-time gangster's coffin was brought out of his house. He was surprised to see Yiddle being given an Orthodox funeral. Bearded men in prayer shawls, fur hats, and dark overcoats carried the coffin to the limo; they were followed by Yiddle's family.

Mike had never seen the gangster's wife. A small, dumpy woman who looked like a peasant, she was considerably different from what he had imagined. She seemed dazed by the fuss, unable to comprehend why someone would want to murder her husband. While all about her wailed, she moved into the widow's limousine without uttering a sound.

All the Lower East Side gangsters were there: Farvel Kovalick, Louis Kravitz, Ben Siegel, Lepke Buchalter, Meyer Lansky (the man they called Johnny Eggs), and Little Augie Orgen, the king of the district racket boys. Mike caught sight of his brother, Harry, sharing a car well down the line with a group of low-level punks.

The procession started out for the cemetery in Brooklyn and Mike returned to his tenement. On the stairway he encountered Jackie Foster in a tuxedo. He had a fixed smile on his face. "I set Yiddle's birds free. That's the least I could do." Then he hurried outside to join the funeral procession.

Mike Roth was filled with sadness at the idea of the dead man's pigeons wheeling above the tenement as day faded to dusk—hovering, wheeling, waiting, waiting. And the single being that gave meaning to their world would not come, not that night nor the next nor ever.

In the evening he went with his father to Militinu's speakeasy on Rivington. Harry met them there. Things had been going badly for Charlie Roth: his reputation as a troublemaker had made it increasingly difficult for him to get work with the contractors in the area. Harry had been giving him money, and it was devastating for him to accept gangster earnings, but he had no choice.

"It's a crime that a rotten piece of humanity like that Yiddle November should get a funeral like he got," Charlie said.

"He was a harmless old guy," replied Harry. They were drinking red Rumanian wine and eating pickles, raisins, and nuts while Sam Militinu played his Gypsy cymbalon and sang songs of dark-eyed women, horse thieves, unrequited love, blood feuds.

"You would like that, wouldn't you?" said Charlie, brooding. "A gangster's funeral. Keep working at it, you'll get it."

He turned away from his elder son. Earlier Harry had slipped him some money. He had accepted it without thanks, not even acknowledging he had received it. He sat gloomily listening to Militinu play the cymbalon, drank his wine, ignored his sons.

Mike felt a responsibility to his father, but what could he do? He was working on the docks down at South Street. Most of his pay he contributed to the house but it wasn't much.

Out of high school now, he had no idea what direction to move his life. He still did a good deal of sketching and fantasized about becoming an architect, a foolish dream. In the evenings he would visit the Rutgers Square Settlement House, although he didn't box much these days. He sat in on the art classes and lectures, spent hours in the library. He read all the plays of Shakespeare and memorized great sections of them. He read Balzac, Dickens, Mark Twain, Frank Norris, Jack London.

He dreamed of a world better than the one he knew.

"It's an ugly world," Harry said to him now, leaning close. "Look what they did to Yiddle. He wasn't a bad guy. You know who it was killed him, don't you?"

"Who?"

"Jack Foster," Harry said softly.

Mike sat horrified at his brother's revelation about Yiddle's murder. Jack Foster! "Why?" he asked.

"They don't need a reason. They have their own reasons."

Mike started to say something, but Harry put his fingers to his lips. "The walls have ears." He rested back in his chair. "So what are you up to these days?"

"The same."

"How are the hands?"

Mike shrugged. The hand he had injured in one of his amateur fights had healed badly. He had broken it several times, then broke the other hand. He accepted it as a sign that a boxing career was not to be his.

Moe Kotovsky had taken it harder than he had. Kotovsky had dreams of developing him into a champion, but Mike vowed never to fight again, and was relieved. Everyone expected so much from him. He had expected so much from himself. Now that it was impossible to fight, he was forced to look for another direction for his life. He had not found it yet.

"Mikey, that Irish kid you fought on the docks, McGrath, everyone's talking what a great prospect he is," Harry said. "They're talking he's going to make a fortune. And you can beat him, Mikey."

In recent years Harry had become increasingly more desperate. All his cronies had moved up in the rackets, but he was still thought of as a small-timer, a hustler without the requisite viciousness to become anything more. He hung on the periphery of the mobs, curried favor with the big shots, picked up a few crumbs here and there.

"Mikey, there's money to be made out in Brooklyn and Long Island in real estate. But you need capital to get started. If you went back to boxing, turned pro . . ."

Mike spread his hands on the oilcloth of the table. His knuckles were raised lumps, red, distorted. "I don't have the hands. You don't have the hands, you can't fight. What can I do, Harry?"

Charlie stood up. He was drunk, although he didn't show it. "Big shots," he said loudly. "Gangsters, prizefights, real estate! I spit on the two of you!" He held out his hands toward his sons. Blackened with tar, gnarled, callused, they trembled with his anger. "These were made for one thing—to work with! Not to fight, not to kill. You work with your hands—or you play music like Sam Militinu." He moved to Militinu and hugged him and kissed him on the side of the head, then did a little dance around the tables and without saying good-bye to his sons left the speakeasy.

The next day at the settlement house Mike tested his hands on the heavy bag. It was no good. As soon as he hit full out, the pain was excruciating.

A well-dressed man had entered the gym. He stood watching Mike for a while. "Feel like going a few easy rounds?" the man asked. He was middle-aged but in good shape.

"I'll have to take it real easy."

"That's fine."

The man changed into a pair of trunks and he and Mike sparred on the mat. Moe Kotovsky entered the gym and watched. The man had a nice jab and was clever. For his age, he boxed quite well.

Mike did little more than block and slip punches and occasionally throw a jab. They both worked up a heavy sweat.

"You know what you're doing," Mike said after they had finished.

"I used to box in college, Princeton—long time ago." He shook his head and laughed. "I was AAU lightweight champion in 1905."

There was an icebox in the corner of the gym, and Mike took out some chunks of ice, put them in a bucket, and soaked his hands. "Bad hands," he said.

"That's unfortunate, because you're very good." Kotovsky joined them, and the man said to him, "He's quite a stylist."

"He had a punch too. He could have had some career."

"It's better like this," said Mike. "Maybe I'll do other things."

"He draws real good. He can draw a straight line like nothing, without a ruler or nothing."

"What would you like to do?" the man asked.

"He wants to become an architect."

Mike laughed and shook his head. "I like to sketch buildings and things, but to be an architect you need school. I have to earn a living."

The man grew thoughtful. He pushed the heavy bag, watched it swing back and forth. After he showered and dressed, he approached Mike and handed him his card. "If you're looking for a job, I might be able to help you."

"Who is he?" Mike asked after the man had left.

"His family are big contributors to the settlement house. A lot of money," answered Kotovsky. "His name is Jason Karl."

11

Tony McGrath and Laura Maddox, elegant in rented formal attire, danced late into the night on the roof garden of the Ritz-Carlton Hotel on Fifth Avenue and Forty-seventh Street. They danced to Vincent Lopez' Orchestra playing "Meet Me in St. Louis, Louie," "Waltz Me Around Again, Willie," and "Rings on My Finger."

All about them, visible through great tall windows, night lights of the city spun gently as they danced. It was snowing; the city looked achingly beautiful, dreamlike.

"My mother always told me you could tell what kind of a lover a man would be by the way he danced," Laura said.

"How will I do?"

"It takes my breath away just thinking about it," she said, pressing close to him.

It was past midnight when they returned to their room, the honeymoon suite, which they had rented for fifteen dollars. For an extra dollar slipped to the bellboy they had been provided with a bottle of bootleg gin.

They had registered as Mr. and Mrs. John L. Sullivan. "Any relation to the Boston Strong Boy?" the clerk had asked.

"He was my uncle," Tony said, and Laura struggled to keep from laughing.

They toasted each other with the bootleg hooch, then he took her to the great wide bed and carefully undressed her.

She stared at him, and her eyes were moist with tears. "What's the matter?" he asked.

"I love you, Tony."

"I love you too."

"I don't want you to think I'm a tramp or anything."

"No, no," he said, pressing his fingers to her lips.

Her skin was milk white and soft as velvet. Her breasts, though not large, were perfectly formed.

He gazed in awe at her body. "You're so beautiful."

He bent down and kissed her breasts. He ran his hands over her body. The hair of her sex was a delicate blond, fine as silk. He slid his finger into her and she moaned and pressed hard against it.

He moved on top of her and entered her, and the tremor and warmth of her was exquisite. He moved slowly in her. He fought to keep his mind on something other than the moistness, the warmth, the passion of her. He came quickly and just as quickly was aroused again.

He made love to her throughout the night, and it was a magical time, as close to paradise as he would ever attain in this life. The fragrance of her, the feel of her as he pressed inside her, the tightening of her body against his, the taste of her mouth, the delicacy of her lips, the soft moans, the sharp animal cries—his whole being was flooded with her, the passion and beauty of her, his love for her.

As dawn light washed the city and glints of gold and silver reflecting the sun shimmered off rooftops and windows, they rested back in sweet exhaustion. She stared at him with great wide blue eyes. He smoothed her hair and held her to him. "I want to marry you." His voice sounded unreal.

She smiled a kittenish smile but did not answer.

"Did you hear me?"

"Let's sleep," she answered. "We'll have a long talk about it later."

"Marry me."

"I want to. I swear to you. But there are other things to consider."

"What things?"

She didn't answer. She pressed close to him. She held on to him tightly. They fell asleep in each other's arms, and no doubts stirred within him. She would marry him. She would. It was the sweetest sleep Tony had ever had in his life

Through the spring and summer Tony McGrath had matches every week. He moved up into the light-heavyweight division. He fought in arenas like Boyle's Thirty Acres in Jersey City, Clairmont Avenue Ring in Brooklyn, South Side Market House in Pittsburgh. He fought in Toledo, Ohio; Michigan City, Indiana; Joplin, Missouri.

He was getting main events now and scoring impressively against boxers with either too little experience or too much. He beat Mike McTigue, Johnny Risko, and the amazing Battling Levinsky, the ex-light-heavyweight champion who had once fought and beaten three opponents in the same day.

Since Johnny McMahon had pressing business and political obligations and Bill O'Dwyer had finally left the police force to set up a law practice in Brooklyn, Frank Matthews handled the day-to-day managing of Tony's career. His reputation was growing: he was a devastating puncher, a scrappy and adept boxer. He had all the tools, but in Matthews' estimation his greatest asset was his intelligence. "Fists is good, brains is better," he told him. "Put 'em together, you go to the top—just like the real McCoy!"

Laura Maddox had taken her own apartment on Lower Fifth Avenue, where Tony stayed when he was back in town. He wanted to help her with the rent, but she refused. She was earning a good living now as Jason Karl's private secretary. More and more he depended on her. He would tour the city and its environs in one of the governor's limousines and she would be with him wherever he went, taking notes, helping him to write up his ideas. "Mr. Karl has a special assignment from the governor," she told Tony. "He's completely reorganizing the New York park and highway systems."

She had to accompany Karl on trips to the state capitol in Albany, and during those times Tony would be torn with jealousy. "That's foolish," she would explain to him. "It's my job. I'm not jealous when you're out on the road boxing, am I?"

What really bothered him was her refusal to commit to marrying him. Whenever he brought it up, she would grow uneasy. "You're just getting started in your career, Tony. What do you want to be saddled with a wife for? We're both doing so well now. Let's wait—"

"I'll wait. But just promise me—"

"Please, Tony. Don't pressure me like this. We'll work it out one of these days soon."

"Promise?"

"I promise."

Though he was doing well financially and the family's burden was easier, things were not going well at home. Paddy's drinking was worse than ever; Rose Ann's condition had deteriorated.

With Tony on the road much of the time, Bessie in the thick of an upcoming mayoral campaign, and Emmett working with John McMahon's construction company, responsibility for looking after Rose Ann rested with the two younger brothers, Jim and Willy.

She had grown very thin. She rarely talked, and when she did, it was to rave about sin, her sin, the world's sin. She had built a small altar in her room, a wooden crucifix surrounded by candles. She would sit in front of it for hours whispering to herself.

Often she would wander from the house. She would disappear for long periods of time. The young McGrath boys would search throughout the neighborhood for her, up and down the West Side waterfront. When they would find her she would be disheveled, bruised, incoherent.

The family discussed the possibility of putting her in a hospital. Bess would not hear of it. It was a passing thing, she insisted, fighting to convince herself that her daughter was not lost. She only needed love and patience and understanding.

Nevertheless, feeling increasingly inadequate in the face of madness, Bess spent more and more time away from the house. A furious battle was raging in the back rooms of the United Irish Club. People were choosing up sides between Al Smith and James J. Walker. "Something must be done with the Talker and his whore," Bessie proclaimed. "The governor will never support him in this election, and without Algie's support, Beau James doesn't have a Chinaman's chance."

She was delegated to talk with Walker. She met him at Tammany headquarters on Fourteenth Street. He was tense, evasive. Bessie would not let him off the hook. "You have a fine, loving wife and you're humiliating her,

Talker. Our people are on her side, and if we can't get our friends and neighbors to support you, who in heaven will? You must do something, and fast."

"What do you suggest?"

"Give up the hussy!"

"Do you think Algie will support me then?"

"I know he will."

"But he won't talk with me!" Walker complained.

"Give her up and he'll talk."

"Can you set up a meeting?"

She said she would try. She spoke with Governor Smith on the phone. He was cool to the idea.She pleaded with him. "There's not a man in this city can bring in the votes like Beau James when he behaves himself."

"He's a Peck's Bad Boy, Bessie. He'll never behave himself."

"Just meet with him. He's changed. I know it."

"I'll do it, Bessie," Al Smith said at last. "But only for you."

One evening when Tony was in town, Bess arrived at the apartment late, bubbling with excitement. Al Smith had given his blessing to Jim Walker's aspirations. "They had a get-together at the Half Moon Hotel in Brooklyn, and Beau James gave Mr. Smith his solemn promise to stop acting the playboy. He's forswearing the sauce and he's dropping that hussy like a hot potato."

"Do you think he means it?" Tony asked.

"He gave me his word."

Tony knew this was not true, that Walker wouldn't change. He learned from Bill-O that Walker was conning Al Smith: he had set up his mistress in a penthouse apartment, then given Smith his promise he wouldn't run around. Well, in truth, he would not be running around—his mistress would be waiting for him in their love nest.

Bill-O was annoyed at the deception but made peace with it. The city organization was controlled by Beau James. Bill-O's fledgling law practice depended on city workers, cops and firemen, who had run afoul of regulations. He could not afford to buck the machine at this stage of his career.

He confessed his dissatisfaction to Tony. "You give 'em an inch, they take a mile, lad. Soon the Talker will be running the whole shebang in this town." He shook his head sadly, then smiled his shy smile. "But like they say, 'The Hall is mother of us all!' "

"What is it that makes the Talker so good?" asked Tony.

"He's not overly burdened by scruples. He's charming as the devil himself, and he has no time for thought. He just does."

There was a sound of grudging admiration in Bill-O's comments about Walker. "Sometimes I think about getting into the political rat race, but I don't have the stomach for it, Tony. That's another thing Jim Walker has—a very strong stomach. He has no shame."

Tony's next fight was set for Camden, New Jersey, that weekend. Two nights before the fight as he was sparring at the Greenwich Village Settlement House, he was called to the phone. It was Jackie Foster. "I'm over at my mother's place. You better get over here."

"What's the matter?"

"Your father. Something's happened."

Tony rushed from the gym in his boxing togs. He ran all the way to the Bowery. Jackie was waiting in the hall outside the apartment. "They were having a drink in the kitchen and he said he felt tired. He lay down in the back room. They couldn't get him up."

A uniformed policeman and a man from the coroner's office were talking in the kitchen. Tony was taken into the back room. His father, fully clothed, was propped up on the bed. It was astonishing to see how death had shrunk him. When Paddy was alive, his drunkenness provided a feisty spark. With the spark gone, he appeared hollow, a balloon without air.

Tony sat beside him on the bed. He stared for a long time at his father, adjusted his tie, brushed a hair back from his forehead.

There was one consolation: Paddy had not been in pain at his death. The paralysis of his face, which in life had given a grotesque twist to his expression, had eased in death. He died smiling.

Paddy McGrath was buried in St. John's cemetery on St. Luke's Place, in the same few blocks where he had lived most of his life since coming to America.

Because of Bess's position with the United Irish Club, Tammany figures from all over the city attended the wake. Boss Flynn came from the Bronx, and McCooey from Brooklyn. Boss Ahearn was there, of course, as well as Johnny McMahon with his whole family. McMahon's daughter Theresa, a plain child, now an even plainer adult, arrived with her fiancé, a serious fellow by the name of Quigley.

Bess McGrath, who rarely touched alcohol, got drunk that night. She wailed disconsolately that a whore had killed her husband.

A limousine pulled up to the building and a group of people entered the house: Senator Walker and his wife, Allie, a chubby, pleasant-faced woman Tony knew from the neighborhood. Also, Walker's brothers, William and George, with their wives.

Behind them in another limousine, arrived a short man in a derby hat with a cigar jammed in his mouth—Governor Al Smith himself. With him were Jason Karl and Laura Maddox.

Laura, always subdued when she was with Karl, conveyed her respects with reserve. She hugged Bess primly and introduced Tony to Karl as "an old friend from the neighborhood."

Al Smith approached Paddy's casket. "I'll never forget the time we appeared together in Dion Boucicault's *The Shaughraun* at St. James. Remember that, Jim? I was the villain Corry Kinchella and Paddy played the part you later did at the London Theater over on the Bowery—Bob Folliot, the hero. Paddy was a dashing hero in those days."

"I remember, Algie," Walker said as he brushed a tear from his eye. "My only regret is that when I'm mayor old Paddy won't be there to carry me up and down on the elevator!"

"Play us a song, Jim," asked Boss Ahearn.

James J. Walker went to the upright piano next to the casket and played "Sweet Genevieve," while everyone sang along with him.

"Ah, Jim, that was Paddy's favorite, and I know it was your father's favorite," said Bess.

Next Walker played "Will You Love Me in December As You Do in May?" then "Sidewalks of New York" and "The Bowery," and everybody sang and laughed and cried a little.

Bess leaned over the casket and kissed Paddy's face and laughed while tears rolled down her cheeks. "Paddy, Paddy, all your old friends are here— Jim Talker and Algie and Boss Ahearn—and you know what they're saying? Jim Talker will be the next mayor of New York. Oh yes, Paddy my love. And he regrets the fact that you won't be there at City Hall to welcome him."

Late at night after everyone had gone, Rose Ann got up and walked to the casket. She began to hum. She danced in front of the coffin.

Tony was dozing in a chair. He opened his eyes to see his sister in front of the casket, slowly removing her clothes.

He halted her and led her back to the couch. She smiled and pursed her lips and said, "He knows. He knows all about me. It's all right now."

12

Through Jason Karl, Mike Roth secured a job as a draftsman's apprentice in the city planning office. Two nights a week he would walk across the Williamsburg Bridge to Ryerson Street in Brooklyn, where he sat in on a course in basic architecture at the Pratt Institute.

The teachers were recent immigrants from Europe, the ideas new: rather than being thick and ornamental, constructions should soar in harmony with their natural surroundings, function and form tightly intertwined, indivisible. Space could be an expression of man's spirit, ingenuity, aspiration—a work of art, yet art of a very practical sort.

The concept of openness and light stirred Mike Roth; he was consumed by passion for the work. He spent his spare hours sketching plans to transform the Lower East Side, to tear out the tenements and create an area of clean, bright housing, playgrounds, parks.

Whenever Jason Karl was in town, he and Mike would meet at the

Rutgers Square Settlement House and spar a couple of easy rounds. After, they would go around the corner to the Zum Essex Café for a glass of tea and a sweet roll. Mr. Karl would ask how his classes were going, what books he was reading, what he thought about the problems of the neighborhood.

Mike would tell him of the changes he would like to see; he outlined some of the ideas he had been working on. The tenements should be opened up. Sunlight, trees, grass, should fill the neighborhod.

Karl listened to him with great interest and it filled Mike with pride that a man of his learning and accomplishment should take his ideas so seriously.

One night he arrived with his secretary, Laura Maddox. They drove in Jason's limousine to Sweet's Restaurant on South Street.

Jason Karl pointed out where Al Smith was born: "Just down the block there, in the shadow of the Brooklyn Bridge." Over dinner he spoke about the governor with passion and respect. "I knew Al Smith way before he went up to Albany. As a man he's the best there is. In the old days the Irish toughs of the area used to beat up the old Jewish peddlers, throw rocks and garbage on them from the rooftops. Algie would hunt the thugs down and give them a good thrashing. Oh, he's a tough little guy! He loves and cares for the poor people of this city."

Laura Maddox was attractive and pleasant, but Mike felt vaguely uncomfortable with her along. With her pale beauty and quiet, watchful gaze she reminded him of Rose Ann. She had been staring at him all evening. "I remember you now," she said. "I was just a kid. There was a gang fight. A group of boys from the Lower East Side invaded Hudson Street. You were their leader. You fought with someone from the Irish gang."

"Tony McGrath."

"Yes," she said, smiling. "Tony McGrath."

After dinner they dropped Laura Maddox at her apartment, then drove over to the Lower East Side. "What do you think of Laura?" Jason asked.

"She's very beautiful."

"And more," Jason said. "She has a maturity way beyond her years. She's bright and eager to better herself. She works very hard for me." The great dark offices and loft buildings of Lower Broadway gave way to gray tenements. At Allen Street whores lazed in doorways, lounged against iron stanchions in the shadow of the elevated tracks, leaned out tenement windows hustling their charms to passersby. "This world is going to be yours," Jason said. "I'm interested to know how you want it to be. We have to change things. My family has been in New York City for nearly a hundred years. I've been involved with the poor people of the ghetto all my life. It's my dream to do as much for them as possible. I want you to help me, Mike."

Mike Roth grew flustered. "How can I help you?"

"You've told me your dreams for this area. I have dreams too. And I'm committed to making those dreams a reality." He gazed at the bleak tenement buildings. There was sadness in his look, and determination. "Politics being what they are, it won't be easy to accomplish. But whatever influence I have with Governor Smith will be used to wipe out the misery of the people of the Lower East Side."

"I don't know what I can do ..."

"You know this world. It's in your blood. You have good ideas. I want to learn from your experience. And you're a leader among the young people down here."

"I don't feel like I'm a leader: I feel like I've let everybody down. They expect me to fight." He studied his battered knuckles. "They keep waiting for me to fight."

"One of these days maybe you will."

"I don't think so. I don't want to."

The limousine turned onto Mike's block. "Could you let me out here?" Mike asked. "People seeing me in a car like this, they'll think there's been a funeral." He laughed, embarrassed.

Jason had the chauffeur stop the car. "I'm a Jew, as you are, Mike. But the distance between upper Fifth Avenue where I was raised and your neighborhood here is light-years apart. I have important plans for this area. I need your help."

"I'll do whatever I can," Mike Roth answered, feeling desperately inadequate.

Through the winter and into the spring, Mike Roth continued his job with the city planning office; he worked hard on his studies at Pratt Institute. And he spent much of his free time with Jason Karl.

After work or his classes at Pratt he would go to the settlement house, where he and Karl would spar a few rounds, then stroll through the neighborhood.

Jason Karl would talk of his ideas for the area: the Lower East Side from East Broadway to Houston Street would become a shining, self-contained model city. The tenements would be demolished to be replaced by open, airy, functional apartment complexes. The core of the slum would be given over to parks, ballfields, playgrounds, and youth centers surrounded by the housing units. There would be theaters, concert halls, sports arenas, libraries.

Mike would arrive home dizzy with possibilities for the future. At times he would stay awake all night sketching variations on Jason's theme, adding ideas of his own, building an intricate, sparkling city within a city.

After accumulating a series of sketches, he showed them to Jason. Karl studied the drawings, then made a few notes. He asked to keep them for a while: he wanted to show them to his staff. He liked the sketches! "This is the future, Mike. It might not happen in my lifetime, but it will certainly happen in yours. We'll have to awaken the people. They must be aroused to see a purer, better life for themselves. They are the ones who must demand this."

This was the power of Al Smith, he explained. Al Smith loved the people and could communicate with them. And Mike must communicate to them also. The people had to be wooed as one wooed a girl he loved.

And so it went week after week, up and down the tenement streets, sometimes just the two of them, sometimes accompanied by Laura.

This dream became Mike's refuge. He retreated to it from the ugliness and stink of his tenement existence. Occasionally he became discouraged, overwhelmed by the meanness and brutality of the life around him. It's foolish to think anybody can change this, he would say to himself. All of this is crazy. I'm crazy. Jason is crazy.

The next evening, though, he would walk with Jason or have tea with him in the Zum Essex Café and the spark of their shared vision would light up everything. Mike would be filled with hope.

In the fall of the year Al Smith was elected for his fourth term as governor of the state of New York. James J. Walker, with Smith's support, was elected mayor of New York City.

"In '28 Mr. Smith will be seeking the presidential nomination," Karl told Mike. "And this time he'll get it. He'll be elected President of the United States and everything we dreamed about will come to pass. The Lower East Side will be transformed!"

Mike Roth had never seen him so happy. In their walks and sparring sessions, Jason exhibited a fire and energy that was extraordinary. Ideas poured from him. He could hardly contain himself.

"I'm reborn," Jason Karl said to him suddenly one evening as they walked along the East River. "I can't tell you how fortunate I am! You know the years since my wife died have been lonely ones. Loneliness is a terrible, killing thing. All that's past me now. I'm a lucky man! Oh, how lucky!" He turned to Mike, his expression radiant with joy. "No one knows this, but in two weeks I'm to be married. Laura has consented to become my wife!"

13

Tony McGrath was scheduled to go ten rounds with Dutch Weimer in St. Louis, Missouri. The day of the fight he learned from the newspapers that Laura Maddox had married Jason Karl.

He had had no preparation for the news, and was devastated by it.

He and Laura had been together two weeks earlier and things had never been better. Thinking back, he realized she had been too accommodating.

Their time together had been perfect, and that should have put him on guard: perfection existed only in heaven.

He tried to understand what had caused it, struggled to come to terms with it. He tried to call her, but there was no answer at her apartment and he hadn't really expected one. The newspaper said she and Karl would be honeymooning in Europe.

He thought about how reserved she had always been toward him whenever Jason Karl was around, and now it made perfect sense: she had been carrying on with him all that time.

But why tell him she loved him? And not once, but over and over again? Were his perceptions of her so distorted that he could not recognize she had been playing him for a sucker?

The Dutch Weimer fight was an important step up in his career. Over the year he had built an impressive record but had not gone up against a front-rank fighter. Frank Matthews' plan had been to bring him along slowly, and when the time was ripe, they would make a push for the top. After the Weimer fight they would challenge the leading contender, Dave Shade, then strike for the light-heavyweight championship.

Beating Weimer was a key element in Frank Matthews' grand scheme.

It did not work out. Tony entered the ring that night, and he was not ready to fight. He couldn't get Laura out of his thoughts. His whole world was crumbling, and Dutch Weimer helped it along.

He was knocked out in the fifth round. He didn't see the punch that hit him, nor did he feel it.

He didn't remember leaving the ring. He sat in his corner crying and he continued to cry in the dressing room. He remembered none of this, nor did he remember showering and dressing.

His head cleared as he and Matthews and Soldier Noonen were walking back to the hotel. "Who won?" he asked.

"Whoever it was," Matthews said, "he weren't no Irishman."

He laid off three weeks. When he came back, something was missing. He won against a few stumblebums, uninspired victories over men he should have toppled with the first good punch.

One evening he met Theresa McMahon walking along Hudson Street. She seemed hesitant to talk with him, but forced herself. "I'm sorry about what happened," she said.

"I'm coming back fine. I won my last three fights. The Weimer thing could have happened to anybody."

"I mean about Laura. You loved her, didn't you?"

"Yes."

"It was terrible what she did to you. I don't know why she would have done that."

She was genuinely moved by the bitter turn in his life and her concern touched him. She was a plain girl, a year younger than Tony and painfully shy, and he knew how difficult it must have been for her to talk with him like this.

She had always been homely. She wore glasses over narrow, slightly irregular eyes. She had thin shoulders and a retiring, studious manner. But she was an intelligent, gentle, good person.

They walked along Hudson Street. Theresa's discomfort was palpable. She stared straight ahead, peering out through thick-lensed glasses. He could sense she was trying to think of something more to say but couldn't. He could feel her regret in having approached him.

He thought how peculiar it was that Johnny McMahon should be so warm and outgoing and his daughter so backward. Still, there was a fineness in her that set her apart from the other girls in the neighborhood. A strange flower, he thought, to have grown up here in this rough place at this time. He understood why she and Rose Ann had been so close.

Theresa never visited the house anymore. His sister's breakdown had affected her deeply. She had tried to remain a friend, but Rose Ann's madness had at last driven her off.

"How are things with you and that Quigley fellow?" Tony asked. For years Theresa had been going with a fellow as introverted and plain as she.

"He has decided to enter a seminary."

"I thought the two of you were going to be married?"

"Yes."

"I'm sorry."

"Things don't always work out," she answered. "Who can understand these things?"

"Yeah, they just happen," he said, trying to put up a brave front.

"I just want you to know that you're too good a man to let someone so thoughtless get you down."

"I appreciate your coming to talk to me, Theresa. Thank you."

Later he made a halfhearted effort to reach Laura. After talking to her mother he gave it up. Her mother told him Laura was doing beautifully. She had never been happier in her life.

A meeting was held at Johnny McMahon's speakeasy. Boss Ahearn was there, as well as Bill O'Dwyer, Frank Matthews, and of course McMahon. They sat at a rear table.

Boss Ahearn lit his cigar and let the smoke curl toward the green-shaded light above the table. "Your mother is one of the saints of the world; I love her as I loved your father, bless his soul, as I love you, Tony. You're like my own flesh and blood. Now, as Frank sees the situation, and I for one concur, there never was a time when we've been in a better position to make a run on the light-heavyweight title. Except for one rotten thing: you can't fight worth a tinker's damn no more."

"You're being too rough on the boy," said Bill-O.

"The truth's the truth, Bill-O. We've matched him with nothing but old ladies, and he had his hands full."

"There's no way we're going to get him a title shot unless he starts looking better," Matthews said. "Do you hear me, Tony? I couldn't in all conscience put you in the ring with some of the better boys now."

Tony sat in silence.

"You've lost your fire," McMahon said.

"Something's got to improve," agreed Matthews, "or we can pack the whole shebang in."

After, Tony walked with Bill-O to the subway on Seventh Avenue. "What's bothering you, lad? Is it problems with your sister?"

"I've been involved with a woman. Things went sour between us."

Bill-O lit a cigar and stood on the corner thinking. "How old are you, Tony?"

"Almost twenty-one."

"It's time you contemplated taking a wife. A good sensible Irish girl. None of this romantic stuff. Oh, it's fine to read about it and dream about it, but when you have to go about the business of life, it takes too much time and effort to reach for dreams. Get yourself a good, solid family woman. Prize fighting is a noble art, lad. You have a talent there. Don't be throwing it away." He held Tony by the shoulders and gazed directly at him. "If it weren't for my Kitty, I'd still be working as a damn bartender or longshoreman. She straightened me right up." He smiled and hugged Tony to him, then hurried down the stairs into the subway station.

For the next several weeks Tony went about his training in a serious, methodical manner. He pondered what Bill-O had told him, and he let go of something within him, that dream of Laura Maddox. Bill-O was right: she was a dream. He had his reality to deal with, the reality of his talent and ambitions. He must get on with the business of his life.

He thought about the women he knew, the girls he had gone to school with, the girls in the neighborhood.

One day he showed up at Johnny McMahon's house on Perry Street. Mrs. McMahon, a birdlike woman who wore a henna-dyed wig, answered the door. "Johnny is down at the saloon," she said.

"Is Theresa in?"

Mrs. McMahon looked surprised. "Yes, yes, she is," and she called her daughter, who came out of the sitting room.

"Theresa, I'd like to talk to you for a moment."

Theresa appeared uncomfortable. She looked at her mother for assistance. "Of course, Tony," Mrs. McMahon said. "Why don't the two of you go into the sitting room. I'll make some tea."

In the sitting room Theresa struggled to find something to talk about. She didn't know what to do with her hands. She had been working at needlepoint, a tablecloth, and displayed it for Tony. He admired it. She asked how his fight career was doing. He told her it was coming along. "I never see Rose Ann anymore," she said. "Is she well?"

"She has her spells."

"I pray for her. I pray every night."

Mrs. McMahon entered with a pot of tea and two cups on a tray. She set it on a hassock between the two of them, then left the sitting room.

"I was sorry to hear about you and that Quigley fellow. Has it been painful for you?"

"I loved him very much," she said, staring down at her tea.

Neither of them spoke for a long time. "We've both had our disappointments," Tony said at last.

"Yes."

"Theresa, my sister takes a great deal of watching after and my mother is having a difficult time of it. She's very much involved with the United Irish Club and it takes too much of her time. And I'm forced to leave home for long periods of time. I think you're a fine girl—I've always thought it. I like your father very much and I believe he likes me."

"He thinks very highly of you."

"Yes. Well. With your permission, I'd like to talk to your father to ask him for your hand in marriage."

Theresa was holding her teacup, raising it from the tray. Her hand began to tremble and the teacup rattled loudly against the saucer. She blushed deeply and replaced the cup on the tray.

"I know this is a great surprise. It's not possible that you could love me now, and I can't pretend that I love you. But I know that you're a fine girl from a fine family, and I care for you and your family a good deal. I think we could have a successful marriage. I have no bad habits, as you no doubt know. I would dedicate myself to your happiness, and if you and your family approve, I'm reasonably certain I could make you a fine husband."

She sat there staring down at the tea tray. When she spoke, her voice was so soft it was hardly audible. "I know I'm not a very pretty woman. Men have never been attracted to me, and I'm not really comfortable with many people. I'm stunned that you should think of me in this way, Tony. I've never thought about you—I mean, it never would have seemed possible to me. I'd been seeing Darryl Quigley since high school. He's a serious, intelligent fellow, a spiritual person. We had—I still think we have—a deep love between us. It wasn't a physical love but a love between kindred spirits, one that was very close to God. I'll love Darryl all my life, but I've lost him to Christ. When I learned he was entering the seminary, I made up my mind I would never marry. His life would be with Christ, and mine . . . well, mine would be a complement to his life and love. I would devote myself to people. I would purify my actions. But your offer reaches out to me, surprising as it is. I agree we could have a successful marriage, because I'm sure you would make a fine husband—not just to me but to any woman you marry."

Tony stood. "I don't expect an answer at once. I'll stop by early next week for your decision."

"There's no need for that. You can speak to my father now. I'd be honored for you to ask for my hand in marriage."

Mrs. McMahon entered the sitting room carrying a plate of tea cakes. "Thank you, Mrs. McMahon, but I must be going."

"Oh, I'm sorry. Well, your visit has been a lovely surprise. Come again, Tony."

"I certainly will, Mrs. McMahon."

An astonished Johnny McMahon gave his permission for Tony to marry Theresa, and in the spring of 1927 they were wed. It was a large and lively affair. A number of the old-time Irish saloonkeepers were there, as well as a full complement of Tammany politicians. Al Smith was in Albany and couldn't attend, and neither could Mayor James J. Walker. But Judge Olvany was there, and Boss Flynn from the Bronx and Boss McCooey from Brooklyn, and of course Edward L. Ahearn, leader of the United Irish Club.

The whole McGrath family was there except for Rose Ann, who became violently ill that morning. She began to scream and wail and couldn't hold her food down. She was left in the care of a neighbor while the rest of the family left for the church.

Jackie Foster, though he was not invited, showed up and stood at the rear of the church throughout the ceremony.

Afterward, at the reception held in the McMahon house, Jack approached Tony. "I don't know what to get you as a gift, Tony, so please take this." He handed Tony an envelope, shook his hand, and left.

Inside the envelope was a thousand-dollar bill.

Through his construction company, Johnny McMahon had been renovating buildings on Christopher Street. Tony and his new wife were given two floors in one of the buildings at a reasonable rent, with an option to buy. Tony and Theresa moved into the ground floor and Bess, Rose Ann, and the boys occupied the second floor. Tony's brother Emmett, now seventeen, got a job with McMahon construction company.

That summer Tony began to fight with his old passion and skill.

In September he had a rematch with Dutch Weimer at the new Madison Square Garden at Eighth Avenue and Forty-ninth Street and knocked him out in the third round. In Philadelphia in October he went up against Dave Shade, the top contender for the light-heavyweight championship, and demolished him in five.

A fight for the championship was set to take place just after the first of the year.

Tony McGrath's life was back on track again.

14

On October 16, 1927, Jacob Orgen, known as Little Augie, was shot to death on the Lower East Side in front of 103 Norfolk Street, between Delancey and Rivington streets. With him at the time was his bodyguard, a

Philadelphia Irishman born Nolan but known by the name of Jack "Legs" Diamond. Diamond took two bullets in the chest and survived.

The word around the neighborhood was that Lepke Buchalter and Jackie Foster had killed Little Augie in a dispute involving the painters and plasterers' union.

The funeral for Little Augie was a grand affair. Once more the cream of the Lower East Side gangsters showed up, though this time Jackie Foster was conspicuous by his absence.

The coffin was massive—cherry-red, lined with white satin. On a silver plate embedded in the lid of the coffin it said: "Jacob Orgen, Age 25 Years."

Charlie Roth, who had been friends with Orgen's father, insisted his sons attend the funeral with him. Afterward, he said to Harry, "How old was Jacob Orgen?"

"The sign on his casket said he was twenty-five, but I know he was older."

"He was twenty-five when his father found out what he had become. To his father he was dead at twenty-five. Do you understand me, Harry?"

"I'm not a gangster, if that's what you mean," Harry said morosely.

After the funeral, Harry invited Mike to Steinberg's candy store for an egg cream.

Steinberg's was a hangout for the local boxing crowd, and Mike always felt uncomfortable there. On the walls were pictures of East Side fighters— Sid Terris, Charlie Beecher, Jackie Hausner, Benny Leonard, and Leach Cross.

There was also a picture of Mike Roth, and whenever he was there the candy-store jockeys would rib him: the picture was gathering dust, it should be taken down. He had once been known as "The Pride of the Ghetto." When he broke his hands and failed to live up to his promise, they began to call him "The *Shunda* of the Ghetto"—the shame of the ghetto.

Harry and Mike sat at one of the round marble-top tables at the rear of the store. Harry, who possessed an incurable sweet tooth, ordered a chocolate sundae and an egg cream; Mike settled for a glass of plain seltzer.

Harry had always been husky; now he was running to fat. His darkly handsome face was bloated and his gut bulged against the narrow-waisted suits he was partial to.

"How much do you make a week, Mikey?" he asked, greedily spooning up the sundae.

"Thirty dollars."

"You're a real *putz,* you know that? That kid McGrath is going for the light-heavyweight championship. He'll win and move up to heavyweight, and he'll be worth a quarter-million dollars a fight."

"So?"

"You could beat him."

"Harry, please . . ."

Harry leaned close to him. "You don't have it *here,*" he said, tapping Mike over the heart.

"From where you sit on your fat ass, maybe."

"You got a talent. You owe it to yourself—"

"While you were working on a case of sugar diabetes I did a little damage to myself, remember?" Angrily Mike held out his fists. "These hurt so bad they keep me awake at night. I don't want any of it anymore, so just drop it."

"We have connections now, Mikey. We can move you right to the top."

"Who's that, Lepke? Ben Siegel? Jackie Foster? You want me to get involved with them? Don't you remember Jake Orgen?"

"It's not like that."

"How is it different? You get in bed with those guys, they're going to *shtup* you."

"They only kill when it comes to business."

"They got a piece of a fighter, that's business."

"You grew up with Lep and Benny and Johnny Eggs. They like you."

"They *loved* Jake Orgen and Yiddle November. They were practically raised by those old guys. And look how they paid them back—beautiful funerals." Mike stood up. "I'm doing something I'm happy with."

"I never knew you were so dumb, Mikey." Harry waved Mr. Steinberg over and ordered another sundae. "I thought you had heart."

Mike left his brother in the candy store. Harry belched and loosened his belt. He sat there brooding. He aspired to a place in the world he knew he would never attain. The sundae arrived and he attacked it as though it were the last food he would ever know.

Jason Karl's vision for the Lower East Side gradually began to take form. An area of tenements between Suffolk and Essex streets had been purchased by a group of Tammany allies—a fancy boondoggle that was engineered by Boss Murphy just before his death. The plan had been to raze the slum and replace it with a middle-class housing development. James J. Walker, in one of his first speeches upon becoming mayor, spoke of the glorious city within a city which would be erected in the area. He never carried it out.

Jason Karl now prevailed upon Al Smith to have the state buy back the tenements, tear them down, and use the area for a park and cultural center—the first step in the realization of his dream. The planning commission where Mike worked was even now drawing up blueprints for the section's development.

The actual move toward laying claim to the land was delayed while Al Smith made preparations for another run at the presidency.

In March of 1928, with Mike Roth spending his days working over blueprints in the planning office on Center Street, Tony McGrath was preparing to fight Jack Slattery for the light-heavyweight championship of the world.

The championship fight took place in the new Madison Square Garden.

Early in his career Jack Slattery had been managed by Frank Matthews and Matthews knew exactly how to fight him. "He's a boozer," he told Tony. "They'll be filling him with brandy from the water bottle. You could hit him with a sledgehammer and he won't feel it, but by the fifth round he won't be able to stand, neither."

Tony stayed clear of him for four rounds, then went to work in the fifth. The next round, Slattery went down before Tony even had a chance to get a punch off. He was in Tony's corner, directly above Frank Matthews, struggling to rise. Matthews yelled for him to stay down. In his dazed and drunken state, Slattery understood Matthews was still his manager and followed his advice. While his true manager screamed hysterically for him to rise, Jack Slattery took the count.

Tony McGrath was light-heavyweight champion of the world.

Later that night at Billy LaHiff's tavern on West Forty-eighth Street, among Broadway touts, Zeigfeld girls, newspapermen, whiskey runners, sports figures, Tony celebrated.

Mayor Walker, who had been at the fight with his newest mistress, Betty Compton, an actress appearing in the Broadway musical *Funny Face,* joined Tony at his table. With him was James A. Farley, head of the State Athletic Commission. Farley owned a building-materials company, and was a staunch Tammany ally. "Tony, you're a great fighter, no doubt about it," Walker said, "but I think we'll score that victory for John Barleycorn! What do you think, Commissioner?"

"I think there should be an investigation, but not by the boxing commission, by the treasury boys. Mr. Slattery has obviously violated the Prohibition Act!"

Tony left the celebration early. Theresa was squeamish about his boxing and had not attended the fight; she was waiting for him at home.

Bill-O drove Tony downtown. "You're light-heavyweight champion of the world, lad. How does it feel?"

"I don't feel much," Tony answered. The fight had depressed him. It had been foolish and ridiculous, a disgrace.

He realized that though he loved to do battle, it was never the winning that made him happy; he got the greatest joy out of anticipating victory. The striving was all. "It's still not the heavyweight championship, Bill-O. That's the one I want. That's the one that counts."

In June of that year the United Irish Club offered Bess McGrath an opportunity to travel down to Houston, Texas, as a delegate to the Democratic National Convention. Boss Ahearn would be going, as well as John McMahon. This was to be Al Smith's year, and the drumbeats for his nomination were starting to sound.

"We'd like you there, Bess," said Boss Ahearn. "Algie would like you there."

He had come to visit her at the house. They sat together in the kitchen, drinking tea. "It's a great honor, Boss. It would be the greatest thing in my life to be present for Algie's nomination."

"Sure it would."

She sipped at her tea. "We're going to win this one. Algie's going to get the nomination and the club is going to turn out the whole district for him."

"You can take that to that bank, Bessie."

"But I won't be able to go, Boss. I can't leave my Rose Ann like that."

"You have the boys to watch her."

"And who's to watch the boys?"

"Bess, leave her be. Your not being here for a week or so isn't going to hurt her."

"I just can't do it."

Boss Ahearn puffed on his cigar. "Since Paddy's gone, you've lost some vinegar."

"I suppose I have." She smiled, and her face brightened. "But come election time, Boss, you'll have no worry!"

And so while a delegation from the United Irish Club traveled to the convention, Bess remained behind in New York. She, Tony, the younger boys, and Rose Ann all gathered downstairs at the United Irish Club and listened to the convention on a static-filled superheterodyne radio set. The room was packed with low-level party regulars. All the big shots were either in Texas or up in Albany with Al Smith, following the proceedings on radio in the governor's mansion.

The loyals of the United Irish Club cheered lustily, waving schooners of bootleg beer in the air. They yelped and hollered and threw their arms about each other as Franklin D. Roosevelt, in ringing tones, offered Al Smith's name in nomination: "One who has the will to win—who not only deserves success, but commands it. Victory is habit—the *happy warrior!*"

Amid the euphoria, as Al Smith gained the nomination on the first ballot, Rose Ann McGrath sat quietly in a corner, a sad half-smile on her face, staring blankly ahead.

As light-heavyweight boxing champion of the world, Tony found himself suddenly in demand. Throughout the summer Tammany sent him from political rally to political rally, where he took a place on the podium with other celebrities for Al Smith. He would be introduced, stand up, wave to the crowd, and smile while the speaker offered variations on how Al Smith would knock out Herbert Hoover even as Irish Tony McGrath had whipped Jack Slattery.

He felt foolish and used, though he believed in the cause. His boxing career was in suspension: all those about him were just too busy battling to get Al Smith elected. But John McMahon did tell him there were big things in the works: he and Bill-O and Frank Matthews were lining up an assault on the heavyweight championship.

At a rally in the Bronx, Edward J. Flynn, the Tammany boss of the area, came to Boss Ahearn, McMahon, and Bill-O just before the speeches. "Frank Roosevelt is going to be here. I'll be downplaying Smith tonight. After all, we have to begin scoring some points for Frank." Franklin D. Roosevelt, protégé of Smith, had been picked by him to run for governor.

Boss Ahearn, McMahon, and Bill-O huddled at their end of the table while Tony looked on.

"They're looking to skunk Al," Boss Ahearn said. "It's as plain as the boil on Mrs. McGillicuddy's ass."

"With the booze and Catholicism against him, Algie should have put distance between him and the Hall," said Bill-O.

Franklin Roosevelt, former state senator and vice-presidential candidate on the Cox ticket in 1920, was Protestant and, despite his closeness to Smith, felt to be essentially anti-Tammany.

"The pros are thinking: What if Al loses the presidency? Let's make sure Frank becomes governor," said Boss Ahearn. "I'll tell you something, boyos, I'll hedge with the best of them, but not when it comes to Algie. I ride the ship to the bottom."

"Jim Farley's playing this one beautiful," put in John McMahon.

Farley controlled the issuance of "Annie Oakleys," passes to the boxing matches and other athletic events, and Boss Ahearn and McMahon depended on the free tickets to keep the United Irish Club regulars happy. In addition, McMahon's construction company did business with Farley's building-supply outfit. Farley made sure government jobs came his way, and both profited.

Farley, a large, bluff man, was seated on the rostrum next to Roosevelt. They were engaged in some good-natured banter. Farley waved at Boss Ahearn down the table. "Look at him. He's got his nose up Frank's butt while jerking our chain with both hands," said Boss Ahearn under his breath to McMahon.

Some years earlier Roosevelt had been crippled by polio, but the seriousness of his condition had been kept a secret. Now, as he prepared to address the gathering, Tony could see just how severely afflicted he was. One of his aides lifted him to his feet, and while he grinned and waved at the crowd, a second aide snapped his braces in place out of view of the audience so that he could stand and acknowledge the ovation. From the waist up the candidate for governor appeared completely at ease and in control; beneath table level, Tony witnessed the prodigious effort Roosevelt exerted, as he fought to maintain his balance—his legs trembled with the strain.

Midway through his speech, two people in evening clothes entered the rear of the hall. Jason Karl and Laura.

She wore a strapless white gown, and a diamond tiara gleamed in her marcelled blond hair. She looked unimaginably beautiful, queenly.

In Tony's eyes she seemed to float into the room. A curious weakness spread through him, and he felt as though he could not breathe. He experienced a deep sense of shame that he should be so shaken by her presence. He'd always known that someday he would run into her, but he wasn't prepared for his reaction.

She saw him and stared at him across the large hall. He gazed down at the tabletop. He could not bring himself to look at her. When he was introduced to the crowd, later, he waved and kept his eyes averted from Laura, though he could see her out of the edge of his vision. After the speeches were over and the party faithful began to mingle with the people on the rostrum, Tony said to Bill-O, "I have to get out of here. I'll catch a cab downtown."

"I'll drive you."

They started for the door, but McMahon came running after them. "Tony, Frank Roosevelt would like to meet you."

Tony tried to beg off, but his father-in-law insisted on bringing him over to Roosevelt. With Roosevelt were Boss Ahearn, Boss Flynn, and James Farley. "Good to see you, Tony," Farley said. "Meet the next governor of New York, Frank Roosevelt."

Roosevelt, who was in heated discussion with Jason Karl, looked up, saw Tony, and smiled broadly. "Glad to see you're in my corner." He was a handsome man with a brilliant smile. They shook hands while photographers snapped pictures. Roosevelt's grip was surprisingly powerful.

Beyond the photographers Tony could see Laura watching him. He attempted to get away from the crowd around Roosevelt. Laura moved next to him. "Tony . . . hello."

He couldn't speak. He felt an involuntary muscle twitch at the corner of his mouth. "Hello," he said at last. His voice was unnaturally hoarse. He could not look her directly in the eye.

"Can we talk for a minute? Please, I have to explain to you . . ."

She led him to several chairs off to one side. "I don't know exactly what to say," she said after they were seated.

He didn't answer.

"I'm glad things are going well with you. I heard you're married now. Kids?"

"Not yet."

"Where's your wife tonight?"

"She hates these political things . . ."

"Yes." She didn't speak for a moment. Tony still could not look at her. He focused his gaze on the red exit sign at the far end of the room.

"Tony, I never wanted to hurt you," she said quietly, simply. "I loved you very much. But my family had nothing. I could see only a life of continuing poverty for them. Jason gave me a way out of that. I know it doesn't sound very nice. It sounds as if I sold myself—"

"I would have given you a way out." His voice was tight and unnatural and he was embarrassed by it, embarrassed by this encounter. He could not get himself to leave.

"You're doing well now, but then . . . I just couldn't see myself the wife of a small-time prizefighter. I suppose I was wrong. I think about it all the time. I think about you all the time." She covered her face with her hand. "I'm doing this so badly."

Neither of them spoke for a long time.

"Will you ever forgive me, Tony?" she said at last.

He couldn't bring himself to say anything. He could see Bill-O waiting for him at the exit. He wanted to rush from her, but he couldn't move. He felt stupid and filled with shame.

"Tony, please." Her hand rested lightly on his thigh.

"Everyone is out for themselves," he heard himself say, and he wanted to stop the words, but they came out. "In everyday life, just like politics. Smith, Roosevelt—all of them. They use each other for the moment. When they see something better come along, they jump for it."

She shook her head and tried to speak but couldn't.

"We really have nothing to say to each other," Tony said.

Jason Karl had separated himself from Roosevelt and was on his way over to them. Laura composed herself and said with forced brightness, "You know Tony McGrath, don't you, darling?"

"Of course. Our new light-heavyweight champion." Jason smiled tensely. He was obviously upset after his talk with Roosevelt. "Are you a Frank Roosevelt man, Tony?"

"I'm an Al Smith man."

"Well, you must know then that Mr. Smith is about to get his tail whipped." He nodded in the direction of Roosevelt. "That man over there has braces on his legs, but in rough-and-tumble he'll beat anyone. He's Al Smith's boy, but Algie's about to learn a bitter lesson."

Tony stood. "It's been nice talking with you, but I have to be going."

Jason Karl misunderstood Tony's abruptness. "I'm sorry if I sound harsh about Roosevelt. It's just that Frank was in Smith's pocket when Algie was a winner. Now that he's about to lose—"

"I don't know much about politics, Mr. Karl," said Tony. "I know that people in general don't have very much loyalty."

"No, they don't these days, do they?" answered Jason. Roosevelt was looking in their direction. He waved and smiled, signaling thumbs-up. Jason looked away.

Tony hurried away from Laura and her husband. He didn't look back at her, though he felt her eyes on him. His face burned with shame.

On the drive downtown in Bill-O's car, Tony remained quiet.

"You noticed what was going on back there with Roosevelt?" Bill-O said.

"I have an idea." Tony wasn't thinking about it at all. He was thinking about Laura. She had said she loved him, and yet . . .

"The shifting sands of power, Tony. Algie will lose and everybody will jump from him like fleas from a dying dog. The Man with the Derby made a few mistakes. He threw in with this millionaire fellow, Raskob. Raskob is a papal knight and the bigots are having a field day, saying if Smith is elected the Pope will control the United States, garbage like that." Bill-O smiled a quiet smile. "I would have done it differently. I would have parted company with the Hall. The Hall can't do Algie one bit of good in this election."

"But how can you go it without the Hall?" Tony forced himself to talk. His mind was elsewhere. His mind was on Laura and the past. "The Hall has the power where it counts."

"That's the trick, lad, walking that tightrope."

"Think you'll ever give it a try?"

"When my stomach is tough enough, Tony. Only when my stomach is tough enough. You have to kill the shame in you. Do you see what I mean?"

Tony did see, but he didn't answer.

In November Al Smith was resoundingly beaten for the presidency, while Roosevelt captured the governorship of New York. No sooner was he installed in the mansion in Albany than he began to put distance between him and Al Smith, just as Bill-O and Jason Karl had predicted.

Jason paid Mike Roth a visit at the city planning commission. He was deeply discouraged. "The Lower East Side project is being disbanded. Roosevelt is sweeping out all the Smith people. I'm leaving, and after the first of the year, you'll be out of a job."

"What will you do?"

"John Raskob has promised Smith a position with him. They're going to be putting up a large building at Thirty-fourth Street and Fifth Avenue where the Waldorf-Astoria now stands. It's to be called the Empire State Building and Smith will head the controlling company. He promised me a position, but I have no idea when all this will take shape. I'll see if I can find you a job someplace else, but it might take a while."

And so dreams were deferred.

15

Early in 1929 Tony McGrath relinquished his light-heavyweight title and moved up to heavyweight. He demolished the two top contenders and by early summer was putting on serious pressure for a shot at the heavyweight title.

Henry John Laws, the first black heavyweight champion since Jack Johnson, had taken the crown by default and was not popular. He was deceptively awkward, a spoiler whose fights were never very exciting. He won by making his opponents look bad. Clamor went up for a new white hope, and Tony McGrath was the boy. A championship fight was set for September in Madison Square Garden.

Bitterness had begun to infect the United Irish Club, a fallout from Al Smith's defeat. In addition to Roosevelt shunning his old ally, Beau James Walker also turned against Smith. Exactly why was unclear. Some felt he was afraid the Man with the Derby would enter New York City politics and go after the mayor's job, others that he resented Smith's disapproval of his mistress and ever-present army of hangers-on.

Whatever the reason, Walker moved against Tammany head George W. Olvany and replaced him with John Curry, his own man. In doing this he usurped Al Smith's position as titular head of the Democratic party. Not only had Jimmy Walker turned on Smith, his friend of years, but he also used Olvany poorly: Olvany and Walker had been boyhood friends. In the early years with Al Smith they had regularly attended mass together at St. James Church, appeared in amateur theatricals, taken part in Irish sporting events.

Boss Eddie Ahearn was appalled, and he jumped in as a Smith man and attempted to gain leadership of Tammany; Walker beat him back, and John Curry was the new sachem of the Hall.

In September, before a disappointing crowd of slightly more than fourteen thousand people, Tony McGrath knocked out Henry John Laws in the fifth round to become heavyweight champion of the world.

James J. Walker toasted him at Billy LaHiff's afterward and tried to sing a duet with him of "Sidewalks of New York." Tony declined. He was still a Boss Ahearn-Al Smith man.

"You were right," Bill-O told him afterward. "Beau James has been behaving badly."

In early October workmen began to tear down the old Waldorf-Astoria Hotel at Thirty-fourth Street and Fifth Avenue. John McMahon, through Boss Ahearn and Al Smith, managed to secure work for his construction company on the project. Tony's younger brothers were all employed by McMahon now.

Emmett was twenty, Jim eighteen, Willy, sixteen—big, strapping boys. Tony would often look at them in wonderment: they had a clear-cut, no-nonsense approach to life, none of Tony's romanticism. Whereas he plunged into situations with no thought of the consequences, his brothers were constantly aware of the balance sheet, what could be gained or lost. They possessed ambition without dreams: the ambition was to become as wealthy as possible in as short a time as possible.

At the end of the month the final demolition work on the Waldorf-Astoria was completed. As its shell came roaring down to make way for the Empire State Building, the reverberations were the herald of another graver collapse. On Thursday, October 24, 1929, the stock market crashed.

One week later, Jimmy Walker, promising to keep the subway fare at a nickel, was reelected mayor of New York City, beating fiery, unpredictable Fiorello La Guardia.

An immediate victim of the Wall Street crash was Mike Roth. Jason Karl had secured a job for him working with one of the Empire State Building architects. Suddenly the project was swamped with people thrown out of work and Al Smith was forced to pay off old debts. Architects and engineers were particularly hard-hit by the effects of the crash, and Mike's position as a draftsman's assistant was taken over by a full-fledged engineer.

Mike's brother, Harry, also had problems. For the past several years while making book for Siegel and Lansky, he had invested his profits in Brooklyn real estate. Overnight he was wiped out.

He called on Mike at the Ludlow Street apartment. They strolled over to Rutgers Square and sat on a bench. Harry looked godawful. He hadn't slept in days and his pudgy face was gray with fatigue and worry. "I'm in deep trouble, Mikey. I've been speculating, using money that didn't belong to me."

"Who does it belong to?"

Mike noticed Harry's hands were trembling. "Benny Siegel and Johnny Eggs. Last night they sent Jackie Foster around to talk to me. They want to be repaid, but how am I going to do it? No one is betting on the streets these days. Who has the money? What can I do?"

"Harry, you know what my situation is . . ."

Harry stood up, his face red with anger. "You have to fight, goddamn it! You have to save me! McGrath—he's heavyweight champion of the world now. He's good for more money than God. And you can beat him!" Harry moved away, trembling. He came back, fighting tears. "Mikey, don't you see—I'm desperate. Help me!"

Wind whistled across the square, scattering leaves, bits of newspaper. A man at a garbage basket poked through the debris.

"I'll have to do something with these," Mike said, holding up his twisted knuckles.

"I can get you fights. I have the connections."

"I'll go back, Harry, but I'm not going in with Lansky and Siegel and those guys. I'll fight, but I do it alone, my way."

"Oh, Mikey, if you get me out of this, I'll pay you back. I swear it to you. I swear it."

Throughout the winter, Mike Roth spent most of his waking hours in the gym at the Rutgers Square Settlement House. He told Moe Kotovsky of his decision. He would go full-out in pursuit of a boxing career and he asked Kotovsky to manage him. The one-eyed ex-fighter was pleased and proud to accept the offer.

There were serious problems, though. His hands continued to trouble him, and his size. He was determined to compete where the big money was, as a heavyweight. He was determined to challenge McGrath. Though nearly six feet tall and well-muscled, he had a small frame; his natural weight was barely a hundred and seventy pounds. To compete as a heavyweight he would have to add fifteen or twenty pounds.

He trained hard, and it was grueling, discouraging work. Whenever he punched full-out, his knuckles gave way. In February, sparring in the gym, he broke his right hand again.

Harry showed up at the gym one day with a friend. Mike, resting his reinjured hand, was going through a light workout, rope jumping, calisthenics. "This is Abie Reles," Harry said. "He does some work for pals of mine." Reles was short and mean-looking, several years younger than Mike, a kid dressed to look like a man in a dark overcoat and hood's fedora. He was swarthy with a flat, tough face, kinky hair. "Abie's been helping me out with some real-estate problems."

Abe Reles smiled. "We hear good things about you from your brother." Reles spoke with a peculiar lisping thickness.

"How's the hand?" Harry asked.

"It's all right."

"The kid has bad hands," said Harry to Abie Reles.

"That's why I like to use an iron pipe," Reles lisped, laughing. "You'll never mess up your hands that way. So you're friends with Jackie Foster?"

"We know each other."

"Jackie's a *shtarker*. So when will you be ready?"

"For what?"

"Harry says your fists are solid *gelt*."

"Abie here has influential friends, Mikey. Everyone's waiting to get behind you—"

"So they can shove it in," Mike said angrily.

"It's not that way," answered Reles. "The thing of it is, Harry has his problems. Some problems are tougher than others. Cancer is more tougher than a head cold. Harry has tough problems."

"What did you bring this *vantz* around here for?" Mike said to his brother.

"We were just in the neighborhood."

"You don't like me, Mikey?" asked Reles.

"I don't like you at all."

"You think I'm a kid. But I done some *shlammin*. Tell him, Harry."

"He's done some *shlammin*."

"You get under my skin," Mike said. "Why don't you get out of here?"

Abie Reles held up his hands in mock terror. He had thick, stubby fingers. "Don't *shlam* me, Mike. My head is like a rock, you'll break your other hand." He laughed, snorting through his nose, then turned and walked to the door. He had an awkward, floppy walk, as though he were trying to kick off his shoes. "Mike," Abe Reles called across the room. "I learned one thing—no matter how tough you are, there's always someone tougher."

"Jackie Foster teach you that?"

"How'd you know?" Reles laughed. "Jackie teached me a lot of things. Come on, Harry, I got to get back to Brownsville."

He started out the door. Harry hurried after him.

Angry, Mike returned to his workout. He lashed his skip-rope in furious cadence, burning off his annoyance at his brother: Harry, Harry, foolish, driven Harry, hopelessly infected by the gangster bug, hustling to make it in the hoodlum world, yet always a step behind everyone.

Later Jason Karl came to see him at the gym. "I want you to meet someone," he said. They walked toward Washington Square, crossed it and walked uptown on Fifth Avenue. "I've been thinking about your hands," Jason said. "A fellow I fought with in college had the same problem. He worked one summer cutting timber in Canada. He never had trouble after that."

Waiting for them at Twelfth Street was a stocky middle-aged man in a brown overcoat and derby hat. He greeted Jason with a broad smile and gruff hello. He had a fleshy nose and cigar-stained teeth; several of the teeth were gold-crowned.

It was Al Smith.

Jason introduced Al Smith to Mike and the three of them began to stroll up Fifth Avenue. The ex-governor's manner was friendly and open and Mike felt immediately at ease with him. He insisted Mike call him Al. In a few minutes Mike felt as though they were old friends.

"I'm not much of a sports fan," Al Smith said, "although in my youth I could give as good as I could take. Jay tells me you have trouble with your mitts. You could use a job to condition them."

"I need to do something for them, sir."

"And if you call me 'sir' I'm not going to do nothing for you. Frank Roosevelt is a guy you call 'sir,' one of those guys with a snooty voice. Never trust a guy with a snooty voice, you understand, Mike?"

"Yes, Al."

"Frank and I aren't as chummy as we once were, but I think I could swing a state job for you cutting roads through the Adirondacks. The state's putting through a whole park system up there—roads, trails, campgrounds—and there's lots of timber to be chopped. If that would help you out, I'll get you on up there."

"That would help me out fine."

"Jay says you're a bright lad. Worked in the city planning office. Wanted to be an architect or engineer or something."

"I thought about it, but with the economy the way it is . . ."

"It's not a time for architects now, that's certain. But this prizefight game is a tough, dirty business."

At Thirty-fourth Street the corner was filled with construction equipment. They were at the site where the Empire State Building would be going up. "I've become an expert sidewalk superintendent," said Al Smith, grinning. "Picture this now, Mike: a building rising up one hundred and two stories. A miracle, right?"

He gazed out over the immense excavation that had once been the Waldorf. The rubble had been scooped out, exposing the dark granite rock of Manhattan Island. "I've lived to see some astonishing changes in this city," Al Smith said. "I remember when New York was like a small town. I remember it like it was yesterday when they built the Brooklyn Bridge." He smiled, thinking back, then grew somber. "Everything changes. Politics. Everything. Like Bill Shakespeare said, whatever you win, they finally steal away from you. Jay, I'm a little thirsty after that walk. What do you say we wet the whistle?"

"Lead the way, Governor."

16

It was the end of February when Mike Roth reported to work at a road-commission camp north of Porterville, near Schroon Lake in upper New York State. The camp was in the Adirondack Mountains and at this time of the year the ground was heaped with snow. The work was cold, bitter, grueling.

The men set out just after dawn with axes and saws and worked until sundown cutting black spruce, jack and pitch pine, until they had cleared a wide corridor through the forest. They were followed by crews who dug out a primitive road while still others constructed fences and temporary shelters with the felled trees. The timber that was not used on the site was loaded into flatbed trucks and hauled south to Lake George.

The workers lived in barracks housing twenty-five men each. Mike, whose only experience in the wilderness had been a trip to Bear Mountain when he was small, had difficulty adjusting to the camp. He missed the crowded streets, the noise, the crush of people. The stink and hustle of the ghetto seemed beautiful to him in this dark, desolate country.

He yearned for his own kind, longed to see swarthy Jewish faces, bearded rabbis, bustling, hysterical housewives; to smell the odor of cooked cabbage, garlic, beets. Even the memory of garbage piled in the streets contained a nostalgic charm for him.

The men he worked with were taciturn mountain folk—clannish, mean. As an outsider he was forced to endure petty harassment and was generally shunned. He was given the toughest jobs to carry out and constantly criticized for his performance of them.

The foreman of his work gang pushed him mercilessly, goading him to quit. This giant, a professional woodsman, seemed to take a perverse delight in needling a man until he flared up, then whipping hell out of him. He insisted on calling Mike "Ikey," and no matter how often Mike corrected him, he would come back with it. Mike tightened his resolve and swore to stick it out.

The forest was cold and dank even in midafternoon, and a sense of gloom settled into him and never left. At night, returning bone-weary to the barracks, he would stretch out on his bunk. Despite his fatigue, sleep would not come, and he would light a kerosene lamp, take up his sketchpad, and attempt to rekindle images he had once had for transforming the Lower East Side. They eluded him now, and he ended up drawing meaningless patterns, eccentric geometric shapes. At last he would drop off into a restless doze filled with disturbing dreams of his sister, of Rose Ann McGrath, and of boxing.

Spring arrived. The days grew warmer. His mood lightened and he began to enjoy the work, the challenge of physical exertion. He had acquired some proficiency with the woodsman's ax, and no matter how hard the foreman drove him, he was equal to the task. His hands grew rough with calluses, the muscles of his arms and shoulders thickened. The food in the camp was simple and plentiful. He gained weight and knew it was good, hard weight. His hands felt good. He refrained from hitting full-out with them, but he sensed they were knitting up, toughening.

The foreman rode him constantly, and several times they almost came to blows. Always, though, Mike walked away.

One morning in early summer as he prepared to set out with a trail crew, the foreman started up with him again. "Hey, Ikey, let's move it!"

Mike ignored him; he continued slowly lacing up his workboots.

"Did you hear me, Ikey? I said hurry your ass."

"If you want something from me, call me by my name."

"I thought that's what they called all you guys. Ikey."

"Which guys?"

The foreman moved from his position at the trailhead back toward the barracks porch. "Kikes." He stood above Mike. "Isn't that what you are? A long-nosed yellow Hebe?"

Mike finished lacing his boot and started to rise. The foreman was now on the porch directly above him, and Mike moved on by him. The foreman swung out, a sucker punch.

Mike ducked, then countered with a left hook followed by a blistering flurry of punches. The foreman's head snapped back. He sagged against the porch railing.

The other men of the crew moved from the trailhead close in to the porch to view the action.

The foreman grabbed at Mike, and Mike caught him coming in. The punch cracked across the bridge of his nose.

There was a soft sound like a fresh twig snapping, and the foreman's nose was now pushed at a crazy angle across his face. Mike hit him again, and he went down without a sound. He hit the porch hard and didn't move.

The men of the crew looked on, awed. Mike walked to his ax and saw, which were resting against the barracks wall, and tossed them to the ground.

The foreman stirred, tried to rise, fell back. "Tell him when he gets up that Ikey quit."

Mike went into the barracks and began to pack. He felt fine. His hands had never been better.

17

As the country continued its slide into the depression, Mike Roth embarked on a campaign to gain a chance at Tony McGrath's heavyweight title.

He persuaded Moe Kotovsky to give up his job at Rutgers Square Settlement House and come on the road with him as manager. Then he contacted Jason Karl to ask for a loan. It pained him to do it, but he had been unable to find another way. "We figure we need a thousand dollars," Mike said.

"Why did you wait so long to ask?"

"I just don't feel right about it," Mike said. "And, Jay, whatever I win, you're my partner. You get your share."

Over the next month he trained with brutal dedication at the settlement house, while he and Kotovsky made final preparations to head west in search of fights.

He approached his boyhood friend Nig Kottler to come with them as a training companion and second. He could only offer expenses, but Nig, who hadn't worked in months, leaped at the opportunity.

When he heard Mike would be leaving town again, Charlie Roth flew into a rage. "You ought to be here with us! You ought to be helping!" Charlie hollered.

"There are no jobs. With boxing I have a chance."

"You have a chance to lose an eye like Kotovsky, to make mush out of your brains like Kayo Jakie Cohen, who steals food from garbage cans!"

Things had been going badly for Charlie; it had been nearly a year since he worked. Florence had managed to get a part-time job in a bakery, and she and Charlie lived off her meager pay.

He was drinking heavily these days, homemade wine that he brewed in the cellar. His temper, which in the best of times had been terrible, now often raged out of control.

He had aged beyond his years. Still a large man, now he had size without power; he had lost confidence in himself and the world around him.

"It's the only way," Mike said. He was weary of the arguments, the bitterness, the recriminations. "I've thought about this. It's the only way. For me and for all of us."

"Go, go," Charlie said. "Get yourself killed. I spit on you!"

Mike and Kotovsky formulated a strategy: stay out of New York, fight as often as possible all across the United States, gain as much pro experience as possible. When they both felt he was ready, then make a push in the East and challenge McGrath. Keep on challenging him. A match between a Lower East Side Jewish heavyweight contender and the Irish champion from Greenwich Village would have enormous appeal and drawing power.

But first Mike needed to gain experience, seasoning.

In the old days Kotovsky had crisscrossed the country fighting, and he knew promoters in tank towns that weren't even on the map. He had also contacted Leach Cross in Los Angeles, and Leach assured him that if Mike could reach California, he would line up fights for him. So in August Mike, Kotovsky, and Nig Kottler were ready to embark on their quest for the heavyweight championship of the world.

The night before they left, Sammy Militinu threw a party for Mike at his speakeasy on Rivington.

Charlie Roth got drunk and sat in a corner brooding. Harry, in a tuxedo shiny with age and looking like a waiter from a dairy restaurant on Second Avenue, wandered around shaking hands and telling bad jokes.

A few of the old Ludlow Street Nobles showed up—Fat Kishke, Crazy Saltz, Yoodie Greizman—but they seemed like strangers to Mike.

Uncomfortable with their old leader, they stuffed themselves with food, chopped eggplant, herring and onions, pickles, *mamaliga* with *brinza*—and drank themselves stuporous.

Crazy Saltz got his hands on a bottle of seltzer and ran around *shpritzing* everybody. Yoodie Greizman insisted on reciting a poem, "The Face on the Barroom Floor." He couldn't remember the words and grew belligerent when his audience began to hoot at him.

Nig Kottler downed a full bottle of slivovitz, did a tap dance on the top of a table, fought with a *Galitzianer* cabdriver, and passed out with a smile on his face.

At dawn Nig, Kotovsky, and Mike drove the Model T through dolorous Manhattan streets to the West Side, where they loaded it on the ferryboat to New Jersey.

Even at this early hour the day was steaming. The breeze off the Hudson was thick and humid.

As the boat plowed its way across the river, Mike could see huge pilings and steel ribs protruding from the water upriver, the skeletal superstructure of the George Washington Bridge. The suspension bridge, a miracle of its time, had been under construction for three years. It still was not finished.

He felt sadness at the sight of the incomplete span. What he loved in bridges was their sweep, their aspiration, the joining of sundered landscapes. An unfinished bridge was a gap in man's dreams. He yearned to *construct*, bring a vision alive, watch as it was given its form in the world. And now, as he moved into the West, he was unhappy with himself. He would not be building: he would be smashing, destroying. That would be his life, and it pained him.

Through late summer and early fall Mike Roth fought in Pennsylvania, West Virginia, Ohio, in every coal and mill town within a hundred-mile radius of Pittsburgh. As fast as the palookas were sent up against him, he disposed of them.

He was not flashy but exceptionally efficient. As a badge of his pride he fought with the Star of David on his trunks, and the verbal abuse he endured was extraordinary. He had come to expect it, even enjoy it. It gave his punches a nice edge of anger.

His purses increased, but they were just breaking even and he, Kotovsky, and Nig continued on, traveling a bare cut above hobo class.

The work paid other dividends, though. Mike was testing his skills, honing them, learning all the slick, mean tricks that tank-town brawlers could teach.

He was hitting harder than ever and his weight had stabilized at an even one hundred and eighty pounds. His speed was fine.

Kotovsky felt it was time to step up in class. He traveled into Pittsburgh to meet Johnny Dime, a local promoter. Dime had seen Mike in several of his battles and was not very encouraging. "He's too brainy. He's going to make any fighter look bad. I don't think I can get you a fight here with any boys who are ranked."

"The kid has everything," Kotovsky said. "Why wouldn't you put him on?"

"A word of advice. People come to a fight to see someone get destroyed. Work with him only on a knockout punch. Tell him to save the brainy stuff."

It was autumn now, and they decided to move west. The newspaper sports pages were filled with stories of Irish Tony McGrath. He fought almost every month, took on all ranked comers, demolished them.

The sportswriters were pushing now for an opponent worthy of McGrath's skills. He had triumphed decisively over all the top-rated boys. Was he unbeatable? A champion with no challengers was effectively no champion at all. What could thay write about?

Harry Roth had written Mike an impassioned letter urging him to come back to New York. The time was ripe for him to make his move at the title. In a postscript he mentioned he needed money; bad days had come again. Ben Siegel threw him a bone from time to time, but Siegel's patience was wearing thin.

Mike Roth held back—it would be premature to attempt to get a title shot now. Johnny Dime was right: he was a spoiler who made opponents look awkward. His fights were dull. If he were to gain a title fight, he would have to develop a more popular style.

Moving westward into the tank towns of Indiana, Illinois, and Missouri, Kotovsky concentrated on opening up his style. He trained on the heavy bag, mastering a brutal combination taught to Kotovsky by Joe Choynski, one of the best punchers of his day: jab, straight right, body punch, body punch, double hooks to the head. He practiced it, ripping it off faster, faster, until it came with blinding speed.

He was fighting better boys now and scoring impressively. Choynski's combination was spectacularly effective; opponents began to fall like pins in a bowling alley.

He gained a reputation as a knockout artist. The news got around to the larger cities of the Midwest. Promoters started seeking him out: a kayo artist filled arenas.

He built up a string of early knockouts in Indianapolis, Chicago, and St. Louis.

He continued to wear the Star of David on his trunks. The anti-Semites and Ku Klux Klanners flocked to see him beaten. He never was.

In Chicago he was matched with Shamrock Jimmy O'Brien, the pride of the city's heavyweight division, a rangy redhead who hit with both hands and had never been knocked off his feet. He was considered indestructible, but Mike beat him easily in two rounds.

On the trek west, Mike fought in Columbia, Missouri; Salina, Kansas; Grand Junction, Colorado. He fought in mining towns in Nevada, logging camps in Oregon. He took on seasoned pros and roughneck amateurs, town bullies, barroom brawlers. Often he would fight three times a week, and there were days when he would show up in a town at sunset, go right to the arena, fight, and shove off for the next town. Sometimes Mike would beat the local tough guy in the ring, then with Moe and Nig whip his friends in order to get out of town with their skins intact.

He went up against an astonishing variety of styles and situations and each time won out. He was polishing his skills, honing his craft. Pridefully, Kotovsky watched him develop. It was beautiful to behold.

Choynski's combination had given his technique a brutal dimension. He could carry the best of fighters, then, in a single blistering assault, take them out. He chose the moment, and with an artist's sense of drama created a fine tension in the ring.

His battles became spectacles of suspense: when would it happen? Cities of the Midwest crowded their arenas to witness his explosive artistry.

In California, through Leach Cross, he landed a fight with Cowboy Rawlings, a ragged slugger considered one of the best heavyweights in the state, a man with a national reputation. Only the awesome Wo Duck, a Chinese from San Francisco, was considered better. Mike Roth fought Rawlings in Los Angeles and beat him senseless in three rounds.

After the fight Leach Cross showed up in the dressing room with a man named Ortiz, a Mexican-American who looked like Pancho Villa. "This is Wo Duck's manager," said Cross.

"The Duck will fight you in two weeks in San Francisco. You get a thousand dollars."

"That's a not a helluva lot of money," replied Kotovsky.

"Just be happy the Duck is giving you a fight. He's very particular about the people he mills with. Them Chinks can be very fussy."

Kotovsky, Mike, and Cross talked it over. "He's a real tough boy," Cross said. "Used to work laying track for the railroad. Hits with both hands, and they're like sledges. He's never been beaten."

"What do we have to gain?" asked Kotovsky.

"He's the best heavyweight we have out here. If you're looking for a reputation, this fight could make you. But he's one tough apple—for a China-man to become a pro scrapper, he has to be something special."

"Take the fight," said Mike.

The fight was held in the Cow Palace, a cavernous hall used for horse and cattle auctions, rodeos, occasional prizefights.

Just before the fight, Ortiz visited Mike's dressing room. "One thing I forgot to tell you. The Duck has this following of Chinks—two Tong so-cieties, On Leong and Hip Sing. They hate each other's guts, live only to kill each other. They're all out there tonight, thousands of them. What I'm trying to say is, even if you can, don't beat the Duck tonight. Not with that crowd."

"The crowd never got in my way." Mike said. "It's the guy in the ring who's the problem."

"You ain't never seen no Chink crowd," answered Ortiz.

As Mike, Kotovsky, and Nig Kottler moved down the aisle toward the ring, a sense of unease worked at them. The place was packed to the rafters, yet there was scarcely a sound in the huge arena. It was filled with Chinese. They sat very still and very straight, staring ahead. Many wore pigtails and Oriental robes. It was eerie: the silence, the impassive stares.

Most unsettling were the weapons they carried—knives, clubs, staves, hatchets—held in plain view across their laps or leaning against their chairs.

"Holy, holy shit," said Nig.

There was a handful of cops in the arena, standing nervously at the exits, poised to bolt at the first sign of trouble. "Make this one fast, Mikey," Nig said. "I think we bit off more than we can chew."

"Don't get cute. Just the basic stuff," Kotovsky advised, gazing nervously about.

Wo Duck was not a large man, barely a heavyweight, but each pound was muscle. He had the thick shoulders and broad fists of a natural puncher. His face was boney and flat and he had very narrow eyes. He gazed at Mike with indifference. At the end of the referee's instructions, he shook hands with elaborate formality, then pinned Mike with an ominous stare before returning to his corner.

For six rounds the Duck ate him up, took his clockwork technique and turned it inside out. Mike fought the Duck's fight and was losing badly. In desperation he threw away all logic and beauty, all calculation, and went right at the Duck as brutally as any barroom brawler.

It was ugly and it was desperate and it violated all sense of rightness within him, but he was beyond considerations of stylistic propriety. He was operating in that muddy, bloody limbo of survival. He had to beat the Duck to get to McGrath. It was that simple, that brutal. The Duck attempted to reimpose his rhythm on the fight, but Mike rushed right at him, caught him and knocked him into the ropes. Groups of Chinese moved down the aisles and stared with eerie impassivity at the action. Before the Duck could recover, Mike jolted him with a vicious combination and Wo Duck went down. He landed on his side, rolled over on his back. His right leg jerked spasmodically. He did not get up. The twitch of his leg slowed down, then stopped altogether.

And then the fight was over and the referee was raising Mike's arm in the air.

As one, the crowd pressed toward the ring.

"What do we do, Mikey?" asked Nig plaintively. The ring was surrounded.

Wo Duck was now seated on the canvas and his handlers were trying to get him up. His eyes cleared. He rose unsteadily and started across the ring to Mike. His face was a mask displaying no emotion.

He reached Mike and took his hand and slowly, ceremoniously shook it. Then he turned to the crowd, said something in Chinese, and they began to back off. They formed a corridor up the aisle, and Mike, Nig, and Kotovsky hurried from the ring.

The police were gathered in the hallway leading to the dressing rooms. They did not permit Mike to change. They grabbed him and hustled him outside, with Nig and Kotovsky following.

In an alleyway a police van waited. As the three were bundled into it, all hell broke loose inside the Cow Palace. Gunshots, screams, shrill yells. A fierce ululation erupted, a chilling wail in the night, many voices sounding as one.

"Tong war!" one of the cops hollered. "Tong war!" And his voice was filled with terror as the van sped away.

The knockout of Wo Duck by Mike Roth was buried in the sports pages of the San Francisco papers the next day. The main news was the bloody war in the Cow Palace that had erupted after the fight. Wo Duck had suffered his first knockout in the ring. After, he had been stabbed five times and left for dead. Three people had been killed in the Tong war that night, and a dozen more in the days that followed.

Mike Roth, Nig Kottler, and Moe Kotovsky viewed the occurrence as an omen: they had outlived their welcome on the West Coast. They were going home.

18

Tony McGrath, heavyweight champion of the world, defended his title with regularity, beating all challengers. He took his considerable earnings and purchased controlling interest in his father-in-law's construction business. He put in his brothers, young men now, to operate it.

It was a period of great economic difficulty and Johnny McMahon was only too happy to take a backseat in the business. The brothers, large and brash, ran the company aggressively. Though opportunities were few, they made the best of what came along. With Tony's capital behind them, they were able to take advantage of other people's ill-fortune, buy up property on the cheap, bid low for available jobs.

It was a brawling time, and often a contract was decided by how much muscle a builder could bring to bear on the situation. The McGraths worked with remnant elements of the Young Dusters. It soon became an axiom in the building trades that if you wanted peace on a construction job in lower Manhattan it was good business to deal with the McGrath boys.

They put the best face on their actions, and neither Tony nor Bess knew the extent of their ruthlessness. Tony tried to keep them under control, but they had plans of their own. If one was tough enough and shrewd enough, there was money to be made, and they went at it with a passion.

They warred with other, smaller operations, made advantageous deals with desperate suppliers, employed Bess's influence in the United Irish Club, and through the club with city agencies, to their own gain.

Ugly reports on how her sons were operating came back to Bess. She called them all together around the kitchen table. She had prepared tea and biscuits with jam. "Boys, I have a crow to pluck with you. People tell me now my sons have become a swarm of barracudas."

"We don't do nothing no one else doesn't do!" Jimmy said heatedly.

"Are you playing the bully?" asked Tony. "It's one thing to be hard-driving in business, another to be pushing people around."

"It's a thin line," Emmett said. "We operate by the rules of the street."

"Don't give me that Jesuit talk!" Bess replied angrily. She buttered a biscuit, smeared it with jam, then pushed it away.

"You're my brothers and you must behave like brothers of a champion," said Tony. The boys were a sore disappointment to him. Thick, sullen, aggressive, they answered his generosity with resentment, went their own way. He often wondered how they had turned out as they had.

Emmett scowled. "You put us into this thing, and we're bound to make a go of it. It's a dog's world out there."

"I raised you to be human beings, not dogs!" said Bess with passion.

"Old Paddy—he was a human being. Look what it got him," shouted Emmett. "Not even a gold watch from City Hall."

"Your father had the respect of every mayor he served. He had the respect of the Hall, and that's worth a thousand gold watches!" answered Bess with fire in her eyes. "Either you play the game proper or I'll run you out of the house. What kind of toy did you buy them, Tony?"

Tony spoke reasonably, mediating between his mother and brothers. The boys promised to soften their avarice. Nevertheless, he was uneasy, discouraged: his brothers had turned into vultures.

It was impossible for Tony to do any more than keep a casual eye on the business. The demands of his career kept him in a constant whirl. As heavyweight champion of the world he was sought after for civic functions, political affairs, award ceremonies. He depended on McMahon's good sense to watch over his brothers. But McMahon was pleased with the state of things. In his estimation the direction of the business was just fine. The McGrath boys had brought an energy and drive to it that were exactly what the moment demanded. It was an era in which a man could grow wealthy if he had the stomach for it.

Tony had gained a reputation as a man-about-town. He could be found most nights at the Broadway-area speakeasies. Billy LaHiff's, the Central Park Casino. There were wild rumors of affairs with showgirls, trysts with society ladies—all of them unfounded. He flirted, but never fell.

His wife drew into the background. She hated the night world of clubs and speakeasies and avoided it. Sensing that Tony was not comfortable with her around, she busied herself watching over the house, seeing the boys were fed, looking after Rose Ann. Her days and nights were terribly lonely and she thought often of Darryl Quigley and the peculiar turn her life had taken. The wife of a champion boxer! Never in her dreams could she have imagined it. The gulf between her and her husband was an immense chasm. He was a stranger to her, and this was the greatest pain of all.

The demand for a worthy challenger for McGrath was spreading when word of Mike Roth filtered back from the West Coast. His impressive wins there were trumpeted: he had destroyed Cowboy Rawlings, knocked out the awesome Wo Duck. A powerful excitement began to grow over a match between the Pride of the Ghetto and Irish Tony McGrath.

Tony was eager for it. He loved a good fight, and Roth could give him a war. His only satisfaction was in beating someone who could really do battle with him: it had been a long time since he had felt pride in a victory.

"In a fight like this," said Boss Ahearn, "there are a number of things to consider. We have to hold the control. There are votes to consider, Jewish votes, Irish votes. Do you see what I mean?"

There were political details to be worked out, and Boss Ahearn of the United Irish Club knew that would be no problem.

* * *

Despite the depression, Mike was earning good money. People channeled their despair into viewing combat; boxing was more popular than ever. Since returning from California, he had been fighting up and down the East Coast, and the purses were handsome. Johnny Dime had been right: the big purses came to the big punch.

Mike rented an apartment at 214 Henry Street, one of the best houses on the Lower East Side. It was a four-story gray-stone building with the name "Powhatan" cut in block letters over the entrance. He moved his parents into it.

Though the apartment was bright and spacious, neither Florence nor Charlie felt comfortable in it. Charlie would sit and stare out the window for hours. A thin wedge of the East River could be seen between the buildings to the south on Madison, Monroe, and Cherry streets. Something was missing from his life, and the success of his son had not filled it.

Florence yearned for the old neighborhood. It was only three blocks to the east, and yet it seemed to her a continent away. Her friends avoided her. They were no longer relaxed with her. The Powhatan was considered to be another world, another class.

Harry, still plagued by hard times, was forced to move in with his parents. He had been living with a woman in the Brownsville section of Brooklyn and had fathered a child by her, then ignominiously departed under the weight of mountainous debt. Now he spent all his hours hatching schemes to escape once more from the Lower East Side. His brother's chance at the heavyweight title brought him a promise of redemption.

He met with Ben Siegel, then phoned Mike. "I have a great deal for you, a deal for everybody," he said, his voice rich with unctuous con. "Meet me by the dairy restaurant on Essex."

Mike showed up with Kotovsky. Over *kasha varnishkes,* Harry explained the facts of life to them: "McGrath is controlled by Tammany. Siegel and Johnny Eggs work hand in glove with the Tammany organization down here. There's no way you'll get a fight unless you deal with Tammany."

"What do they want?" asked Mike.

"Votes. Don't you see how it works? They have the fighter, they have blocks of tickets. Tickets go to the people who vote the right way. Siegel and Johnny Eggs just want one of their boys handling things with the Hall."

"I won't fight him. Not like that."

"They have to come to Mikey," Kotovsky said. "There's no one else."

"Don't you see? Ben and Meyer are willing for it to be me!" Harry was agitated; food dribbled from his mouth. "I become one of your managers and I'm the man in the middle. They just want assurances they can get the Annie Oakleys. Sure, McGrath might come to you—after he's fought every garbage collector in the United States. Why make it tough on yourself?"

Kotovsky pondered this. "You'll have to deal with someone, Mike. If we can deal with Harry, we keep it in the family."

"Better to keep it in the family," assured Harry.

It rankled Mike to have strings attached. Nevertheless, he felt responsibility toward Harry. His brother tried, failed, kept on trying. Nothing worked for Harry. More than a year on the road had shown him the folly of going up against men who held all the cards. You always had to cut one deal or another; it was a fact of life.

"All right," Mike said. "After I beat McGrath, though, things will be done differently."

"Right, Mikey."

"I'm dealing with you. I'm not dealing with those other guys."

"You call the shots, Mike. Whatever you say."

Harry wolfed down his *varnishkes,* followed them with a healthy slice of cherry cheese cake. His appetite, lately languishing, had suddenly returned. Once more the world had become a beautiful, habitable place.

The fight was set for Yankee Stadium in April. A mythic aura surrounded it—the Ghetto's Pride against the Irish warrior, Tony McGrath—and the public streamed to the ticket offices. Within two weeks of the announcement, seats were impossible to come by. Everyone chose sides, and New York found itself divided between Irishman and Jew.

The pols of Tammany, working both sides of the street, sold, bartered, and gave away enormous batches of Annie Oakleys. Each ticket brought with it a promise of votes.

Mike Roth set up training at Madame Bey's, a fight camp near Summit, New Jersey, run by the wife of a former Turkish diplomat, while Tony McGrath prepared at a health farm in Pompton Lakes, New Jersey.

People flocked to the training camps—reporters, fans, theatrical celebrities, athletic stars. A special package was organized, and for a dollar a person could watch Tony McGrath at work in Pompton Lakes, then be taken by bus twenty miles south to view Mike Roth.

McGrath's camp was a much livelier place. He was the champion, and the health farm abounded with Tammany politicos, show-business notables, Broadway touts, speakeasy regulars. Tony was in an easy, playful mood and went about his training with exuberance. He sang, joked, signed autographs, had a friendly word for everyone. Music blared constantly from a phonograph next to the sparring ring, sentimental songs sung by John McCormick.

Mike Roth's camp was businesslike, serious. He worked without letup from early morning until dark.

The styles of the two fighters were a study in contrast: McGrath's was broad and explosive, Roth's fierce and dry. McGrath scored by taking chances, while Roth worked to achieve the maximum effect within the narrowest confine, an approach that was cautious and shrewd.

In the evenings Mike went for long walks in the wooded area surrounding the camp. He tried to keep his mind on the fight, but at times it wandered to other things: he saw buildings, complexes of apartments, parks, playgrounds—shadows of his old dreams. He carried his sketchpad with him and by flashlight filled the pad with rough drawings.

At these times he felt a wrenching ache, a terrible emptiness. What was his life now? Where was it going? Why? He put the pad away and struggled to keep his attention on the business at hand: he had a job to do, and if it was one of destruction, well, that had been his choice.

Two weeks before the fight, Jason and Laura Karl visited his camp. Mike had not seen them in nearly a year.

He showered after his workout and the three of them sat on the rear porch of the farmhouse. A broad lawn swept down to a pond where a flock of ducks strutted and splashed. The evening sun was dying. Night insects flitted above the water, swarmed about the porch light.

They avoided talk of the fight and instead spoke of politics. Tammany was having a rough time of it, Jason explained. Jim Walker's freewheeling ways had at last brought everyone to the brink of ruin. Judge Samuel Seabury, a minister's son and lifelong enemy of Tammany, had gone after Walker, and a major scandal threatened to shatter his administration and all involved with it.

Al Smith, too, was in trouble. Tammany's plummeting fortunes and his break with Walker and Roosevelt had severely crippled him politically. He would like to make another run at the White House—the economic situation all but guaranteed the election of a Democrat—but his chances of getting the nomination were negligible. He no longer had the power base.

Mike was saddened by what he heard. Beneath all the talk was a sense of Jason's disillusionment. He had a vision for the Lower East Side, a vision tied to Al Smith's future for better or worse. It would never be realized now. All his passion, all his commitment, were as dust.

It grew dark. Bullfrogs sounded at pondside, a low pulsating drone, relentless heartbeat of night, time eroding, dreams dying.

Jason and Laura rose to leave. Mike walked them to the front of the house. Three men were waiting beside a parked roadster: Jackie Foster, Abe Reles, and Ben Siegel.

They smiled when they saw Mike, and each smile seemed a carbon copy of the other and there was something mocking in the smiles. Mike felt a great anger.

"Can we talk, Mikey?" asked Siegel.

"What about?"

"We have business."

Jason took Laura by the arm and steered her to their waiting limousine.

"What business?" Mike said, tense.

Ben answered, "We're lovers, Mikey. We're all in bed together."

Jason and Laura paused by their limousine and watched.

"Someone's telling you stories, Ben. I'm not in bed with anyone."

Siegel stared at Mike. The anger in his eyes was like a thin, hazy film. His face flushed. A prominent vein stood out on his forehead. "Don't do this to me, Mike." His voice trembled with anger. "Don't treat me like this."

They were standing very close now, and Siegel's eyes were narrow with rage.

"Get out of here. Now," Mike said very quietly.

Siegel blinked, and suddenly the anger was gone and he was smiling. He shrugged. "I don't know what it is with you, Mike. You always give me aggravation. Why do you treat me like this?"

"You and your *gunzles* have no reason to be around here."

Ben Siegel continued to smile. *"Gunzles?"* He turned to Laura and Jason. "You hear how he talks, how he insults? You're a *chaye,* an animal, Mike. We have serious business to discuss, and you call us names? You're under pressure. All right. I understand. We'll straighten everything out later."

"There's nothing to straighten out."

"Whatever you say, Mike." He walked toward Laura. "People nowadays have no respect for nothing, for friendship, for business ethics. A man's word used to be gold." He shook his head sadly. "No one respects me. People lie to me and I take it. What else can I do? I like to think of myself as a civilized man. Look at this man here," he said, indicating Reles. "He wears dirty underwear. I can't stand dirty underwear and yet I put up with this man. What does that say about me, that I'm too civilized? What can I do? That's my nature."

Reles laughed thickly, and Foster snickered. "Sure, everyone laughs," Siegel said, "but I'm the one who suffers." He started toward the roadster. Reles and Foster followed. "Everything will be straightened out," he said as though to himself. "There's time. There's time for everything."

After they had gone, Jason, Laura, and Mike stood in the driveway. "That's the man they call Bugsy, isn't it?" asked Laura. "What did he want?"

"He has business with my brother."

"He seems to feel he has business with you," said Jason.

"Damn, Harry! Damn him!" Mike said in a fury.

"Is it serious?"

"They have no claims on me!" Mike knew, though, that Ben Siegel had other ideas.

In the week before the fight, a gloom that had nothing to do with boxing settled over Tony McGrath's camp. Jim Walker was in trouble, and it affected all the Tammany folk.

In the basement card room after dinner, Bill-O, McMahon, and Boss Ahearn gathered with Tony. Emmett was there, carrying a thick sheaf of bills. "Suddenly nobody wants to do business with us," Emmett said heatedly. "I don't understand. I have cement on order. I have crews to pay."

"Don't bother Tony with this now, Em," ordered Bill-O.

"He's right," McMahon agreed. "Don't bother your brother."

"Nobody'll do business with any of us," said Boss Ahearn morosely.

"Another thing," Emmett said, "we had sewer contracts—"

McMahon put his fingers to his lips to shush Emmett.

"Rent them as apartments, 'cause the sewers is where we'll be living!" Boss Ahearn yelled. "I've known Sam Seabury since he was a little Catholic-hating prig who'd stand on the corner opposite Tammany shouting hell, fire, and brimstone about what devils we were. We're dealing with a preacher's son and they're all nutty as fruitcakes. That was the wisest thing the Church ever done, forbidding priests to marry." Boss Ahearn's tongue was thick from drinking. The Seabury investigation, building over the last eight months, threatened to bring everyone down. McGrath and McMahon Construction wasn't the only one who would be affected by it. Boss Ahearn had his own pots bubbling with the city.

"You had a winning game, Boss," Bill-O said. "You should have played by the rules."

"They changed the rules in the middle of the game," Boss Ahearn came back. "A favor now is not a thing of goodwill between old friends, it's something filthy—graft. I hate that word."

"Isn't that what they always called it?" Bill-O said, smiling.

"I'd rather they cut off this hand," replied Ahearn, shaking his right fist melodramatically, "than accuse it of taking what didn't belong to it."

"You can't go wrong if you play by the rules," said Bill-O again.

"What are you suggesting, Bill-O?" asked McMahon. "I know you, and you're a bright lad. You must have something up your sleeve."

"Do you want to ruin Tony? Do you want to bring this whole thing down on his head?" said Bill-O. "You have to clear out of here, all of you. John, you have to put distance between you and Tony. You have to eat your losses on this construction stuff and leave Tony out of it."

"I told you to play the game straight, didn't I, Em?" Tony asked angrily.

"But we had these orders. They were legitimate orders—"

"I admire your dedication to the business Em," McMahon said, "but don't bother Tony with none of this."

"You all have to separate from Tony," repeated Bill-O.

No one spoke for a while. "He's right, Boss," McMahon said at last. "Bill-O's clean as new laundry. Let him stay here. He'll look after our interests."

"Whatever happened to the old values?" Boss Ahearn said sadly. "These damn hypocrites are making it a dog-eat-dog world."

19

Yankee Stadium at East 161st Street and River Avenue in the Bronx
loomed like a great ocean liner in a gray tenement sea, tier upon tier
rimmed with white and red light. On foot, by taxi and limo, automobile
and elevated train, people poured toward it.

The day had been unseasonably hot, but toward evening a refreshing
coolness moved in off the Harlem River.

In late afternoon a trickle of spectators began arriving. By dusk, with the
preliminary fights under way, the red and white tier lights glowed and the
great white ring lights illuminated the roped square in the center of the stadium. The trickle became a torrent: businessmen and working people, politicians and show-business folk, sports figures, hustlers. As dusk shifted to
night, the ring appeared magical, unreal, a blazing platform of pure white in
the center of the universe.

Joe Humphries, the ring announcer, entered the square and a low rumble
started in the far bleachers, spread through the yawning horseshoe canyon
of the stadium, built to a roar which engulfed the bright platform at its center.

Humphries, fat, bald, with a great bulbous nose, proclaimed in a raw
voice: "Ladies and gentlemen, there are some folks at ringside for this mo-
mentous battle. I'd like to introduce the great Al Jolson, that fine lightweight Lew Tendler of Philadelphia, the very colorful George Jessel ..."
His voice was drowned out by the sound of the crowd. He went on for a
while introducing notables, then left the platform and conferred at ringside
with James J. Walker and Boss Curry.

The roar of the crowd grew louder still. The stadium reverberated with it.
Mike Roth, in a blue-and-white robe, came down the aisle toward the ring.
He climbed through the ropes, danced in the resin box and worked his
shoes in it, then shuffled in a tight circle, chopping out short, sharp
punches.

And now Tony McGrath moved briskly toward the ring. The roar in the
stadium, continuing to grow, was thunderous. He bounded up onto the
apron and waved at the crowd. Inside the ring he moved in an easy glide,
limbering up. His handlers took off his robe, green with a large white shamrock.

Joe Humphries was back in the ring now. Slipping his false teeth into a
side pocket of his tux jacket, he announced: "Ladies and gentlemen, fifteen
rounds for the heavyweight championship of the world, in this corner one
hundred and eighty-two and one-half pounds, from the Lower East Side of

New York, with a record of twenty-seven wins and no defeats, the Ludlow
Street Assassin, the Pride of the Ghetto, Mike Roth!"

The roar was constant now, a steady wave of sound assaulting the bright
white square. "And in this corner, at one hundred and ninety pounds, fifty-
six wins, one defeat, also from New York City, the Shamrock Slugger, the
Greenwich Village King of Kayos, Heavyweight Champion of the World,
Irish Tony McGrath!"

The referee motioned both fighters to the center of the ring for instructions: they could hear none of it. The sound of the crowd buried everything.

The bell to start the fight cut through the roar.

McGrath came out fast to set the pace. He moved crisply through the
first round, jabbing and dodging, slipping punches, countering.

He appeared large to Mike, thicker, more muscular than he remembered
from earlier days. His fists were much quicker; his punches had a kick to
them, even the ones Mike blocked.

Tense, Mike had trouble getting started. He tried to put together a few
combinations, but McGrath countered them in stinging rebuke.

Between rounds Kotovsky deftly swabbed down Mike's face, smeared pe-
troleum jelly across his brow and over his cheekbones. Nig Kottler held a
cold sponge to the nape of his neck, the water poured down his back. "Get
inside him, Mike," Kotovsky said.

"Dig for it, Mikey," Nig agreed. "The *kishkes.*"

Kotovsky pried his mouth open and inserted the rubber teeth protector.

The second round went much like the first, McGrath forcing the fight.
Several times he lashed out with a ferocious, whipping assault of punches.
Mike ducked under them. The crowd screamed as though he had been hit.

Mike came back with a nice, digging combination at the midsection,
then went for the head, but McGrath took the blow on the shoulder.

Just before the bell, McGrath whacked in a murderous punch to the side
of Mike's head. He caught him on the ear, and the sound of the crowd rang
in his head in harsh dissonance, echoing the bell, and continued to reverber-
ate as he returned to his corner.

"You gotta go under, Mike. Under!" Kotovsky said. His expression was
serious as he demonstrated a digging punch to the body.

Nig applied ice to his ear. "It won't cauliflower, Mikey, don't worry,"
Kottler said.

"The *kishkes,*" repeated Kotovsky. "That's where paydirt is."

In the third round the fight began to find its groove—brisk probes, suddenly explosive exchanges, McGrath working outside with powerful, arcing
punches, Mike banging in close. They had each found the other's range and
with regularity were landing stinging blows that popped in the night air.

Mike felt an edge of concern. He was hitting McGrath but not hurting
him. He was in superb condition and Mike realized it would not be easy to
put him down. He would just have to keep at him, wear him down.

And McGrath's punches hurt. They started wide and Mike would look to go under them and then they would slam in hard. He could feel his arms and shoulders swelling where he had blocked them.

His face was numb. The tissue about his eyes began to puff up.

Over the next two rounds Mike battled back, gave as good as he got, and yet McGrath appeared unfazed.

In the sixth round he put together a beautiful combination—a half-dozen short, solid punches that drove McGrath against the ropes.

A roar exploded from the crowd, remained constant. Mike kept McGrath on the ropes and chopped away. A ripping punch caught McGrath's head. Sweat sprayed from him. He was not hurt though: his eyes were clear and he bounded back swinging. Mike took a punch high on the head that caused him to retreat.

Between rounds Mike said, "I can't hurt him." There was despair and confusion in his voice.

"He's feeling 'em, Mikey. He's feeling 'em," Nig insisted.

"Keep coming at him," said Kotovsky. "No letup."

"He's feeling 'em," Nig said again. "Take it to the bank. He's feeling 'em."

Tony McGrath was on his feet before the bell. He had an ugly red welt on his cheekbone but didn't look tired. He was smiling down at someone at ringside.

The bridge of Mike's nose was swollen. He breathed in and had difficulty getting air through the passageways.

At the bell, McGrath came out fast, moving in a circle around Mike. Mike attempted to go inside to work at the midsection, but he was stopped by a sudden jolt, a punch he hadn't seen. And now the ring was fuzzy, a soft nimbus blossoming about the overhead lights. Mike tried to tie McGrath up, but McGrath caught him with a left hook. Two more punches whipped in, punches Mike hadn't seen, and he realized he was hurt.

He backpedaled. McGrath pressed in on him. Mike couldn't see the punches but felt them. Each exploded a halo around the ring lights. The ring was now a circus of halos before his eyes.

The rock-hard roar of the crowd crashed against him, and his world was now harsh sound and exploding light. He tucked his chin low and tried to get under the arc of McGrath's punches, ripping at him with punches of his own.

He hit McGrath a lovely combination, short and clean, and McGrath went back surprised. Now there was a split in Mike's attention: should he go after him or conserve his energy? How much did he have left? The fuzzy halos continued to dance in his vision, and he punched through them, pressing after McGrath. His arms were devoid of strength and feeling, and yet he continued to punch out.

And then McGrath staggered him, hit him with a devastating punch, and the halos slid to one side and bounced about and he realized he was on the canvas. He could smell the liniment and perspiration. The canvas felt rough under his back. He saw the bright leather of the referee's shoes, the sheen of his trousers.

He was tired, very tired. He tried to get up, but his legs wouldn't work. The yells of the crowd fused with the referee's count, and the sound seemed to be driving him down into the canvas.

At six he managed to get up on one knee. It became the most important thing in the world for him to get up. He tried to push off his knee, but his leg had no spring to it. He heard the referee count nine, and he flung himself upward. He was on his feet, but there was no hardness to the floor. It pitched at an angle away from him. Inside, he rolled with nausea and felt himself falling toward the ropes. The referee grabbed him and pushed his face upward so that the overhead lights exploded in his sight, halos bursting about the referee's face. The ref said something to him, but the sound of the crowd made it impossible to hear. "I'm all right," he yelled. He could see the referee studying him, and then he was pushing him forward, back into the fight.

McGrath hit him again, but he didn't remember the punch. He was sitting on the stool in his corner and Nig was screaming something at him, but all sound had become stone and he couldn't hear anything.

He didn't hear the bell for the eighth round, but the stool was suddenly out from under him and someone was pushing at him and then he was out in the center of white light; the smaller halos had stopped and were replaced by one huge white halo and he knew there was danger at the center of that halo but couldn't figure out how to avoid it.

After, he lay on the rubbing table staring up at a white light and he realized the fight was over. Kotovsky worked above him with swabs of cotton and towels. There was great noise and commotion in the dressing room. He forced himself up onto his elbows. Nig was at the door trying to hold back a crowd of people. He finally managed to get the door shut.

"What round did it end?" Mike asked.

"You don't remember, Mikey?"

"After the seventh round I don't remember anything."

"It went three more rounds."

"What did I finally go down on?"

Nig looked stunned. "Go down? You didn't go down! You beat him, Mikey! You knocked him out! You're the heavyweight champion of the world!"

Some days later Mike saw the fight in a newsreel theater on Broadway. He watched himself as though viewing a stranger. From the seventh to the tenth round he had been out on his feet. He had taken everything McGrath had thrown. Fighting on instinct, he had managed to clinch, slip punches, mount an offensive of his own.

In the tenth round he cracked off a clockwork combination, Choynski's combination, learned in the tank-town belly of America.

McGrath took the first two punches in surprise. He stood stock-still in the middle of the ring as though rooted there. His head snapped backward. His eyes clouded over. He lunged at Mike, laid an arm across his shoulder, and kept on going. He sprawled on the canvas, facedown. At eight he rolled over, shielding his eyes with his gloves.

Mike wondered if he had seen halos above the ring.

20

"Tony, it's all for the best," Theresa said. "We have all the money we need now. My dad says the boys are doing good with the business. It's a sign from heaven that you're supposed to quit!"

She came to him in the parlor of the house. Though it was the middle of the night, he had not yet been to bed. Since losing the title he had been trapped by depression. He could not shake it. Losing was not part of his world. He couldn't accept it.

It had been this way ever since the fight. Every night he would stay by himself in the parlor or take long walks down by the waterfront.

He buttoned up his shirt now, pulled on his shoes. "Where are you going?" Theresa asked. He didn't answer. "I want to help you—"

"You can help by leaving me alone."

"Why did you marry me? You don't confide in me. You treat me as though I don't exist. Why? Why did you marry me?"

"Theresa, please. Leave me alone. I have things to figure out."

"You were beaten. It happens to everyone at some time—"

"He didn't beat me!" He started for the door.

"You have to put it behind you," she said.

"I'll never do that. It's just not my way." Outside, he walked toward West Street. It was quiet and cool out, and he moved along the waterfront. He stood at dockside watching the dark water lap against the pilings. A buoy bobbed at the end of the dock, clanged in the night.

He went over the bout blow for blow, as he had every night since losing the fight. He had Roth staggered for nearly three rounds and couldn't put him down. In his mind's eye he saw in bold detail the punch that led to his knockout. The glove appeared enormous, a watermelon; it moved agonizingly slowly; he saw it but couldn't avoid it. It was as though a switch had been thrown. An electric jolt went through him; then everything went black. Next he was in his corner kneeling. There was a stabbing pain in the center of his skull between his eyes. He felt the pain for the next two days.

How could it have happened? How? What should he do now?

It was dawn when he returned to the house. His mother was sitting with Theresa in the kitchen. "You have to stop this, Tony," his mother said. "You're going to give this poor woman a breakdown."

She had made tea. He poured himself a cup from the pot on the stove and sat at the table.

"It's not like you, Tony," Bess said, "making everybody miserable this way. You're the luckiest man alive. You have money, your health, a good wife who cares for you." She got up from the table and began to slam around the kitchen. "Who wants some breakfast? Theresa?"

Theresa shook her head.

"You have no problems except what's in your head! I'm not going to have you around here pouting like a baby! You lost one measly fight. For a few minutes one man was better than you. What's the tragedy there?"

"I never said it was a tragedy—"

"You're walking around here like it is, and it makes me sick to my stomach. There are more important things in this world than winning a boxing match, beating up other men. There are mothers can't feed their children, there are men who don't have jobs, there are people who are sick. The whole country is sick, and you walk around here like Prince Hamlet himself! It's a sickening spectacle, Tony! If you feel that low, go down by the breadlines where you'll have plenty of company—"

"Bess," Theresa interrupted softly.

"Don't Bess me, Terry. The boy needs a good kick in the behind, that's what he needs."

Tony looked up and smiled. "You're one tough old chicken, aren't you?"

"Tough as shoe leather."

Tony got up and started for the rear of the apartment.

After he left the room, Theresa said, "It's my fault. I should have been able to help him. I just don't know what to do."

Tony appeared in the doorway carrying his leather equipment bag. He looked sheepish.

"Where are you going?" asked Theresa.

He shrugged, embarrassed. "To the gym. It's time I got back in training."

The next weeks he spent almost all of his time in the gym. He trained furiously, working off his unhappiness, mauling his sparring partners. He hadn't consciously decided to fight again, but deep down he knew he had no choice. He would challenge Mike Roth.

He discussed it with Bill-O and John McMahon. "What is it you want, Tony?" McMahon asked.

"Get Roth. The sooner the better. June if possible."

There were meetings, and Bill-O returned discouraged. "He's in no hurry, Tony. He feels there are Tammany strings attached to you. He wants all strings cut."

"Give him what he wants."

"No more Annie Oakleys for the pols . . ."

"Fine. Just get me the fight. Any way you can. Just get it."

Toward the end of May, Mayor James Walker, battling for his political life, organized a march in opposition to Prohibition. He called it the Beer Parade.

Tammany would be marching of course, and Boss Ahearn put pressure on Tony to take part in it. Tony begged off. He wanted nothing to do with Tammany now, nor Jimmy Walker.

Bill-O agreed. "Roth doesn't want the Hall to have any part of the next fight, Boss."

"We stayed out of the last one."

"The Hall had their seats, all the same. And a healthy batch it was, too. Roth is the champion now, Boss. He calls the shots."

"This town belongs to us—"

"If Beau James sinks, who knows who it'll belong to."

"It'll belong to us!" the Boss said with anguish in his voice. "What should we do, Bill? What should we do?"

"I'd keep my distance from Beau James. I'd skip this beer parade."

"Ah, Bill-O," said Johnny McMahon, "it's going to be a lovely party. Why should we miss it? It's going to be like the old days when Dry Dollar Tim Sullivan would throw a bash. Remember them days, Boss?"

"Sure, I remember," the Boss said, moved at the thought of less compli- cated times. "It's a family party. You can't snub your own kin. The Hall is your family, and don't you forget it."

Against Bill-O's advice, Tony agreed to participate in the parade. Bess had swayed him. "I have no respect for Jim Talker now, but we can't turn our backs on him at this hour. Remember how he came to your father's wake? That was a manly thing he done. We have to march in his parade."

The Beer Parade! The whole family was caught up in the idea. Even Rose Ann seemed cheered by it. Bess, Theresa, Tony's brothers—they would talk of nothing else. For them it had become Fourth of July, St. Paddy's Day, and New Year's all rolled into one. It would be a throwback to the grand old Irish celebrations, the wild brawling time when Tammany ruled the town unchallenged.

The parade was due to set off at eleven o'clock in the morning. Mayor Walker, who was to lead the march, was late as usual. "He'll be late for his funeral, don't you know it!" Johnny McMahon called over to Boss Ahearn, who would be marching on foot in the rear of the Tammany group.

Tony, Theresa, Rose Ann, and Bess occupied a horse-drawn hansom cab next to one with McMahon and his wife. Bess was furious. The United Irish Club contingent had been forced to the back of the parade because of their support for Al Smith in his feud with Walker. "Look at the way they're making Boss Ahearn walk like that, pulling up the hind end like a horse's ass," she huffed.

Bubbling with excitement, Theresa shifted about, trying to take in every-thing at once. Rose Ann, looking lovely but thin, sat very still and quiet. Theresa struggled to get her attention. She gazed about, but seemed to see nothing. Her face set in a wan, secret half-smile.

It was nearly 11:30 when Mayor Walker arrived, cool and unruffled in formal morning coat and striped trousers, white shirt with stiff white collar, and a derby. A Department of Sanitation band started a raucous rendering of "There Is a Tavern in the Town," while the Fire Department band across the street came in with "How Dry I Am," and the parade was off, heading downtown from Seventy-ninth Street along Fifth Avenue.

A group of kids trailed alongside Tony's hansom, pressing scraps of paper at him to autograph. "When are you going to fight the sheenie again?" one of the kids yelled.

"Soon," Tony hollered back.

"You're going to be champ again, right, Tony?"

"Tell everyone to bet on it."

An airplane lazed in the sky above, blaring out announcements over a loudspeaker: "Hello, everybody, this is the voice from the sky! We want beer up here and we're willing to pay taxes for it! Hello, everybody, this is the voice from the sky! . . ."

The parade continued down Fifth Avenue. There were performing dogs, clowns, acrobats, Broadway chorus girls walking alongside Tammany floats of huge kegs of beer, vaudeville and show floats, industry floats like the huge papier-mâché fish from the Fulton Market and the laundry workers' float with the sign "No Suds, No Wash." People blasted noisemakers, danced, passed flasks of booze around right under the view of smiling cops. Horns honked, sirens screamed, bells clanged.

At Thirty-fourth Street and Fifth Avenue the parade arrived at a review-ing stand erected in front of the sleek new Empire State Building. The building rose in awesome majesty above the avenue, and Bess and Theresa craned their necks to see the top. Though McGrath and McMahon Con-struction had done considerable work on the building, it was the first time they'd seen it close up and they ooh'd and ah'd in astonishment at its mag-nificence.

Bill-O brought a reluctant Tony McGrath to the reviewing stand. He took his place at the far end of the rostrum, thinking: I should be standing here as heavyweight champion of the world. Instead, I'm in disgrace. Be-yond Jim Walker he could see Mike Roth, the man who had beaten him. Jason and Laura Karl were with him. Laura was watching him; she smiled, and he smiled back, his feeling of desolation deepening.

He had lost to Mike Roth. *He had lost.* How? How?

Jim Walker was at the microphone now, addressing the crowd: "There's a commission in this town been delving into our sins, and some people feel I haven't been as lily-pure as they'd like me to be. In a couple of weeks they're going to be dragging me in front of their inquisition, and I intend to take a lesson from the great athletes of our town—the Babe Ruths, the Tony McGraths, the Mike Roths—one day you hit a home run and get the cheers, the next day you strike out and get boos, and that's spelled b-o-o-s!"

The crowd screamed its approval. The bands broke into competing renditions of "How Dry I Am" and "There Is a Tavern in the Town." Walker waved his arms to quiet them.

"I don't want to bore you with my problems. We're here for fun today. Six weeks ago the great Irish Tony McGrath had his block knocked off by the superb Pride of the Ghetto—" A tumultuous roar went up. Before the bands could start in, Walker, laughing, made a mock conductor's move to silence them. "Well, Tony McGrath picked himself up from the canvas, and I intend to do likewise, no matter what the prigs say about it! No one, let me repeat, no one, is going to keep this Son of Erin down!"

The bands blared out again, one doing "Sidewalks of New York," the other "Will You Love Me in December As You Do in May?"

Mayor Walker laughed and waved Tony to the podium. Tony resisted, but the crowd shouted for him and he made his way toward the Mayor. Walker had Mike Roth by the arm and brought him to the microphone.

Tony and Mike shook hands. The bands finally quieted down, and now Walker said, "Mike, you knocked our friend Tony's ears into his socks over in Yankee Stadium, and I want to say that was some job and I have a favor to ask of you: will you stand behind me when I go up against old prune-face Judge Seabury next month?"

Everyone laughed, and Mike smiled uncomfortably. "I'm just a fighter, not a politician, Mr. Mayor." Walker covered his dismay with a forced smile. "But I appreciate your asking. This is a great day and it's a sincere pleasure being here."

"The boy's learning," Walker said. "See how well he speaks out of both sides of his mouth."

"You taught him, Jimbo!" someone yelled from the crowd, and Walker laughed heartily, but his eyes were wary.

Walker eased Tony to the microphone. "It's also a great pleasure for me to be here. I was just getting over the headache Mike here gave me, but I think these two fine bands have brought it back!"

The crowd loved it. They laughed and applauded.

"Mike is a great fighter," Tony said. "It was a privilege to meet him in the ring. You beat me, Mike. But I want another shot. I deserve it. You're wearing that crown now, but it belongs to me, and I'm going to get it back. Will you give me that chance?"

Mike appeared uneasy. "I don't want Tony to feel I'm ducking him. Of course I'll fight him again, but I want no strings attached. I want the politicians and chiselers to keep their hands off this fight. Sure, Tony. You have your fight. Anytime you want it."

Jim Walker looked sheepish. He forced a smile and said with mock horror, "When he mentioned chiselers, was he looking at me?" The crowd roared with laughter. "It'll be a great fight, I'm sure, and this has been a great day. I'll be looking forward to seeing all of you down at the court-house two weeks from today! It'll be me against Sam Seabury, and may the better man win!"

People screamed, shouted, laughed. The two bands blared away at each other. Mike turned from the microphone and made his way toward Jason and Laura. Laura was staring past her husband, past Mike, who turned to look in the direction of her gaze.

She was watching Tony McGrath moving away through the crowd.

21

The details of the match were finally settled. Mike Roth and Tony McGrath would meet again in Yankee Stadium at the end of June. Bill-O guaranteed that Tammany would have nothing to do with the fight. The control of free tickets was taken away from the athletic commission.

Bill-O informed Tony that after this fight, win or lose, he would no longer be managing him. "I'm going for a judgeship," he explained. "If the Talker resigns, I'll have it." His expression was solemn, as though he were already sitting on the bench.

Tony had recently noticed a change in Bill-O. As he began to move up in the world, the twinkle in his eye was replaced by something cooler, more impatient and businesslike. Tony didn't like the change. He preferred the old Bill-O, the fun-loving ex-longshoreman who would sit around with the boys for hours telling riotously funny tales of his early days on the docks and the police force.

"How will you swing it, Bill?"

"I've thrown in with Joe McKee." Joseph V. McKee, known as Holy Joe, was president of the board of aldermen. He was an anti-Tammany Democrat and by law would become acting mayor if Walker was forced to leave before his term was up.

"You're kissing the Hall good-bye, then?" asked Tony.

Bill-O smiled sadly. "I might be leaving her, but she won't be leaving me. Like they say, lad-o, she's the mother of us all."

Once again Mike Roth set up training at Madame Bey's, while Tony returned to Pompton Lakes. At McGrath's camp the colorful hangers-on, the Irish songs, the horseplay, were still around, but there was a change from the earlier fight—the Tammany boys were absent, Boss Ahearn, Johnny McMahon, James J. Walker's crowd. Bill-O had sent the word out to keep Tammany away. Tammany had problems of its own and was happy to tend to its gardens close at home.

The reporters still treated McGrath as champion. Mike's victory was regarded as a fluke—he had been beaten badly and had only come back with a miracle to win the fight.

Mike accepted this judgment. At his training camp all was serious purpose. He knew that if he was to keep the title he must drive himself brutally, work harder than ever before.

He and Kotovsky discussed strategy. They decided that their approach in the first fight, to bring the battle to McGrath, had been wrong. This time they would attack him differently. Harry sat in on the strategy meetings and was a constant source of irritation. He and Kotovsky argued about everything from Mike's training schedule to the color of his boxing shoes.

Harry accused Kotovsky of being responsible for Mike almost losing the first fight—he hadn't enough top-level professional managing experience. "This is the heavyweight championship, not some club title," Harry insisted.

"Do you want me out?" Kotovsky asked Mike. "Maybe Harry's right. Maybe I'm in over my head."

"Whatever trouble I had in the first fight was my own fault. I'm nothing without you, Moe."

One day Harry showed up with a small, wiry, middle-aged man with ferret eyes and a punched-in nose. It was Abe Antoff, the great Abe Antoff, former featherweight champion of the world. Along with Leach Cross and Joe Choynski, he had been one of the legendary Jewish fighters who performed so spectacularly in the era before the Great War. He had been a master of the craft, his style one of great elegance and innovation. He was an encyclopedia of all the little tricks and quirks of the game, a formidable stategist. What he hadn't invented, he knew; and what he didn't know, didn't exist.

Harry pleaded with Mike to take him on as Kotovsky's assistant. Surprisingly, Kotovsky agreed. Abe Antoff was hired. There was only one disquieting drawback: he was a close friend of Ben Siegel and Lepke Buchalter.

Things went well for a time. Antoff was content to let Kotovsky do most of the day-by-day work with Mike. Occasionally, he would make a suggestion. His ideas, simple on the surface, were undeniably brilliant in execution: a hitch here, an eccentric twist there, a stunning reversal of the expected. He was a great one for having his man play possum, lure an opponent by a seeming blunder, only to turn the whole thing around with a startling array of counters.

In the last weeks of training, he and Kotovsky began to disagree. Antoff pressed Mike to go at McGrath's strength, "beat him where he lives." On the basis of the first fight, Kotovsky felt this would be disastrous. McGrath was too smart, too strong.

Antoff grew testy. He began to override Kotovsky. He continued to counsel bringing the fight to McGrath. "You make him think you learned nothing the last time. It's a ploy, don't you see?"

Tension in the camp grew. Kotovsky became upset. Antoff dominated the training sessions, insisting that Mike make a fight of it. "He'll never win by staying away, and he won't have nothing. You make the fight exciting, you'll stay in this business forever. It's show business, just like anything else. It's tigers that dominate, Mikey; hedgehogs end up buried in the ground." It was Pittsburgh Johnny Dime talking all over again.

"If they want fun and games, let 'em go to Coney Island," Kotovsky said heatedly. Mike had never seen him so upset. "You have the championship. If he wants it from you, make him come after it."

The arguments grew more bitter, personal. In their heyday Antoff had been a champion; Kotovsky was nothing more than a run-of-the-mill pro. "I have both my eyes!" Antoff yelled one day. "What do you know about how to fight?"

That night Kotovsky came to Mike's room carrying a suitcase. "I'm leaving, Mikey. I believe in my heart if you mix it with McGrath he's going to carve you up. Abe is setting you up for a terrific beating."

Mike tried to talk him out of leaving. He was torn between his loyalty to Kotovsky and his great respect for what he had learned from Antoff. There was no doubt in his mind that he was a better fighter for having had Antoff in camp with him.

"I'm not questioning his tactics," Kotovsky insisted. "I'm talking about overall strategy. You can't go head-on at McGrath."

"It's a ploy—"

"After the ref's counted you out, tell McGrath that. Tell the crowd, the reporters. I'm saying to you, something's not kosher here."

There was nothing Mike could do to persuade Kotovsky to remain. He was adamant and he left camp immediately.

With Moe gone, Mike suddenly felt lost. Since he had started fighting he had had no other trainer. He missed him desperately, missed his concern, his obvious love.

"Don't worry about Kotovsky, just listen to Abe," Harry said. "Abe knows what's good for you."

Mike prayed he was right. He was not so certain now.

22

Bess McGrath stood outside the courthouse in downtown Manhattan with a contingent from the United Irish Club carrying signs in support of James J. Walker. She waited without any deep sense of commitment, a political workhorse going through the paces.

"Walker, Walker, he's the one! Seabury's a sourpuss, he's no fun!" the

United Irish Club chanted as they paraded up and down the sidewalk.

The morning was hot. An old man was doing a brisk business selling Italian ices from a cart. A fire hydrant had been opened on the corner, and from time to time someone wet a handkerchief and passed it around.

James J. Walker, the mayor of the city of New York, was due to testify this day before Judge Samuel Seabury and the Joint Legislative Committee on corrupt practices. Bess felt increasingly downhearted as time for the hearings drew near. She sensed that Walker was about to bring disgrace upon all of them, or her friends and neighbors, on the political party she so loved. He would desecrate the sweat and toil she had poured into Tammany these many decades.

Beau James arrived at the courthouse. He alighted from his limousine, waved jauntily to the crowd, and blew kisses at the United Irish Club pickets. He was dressed in shades of blue—hat, shirt, suit—all a complement to the china blue of his eyes.

The eyes, though, reflected an anxiety that his jauntiness could not conceal.

He spotted Bess and came to her. "Bessie, there are three things a man must do alone. Be born, die, and testify. Wish me luck."

"I wish the Lord's mercy on you, Talker. I wish you to be true and honest. I wish you not to disgrace us all!"

Walker looked stricken. "You're hard on me, Bess," he said softly.

"I wish the best for all of us, Talker."

Walker, seeing a gathering of reporters moving toward them, forced a smile. He kissed Bess on the cheek, then winked at the crowd and hurried into the courthouse.

Over the next two days Bess watched the hearings. The miracle she had prayed for did not occur. Walker's political skills were intact, and in sparring verbally with Seabury he won several minor skirmishes by force of wit. But the strength of Seabury's ethical arguments, the power of the facts, demolished him. At the end of his testimony, as he headed for his limousine, women strewed his path with roses. Nevertheless, it was obvious to all that James J. Walker was through as a political force in the city of New York.

Bess returned to the Christopher Street apartment deeply shaken. Tammany, her life, her passion, had been dragged through the mud. What could she do now? What could she salvage? What would become of the United Irish Club?

Theresa tried to comfort her. "It was bound to happen. Beau James was a scoundrel from the first to the last."

"He fooled us. He fooled so many of us for so many years."

"It's tough for these men. The temptations are so great ..." And Bess realized Theresa was talking about her son, also.

They sat in the parlor. Theresa worked on her needlepoint. Bess still wore the clothes she had had on at the courthouse. She smoothed the linen flowers of her hat over and over as though to press out all the wrinkles in her life. Rose Ann sat silently in a corner of the room.

"You should be starting a family," Bess said. "It would be good for Tony, children."

"I don't believe he wants a family. Not just now." Theresa stared down at her needlepoint. Her face was flushed. "He doesn't touch me very often. But perhaps I'm not attractive to him."

"Does he mistreat you? Does he holler or threaten you?" Bess asked.

"No, he doesn't mistreat me."

Bess nodded, thankful for that. "These men, Terry, are nothing but overgrown children." She sighed. Suddenly she said, "Where's Rose Ann?" Unnoticed, Rose Ann had slipped from the room.

"Rosie!" Theresa called. "Rosie!"

The two women searched the second-floor apartment but couldn't find her. They ran downstairs. The front door was open.

Rose Ann McGrath—beautiful, mad Rose Ann. Barefoot, wearing only a thin cotton dress, humming and laughing, she wandered down Christopher Street. She turned down West Street and continued south past the New York Central railroad terminal, through the dock area bordering the Hudson.

She strolled past cheap lunchrooms and waterfront saloons, pawn shops, secondhand haberdasheries, junk stores. It had been a while since she'd been in the area, and the sudden rush of people—sailors and dockworkers, derelicts, street-corner pitchmen—was dizzying and exciting. Her body tingled with the thrill of so many people. She moved through the teeming crowds, skipped and laughed, her feet light as motes of dust.

The sun died with a last explosion of blood red over the river. Its final flare caused her to gasp and clap her hands. The day grew cool. Great shadows of warehouses and slabs of highway above created pools of black in the confusing angles of the dock area. I am the daughter of God, Rose Ann McGrath sang to herself.

She was aware of a man following her—a Portuguese or Spaniard with long slick black hair, a mottled face, a dagger-thin mustache. He was a sailor. Lithe as a ballet dancer, he wore tight white bell-bottoms and a black jacket and black cap.

Rose Ann looked back at him and laughed and sang her song: I am the daughter of God!

He came up behind her and pressed himself close to her, and she danced away and he rushed after her, down an alleyway, moving in a serpent's path through concrete and steel, the stanchions of the fractured highway above.

She began to run, laughing. He continued close behind. She slipped into a black opening in a dark warehouse. She moved between high bales of burlap and found a square of open floor beneath a bare bulb which burned on high.

She stood in a circle of light and lifted her dress. She wore nothing underneath. "I am the daughter of God," she said aloud as the dark sailor moved toward her.

His eyes were opaque and empty, and for an instant she felt a pulse of fear within. Why was she here? Who was this man?

I am a sacrifice, she thought. He is here to help me atone with my blood. She breathed a sigh of acceptance and opened her arms to receive him.

The next day a warehouse worker found the mutilated body stuffed among the trash bins. The detectives assigned to the case, Irish lads from the neighborhood recognized the woman. It was a terrible thing for them, notifying the family. They knew the home, the people.

"Bess, something has happened to your daughter," one of the detectives told her. "Something tragic."

Bess McGrath stared. Her eyes grew wide. She knew.

"She's been murdered." The detective hated what he had to say next, to describe how she had been killed. There was no need for that, however. The screams of Bess McGrath drowned out whatever he might have said.

Tony McGrath took the death of his sister desperately hard. Though the fight was little more than a week away, he couldn't train. He couldn't sleep. He felt responsible for what had happened. He tried to deal with the events leading up to her death. It had started with her breakdown. No. No. Before that. It started with Mike Roth. He had her and then threw her over, and *then* she broke down. . . .

The words of Jackie Foster, spoken years before, came to him now: *The kike done it, Tony. The kike done it.* . . .

The wake and funeral were over. Bess was sedated and asleep in the back room. Theresa was with Tony in the parlor, her face streaked with tears. "It's all for the best, Tony. It's all for the best." Over and over she said it. "It's all for the best. Her suffering and madness are over. It's all for the best."

"Why did she have to suffer like that?" he asked. "She never harmed anyone. Why?"

"God has his reasons. It's all for the best."

He sat there thinking of Mike Roth. Theresa came to him and he held her, but he was thinking of Roth. He had been the one, the cause.

The next day he returned to his workouts. He was murderous in the sparring ring. Bill-O and Frank Matthews were pleased that he had come back to training, that he was hitting with such ferocity.

There was something troubling, however. He rarely spoke. And the murderous look in his eye never left him.

Five days before the fight, Moe Kotovsky visited Mike Roth in his training camp. Jackie Foster was with him. Kotovsky's expression was serious. Jackie was smiling.

Kotovsky asked if they could talk away from everyone. Foster, Kotovsky, and Mike walked to the woods nearby. They paused by a creek. "Tell him, Jack," Kotovsky said.

Jackie's voice was soft, reasonable. "They've set you up to lose, Mikey. Your brother. I tell you this because I love you. What they're doing to you is a terrible thing." He was not smiling now, but there was something laughing behind his eyes.

"I don't understand," Mike said, looking over at Kotovsky.

"I knew something was wrong, Mike. Too many people are betting against you—neighborhood people who would never do such a thing unless they knew something. They've set you up."

"Antoff is their man," Jack Foster said.

"Whose man?"

"I don't have to mention names. You know these people as well as I do. Harry is owned. Harry says he can deliver you."

"Why are you telling me this?"

"You're more than a brother to me, Mikey," Jackie said, the smile still behind his eyes.

Mike left Foster and Kotovsky in the woods and ran back to camp. In the office he found Antoff and his brother having a drink. "I just heard something. I heard you and Abe set me up to lose."

Harry looked startled and grew pale; his eyes darted anxiously about. He recovered and began to rant. He swore, threatened, pleaded. "How can you believe that, Mikey? I'm your brother! How could you believe that?" He paced the room, slamming things about. Antoff looked uncomfortable.

"Tell him, Abie. This whole thing is lies."

Antoff didn't answer, and Mike knew that what Kotovsky and Foster had said was true.

"I think you better pack up, Abe," he said.

"If that's the way you want it. The truth is, none of us does what we want to anymore. Ever. You hear me, Mike? I was the featherweight champion of the world, and they came to me and said, 'Abie, you had a good time, now you let someone else have a good time.' What did I do? I kissed their butts, championship and all, and that's the way it goes—free for nothing, nothing for free." He held his hand out to Mike. "I had nothing personal against you, Mikey. You're a good fighter, but you can't win this one."

Mike ignored his hand; Antoff left the office.

"You don't believe all that, do you, Mikey?" whined Harry. "He's punchy. I never realized it—"

"Get out of here."

"Lies! It's all lies!" Harry's eyes were fearful, his expression pathetic, a whipped, cornered dog.

Yes, Mike thought, he tried to sell me out. He brought in Antoff and they trained me so I would lose. "Go, Harry. Now."

"It's not me you're dealing with. It's other people. They have you, Mikey."

"Not me. You. Now, go back to them."

"What can I tell them?"

"That's your problem, isn't it. Harry?"

After he had gone, Mike sat thinking for a long time. For more than a month he had dedicated himself to a training strategy that would assure his defeat. What could he do now?

He had five days to try to remedy the damage. He would work with Kotovsky. Five days. It would be an impossible task, but he could only try. What else could he do?

In the eyes you could see the murder. Outwardly calm, Tony McGrath's eyes betrayed the rage within him. They were very bright and he looked at people with a startling directness; in the center of the eyes were pinpoints of hate, murder.

He thought of his sister constantly. The blood pounded behind his eyes. The world about him pulsated with blood. He would kill Mike Roth in the ring. *The kike done it, Tony. The kike done it.* It would not be a fight. It would be a killing revenge.

The flow of traffic approaching Yankee Stadium had come to a standstill, was backed up for miles. Seventh Avenue and Broadway leading north, the 155th Street viaduct in Harlem, were jammed with limousines, Tin Lizzies, taxis, flatbed trucks, buses. The air was heavy with exhaust from the vehicles. Horns blared without stop. People pushed forward toward the stadium gates. Scuffles broke out. Beleaguered gatemen fought back the crowd.

Those who could not buy their way into the arena searched for other ways to get in. They scaled a section of fence to the north. Near the bleachers on the east a group of entrepreneurs set up a ladder; they charged a buck a head for anyone who wanted to climb in.

At the beginning of the week, betting had been heavy for McGrath. At fight time, with rumors abounding, the odds dropped and now stood at even money.

The night was hot and humid. A storm threatened and the sky was heavy with dark clouds, the damp air charged with electricity. Thunder rumbled in the distance.

The crowd was strangely quiet. They had heard stories. They knew of the death of McGrath's sister. They sat through the preliminary fights with a sense of hushed expectancy. As Tony McGrath moved down the aisle there were no cheers, no hysteria like the first fight. People watched and waited.

McGrath entered the ring. He didn't move about. He stood in his corner, staring straight ahead. His blue eyes were cold and serious.

Roth entered a moment later, tense. He didn't look at McGrath. McGrath stared at him throughout the referee's instructions. Roth gazed at the floor.

There was death in McGrath's eyes—bright, cold death.

At the bell he came out quickly, moving straight ahead. He punched out, pressing forward at Roth. He didn't waste a motion. His punches were crisp, efficient. He was a man with a job to do, and he went at it with dispatch.

It was a job of killing.

The hate within him was immense. He thought: Kill him. Kill him. You must kill him.

Roth jabbed and moved away, trying to get loose. His neck and shoulders were stiff with tension. He felt out of rhythm, awkward.

McGrath shuffled after him, cut down the ring, pounded him. The punches came in with terrible fury. He landed a straight right, followed it with a hook, and Roth's knees sagged and he attempted to clinch. McGrath kept at him with slashing combinations, hit away without letup.

Kill him, McGrath said to himself as he whipped in punch after punch.

At the end of the first round Roth stumbled back to his corner, his face swollen and bleeding.

The crowd was quiet, uneasy. There was nothing of sport in this fight. They were witnessing a savage presence in the ring, and they were hushed before it.

Kill him, kill him, a voice sang in McGrath's head.

In the second round, then again in the third, he mauled Roth on the ropes. Roth attempted to elude him, but McGrath kept him there, punishing him with punches of cold fury.

His eyes were ice, his heart was ice. Nothing touched the ice within him. Kill him, the voice sang within him. Neither the crowd nor the referee, nor the ring lights or Roth's battered helplessness, swayed him from his murderous purpose. Kill him.

Roth struggled to fight back, to get away. McGrath kept him on the ropes, bored in, slashed at him.

The punishment went on round after round. The crowd remained silent, sickened. McGrath went about his job with the brisk efficiency of a professional killer.

The swelling about Roth's nose, his mouth, his eyes, was ugly and terrible. There were gashes on his cheekbones; blood streamed from the folds around his eyes.

"Mikey, I want to stop it," Kotovsky said between rounds. "Mikey!"

Roth couldn't speak. He was aware of everything, of McGrath's fury, his own pathetic condition. He could do nothing. The cold rage of the man in the ring with him was stunning.

"Let me stop it," Kotovsky pleaded.

Roth shook him off and went back into the fight.

Through the seventh round, the eighth, into the ninth, McGrath continued the business of slaughter. In the stadium the crowd, repulsed by the ugliness of the beating, began to call for the referee to stop the fight.

The referee pulled Roth to a neutral corner, where the ring doctor examined him. His eyes were swollen almost shut. Blood came from his nose, and his lips were caked with it. And yet he knew where he was. He wanted to go on. The referee permitted the fight to continue.

McGrath moved back in on him, slicing at him. Kill him, the voice cried in his head. His sister was dead, raped, mutilated. *The kike done it, the kike done it.* . . .

He had Roth against the ropes once more. He leaned in, ripping punches to the body, to the head. The referee pulled him back, but he came on again and mauled Roth into the ropes.

Roth hung on. McGrath, his head close to Roth's, heard his own voice, and it was strange to him: "I'm going to kill you, dirty kike!"

Roth leaned against him, fighting to get his breath. His blood spattered McGrath's chest. "I'm going to kill you," McGrath said.

Roth was helpless. He couldn't escape. He couldn't see. He couldn't breathe. He could hear, though, and it was McGrath's voice coming at him over and over. "I'm going to kill you, kike, I'm going to kill you. . . ."

And now Mike was seized with a terrible shame. McGrath had stripped him of everything. And more: he was trying to kill him because he was a Jew.

The round had ended, but Mike wasn't aware of it. Kotovsky was trying to stop the fight, but he was not aware of that either. He was aware only of his need to survive.

He's trying to kill me, Mike thought, his brain embracing that awful fact. He's trying to kill me because I am a Jew.

He will not kill me. He will not kill my people.

At the bell, he shook Kotovsky off and rushed forward. He lurched forward to the center of the ring, punching out. He was hit, but he didn't feel the blows. He could see nothing for the blood in his eyes. Blood washed the ring, the stadium, and he punched and punched and punched.

He knew only that stubborn need: to keep on punching, to never stop, to never back off. His soul's survival hung in the balance. I will not die, he told himself. My people will not die.

Now he was aware of a low sound that swelled and in a dim memory of all his fights he realized it was the voice of the crowd. The crowd which had been so quiet all night was now screaming. He continued to punch.

And then he realized he was swinging at air. There was nothing there for him to hit. Someone was pushing him back, the referee.

He struggled to see, but the blood in his eyes distorted everything. The world was a red haze. He could not breathe.

He tripped over something. Someone pushed him back. He reached out and grabbed at a shadow, dark, red, wavy. It was a strand of rope, and he hung on to it. He was aware of a reddish form on the canvas, and the crowd's screams whirled about him.

And then people were pulling at him. Someone thrust a microphone at his mouth. Kotovsky's face was close to his, but he could only see him indistinctly through a red haze. "I'm blind," he heard himself say. "I'm blind."

He realized, then, that he had beaten Tony McGrath again. And he was blind.

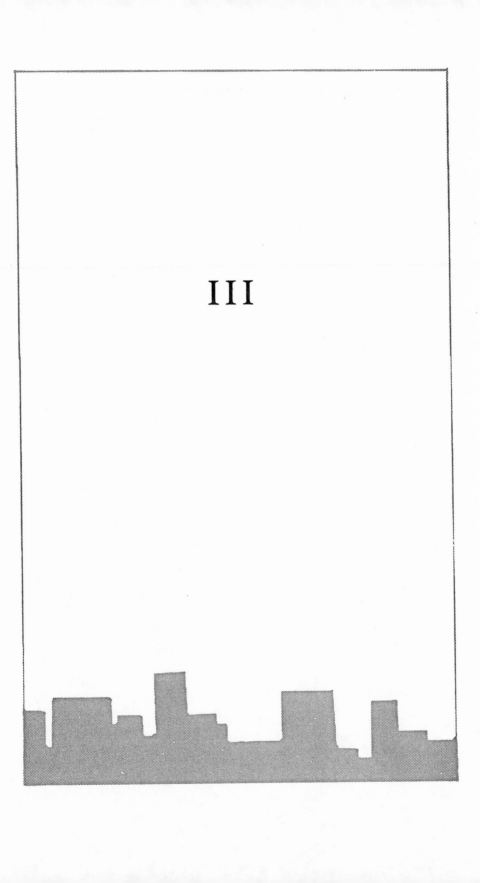

III

23

Mike heard someone enter the room. "The problem is rebleeding," a voice said, the doctor. "You must remain very still. If the bleeding starts again, the retina could be permanently damaged."

He lay in a bed in St. Vincent's Hospital, his eyes bandaged. He had torn the irises. Blood had leaked into the pupils. It would be a week before he would know whether or not he would ever see again.

With the closing down of light, a peculiar peace seemed to overtake him, a banking down of his emotions. Nothing mattered all that much. In losing his sight he had gained a measure of acceptance. It seemed like a miracle to him: we are born with the capacity to accept everything.

After the doctor left, he lay there immobile. He saw nothing in his mind's eye: the cutting off of his vision had somehow severed the pictures in his head. He dozed, wakened, slept again. Waking and sleeping were not all that different. In the deep of the night he awoke, aware of someone in the room. There was an odor of stale cigar. He realized a man was standing by the bed. "Who is it?"

"You don't know me. Your brother sent me." The voice was quiet, intelligent, with a light New York accent.

Something cold was pressed against Mike's cheek—the barrel of a revolver. The man moved it slowly across his face. "Come with me."

"I'm not supposed to move."

The gun was pressed very hard into his cheek. "Get up."

At the side of the bed was a button to summon the nurse; Mike slid his hand down, found the button, and pressed it.

"Well, Mr. Roth, I see you're awake." It was the voice of the night nurse. Mike could feel the revolver, in the man's jacket pocket now, pressed against his shoulder. "Dr. Weiss here has authorized you to be transferred. They'll be moving you to a new hospital. Let me help you into your robe."

"Yes," the man said. "It's perfectly all right for you to be moved."

They walked out into the hallway. There was another man there. He didn't talk, but took Mike firmly by the arm and led him to the elevator.

Mike could feel the blood pounding behind his eyes. He wondered if it were leaking into his pupils. What will happen now? I can't fight. I can't run. I'll be blind.

The night outside was warm, but the breeze chilled Mike. He entered a car waiting at the curb. Who were these men? Where were they taking him?

They drove for a long time. Neither of the men spoke, nor did the driver. After more than an hour the car came to a stop. One of the men led him from the car. A door opened and he was inside. He was taken along a hallway. He could hear the men on either side of him breathing heavily.

Now he felt hands on him. He was pushed into a chair. Someone yanked at his bandages. He tried to grab at the hands on the bandages, but someone else held his arms. The bandages were torn from his eyes. There was a bright light focused directly at him, and the sudden glare was like a knife in his eyes. He could see nothing but the brightness; then the lamp positioned on his eyes was moved and he realized he could see.

He was in a bare room save for a chair opposite him. Seated in the chair was his brother Harry. Handcuffed to the arms of the chair, he was almost unrecognizable. He had been beaten about the head; his face was a swollen mass. His eyes were closed, and Mike thought he was unconscious, but then he saw his brother's lips working slowly, painfully. He spoke, and his voice was a whisper, almost inaudible. "I'm sorry, Mikey."

A man was in his view now. He was young, handsome in a pretty way. It must have been the man who came to him at first. He looked as though he could be a doctor. The two other men looked like young Jewish businessmen.

"Harry's a cutie-pie," one of the men said. "Full of fun and games." He had a thick Brooklyn accent. "He's partners with some people. He takes all the money from the deal, throws it up in the air. What stuck to the ceiling, he gave back to them."

"A half-million dollars," the pretty-looking man said.

A half-million! Mike Roth thought. What could he have done with it? "Who does he owe? Lansky? Ben Siegel?"

"What does it matter? People are people, the way I look at it," the man with the Brooklyn accent said.

"What did you do with the money, Harry?" Mike asked.

"He spent it on cheesecake and sundaes," said the man with the Brooklyn accent. He didn't laugh.

"He took from Peter to pay Paul," the pretty-looking man said. "He led these people to believe that you would lose a fight. He had no confidence in you. On his word, these people not only didn't collect a debt, but invested funds. Good money after bad. You won. Now they're getting *gridgins* in the gut from aggravation."

"Let them kill me, Mike," Harry said. His head sagged forward like a piece of battered meat.

"No one's talking about killing. That's a depressing subject," said the young man.

"What do you want from me?" Mike asked.

"Pay off the man's debts," said the man with the Brooklyn accent. "You helped get him into this. People tried to explain the situation but you wouldn't listen."

Mike's head ached terribly. The pain in his eyes was excruciating. "I'll pay off his debts," he said.

"That's all we wanted to hear." The young man smiled warmly. "You see, Harry, your brother's a champion. A champion knows how to do the right thing."

He replaced the bandages. The darkness came down over Mike Roth's eyes like cool water.

He was taken from the room and down the hallway. Then he was out in the night air again, being helped into a car. The car rushed through streets he could'nt see. At last it came to a halt. He was taken from the car, and he could hear it pull off. He called out. No one answered. Someone approached him. "I have to get to St. Vincent's hospital."

"You got a ways to go to St. Vincent's," a man's voice said. "You're standing in front of the county morgue."

Mike Roth was wheeled down a hallway in the hospital to an examination room. The doctor was a brusque, efficient man. He turned down the lights in the room, removed the bandages, and peered into Mike's pupils with a lighted instrument. The pain was intense, though bearable.

Mike tried to gain some hint of the doctor's feelings by his behavior, but his imperturbability revealed nothing. Will I see again? Suddenly, for the first time since his injury, he cared deeply.

The doctor completed his examination. He lit a cigarette and made some notes on a file sheet. "I understand the bandages were removed." His expression was grave.

"Yes."

"Well." He didn't speak for a moment. "You're lucky. There's been no rebleeding. You'll come out of this fine. You can even go back into the ring." He walked with Mike to the door. "Will you fight McGrath again?"

"No."

"For all that money?"

"I won't fight again."

A week after he left the hospital, he was visited by Jackie Foster at the apartment on Henry Street.

Foster appeared heavier than when Mike had last seen him: he glowed with health and cheer. "I feel bad about this situation. I tried to advise Harry not to get in over his head. It's a beautiful thing you're doing for your brother."

Foster chattered on. Mike wanted to grab him by the throat and choke the breath out of him. He kept referring to Mike as "Champ," went on about how the two of them were like brothers, closer than brothers. It was a shame that so much money had to be sacrificed because of Harry's irresponsibility, but then, as heavyweight champion of the world, Mike was a money machine; it would all come flowing back.

He made several phone calls. Harry got on the line. "I'm nothing," he sobbed. "I'm just a heap of shit, I'm nothing."

When Foster left the apartment, all the details of Harry's release had been completed.

Mike was stripped of all the money he had in the world.

24

Tony McGrath had never been drunk in his life. He had resented his father's drinking. He had always held himself in control. This night, though, he was off on a monumental bender.

It started at his father-in-law's house—a family dinner with Theresa, his mother, his in-laws, his brothers.

Everything seemed out of joint to him.

That summer Al Smith was beaten by Roosevelt for the presidential nomination. Then Jimmy Walker resigned as mayor of New York. Tammany was sunk in disgrace.

Bill-O had gone his own way, avoiding his old cronies. Acting Mayor, Joseph V. McKee appointed him a magistrate in Brooklyn. He severed his ties to boxing completely.

And Tony McGrath had been beaten again by Mike Roth, who wouldn't give him another fight.

During dinner Bess railed at the Hall, at Beau James, at Roosevelt. McMahon argued with her. Tony drank. He thought of Mike Roth and he drank.

Roth would not fight him again.

After dinner, Frank Matthews arrived. He tried to cheer Tony up. "Roth'll have to give you a fight. He's broke. He'll have to fight you."

Tony had heard the same song for months now, but no fight had been set. He was a wealthy man. He could continue on as though he were champion, and if Roth chose never to fight again, he would be the champion, but that was not enough.

He had to fight Mike Roth again. He had to beat him. And he had to do it cleanly and with style.

At the dinner table talk raged—the fight scene, politics, Roosevelt, Al Smith, Mike Roth, all of it spilling together, everyone arguing, laughing, shouting while Tony brooded.

He realized his resentment toward Roth went beyond his having beaten him twice, Roth's relationship to Rose Ann, the fact that he wouldn't fight

him again. He hated Mike Roth because he was so damn good, so tough.
He hated him because from the first time they had fought Tony knew that
this was a man capable of beating him.

That's what was tearing him apart. He hated Mike Roth because he
sensed he was a better fighter.

He had to fight him again. He had to defeat Mike Roth.

Theresa came to him and tugged at him. "Come on, Tony, let's go
home."

"I don't want to go home!"

"Why are you drinking like this? You never do this."

"Everybody can drink, but not me? Is that it?"

"You're a disgrace, Tony!" Bess shouted from the opposite end of the
table.

"What kind of disgrace?"

"Drunk in front of your wife like this!"

Everyone laughed. Theresa looked as though she would cry. "You took it
for how many years?" Tony asked Bess. "How many? Paddy was drunk
every night."

"Please, Tony, let's go home," Theresa pleaded.

His brother Willy laughed shrilly and tousled Tony's hair. "You go
home, Terry. We'll take care of him."

Bess and Theresa left and the men sat around drinking.

"I want him!" Tony hollered.

"Sure you do," Matthews said. "And you're going to get him. We just
have to talk to the right people."

"Who are the right people?" demanded Tony.

"The sheenie goons own him. Everyone knows that. We just have to get
to the goons," McMahon said.

"Let's get to them, then!"

"Jackie Foster," said McMahon.

"Let's talk to him, the little bastard," Tony yelled. "Hey, look at my
brothers, what big strapping guys they've become."

"Yes, they have," Matthews said.

"I can whip the three of them at one time."

"You're drunk, Tony." Emmett laughed.

Tony staggered to his feet and grabbed Emmett around the shoulders and
pulled him to him. "I love my brothers!" He fell off balance and crashed
against the table.

"Oh, my God, my God," his mother-in-law yelled, hurrying into the dining area. "Louts, wrecking my house. Out of here, all of you!"

They went downstairs to McMahon's speakeasy and drank for a while.
Then Tony abandoned Matthews and McMahon and he and his three brothers went reeling and singing down the street. They visited two more speaks
on Hudson Street, got into a wrestling match in the second place, and were
asked to leave.

"Let's go home," Emmett said to Tony.

"No."

"We're going home," said James.

"Good-bye." Tony blew kisses after his brothers as they moved away up Hudson Street. He wandered through the Village and found himself in a ratty speakeasy with sawdust on the floor and booze that tasted like rubbing alcohol. He railed at a group of bums: "Where's your guts? Where's your goddamn guts? Come on, fight me! Fight me!"

The bartender, a large, smiling man, said to him, "Take it easy, Champ. They're out of your league."

"What did you call me? Champ? I'm no champ. No more. I'm nothing now, just like everybody."

A girl in a loose-fitting red dress was at his side now. She was very young and very thin. Her skin was red and scaly. "Let's go home, babe."

"Who are you?"

She laughed. "You tell me."

"Let me think about it." He put his arm around her and the two of them moved out of the speak.

She took him to a tenement flat around the corner. There was a battered couch in the living room. Tony stretched out on it, with the room spinning slowly around him.

The young girl took off her dress. Tony closed his eyes. He saw Laura Maddox in his mind's eye. She leaned down to kiss him.

He awoke the next day confused. Where was he? What time was it? The shades in the flat were pulled down over the windows and curtains closed over them. He looked down the hallway. In a back bedroom he could dimly make out someone asleep. He was horribly hung-over and couldn't remember anything that happened after leaving McMahon's house.

He hurried from the flat. Outside it was midafternoon. The day was bright, Indian summer: the glare off the sidewalks caused his eyes to ache. He squinted against the brightness.

From a candy store on the corner of St. Mark's Place he called home. Theresa told him Frank Matthews had been trying to reach him. He called Matthews. "Where are you?" Frank asked.

"St. Mark's Place and the Bowery. Candy store on the corner."

"I'll pick you up in half an hour."

Matthews arrived with McMahon in a Hudson roadster. "You smell like a damn garbage truck," Matthews said, drawing away from him.

They traveled over the Williamsburg Bridge, out Flatbush Avenue to Ocean Parkway. "Where are we going?" Tony asked.

"To meet some people," said Matthews.

"What sort of people?"

"Mockie gangsters," answered McMahon.

They arrived at Emmons Avenue in Sheepshead Bay and entered Lundy's Seafood Restaurant. They were taken to a private dining room overlooking the bay. Small fishing boats bobbed on the water below them.

Jack Foster was seated there with Ben Siegel and Abe Reles. They shook hands all around.

Matthews and McMahon ordered lunch. Tony had coffee. Siegel stared at him with bleak eyes. "Tony's very upset," Matthews said. "He doesn't want nothing to do with boxing no more."

"It's a rotten game," Siegel said.

"He only wants Mike Roth."

"Another fight between Roth and Tony would break every record there was," said Foster.

"I don't like to have nothing to do with boxing," Siegel said. "It's double crosses and headaches. I've had dealings with the Roth family—the brother Harry particularly. A fine upstanding man. So there is a relationship there. And if we can work out the numbers, I'm sure I can have an influence on events."

"What numbers?" Tony asked. His head ached. The odor of fish in the restaurant had made him feel sick to his stomach.

"What part of your cut you give to me," Siegel replied.

"There's a mistake. We're not here to make that kind of deal."

Siegel's jaw muscle worked in a rapid tic. "What kind of deal are you looking for?"

"Are you doing business for Mike Roth or trying to cut in on my end?"

"I don't like your attitude, punk!" Siegel suddenly flared. He leaned across the table. His face was flushed; a vein on his forehead pulsated angrily. "I'm trying to do you a favor! And you come to me looking like a scumbag! I put on a fresh suit for this occasion, had my shoes shined. That's because I have respect for a former heavyweight champion of the world. But that doesn't give you the right to come here all fucked up and make derogatory remarks!"

"There's been a misunderstanding," said Matthews placatingly.

"Don't apologize," Tony said. "You're nothing, Ben, you and these two weasels. I came here because I was told you owned Mike Roth. If you don't, we have nothing to say to each other."

"You're condescending and fucking rude!" screamed Siegel. "And why? What did I do to deserve this kind of treatment? You were a heavyweight champion, is that why? You think you're so tough?"

He was standing now, yelling at the top of his voice.

Tony got up and started to walk away. Siegel rushed after him. Reles hurried between him and Tony. Siegel grabbed Reles by his coat and flung him to one side.

"I come to this restaurant three times a week. I always enjoy myself. Now I got gas pains in my stomach!"

Tony waited at the archway for Matthews and McMahon. They still sat at the table, pale and shaken.

Siegel walked to the window, stared out. He turned back into the room.

"I'm not paying the check. Not when I get heartburn like this."

"That's all right, Ben," Foster said. "I'll pay the check."

"No. They pay the fucking check!"

Foster winked at Matthews. "Okay, Ben, they pay the check."

Siegel paced to the far end of the room. He took several deep breaths. He adjusted his tie. When he came back to the table, he was smiling. The transformation was astonishing. "I apologize for anything I spoke out of line. I had some steamers just before you arrived and they always upset my system. We'll do some business some other time."

Tony moved back to the table and picked up the check. Siegel snatched it from his hand. "When you have lunch with Ben Siegel, Ben Siegel pays. You have all my respect, Champ. I'm sorry if I got a little heated." He put out his hand to shake.

Tony ignored it. He, Matthews, and McMahon left.

Siegel grabbed Reles around the neck and hugged him. He kissed him on the top of the forehead. "Why do I put up with this guy?" he said of Reles. He smells like a fucking toilet."

And the three of them laughed.

25

The sportswriters of New York City congregated at Billy LaHiff's tavern on West Forty-eighth Street. They were a gregarious crew and felt great affection for Tony McGrath. It disturbed them that Tony was so glum lately. The boxing scene had been lively when he was champion. Now there wasn't much to write about, so they began to fill their columns with outcries for a Roth-McGrath fight. By the new year 1933, the campaign for the fight was gathering momentum. Mike felt the pressure. He tried to ignore it, but it followed him wherever he went: When would the Pride of the Ghetto give Tony McGrath his chance?

He rarely left the Lower East Side these days. He hung around the apartment on Henry Street, read, went for walks through the neighborhood. His brother had moved back in with his girlfriend in Brooklyn. He avoided Mike.

Mike was offered speaking engagements, commercial endorsements, business deals. He turned them all down. He wanted nothing to do with his championship. He was walking away from it completely. But what would he do now? What would become of his life? He worried about his financial situation, his future, the welfare of his parents. What would he do?

Occasionally he strolled over to the settlement house and watched the kids sparring; he got in the ring with them and gave them pointers. He noticed they treated him with a certain coolness. They asked when he was going to fight McGrath, and when he told them he'd never fight again, they looked at him with disdain, as though he were a coward.

Jason Karl stopped by from time to time and they put on the gloves together and worked up a sweat. Mike's heart was not in it.

One evening Jason asked him to take a walk. Rutgers Square was quiet. The people no longer congregated there discussing, arguing, shouting at each other. Every man was alone these days. It was the Depression. Life, always a struggle on the Lower East Side, was now mired in hopelessness.

"Some people want me to run for mayor," Jason said. "Reformers. The Fusion movement. I'd like to give it a try, but I don't think I can."

"Why not?"

"I'm Jewish."

"What does that have to do with it?"

"Over in Germany that madman Hitler is screaming about the Jews, how they control the world. New York has a Jewish governor, Lehman. I don't want to give ammunition to the anti-Semites."

"That's foolish, Jay. No one thinks like that. If the Fusion people want you, you have to accept. You always said you wanted to do things for this area. As mayor you'd have the chance."

"I have to think it through."

There would be a benefit dance at the Commodore Hotel that weekend, he explained, a yearly affair sponsored by Mrs. William Randolph Hearst for a free-milk fund for underprivileged children. Laura was on the committee.

"I'd like you with me."

"Why?"

"The Fusion people will be there pressuring me for a decision. I want to do the proper thing." He had difficulty explaining how he felt. He groped for the words. "You remind me of the dreams I once had," he said at last.

"I can't face all those people. Not now, with this McGrath thing."

They walked to the far side of the square.

"I think I could accomplish a great deal as mayor, and yet . . ." He hesitated, weighing his words. "A certain fire has gone out of me. That's why I keep coming down here. I'm trying to rekindle that fire."

"I'll come with you," Mike said after a while. "If you need me, I'll come." He knew what Jason meant when he spoke of fires going out.

At the milk-fund benefit Mike sat at a table with Jason and Laura and a group of men from the Fusion party. They were men of power, judges, prominent business leaders. Jason huddled with them as they tried to plot the future of their movement.

Throughout the evening Mike was badgered by a steady stream of people stopping at the table, reporters, sports figures, politicians. They kept at him. The question was the same: When would he fight Tony McGrath?

He sloughed it off, joked about it, but inside he was wire-tense. Laura sat at his side and tried to make things easier for him, but he couldn't get comfortable with himself.

Wayne King and his orchestra played. Men and women in formal dress danced, gliding easily across the ballroom floor, controlled, elegant, the power brokers of the city.

At the far end of the ballroom Tony McGrath and his wife entered. With them were John McMahon and Bill O'Dwyer and their wives.

It was the first time Mike had seen McGrath since the fight. He felt his body grow tense. He squeezed his hands into tight fists. He tried to blind me, to kill me, Mike thought.

"What's the matter?" Laura asked.

He didn't answer.

A while later O'Dwyer approached the table. He leaned close to Mike. "Some reporters are going to try to stir up a confrontation between you and McGrath. Don't pay it no mind, lad."

Behind him, moving fast, was a small, dapper man, lithe as a tap dancer. "How does it feel to be a judge now, Bill-O?" He had a harsh, nasal voice.

"I try to do my job," Bill-O answered.

The little man edged close to Mike. "Can I talk with you for a moment, Champ?"

"This is Walt Winchell, Mike." Bill-O signaled with his eyes for Mike to be careful.

Mike knew the name: Winchell, a former vaudeville hoofer, was a rising gossipmonger with a nasty reputation for vindictiveness in his column.

"Don't you think Tony McGrath deserves a shot at the title?" Winchell asked.

"It's not my title anymore. I'm giving it up."

"Are you afraid, Champ?"

"That doesn't have anything to do with it."

"Let me see if I can get McGrath over here. The two of you should straighten this out face to face." He hurried away from the table. Bill-O moved away after him.

"Disagreeable little runt," said Laura.

"Don't tangle with him," a woman at the table said. "He'll cut you up into very small pieces."

Winchell was back shortly, trailing reporters and photographers. With him were Tony and Theresa, McMahon and Bill-O.

The reporters, led by Winchell, bombarded Mike and Tony with questions while the photographers tried to get them to shake hands. People shouted, shoved, struggled to get close to the table.

Mike didn't look at McGrath. He kept his gaze focused on the dance floor. Jason rose and tried to clear people back from the table. Winchell started on Jason, prodding him about his political aspirations. Tony held up his hand to quiet everybody. "Now's your chance, Tony," Winchell said. "You can have your say here and now."

"I'm at this table for a very important reason. There's things that go way back that I have to settle."

Tony smiled and leaned past Mike. "Mrs. Karl owes me a dance," he said, taking Laura by the hand and leading her onto the dance floor.

Walter Winchell seated himself next to Mike. "Why won't you fight him again? He deserves a chance to win back the championship."

"I told you, I'm retired."

"You have a lousy attitude. You don't want me for an enemy, Champ."

"Why don't you take a walk? You've been eating onions. Your breath is making me sick."

Winchell stood. His face was flushed. "I hope you have a lot of money in the bank to talk to Walter Winchell like that." He moved around the table looking for Jason Karl, but he was on the dance floor with Tony's wife.

Wayne King and his orchestra were playing "Bedelia." "Remember this?" Laura said to Tony.

"The night up on the roof garden of the Ritz-Carlton."

"Yes." She pressed close to him. "Why did you ask me to dance with you?" He shrugged. "Why, Tony?"

"I wanted to see if I still felt anything for you."

"And?"

"I do."

"I miss you," she said softly. "I'm happy with Jason, but I miss you. And how about you? Are you happy?"

"No."

"Is it your wife?"

"Our relationship is as good as it'll ever be. It's not her. It's that man over there, Roth. I won't be happy until I fight him again and beat him."

Tony returned Laura to the table. Without looking at Mike, he took Theresa by the arm and led her to the opposite side of the ballroom.

Jason, in conference again with the men from the Fusion Party, excused himself to join Mike and Laura. "They're pressing me for a decision. If I don't accept, they'll turn to La Guardia. I don't know what to do. I honestly don't know what to do."

A meeting was arranged upstairs in the hotel to resolve things. Jason asked Mike to see Laura to their car, then departed with the Fusion group. People drifted away, and Mike was alone with Laura at the table. The ballroom began to empty, and as Tony McGrath's crowd moved to the door, Laura watched. Tony didn't look back. "You're so much alike," she said, "you and Tony."

"We're not alike at all."

The orchestra began to pack up their instruments. Busboys cleared the tables.

"I'll drive you home," said Laura.

In front of the hotel they picked up her Lincoln Zephyr convertible and drove south on Lexington Avenue. As they neared the Lower East Side, Laura said, "I'm not tired yet. Do you mind if we just drive around for a while?"

They drove through lower Manhattan, circled the Battery area, and drove along South Street, past Coenties Slip and Gouverneur Lane. They came to the Fulton Street area. "I used to work here as a kid," Mike said.

The streets were littered with battered wooden crates. The air smelled of fish and the sea. The Brooklyn Bridge arched in the night ahead of them. Laura pulled the car onto a pier overlooking the East River.

They didn't speak for a long while. Mike stared out at the water, the bridge, the lights of Brooklyn across the river. He thought of Rose Ann McGrath, of their evenings together strolling on the bridge.

He was aware of Laura staring at him. "I love Jason very much," she said. "He is the kindest man I know. But there is something missing between us. Physically there is something missing." She leaned close to him. He could sense the tension in her. She continued to stare at him with a pained expression; there was a childlike look in her eyes, a desperation, and he was moved by it.

She curled up on the seat next to him. He could feel her warm against him, her breath on his arm. He could smell the fragrance of her, violets.

"I've always been attracted to you," she said, "and you've been attracted to me, haven't you?"

"Yes," he said, uneasy at the admission.

He fought within himself not to touch her. He wanted her, yet it had nothing to do with her: it had to do with his youth, with Rose Ann.

Then he was kissing her. It was as though he were operating apart from himself. He was outside watching himself. She held him tight, churned against him, moaning, "Oh, yes, Tony. Yes, yes."

He drew back. She opened her eyes and laughed. "Oh my, that's funny. I don't know why I said that." She sat up, lit a cigarette. "I'm very sorry," she said.

"Neither of us was here with the other one," he answered. "There's nothing to feel sorry about."

The next day Jason called Mike for lunch. They met at the Zum Essex. "I turned the Fusion party down," he said. "They'll run La Guardia and he'll win."

"You could have won."

"I wanted it but I couldn't bring myself to take it. The fire just wasn't there." He remained silent for a long moment. "At any rate, I'll have influence with La Guardia. I'll be able to do a great deal for the Lower East Side. I want you to work with me on this, Mike."

"I'm leaving New York. I just have to get out of here. I spoke with Leach Cross out on the Coast. He might have something for me out there."

"Fighting?"

"No. He'd like to open a gym. I could operate it for him."

"You won't be happy with that. If you stay here, we can still realize some of those things we used to talk about."

"I can't stay here, Jay. I just can't."

"Why not?"

Mike couldn't explain it. It had something to do with the fight game, with the reporters, with Tony McGrath. But more: it had to do with Jason and what he felt about Laura.

He couldn't trust himself to be near her.

26

There was something unnerving about Los Angeles to Mike Roth. It was the quality of the sunlight—it was too bright. It made everything look too clean. There were few overt signs of the Depression here. Everyone smiled; no one seemed in a hurry. It was like a city cut out of cardboard, a child's game, one huge, sprawling Atlantic City. No one battled in this town; no one seemed to work. He was uncomfortable in it.

The pressure of fighting McGrath again was behind him now, an East Coast aberration, and that was a blessing. Yet a question nagged at him: What do I do with my life? He was retired heavyweight champion of the world and he didn't feel like a champion at all. He felt like a failure in his life. He was twenty-seven years old. He had no wife, no children, no income, no savings. What was his future?

After the train trip cross-country he checked into the Miramar Hotel in Santa Monica. Leach Cross lived nearby. Mike had exaggerated in telling Jason that Leach wanted to open a gymnasium with him as manager. They had discussed the *possibility* in general terms. Still it was the excuse he needed to get away from New York City.

Leach called for him at his hotel and took him around the town. They visited gyms in Hollywood and downtown Los Angeles.

As ex-heavyweight champion of the world he had a certain status. People gathered around them wherever they went. Leach seemed to enjoy it.

Mike Roth's mood darkened. It became apparent that Leach had nothing for him beyond serving as a figurehead for someone else's operation.

He would be a glorified towel boy.

That evening on the drive back to the hotel Leach said, "What do you think, Mike?"

"None of this is for me."

"I didn't think it would be. I have another idea. Why don't you try to hook up with one of the movie studios? They like to have athletes around. You could take over the gym, maybe even get some acting work. Cowboy Rawlings? He's working over at Warner Brothers now."

"That's not for me, Leach. I can't be a patsy like that."

"You're right, Mikey. A lot of people come out here like they're going to conquer China and they end up being Chinamen. They use you, Mikey. They use everybody. The people who run this town have no shame."

They agreed to stay in touch, but when Mike returned to his hotel he knew he would see little of Leach Cross.

That evening he walked down to the ocean and watched the waves washing in against the shore. He stood there for a very long time, until the great disk of the sun sliced behind the horizon at the ocean's far edge, spraying the sky with streaks of orange and red.

Anger welled up inside him. What was he doing here? Why had his life become so unreal, insubstantial?

He began to run along the beach. He ran past the Santa Monica Pier. The La Monica Ballroom came into view, an immense Oriental structure of minarets, banners, festoons of electric light. I'm in kiddie-land, he thought. My life has brought me to the Coney Island of the West Coast.

He felt immensely lonely, empty. What would he do?

He returned to the Miramar. There was a message waiting for him: a Mr. Mannix had called.

Who was Mr. Mannix? He tried to think of the people he had met that day with Leach. He didn't remember a Mannix.

He dialed the number. "Mr. Mannix?"

"Yes." The voice was deep, ragged.

"This is Mike Roth."

"Hello, Mike. How are you?"

"Fine. Who is this?"

"Eddie Mannix. We've never met."

"How did you know I was in town?"

"Word gets around fast in this town. We'd like to see you."

"Who is we?"

"The studio—MGM. Mr. Louis B. Mayer. He wants to see you tomorrow."

The next morning a large Cadillac waited for Mike outside the Miramar. Seated in the back was a short, powerfully built man who looked like a prizefighter—Eddie Mannix.

Mike got into the car and they drove along palm-lined streets toward Culver City. "As soon as Mr. Mayer heard you were in town, he told me to check up on you," said Mannix.

"What does he want with me?"

"The man's a genius. Who can read his mind? He said, 'I've always liked the boy. Find out all you can.' So tell me, what's the real story?"

"I don't know what you mean."

"Between you and McGrath. It would make a helluva film. Mr. Mayer said maybe you could play yourself in it."

"If that's what he wants to see me about, forget it."

"Who knows what L.B. wants with you? You'll meet him, you'll talk, you'll see. What do you have to lose? You know, you're a good-looking boy. You could be an actor."

"I'm not interested."

"All right, Clark Gable. We'll get Clark Gable to play you. You'd like Clark Gable to be you, wouldn't you?"

"How'd you like Clark Gable to be *you?*"

"I'd like to be *him*, I'll tell you that much. Yessir." Mannix laughed loudly. Then, having second thoughts, he added, "For one night. He has a small pecker."

The studio, situated behind high, buff-colored walls, reminded Mike Roth of a prison. There was a guardhouse in front, tall towers, a sterile, forbidding look. They drove through the gate and the limousine deposited them in front of a shabby three-story office building. Mannix led the way into the building, to Louis B. Mayer's office, which was immense, painted completely white. Mayer was seated behind a large curved desk. He rose and came around the desk to greet Mike. He was short and stubby and moved with quick, aggressive steps. The first impression he gave was one of dumpiness, a cheerful clothing salesman. He had gray hair thinning in front, a broad face dominated by a sizable sharp nose.

They shook hands. His grip was powerful, a man deceptively strong. "Eddie's my heavyweight champion here," L. B. Mayer said, and Mannix grinned broadly. "Don't tangle with Eddie, he's tough. He used to knock heads, didn't you, Eddie?"

Mayer retreated behind his desk and signaled for Mike to be seated in a chair directly in front of the desk. Mannix sat to one side.

"It's good to see a *landsman* heavyweight champion of the world," Mayer said. "Did you ever think you'd live to see the time when a Jewboy beat an Irishman, Eddie?" Mannix laughed and shook his head. "One of these days you and me are going to tangle, Eddie."

"You're too tough for me, chief."

"Iggy Thalberg's more your speed, huh?"

"That's about it, chief."

"I'd like to see you whip that cheap kike's ass," Mayer said. "Don't take exception to my talk, Mike. There are Jewish men and there are kikes. Take my friend Iggy. He's like a son to me. I made him what he is, which is a pretty powerful person. But he has one serious defect. He loves money more than anything. Quite frankly, that's between you, me, and the wall. There are a lot of people who are more like animals. But I don't have to tell you that."

Mike Roth said nothing.

"So let me see," Mayer said. "I hear good things about you. We have some very good success with boxing pictures. I think we can find a story for you which would incorporate all the elements of an artistic experience as well as human values. And you're a handsome boy. I think we could develop something for you."

"I'm a prizefighter, not an actor."

"There are a lot of prizefighters who became actors. That's what brings the alleycats into the theaters. Acting is selling cock, and prizefighters sell it as well as anybody."

"I'm not interested."

"You haven't heard what I'm paying."

"You couldn't pay me enough to parade around like a trained seal."

Mayer's face reddened. "What are you, one of these artsy-fartsy types? You're too good for the movies? James Corbett, John L. Sullivan, that *shvartzer* Jack Johnson—they were great fighters. Afterward they became actors, and it wasn't beneath them ..." Mayer was shouting now, and pounding the table for emphasis. "Vic McLaglen, stop me if I'm wrong, Eddie. He fought Jack Johnson one time, didn't he?"

"You're right about that, chief."

"So just get off your high horse, young man!" Mike stood and started for the door. "Where are you going?"

"I didn't come to you, you came to me. I told you I don't want to be a clown for anybody. I might not have been a great champion, but I did as well as I could. I don't want to disgrace that. If you called me to talk about kikes and *shvartzers,* I've heard enough of that garbage in the streets. I don't like it."

"Just sit down and let me talk for a minute. Don't mind my mouth." Mayer was apologetic, off on another tack. "I got a lot on my mind, a lot of worries. I have a wife, God bless her, the salt of the earth. She's a very sick woman, bedridden. I have intrigues all around me. I have that weasel Thalberg, I got Nick Skunk in New York. I got a lot of pressures. Sit down."

Mike looked over at Mannix, who nodded as though everything was fine. Mike didn't sit down, but he didn't leave.

"Michael, I'm old enough to be your father. Now, you ask me, why have I brought you in here? Someone told me you were out here looking for employment—"

"I just arrived here two days ago."

"It's a very small town. I know a little about you. I know you're tough. I know you've come up the hard way. I admire and appreciate that. The road for me has not been a bed of carnations. We were a poor family, poor but proud. I don't have to tell you. My mother was a saint and the good Lord took her before she could see what I accomplished in this life." Mayer's voice was hushed and choked. "I hear men talk about their mothers, and they call them whores. I could never understand that, a man speaks of his mother in that way. I lose all respect for a man who calls his mother a whore. What do you think of your mother? How is she?"

"She's a fine woman."

"I knew you'd say that. I could tell that's the kind of son you are. Is she still alive, your mother?"

"Yes."

"Thank God for it, Michael. Get down on your knees every night and every morning and thank God for it." Tears formed in Mayer's eyes. " 'Dear God, I thank you for preserving my mother. She has given me much and I am unworthy of her.' That's the kind of prayer you got to say, Michael." Mayer turned to Mannix. "You hear that, Eddie? He's a prizefighter, he's fighting for the championship of the world. His mother is dying. Just before the fight, he falls down on his knees. This could be great. You could act this film, Michael, because it'll be your own story. Your mother is sick, dying maybe, who knows? And it's the night of the heavyweight championship. Maybe you wanted to be a rabbi. *She* wanted you to be a rabbi. It didn't work out. Now, on the night of the big fight, your mother is dying. You fall on your knees and begin to sing." Mayer began to wail the Hebrew chant, *Eli, Eli*. Mike, struggling not to laugh, looked over at Mannix. Mannix was weeping.

"L. B., that'll be one of the great ones," said Mannix in a voice choked with emotion. "Maybe greater than *The Champ*."

"Look, Mike," Mayer said, "even this dumb ox is crying. You see, we got possibilities here. You could have a career like Wallace Beery."

"You don't take no for an answer, do you, Mr. Mayer?"

"Why should I? What's the matter with you? Your mother's dying! She wanted you to be a rabbi, but you got to fight! Don't you have any heart for a story like that?"

"What do you want from me?"

"I want you here with me."

"Why?"

"You're the toughest man in the world—what other reason do I need?"

"If you have a legitimate job for me, tell me what it is and I'll consider it."

Mayer stared at him. He was not pleased. "You know your trouble? You think you got brains. That's a stupid way to think. All right. Get out of here."

He swung his chair around and faced away from Mike.

Mike left the office. Mannix caught up with him outside the building. "L.B. really likes you. You stood up to him. He respects that. He told me to take you to Iggy—"

"Iggy?"

"Irving Thalberg, head of production. L.B. wants a place for you here, Mike. Come on, I'll take you to Thalberg."

"Why does he want me here? What kind of place?"

"What do you care? He pays in good American dollars."

"What do I have to do for it?"

"Iggy will explain everything to you."

Since arriving in Los Angeles, Mike Roth had found himself unable to come to terms with the outlandishness of the town, the ridiculousness. Everything seemed oversized, forced, silly. Now he was being pursued by the leaders of a major motion-picture studio for a job which no one was either willing or able to characterize. Absurd!

It was an amusement park, a kiddie-land, and as he followed Eddie Mannix, the ox who wept, through the halls of MGM, he watched himself in amazement as he whizzed along on the ride.

Irving Thalberg's office was on the second floor of the executive building. Mannix entered without knocking, and Mike followed him. Thalberg, dark and thinly handsome, was on the phone. He nodded as Mannix entered, and completed his call.

"This is Mike Roth, Irving."

"I know." He had a distracted air about him.

Mike shook hands with him, and his hand was soft and damp. Mike noticed his fingers were trembling. Thalberg picked up a twenty-dollar gold piece from the desk and began to toss it aimlessly in the air, then click it on the desktop.

He stared at Mike, and there was something familiar in the gaze, a certain detachment, a coldness in the eyes. He reminded Mike of someone, and it came to him now: Ben Siegel. The same cold handsomeness, vaguely feminine, remote. "L. B. wants you with us very badly," said Thalberg.

"What for?"

"What does it matter?"

Mike smiled. "Everyone tells me that. I ask, 'What do you want me here for?' And no one has an answer."

"Eddie, do we have someone working on special projects?"

"Nate Katz."

"Does he have a contract?"

"No."

"Fire him."

Mannix shook his head. "He's Nick Schenck's man, Ig, from New York."

"Fire him. L.B. wants Roth. Roth is prestige, Katz is *tsouris.*" He looked at Mike. "This has nothing to do with you. This is just an excuse. What has to do with you is how you're going to be paid. Fifteen hundred a week."

"A man once said to me: free for nothing, nothing for free. What do I have to do for it?"

"All right, two thousand a week, but no questions. We'll find something for you, don't worry."

Mike left the office with Mannix. He had been hired by MGM at a salary of two thousand dollars a week. He had no idea what he must do to earn it. And more—no one seemed interested in telling him what he must do to earn it.

"What did you think of Iggy?" asked Mannix as they walked down the hallway from his office.

"His hands sweat."

"He seems nice, don't he? Don't let that fool you: he pisses ice water."

"What was the problem with this Katz fellow?"

"They sent him out here from the East to spy on L.B., a snake."

The next day a limousine was waiting for Mike outside his hotel. He was taken to the studio and directed to his new office, which was on the third floor of the main building. His name was already on the door: Michael Roth, Special Projects.

He entered the office and sat behind the desk. Special projects? What was that supposed to be? He sat behind the desk for a long time trying to figure out what he should do. He picked up a pad and began to sketch. He drew an amusement park.

There was a knock on the door and a pretty young lady entered. "My name is Ellen. I'm your secretary." She sat in a chair next to Mike's desk.

"I don't have anything for you to do."

"That's all right. Mr. Katz never had anything for me, either. I could give you a blow-job," Ellen said matter-of-factly.

"Maybe some other time."

"Mr. Katz loved my blow-jobs. I'm very good at it."

"I'm sure you are."

The phone rang and Ellen answered it. "Mr. Katz's ... I mean, Mr. Roth's office." She listened for a moment, then put down the phone. "Mr. Mayer would like to see you."

Mike went downstairs to Mayer's office. Mayer was in a fury. He paced his office. "That son of a bitch Thalberg. He's trying to bury me! Who gave him the right to fire Katz?"

"Don't ask me. I'm just in the middle."

"With Iggy, you're always in the middle. I like you, Michael. I want you here. But don't you see what that weasel is doing? All right, Nate Katz is a low-down, slimy snake. I'd like to see him in the ground, dead and buried. Mr. Skunk sent him out here to spy on me—"

"And Thalberg got rid of him for you."

"You're so innocent, Michael, you don't know what's going on. Thalberg does nothing *for* me. He only does things *to* me. In New York they'll say I got rid of Katz to put in my own man. Mr. Nick Skunk won't forgive me for that. Irving has set me up to look like a villain. I was happy to live with Katz. I was playing cat-and-mouse with him. He suffered every day he worked here. Irving had no right putting that man out of his misery. He did it just to get at me." He paused in the center of the room and took in a deep breath. "I need you desperately, Michael," Mayer said with deep feeling. "They're all out to do me in. We'll win out, though. Just stay with me, don't disappoint me."

Mayer suddenly embraced Mike, hugged him around the shoulders. "It's a vicious world, Michael, but the two of us know how to fight it. Don't we?"

Mike didn't answer. What am I doing in this madhouse? he wondered. Yes, he was an innocent. There were complex forces at work. Where did he fit in?

He had found a place for himself, of sorts, but what was it? Of one thing he was certain: L.B. Mayer knew.

27

Summer was growing to a close and Tony McGrath was relieved. He looked forward to the coolness of autumn. The summer had been difficult for him. His defeat by Mike Roth stayed with him and became part of the oppressiveness of summer. He felt as though he couldn't breathe. It was the sense of defeat—he choked on it.

As election time approached, the McGrath house sizzled with politics. Bess had split with the Tammany minions over their candidate, John P. O'Brien, who had served out Jimmy Walker's term after a runoff election. "O'Brien's the dumbest mayor this city has ever had," Bess yelled at John McMahon and her younger boys, all of whom supported O'Brien. "He hasn't learned the simplest political lesson—recognize the problems of the average man and come to his aid with money! All the brains of Tammany were buried in the grave with Silent Charlie Murphy."

She worked with the Democratic party regulars supporting Joseph V. McKee, and this pleased Bill O'Dwyer, who owed his appointment to the bench to McKee. Bill-O came to dinner and tried to win Tony over to McKee's side. John McMahon, Emmett, James, and Willy were there. "You have to balance off your brothers and your father-in-law, Tony."

"They're only interested in the money side," Tony said. "They see rich construction contracts if O'Brien stays in office."

His brothers grinned and shifted uncomfortably in their seats.

Tony was attracted by Fiorello La Guardia. He admired the man's feisty honesty. "God forbid you support that man," Bess declared. "He's a Communist and a Republican and that's as low as a man can get!"

"He's going to win," Tony replied, "and he deserves it."

"You work for that arrogant pipsqueak, one of us moves out of this house," Bess said. Everyone at the table laughed, but she was dead serious.

Bill-O didn't think it a bad idea for Tony to support La Guardia. "That way, whoever wins, McGrath Construction has a foot in the door. The boys go for O'Brien, Bess for Holy Joe, and Tony for the Little Flower!"

John McMahon enjoyed that. His eyes lit up. "You got the bases loaded there for sure," he chortled.

After everyone left, Tony sat alone in the living room. Theresa joined him. "What is it?" she asked.

"Bill-O has changed. Since he took that judgeship, everything is a deal for him. He's become a real politician."

"Why are you so unhappy, Tony? Is it me? Are you sorry you married me?"

"No, no. It's not that at all," he said, pained that she should think it.

"We have plenty of money, Tony. The company is doing well. It's the boxing, isn't it?"

"I don't want to *just* fight. I want to fight Mike Roth."

"Well, you can't have that now, can you?"

"What else can I do, Terry?"

She held him in her arms. They kissed and it was a kiss without passion.

She knew the way he felt. It bothered her, of course, but she was happy just having him there to take care of. She would have liked something more, but she knew it would never be. She did the best she could with what she had.

Tony McGrath knew that he must find something to replace boxing. It wouldn't be the construction company or working for the election of Holy Joe McKee. If he were to commit himself to anyone, it would have to be a man who could win.

He was invited to a meeting of potential La Guardia supporters at an apartment on upper Fifth Avenue, opposite the old Arsenal Building, which now housed the Central Park Menagerie. A butler admitted him to a richly appointed living room filled with people of obvious wealth and position. The hostess approached him.

"Don't look so surprised," she said, smiling. It was Laura Karl.

He felt himself go weak inside at her beauty. Everything inside him sank, and he felt clumsy and embarrassed. "I had no idea . . ."

"That you were coming to my apartment? Does that mean you wouldn't have come if you'd known?" She was staring at him with a flirtatious expression, a look he always associated with her, a look that melted something inside him. He felt as though he were a kid again.

Jason Karl was at the opposite end of the room, talking to a group of people. Laura moved close to Tony. "How have you been?"

"Good. You?"

"Not bad." He could feel her hand against his, trembling lightly. She continued to stare at him with a quizzical look, as though expecting an answer to some unspoken question between them. What did she want? And even as he examined it, he knew the answer and it was what he wanted too. Yet he knew it could never be: time could not be turned back. The past could not be rerouted. They could never be together.

Suddenly there was a stir at the door and Fiorello La Guardia bustled into the room. His dark hair fell down over his eyes and his rumpled suit seemed a size too big for him. He held a large cigar clenched between his teeth.

"My apologies, Jay." His voice was high and shrill, loud. "The lousy cleaners. They lost my tuxedo."

He was small, barely five feet, and overweight. He moved with a wonderful grace, though, and when he began to talk, a magical thing occurred—he seemed to grow, and the force of his personality filled the room.

He greeted various people, then spotted Tony and squared off in a fighter's pose. "Who's that Tammany spy!" he yelled, then did a little boxer's dance over to Tony, threw his arms around him, and hugged him. "This is what a little runt like me needs, a big tough guy like you!"

Someone seated at the piano began to play La Guardia's campaign song, "Who's Afraid of the Big Bad Wolf?" The people in the room picked it up; they sang and clapped and La Guardia puffed out his chest and conducted them in a rousing finale. Then he took off his jacket, loosened his tie, and addressed them. "I am fighting Tammany Hall to redeem this city. I remember when Jimmy Walker raised his salary to forty thousand dollars a year. I said, that's not bad, but imagine what we'd pay if you worked full time!" La Guardia's voice was a shrill shout and he waved his arms as he spoke. "I am fighting for the salvation of this city! The machines must go, the lousy bums must go, the crooks must go, and the people must be given what's theirs! Yes, I'm dangerous. I'm dangerous to crooks, to political hacks, to bribesters and schemers. And I am radical too, radical in fighting against poverty, ignorance, thievery. And so I ask you to join me in this radical, dangerous fight. To the people of the city of New York, I report to duty!"

He finished, took a handkerchief out of his pocket, and mopped his brow. A man at the piano struck up "Who's Afraid of the Big Bad Wolf?" again.

Tony liked him. He liked the sweat of him, the fatigue in his face, the glowing energy, the pugnacity. He was a fighter. And what was more, Tony had the conviction he could win.

La Guardia stayed for a short while longer. He told stories; he badgered people; he argued, as much with himself as with those who crowded around him. He was a bubbling pepper pot of ideas, ideals, prejudices. One theme was at the core of it: the common man in New York must have his day. The cheaters, the frauds, must go.

On his way to the door he grabbed Tony by the arm, lifted up his hand, and formed it into a fist; he held his fist next to it. "What do you think, Champ? Can we knock out the crooks and punks in this town once and for all?"

"I'll take some swings for you."

La Guardia grinned. "We're going to do a job. Oh, this is going to be fun!" He hugged Tony to him. "I admire you, you big Irishman. You're one tough son of a gun!"

And then he was gone and Tony felt a great rush of excitement as though he were about to enter the ring for a big fight.

He saw Laura watching him from across the room and his heart sang within him. He grinned at her. She smiled.

This is it, he thought. I will fight for La Guardia. For a moment he felt free. Mike Roth did not exist.

The next day in the living room of his house he brought the family together and told them he would be working for La Guardia.

His mother grew pale with fury. "All my life I've poured my heart and soul into the Democratic party," she said, shaking with anger. "No son of Bess McGrath is going to work for a Republican!"

"He's a Fusion candidate."

"He's a Republican! He ran for Congress as a Republican. He ran for mayor in twenty-eight as a Republican. I tell you, Tony, you work for that man, you become my enemy. If my son wants to work for a Republican and a Communist, well, he better go out and get him another mother! You hear me, Tony?"

"I hear you."

"Well, that's that, then." She turned and hurried from the room.

"She'll get over it," said Theresa.

No she won't, Tony thought. No. Not ever.

The next day Bess rented a room several blocks away. Tony found her packing her belongings in cardboard cartons. "Bess, this is foolish! I believe in this man. Don't I have a right to that?"

"No! If you told me you believed in the devil, you wouldn't have the right to that neither."

"Ma, listen to me—"

"I will not! You were my son and you now desecrate all that's sacred to me, the Democratic party. The party that put bread in our mouths when we were hungry. It looked after us in sickness. It helped bury your father and sister. And this is how you reward it!"

"What the party did for us, La Guardia wants to do for the whole city. He's a fighter for what's honest and right. And he'll win."

She continued packing. Tony tried to reason with her. She wouldn't speak or look at him.

He went downstairs and told his brothers to watch out for her, to pay the rent at the new place. This breach with his mother tore at him, but he believed in La Guardia. What could he do?

So Bess McGrath moved to a narrow room with the toilet in the hall, a battered dresser, a steel cot, a chipped enamel washstand. On the dresser she set up pictures of her dead husband and daughter, three of her sons. Tony's picture was not among them.

Tony threw himself into the campaign for La Guardia with the same energy and dedication he had brought to the prize ring. He canvassed the five boroughs of the city, working from early morning till well past dark. He spoke to longshoremen, truck drivers, warehousemen, addressed athletic functions, community organizations, appeared at youth centers, boxing matches, picnics, baseball games.

His message was always the same: New York could not survive as the great city it was without Fiorello La Guardia. The people must be liberated from the tinhorns, the grafters, the hustlers and hucksters, and La Guardia was the man to do it. He was of the people, and for them, and as beautiful and tough as they were.

Tammany played down and dirty. They attacked McKee, the regular Democratic candidate, and La Guardia with equal ferocity. Desperate men, these rough ward heelers and party hacks were fighting for their political hides.

Overnight the city was plastered with pictures of La Guardia bearing the admonition: "No Red, No Clown Shall Rule This Town." In the Jewish neighborhoods they accused him of being an apostate to his mother's faith; among the Italians, an anti-Pope rabbi-lover. He was, one and the same, a half-kike, half-wop, commie, fascist, radical reactionary intent on delivering the United States to the forces of international Zionism, Wall Street imperialism and the Russian Comintern.

And yet Fiorello La Guardia won the election by a landslide. Tony felt clean, elated. He loved a good fight, and they had won it handily, he and the Little Flower. That made it all the sweeter.

Six weeks after the election, John McMahon opened his speakeasy to the general public for a grand celebration: Prohibition had been repealed.

Bess wouldn't agree to attend until she was sure Tony wouldn't be there. Theresa told Tony she would call him as soon as his mother had gone home.

Bess, who had been drinking, berated everyone who came near her. "You should have supported McKee instead of that cabbagehead O'Brien," she railed. "The Hall is dead and buried, dead and buried."

Her sons argued with her to move back into the house. "Not as long as that traitor is paying the rent."

"I'm paying the rent!" Emmett yelled back. "Me and the boys have earned it. We built up McGrath Construction, not Tony!"

"He backed the whole thing, and I'll have nothing to do with it!"

She and Emmett hollered at each other while Theresa attempted to calm them. Then his two younger brothers got into it. Bess lashed out at her sons. "You're nothing but bad pennies, all of you! Drunks like your father. You're all grief. Black-hearted Tony and all of you!"

Theresa took her home. She grew very quiet on the walk back to the rooming house. "Tony was as good a lad as there ever was in this world," she said as they reached the house. "That last fight with that Roth fellow injured his brain. He's thrown in with the devil. I pity you, darling Terry. I pity you."

Later Tony arrived at McMahon's bar. Bill O'Dwyer and his brothers were there. Bill-O raised his glass in a toast. "To Tony, the only one who backed a winner. A fine career in politics to you!"

"I don't want a political career."

"What *do* you want, lad?"

"That's the question."

"Aye, that's the question," agreed Bill-O.

Fiorello La Guardia was sworn in as mayor of the city of New York at a minute past midnight of the new year. The ceremony took place in the library of Judge Samuel Seabury's house on East Sixty-third Street. Tony was invited to attend by La Guardia, and he stood next to Laura Karl. Jason had gone to Albany to meet with the governor of the state, Herbert Lehman.

After the swearing-in, La Guardia said, "I have just assumed the office of the mayor of the city of New York. I want the word to go out to all the gangsters, the grafters, the killers: get out of New York City. And to all our police I say: taking even the gift of a five-cent El Creamo cigar shall be considered a dismissible offense."

It was snowing outside. Tony stood by the library window and watched the whiteness falling. La Guardia approached and led him to the far end of the library. "I'm setting up a commission to rid this town of crooks. I want you to serve on it. I need someone who knows how to come out fighting and who will never stop. You're that kind of man. Will you do this for me?"

"Yes, I will. I'd be proud to."

La Guardia smiled broadly and winked. "We're going to have us a humdinger of a time, Tony, these new few years. Yessir!"

He raised his hands palm upward, a boxing manager's gesture. Tony slapped his fist into La Guardia's hand, then raised his palms also. La Guardia slapped off an acceptable one-two. "Yessir," La Guardia said, "we're going to do some job for this city!"

Downstairs the snow was coming down in great sheets. Tony searched in vain for a taxi. There were none to be seen.

"You'll be frozen like a snowman before a cab shows on a night like this." It was Laura Karl, calling to him from her car.

He got in and they drove through the thick-falling snow. The streets were muted, everything muffled. Stranded cars along Fifth Avenue whined and bucked, fighting to free themselves from drifts. The sound seemed very far off, buried.

Laura tried to turn off Fifth Avenue. The car skidded sideways and came to a stop in a snowbank. She shifted into low gear and tried to gun the car out, but the rear wheels spun. She put the car into reverse. Still the wheels spun. They were stuck.

Tony got out, and while Laura revved the motor, tried to push them free. It didn't work. He got back in, soaked with melted snow and perspiration, his trousers splattered with mud.

"Look!" Laura said, pointing down the block. Through the falling snow he could see the canopy of the Ritz-Carlton Hotel, where they had spent their first night together.

She leaned against him, laughing. He kissed her very softly.

"We could take a room there."

He shook his head. She looked wistful, ashamed. "You're right. It wouldn't work. I don't know what I want. I miss you, Tony. I've just never stopped loving you."

He put his fingers up to her lips to silence her. Then he held her close. "What a terrible mistake I've made with my life," she said.

"No. You haven't made a mistake. You did what you had to do."

"A day doesn't go by that I don't think of you."

He kissed her again. "Oh, Laura. My darling Laura."

They stayed in each other's arms for a long while without speaking. They just held on to each other. The snow fell thicker, faster. The windshield was covered now, and the car was dark inside. It was as though they were isolated in a safe magical cocoon.

Her breath deepened. She slept. Tony stroked her hair and tried to imagine what their life together might have been. He couldn't picture a reality with her. She was a dream. She would always exist as a dream for him.

Someone was banging on the car window. He had fallen asleep. Two policemen stood next to their car. They had a shovel, and in a matter of minutes they had freed the car.

Road crews were already out cleaning up the streets. It was dawn when Laura brought him home. He kissed her again before he got out of the car. It was very soft, virginal.

He hurried into his building. He didn't look back.

Theresa was asleep. Tony climbed into bed, and she stirred. Her eyes fluttered open. "How was it?" she asked.

"La Guardia wants me to work in his administration."

"That's wonderful, Tony."

She held on to him, trembling. "What is it?"

"There's something I've been wanting to tell you. I wasn't sure about it until today. I'm pregnant," she said, looking at him with apprehension. "You're not mad, are you? I've never felt that you wanted kids."

"Of course I want kids," he said. Inside, a great ache filled him, an ache at the loss of Laura Maddox, an ache at the loss of his heavyweight championship.

He was growing older, and dreams were dying inside him.

28

Why was he there? No one would tell him. Mike Roth went through the motions of doing a job, but no job for him really existed. He was paid well and given the title "Head of Special Projects." But there were no special projects.

The only thing that was expected of him was to spend a good deal of time with Louis B. Mayer. Mayer was frightened of something, and somehow he felt Mike could ward if off. What he was afraid of was a mystery to Mike.

Mike also functioned as a balancing point between Mayer and Irving Thalberg; he was not comfortable with the situation. The enmity between the two executives was ferocious, yet they were fused to each other, Siamese twins. "Iggy needs me," Mayer would say. "I'm his sounding board and his wailing wall. But his love for money is doing him in. It's his only weakness, and he will try to destroy me to make a bigger buck."

Was that it? Was Mayer in some way *afraid* of pale, fragile Iggy Thalberg?

Thalberg, who enjoyed the prizefights over radio on Friday evenings, would invite Mike over to his house on the beach in Santa Monica to listen with him. He cautioned him about Mayer: "If Louis likes you, look out— it's an embarrassment. If he hates you, just look out!"

Mike probed Thalberg about his position with Mayer: "What does he want with me? Why am I here?" Thalberg smiled and shrugged and never provided the answer, although Mike sensed that he knew it.

There was a subtle competition between the two men for Mike's attention. He was admired by them in a way that great athletes often are by men of lesser ability, and both would confide in him things they would never share with the other.

Why did he stay? he often asked himself. Of course, the money was a consideration, but there was something else—the necessity of knowing why they wanted him. He was being paid handsomely—for what? It had become essential for him to find out.

Dawn light streamed into his bungalow at the Miramar Hotel. He showered, dressed, then walked to the palisade overlooking the Pacific Ocean. A limousine rolled down Ocean Avenue and came to a stop next to him. Louis B. Mayer got out. He approached Mike with short, rapid, purposeful strides.

Mayer had established a ritual in the eight months Mike had been in California: a morning walk just after dawn. Mayer, who had difficulty sleeping, had suggested it; they would discuss Mike's duties at the studio, he said. In the first week it became apparent that Mayer had no intention of talking about his duties. He was frightened and lonely, and he needed someone with him, someone to confide in.

He bared his soul. His relationship with his wife had long ago disintegrated; he went his own way. Mike had trouble taking his confessionals seriously. Thalberg had jokingly cautioned: Louis B. Mayer was that legendary Hollywood mogul who had broken his teeth eating his heart out.

Mayer admitted to Mike he yearned for a woman, but a puritanical streak prevented him from taking up with the young actresses he had access to. "I'm a one-woman man, Michael. I come from a background where my mother stressed to me, 'Louis, do it with a woman only to make babies.' Now my wife, Margaret, has had her organs cut out. Do you know what it is to make love to a woman without any organs? It's like swimming in a lake without water!"

"I slept badly last night," Mayer said as they strode along the palisade, his eyes darting nervously from side to side. "Thalberg and the people at the studio went out to San Bernardino to preview a picture. They left without me." Mayer looked as though he would weep. He paced quickly, and Mike had to hurry to keep up with him. "Last night I was so lonely I couldn't stand it. Joe Schenck and Harry Cohn invited me to dinner. It was torture. All they do is wheel and deal, figure out how to screw someone to make an extra buck. I got home at night, I couldn't sleep. I kept going over everything we said. You got to watch yourself with those tough kikes, Mike. They'll steal my studio right out from under me. Let's shoot some golf."

They returned to the limousine and drove out Pico to the Rancho Country Club, not far from the studio.

Mike, who had never attempted golf before coming to California, had taken it up at Mayer's insistence. He marveled at the man's style. No score was kept; he didn't try to knock the ball into the cup. He played five balls at a time and whacked hell out of them. When Mayer finished on the course, it looked as though a tractor had chewed through it.

He hacked at the balls, charged along the fairways, swore, shouted. He was ridiculous, and yet in a peculiar way Mike found he liked the man. Mayer was a patchwork of contradictions—vicious, kind, sentimental, brutal. It was the foolishness, the fact that Mike couldn't take him seriously, that endeared Louis B. Mayer to him.

Golf with Mayer was just about the only exercise he got these days. When he first started at MGM he visited the studio gymnasium but the attention focused on him there put him off. The old questions came up over and over: When would he fight again? Why had he retired? Why wouldn't he give McGrath a rematch?

It was a nest of intrigue, with actors, producers, directors vying with each other in a mad climb up the slippery pole of film-town power. Tension, fear, obsequiousness, were the behavioral norm. Since Mike was known to be close to Mayer, he was reluctant to turn his back for fear he would find someone's nose up his butt.

His exercise now consisted of calisthenics at his bungalow, an occasional workout with Leach Cross at the Main Street Gym in downtown Los Angeles, and outlandish golf with L. B. Mayer.

They finished eighteen holes. Mayer, positively glowing, was fresher than when they had begun. He practically ran from the limo to the executive building. "Meet me for lunch," he called over his shoulder.

Mike Roth spent the morning studying project possibilities. As head of "Special Projects" he was swamped with ideas that had nothing to do with making movies: a woman in Riverside with thirty trained cats wanted to organize a cat circus, a man had invented a wand for locating oil, another was passionate about organizing a studio polo team. Since he had nothing else to occupy his time, Mike would amuse himself reading these harebrained proposals.

One intrigued him. A man by the name of DuBois, a doctor of some sort, had submitted a plan to broadcast pictures over the airways. He included a list of impressive scientific credentials with numerous unfathomable diagrams. The covering letter was filled with insane rant: plots against him, theft of his ideas, deceptions. It ended with: "Call me a crackpot if you will, but I have at present synthesized a visual scanning device which will make practical the transmission of radiovision pictures (I prefer the term "television") not only in black and white but also in color. The commercial feasibility of broadcast television, including the transmission of motion pictures, is within my grasp." The address accompanying DuBois's presentation was a rooming house in downtown Los Angeles; tacked on was a comment about how the landlady was spying on him.

Mike mentioned the proposal to Eddie Mannix, who knew of DuBois. "He involved us in a lawsuit over a sound-film patent. Mayer vowed to destroy the rascal, and to some extent he's succeeded. Still, DuBois pops up to haunt him every year or so, like a bad penny."

No doubt a madman, Mike thought now, rereading the proposal. There was an addendum scrawled at the bottom of the page: "If there is no interest in my radiovision scanner, I am also at work on a diathermy machine which I am convinced will cure cancer, constipation, diabetes, ulcers, baldness, and arthritis. Since motion-picture executives are notoriously prone to these ailments, they would perhaps have more interest in this invention than the transmission of color motion pictures."

At lunch with Mayer that afternoon in his private dining room just off the commissary, Mike brought up DuBois's project. At the mention of DuBois's name, Mayer reddened. "Why bring up that fake at my lunch table? Someone should have put a bullet in the no good son of a bitch years ago!"

"This radiovision thing could be something worth investigating."

"I know all about it!"

Mike leaned back in his chair. "That's my problem here, L.B. I'm stuck away in a little cubicle with nothing to do. I find an idea that interests me, and you dismiss it. You know all about it."

Mannix started to tell a joke. Mayer cut him off. He thrust his face toward Mike. Behind his round spectacles his eyes were bright with anger. "Why should we get involved with this radiovision thing? Do you think I want people sitting at home staring at some little box? What do you think, I have my brains in my ass? Now, no more of this!"

Mannix completed his joke. No one laughed. Mayer bent his head close to his bowl and rapidly spooned soup into his mouth. He wiped his mouth with a napkin and rose from the table.

"Are you afraid of this DuBois?" Mike asked.

"Why should I be afraid of him?"

"You're afraid of something."

The other people at the table froze. Mayer stared at Mike, and his expression was fierce. "Who told you I'm afraid of anything?"

"It's just my observation."

"You think you're so tough? You're not afraid of anything?"

"I didn't say that. I just want to know what you're afraid of."

Mayer didn't answer. He threw his napkin down on the table and stomped away.

"He is afraid of something. What is it?" Mike asked Mannix.

Mannix stirred uneasily. "Ask Iggy. I just work here."

Thalberg was just concluding a conference when Mike arrived at his office and took a seat opposite the desk. Thalberg didn't look well. He was pale. He picked up a gold piece from his desktop and began to flip it in the air and click it against the desk. His hands trembled. He didn't speak. He gazed at Mike with a faraway, abstracted look.

"I want to get something resolved," Mike Roth said at last. He resented Thalberg's studied remoteness, the vague attitude that Mike's presence was somehow an imposition. "Why is it I'm here? Why did Mayer hire me?"

"I don't have time for this right now."

"Either you tell me what's going on or I'm walking out that door. And I'm not coming back."

Thalberg stroked the gold coin in his hand. "L.B. needs you."

"What for? To carry his golf clubs?"

"He's frightened."

"Of what?"

Thalberg didn't speak for a moment. "Some hoods from the East have been putting pressure on him. They came in here and tried to organize the screen extras. Mayer tossed them off the lot. Since then he's worried about what could happen. He heard a great deal about you, Mike. He respects you. He figures that if he has the heavyweight champion of the world at his side, nothing can happen to him."

"I was hired as a glorified bodyguard?"

"Something like that."

Mike remained quiet for a long while. "I quit," he said at last.

"Don't do that. Mayer has come to depend on you. He really needs you."

"Why are you suddenly so concerned with his needs?"

"I need you too. Before you came, he and I were at each other's throats constantly. You're a good buffer."

"What about the East Coast hoods?"

Thalberg made a small, deprecating wave of his hand. "They backed off long ago."

"If I stay, I'm still the patsy in the middle. I'll think about it."

Mike left and returned to his office. He went over what he had just learned from Thalberg. Mayer was frightened about labor troubles, so Mike was brought in as some sort of talisman to ward off evil gangster spirits: something like that. But why was Thalberg interested in keeping him on? Was it as he had said, because Mike provided a cushion between him and Mayer? Or was it something else?

In late afternoon he received a call from Mayer's secretary; Mayer requested dinner with him.

His limousine was waiting near the studio gate. There were two young ladies with Mayer in the backseat. Mike got in and sat on the jump seat. Mayer was beaming nervously, like a teenage boy on his first date. "This is Miss Gloria Wakefield and Miss Lisa Haynes. Michael Roth, as you may know, ladies, is the heavyweight champion of the world."

Gloria Wakefield, the more spectacular of the two, was tall, blond, with a prominent bosom threatening to leap out of her drastic décolletage. She shifted her weight toward Mayer, sporting her breasts as though they were weapons. Mayer sat rigidly in the corner of the seat, his face flushed.

The other girl seemed shy and was only pretty the second time you looked at her. Uncomfortable in the situation, she had a tense smile fixed on her face.

The limousine made its way through the streets of Culver City. Mike gathered that Miss Wakefield was, of all things, a writer, and the shy girl was an actress under contract to MGM.

Mayer was going on about a project. Slowly Mike came to realize that the buxom blond would be adapting some classic or other from novel form to the screen. "The woman must repent in the end, though," Mayer said. "She must find God."

"Oh, sure," answered Gloria Wakefield.

"The good always triumph in this life. Here! Here! Pull over here!" Mayer screamed at the chauffeur.

They had dinner at the Victor Hugo on Beverly Drive. Mayer launched into his lecture on the pitfalls of Hollywood for poor innocent ladies, the lechery they would encounter, the people who would attempt to exploit them. Gloria Wakefield didn't seem as though she would mind.

Mayer kept his attention on her, darting discreet glances down at her breasts. Occasionally he would look over at Lisa Haynes; he was as uncomfortable with her as she was with him.

To Mike, Mayer's whole behavior this evening was confounding; he had never seen him so tense, so hysterical. He talked too fast, became tongue-tied, blushed, laughed too loud and long at things that weren't funny.

Before coffee arrived at the end of dinner Mayer jumped to his feet. "Let's do some dancing!" he said.

They drove to the Trocadero on Sunset Boulevard. Mayer suggested that Mike escort the women into the club. He would join them shortly. While Mike and the ladies walked through a gauntlet of reporters and photographers to get into the club, Mayer entered by a side door. Mike realized that Mayer had brought him along to serve as a decoy, a beard.

They were seated, and Mayer joined them. He asked Gloria to dance. They moved onto the dance floor, bouncing into a fast fox-trot as the orchestra played "Goody-Goody."

Mike tried to make conversation. Lisa spoke in such a quiet voice that Mike had to strain to hear her. She and Gloria had been showgirls together in New York for Flo Ziegfeld; she was born and raised in Davenport, Iowa. There was a frailness to her, a lack of confidence that Mike found appealing. He felt as though she was a person who needed someone to protect her.

"Why are you so uncomfortable?" Mike asked.

"I'm never very comfortable in these situations—an older, powerful studio executive, his assistant, and two young ladies. I feel cheap."

"Your girlfriend seems to be able to handle herself."

"Yes, she's very good at it."

Mayer and Gloria returned to the table. Mayer was beaming. "Mike, why don't you have a spin with Gloria? She's some dancer!"

Before Mike could protest, Gloria pulled him onto the floor. "Lisa's nice, isn't she?" Gloria said, guiding him skillfully in the dance.

"Very nice."

"She deserves a really special person because she's a very special girl. I find Mr. Mayer a fascinating man. You don't think he'll want to take me to bed, do you?"

"Your guess is as good as mine."

"I certainly hope not. Just think—if I went to bed with him I might end up owning the studio, and what a terrible responsibility that would be." She winked and smiled a shrewd little cat's smile. "I think Lisa likes you."

"How can you tell?"

"Oh, I can just tell."

The dance ended and they returned to the table. Mayer and Lisa had run out of conversation and sat staring into their drinks. A photographer approached, and Mayer tried to shield Lisa. The photographer raised his camera to shoot, and Mayer grabbed him around the neck and wrestled him to the floor. He began to pummel the hapless man.

Mike pulled him off. "I want the name of that son of a bitch!" Mayer yelled. "I'll have him barred from every club, theater, and lot in this town!"

The manager hurried to Mayer's side. "I'm sorry, Mr. Mayer. I'm sorry."

"Take the girls home," Mayer said to Mike, gulping air. "I'm getting out of here!"

Mike could see that Mayer wanted to say something to the girls, but he couldn't get the words out. He'd acted foolishly and he knew it. He was the most powerful man in Hollywood and he had behaved like a six-year-old. As Thalberg had said: *If he likes you, he's an embarrassment.* . . . Mike realized Louis B. Mayer was deeply aware that he was an embarrassment; his whole life was an attempt to escape his own foolishness.

Pale and shaken, Mayer hurried from the club.

Mike took the girls by cab to their house just above Sunset. It was a stucco place, tacky and run-down, with a narrow weedy yard in front.

Inside, Gloria announced she had to be at the studio first thing in the morning and was going to bed. "Mr. Mayer wants me to work on a script of Madame Curie—or is it Madame Bovary?" She smiled. "I'm not sure—I know it has 'Madame' in the title."

After she left them, Lisa hurried to straighten the place. It was a mess, with lingerie, sweaters, shoes strewn all about. Embarrassed, Lisa hastily picked up a pair of panties and a bra, stuffed them into a drawer, then went out to the kitchen.

He seated himself on the couch. Lisa came back with coffee and cookies on a tray. She sat in a chair opposite him.

"This is probably a very stupid question," she said, "but what exactly do you do at the studio?"

"I'm Louis Mayer's baby-sitter. And you?"

"Small-part actress. But not for long. I'm going to be a star." She suddenly grew embarrassed at what she'd said, and stared down at the floor. "That sounds foolish, doesn't it?"

"Do you believe it?"

"It's just something I've always known. When I was a kid I'd watch the silents—Theda Bara, Mabel Normand, Mary Pickford. I just knew I would be like them someday. Carole Lombard. She's my favorite."

There was a touching innocence about her, and Mike was moved. He liked her, liked her shyness, the crazy ambition she had for herself.

"Do you like living in Hollywood?" he said.

"It's lonely."

"Yes."

"Have you been lonely too?"

"I suppose so. I just haven't found my place here yet."

She seemed confused by that. "But you're very important. You're a boxing champion of the world. You're an assistant to Mr. Louis B. Mayer."

"I'm a gold statue he puts on display, like the studio's Academy Awards."

She smiled at him and he realized she didn't understand what he meant. "I'd like to show you something," she said, and left the room for a moment. She returned with a photo album and sat next to him on the couch.

In the album were pictures of her from her high-school-class play (the female lead in *Captain Applejack*), shots taken when she was a Ziegfeld girl, standard Hollywood-starlet photos, and a layout featuring her face in an advertisement in *Liberty* magazine for "Golden Peacock Bleach Creme." In all the pictures she looked vaguely uncomfortable, and Mike was somehow moved by this.

He took her in his arms and kissed her. She yielded against him, then pulled back. "No, please. I don't want it this way ..."

"Lisa ... " He found himself suddenly flooded with emotion for her; he had no idea where it came from, this powerful caring. She was vulnerable and lonely, and he wanted to protect her.

"I'm not one of those fast Hollywood girls. I like you very much. I want it to be right between us."

He held back, though he sensed she wanted him and would be his if he just pressed it. He didn't. He believed her—that she felt for him in some special way. He would not violate the possibility of this purity between them.

"I better leave now," he said.

"You'll call me, won't you?"

"Yes."

In the cab out to Santa Monica his mind was racing. What a strange girl! He felt a powerful clash of emotion within him: he wanted her; he felt something like love for her, at least infatuation, and yet how had it come upon him? At first he'd taken very little notice of her—it wasn't until they were at her house that she had captivated him somehow.

The phone was ringing as he entered his bungalow. It was Moe Kotovsky calling from New York. "I've been trying to get you all night. They murdered your brother."

29

Harry Roth's body was found trussed up in a burning car in an empty lot in Canarsie. He had been strangled and stabbed with an ice pick.

The day of his funeral was gray, cold, the sky threatening snow as the procession traveled across the Williamsburg Bridge to Brooklyn, out Myrtle Avenue to the cemetery.

At graveside Mike realized how little Harry had accomplished in his life, even on his own petty terms. He remembered the funerals of Yiddle November and Little Augie Orgen, jammed with people—not only gangsters, but tradespeople, men from the synagogues, neighbors.

Harry Roth's funeral attracted fewer than a dozen people. Where were Johnny Eggs and Ben Siegel and Abe Reles and all the street-corner tough guys for whom Harry had played the clown, run errands, hustled change?

Not even Jackie Foster had made an appearance.

Back at his parents' apartment, while neighborhood folk gathered for the ritual seven days of mourning, Mike phoned Lisa Haynes in California.

Her voice sounded thin, distant. He told her what had happened to Harry. "But why?" she said.

"Wrong friends."

"Were you close?"

"When we were kids. Not lately. Now that he's gone, it seems as though he hardly existed."

There was an uncomfortable silence. "I'm looking forward to seeing you when I get back to California," he said.

"Yes, yes—I'm looking forward to seeing you again." Her voice was tense, shy.

"Well, there's nothing much really to say."

"I'm sorry about your brother."

"I'll see you when I get back."

The next day Mike received a call from a man in the Brooklyn district attorney's office requesting a meeting. He traveled to Brooklyn that afternoon. An assistant D.A. by the name of Penner was waiting for him. Penner, wiry and nervous, looked like an intellectual but his manner was street-tough. "It's open season on killers in this city now," he said. "It may take time, but we're going to nail whoever it was hit your brother. We think Jack Foster was involved, but making a case against him is going to be rough sledding."

The phone rang. He took the call, then turned to Mike. "An acquaintance of yours is working out of the mayor's office on this thing. Special task force on crime."

Two men entered the office, Bill O'Dwyer and Tony McGrath. McGrath was dressed in a three-piece business suit and carried a briefcase. He had put on some weight and no longer had the hard, chiseled look of a trained prizefighter.

Bill-O shook hands with Mike. McGrath avoided it. They gazed at each other as though they were strangers. "Bad business about your brother," said Bill-O.

"Do you have any questions for him, Judge?" Penner asked.

"After your last fight with Tony, there were rumors concerning your brother."

"He got himself into trouble. I bailed him out."

"Who did he have trouble with?" McGrath asked.

"I never found out."

"Siegel? Lansky? Jack Foster? Abe Reles?"

"He knew them."

"They tried to fix the fight, didn't they?" McGrath said.

"They didn't try to fix the fight," Mike replied. He saw himself in the ring again with McGrath pressing him on the ropes, cursing him, calling him kike, trying to blind him, trying to kill him. "Harry thought I would lose without a fix."

"What was it they wanted from your brother?"

"He was in debt. He gave people the impression he had influence on me. He made them think the fix was in. At least, that's how I saw the situation."

"Is that why you wouldn't fight me again?" asked McGrath.

"No. That's not the reason."

"Who did you straighten out your brother's debt with?"

"Jack Foster was the middleman."

"If the debt was taken care of, why would they want to kill him?" said Bill-O, but Mike didn't answer.

"There's a syndicate of killers operating out of Brooklyn," McGrath said. He continued to avoid looking at Mike. His manner was objective, businesslike. "We feel certain both Foster and Reles are involved. Above them are Lansky and Siegel. We can't make a case against them. If we can break your brother's murder, it could be very important."

"There's nothing much I can tell you. My brother was a harmless guy. He grew up with these punks and envied them. They stabbed him with an ice pick. He should have chosen his friends better."

"No matter what has gone on between us," said McGrath, "I'm going to do everything possible to find your brother's killer. The mayor himself has a personal interest in this case."

Bill-O walked to the window and stared down at the street. "It's a tough one. They've become powerful. Very powerful."

"You work for one of the studios out there in California?" Penner said.

"Metro-Goldwyn-Mayer."

"Were you aware that some of these guys were trying to shake them down?"

"I heard something about it."

"Did they tell you who it was?"

"No."

"Your being hired—did that have anything to do with these shakedowns?"

"Possibly," Mike said, burning with anger inside, humiliated. "They might have felt I could offer them some protection."

"What sort of protection?"

"Nothing sinister. Just my reputation as a boxing champion." McGrath, O'Dwyer, and Penner stood staring at him.

"That's all?" said McGrath.

"Yes." The implication that he was somehow tied in with Eastern gangsters infuriated Mike. He cut off the emotion, maintained his composure. "Who's behind the shakedown?" he asked.

"We hear it's Siegel," McGrath said.

And then the meeting was over. Mike Roth and Tony McGrath parted without shaking hands.

* * *

Mike walked the distance from the Brooklyn district attorney's office to the Lower East Side.

He paused midway across the Brooklyn Bridge and stared out at the bay. He stood there at the railing for a long time. It was night now. He thought about the past, about his future. Where was his place in the world?

Tony McGrath appeared self-assured, prosperous. Kotovsky told him the construction company he had founded with his brothers had become one of the most powerful in the state. He was influential with the city administration.

And yet Mike could feel the tension that still existed between them. McGrath still wanted another fight with him.

For a fleeting moment Mike considered how his life might have been had he continued fighting. When he was in the ring he had purpose. There was a reason for everything he did. He had lost all that.

Did Tony McGrath feel that way?

He thought about Ben Siegel. Of course Siegel would be the one to try a shakedown of a Hollywood studio! The appeal must have been enormous to him—a chance not only to squeeze out money, but perhaps to force himself into the movies. Gangster roles. Tough guy. Did Mayer know when he had hired Mike that he and Siegel had grown up together? Did he believe that Mike could influence Siegel in some way?

The people sitting with his parents were gone by the time Mike arrived at the apartment. Florence was cleaning up. Charlie sat in a straight-back chair, staring at the wall.

Mike made himself a sandwich. He sat at the dining-room table next to his father. "I want the two of you to come out to California. I'll get you a nice little house. The weather is beautiful. You'll like it out there."

His father looked up, his expression flashing the old ferocity. "I don't want to die with strangers." He got up and moved quickly into the bathroom.

"This is our life here, Mikey," Florence said quietly.

His father's anguish had shaken Mike. He didn't want to die with strangers. Mike realized that in his father's eyes he had become a stranger.

30

On the train back to California Mike couldn't get Lisa Haynes out of his mind. The depth of his feeling disturbed him.

It was astonishing. Someone he didn't know at all, whose face he could hardly remember, had somehow worked her way inside him. It was miraculous and frightening.

He tried to phone her from the train station in Albuquerque. There was no answer; then an operator came on the line. The number had been disconnected; no new one had been given.

Across the deserts of Arizona and southeastern California, through sere rock countryside—burning color, waterless desolation—a great emptiness seized Mike, and it seemed that only Lisa Haynes could fill it. By what magic had this girl taken a hold on the core of him?

Back at the Miramar he found a message from Lisa. It gave an address in Santa Monica; no phone number.

Though it was after midnight, he drove there. The house, a large one of white clapboard with a wide porch and vine-laden trellis, was set back from the street. There were no lights on, and he suddenly felt foolish. He hardly knew this girl; suppose another man was there? What was he doing?

He rang the bell, and kept his finger pressed on it. "Who is it?" a voice called out at last, nervous, tentative.

"It's Michael Roth."

Lisa opened the door clad in a flannel robe. She was smiling. "This is very stupid," he said. "I just got into town and there was your message and I had to see you. Stupid."

"It's not stupid."

She led him into the house. "I haven't been able to get you out of my mind," he said, still feeling stupid as he talked. "I tried calling you from New Mexico, and when I learned your phone had been disconnected . . ."

"We just moved in. We don't have a phone yet. Sit down." There were packing crates all over the place, and a brand-new couch. It was the only piece of furniture in the room.

He sat on the couch and she sat next to him. "So many things have happened since you left. Mr. Mayer visited us in our other place and he insisted we move right out. He got us this house, the furniture, everything. It's just . . . crazy!"

"Hello," he said.

"Hello." She smiled and seemed genuinely happy to see him. "I've been thinking about you a lot too."

He took her in his arms and they kissed. There was no resistance; she yielded immediately. They moved together, and their desperation was the same. They made love, and it was as though they had always known each other. She rocked against him, and Mike was confounded. How had it occurred? What had happened to him? Where would it lead?

Love and the world were strange, indeed.

Lisa insisted on keeping the affair secret, and because of this the relationship developed awkwardly, forced into shadow, fraught with tension.

It had to do with her career. She hated the idea that people would think she was carrying on with a powerful man at the studio to advance herself.

She had had a strict Catholic upbringing and she carried within her a sizable sense of sin.

She feared Louis B. Mayer because she was certain he would not approve. Mayer dominated both Gloria Wakefield and her, treated them as though they were his own daughters, advised them, supported them, helped them. With Lisa he was formal, uncomfortable, a bit foolish. He was more relaxed with Gloria, but never attempted anything beyond a few hugs and a peck on the cheek.

Both of their careers were flourishing now. They were Mayer's pets and everyone at the studio knew it. Gloria was placed on a top-level writing project, while Lisa was brought in to test for increasingly more important roles.

Mike was uncomfortable in the situation. He realized that Mayer was tremendously sensitive in his attitude toward women. They were either saints or whores—"alleycats," as he called them. Saints were worshiped, showered with gifts; alleycats were discarded, destroyed. "Lisa and Gloria are princesses," he would tell Mike. "I've never met cleaner, finer girls. I know, Gloria looks a little flashy, but underneath she's one in a million. Do you think a fine young lady like Lisa would have anything to do with her if she wasn't?"

Mike chafed in his role, hated the deception. "Please," Lisa insisted. "Everything is going so well for me now. Mayer's a pathetic, lonely man. He wants to be a shining knight with us. It's touching. We shouldn't destroy that."

He agreed reluctantly, knowing that a time would come when Mayer would find out. When he did, it would not be pleasant for anyone.

And so the charade continued. Once or twice a week the four would go out for dinner and dancing together. Mayer would quiz the ladies on their experiences at the studio. "Has anyone made improper advances? You must tell me. I want only good wholesome people working for me. And we will make only good wholesome films, films that any man can take his children to."

He devoted most of his attention to Gloria, chattering on with her, dancing with her, pawing her occasionally in a pathetic, little-boy way. With Lisa he was always reserved and uncomfortable. "What a pure girl that Lisa is!" he would say when he and Mike were alone. "I'm sure she's a virgin."

"She's a grown woman, Louie . . ."

Mayer blanched. "She would never do anything smutty. That's the kind of girl who would never do anything with a boy unless she married him."

Mike smiled to himself. Perhaps that was it—the only way he could bring his relationship with Lisa into the open: he would have to marry her.

During this period Mike tried to discuss Ben Siegel's attempt to shake down the studio. Mayer laughed it off. It was a figment of Thalberg's imagination, he insisted. "That Iggy, he sees gangsters under his pillow at night. He's such a nervous wreck, that Iggy!"

Had Mayer hired him as protection against the East Coast hoods? Of course not, Mayer said. But he knew that if there was trouble, Mike was the man to handle it.

"What makes you think that, Louie?"

"You're the heavyweight champion of the world. No one messes with the champion of the world!"

One night Mike was called to a meeting with Thalberg and Mayer. He knew it must be important because the two men were barely speaking to each other these days.

Thalberg was pale and perspiring. He looked as though he hadn't slept in days. Mayer paced the office. He had developed a tic on the left side of his face lately, and it was especially pronounced this evening. "They're back," Thalberg said. "The gangsters."

"Siegel?"

"I don't know who's behind it. They're working with some local hoods."

"They've threatened to close down everything," Mayer yelled. "They got their claws on the extras, the truck drivers, the studio laborers!"

"What about your political connections, Louie?" Mike said. "Hoover? The FBI?"

Mayer waved his hand in impatient disgust. "We got big pictures in production, millions of dollars. By the time the government acts, the studio'll be bankrupt!"

"You know these people," said Thalberg. "Talk to them."

"I might know them, but why would they listen to me? Look what happened to my brother?"

"You have to do something, Michael!" screamed Mayer. "They'll ruin us!"

"What do they want?"

"They want to be partners, that's what they want! They want a percentage of everything. Please, Michael, please! I'm paying you good money. You owe me this!"

Before Harry's death Mike wouldn't have considered it. He deeply resented the idea of Mayer bringing him to the studio as some sort of strong-arm protection without even telling him why he was there. But Harry's death at the hands of his boyhood pals had opened a deep scar within Mike. He had paid off his brother's debt, and still they had killed him.

He felt an obligation to do something for Harry.

"Who do I talk to?" Mike asked.

Thalberg made a phone call, spoke with someone, and he wrote out the name of a restaurant for Mike. "The man said he'll see you there at ten."

"How will I recognize him?"

"He'll be carrying a dog."

"A dog!" Mayer said. "See? These are the kind of people we're dealing with. Men who bring a dog into a restaurant."

The restaurant was in the San Fernando Valley, on Ventura Boulevard. Mike Roth arrived shortly after ten.

A small man with a punched-in nose wearing a cowboy hat was seated alone in a room off the main area. He had a bulldog on his lap and was feeding the dog raw hamburger. "Mickey Cohen," he said when Mike seated himself at the table.

"Mike Roth."

"I know who you are. I used to do some boxing myself."

"What do you want?"

"It's not what I want. It's what other people want. I'm just trying to make everybody happy." The bulldog seemed voracious. Cohen fed him handful after handful of meat. "Man's best friend," he said. "I bet the little bastard'll eat my hand up to the elbow if I let him."

"You're working for Benny?"

"I don't work for no one. I'm a middleman, you might say. A broker. If you want to know the truth, Benny gripes my ass. He wants to be a movie star, like his buddy Georgie Raft. I tell him: Benny, you got to have talent to be a move star. He tells me: Bullshit, I'm better-looking than half those guys. I'm better-looking than Raft, Robinson, that guy Cagney. Why can't I be a movie star? I tell him to kiss my ass if he's a movie star. You got to have talent." He yanked the dog off his lap and set him down on the floor. The dog curled up and went immediately to sleep.

"You talk to Benny from time to time, do you?"

"I talk to him."

"Tell him the studio's giving him nothing. Tell him the studio won't even give him a screen test."

"That's a good one," Cohen said. "He won't like that." He parted his jacket. He wore a holster strapped to his waist; in it was a Western-style .45. "You're out of your depth, Champ."

"How many fights did you have as a boxer?"

"Enough."

"Did you ever get a real beating?"

Cohen indicated his .45. "Since I been carrying this, never."

Mike reached down and grabbed the gun, yanked it from the holster and threw it across the room. It hit a mirror on the far wall, shattering it. A waiter came running, sized up the situation, and beat a hasty retreat.

Mike took Cohen by the jacket and pulled him out of his chair. He dragged him across the tabletop and dumped him on the floor. Cohen started to rise and Mike hit him hard. He went back on the seat of his pants. "Wait a minute, here!" Cohen yelled. "I'm just a lightweight. We're not matched." Mike hit him again. The bulldog jerked awake and ran to a corner of the room, where he huddled, trembling.

"Tell Benny I owe him something. Tell him he's a rotten, sleazy creep. Tell him forget about the studio—if he comes anywhere near me he'll have more trouble than he's ever seen."

"You're crazy, you know that?"

"You tell him that for me, you understand?" Mike took the table and overturned it on Cohen, then walked out of the restaurant.

Two days later Thalberg called him into his office. He looked less tired
and he was smiling. "They've called it off. What did you say to them?"

"Not very much."

"You must have said something."

"I said they weren't so tough. They said, yes, they were. We discussed the
matter. Finally they agreed with me."

Over the next weeks Mike waited for something to happen. He knew it
would mean little to Siegel and his associates to kill him. One day Mickey
Cohen arrived at the studio. He came to Mike's office. "I apologize for what
happened between us," he said, much to Mike's amazement. "You have
balls, and I respect that. If Ben Siegel wants to get in the movies so bad, let
him come out here and do his own dirty work." And he presented Mike
with a gift, a pair of hand-tooled cowboy boots.

"I need a hundred thousand dollars."

Mike Roth looked up from his desk. A man had entered the office and
was standing in the center of the room. He had entered so quietly Mike had
not heard him.

He was in his mid-fifties, with thinning gray hair and thick eyeglasses.
Dressed in a baggy dark suit with frayed cuffs and lapels, he carried a battered briefcase.

"If I had a hundred thousand dollars, I might consider giving it to you,
but first I'd have to know who you are."

The man didn't move. He stared directly at Mike through his thick spectacles. His voice was surprisingly deep and resonant, theatrical. "Dr. Elias
DuBois."

Several months earlier Mike had tried calling DuBois to set up a meeting.
He left a number of messages; none had been answered. Now DuBois was
in his office, unannounced.

"Please sit down."

"I prefer to stand."

"Well, tell me about the hundred thousand dollars you need."

"Among other things, I have perfected a system for broadcasting film on
a motion-picture screen."

"If you've perfected it, why do you need money?"

Dr. DuBois hugged his briefcase to his chest. "I can demonstrate that for
you. Can we go to a projection room?"

Mike phoned the projection department and secured an empty room,
where DuBois handed a reel to the projectionist. A bizarre little film, lasting
perhaps eight minutes, came on the screen. DuBois stood in a cramped laboratory. He held a cat in his arms and walked about the room, lecturing to
the camera. The image was reasonably sharp, but you could see it was made
up of a number of horizontal lines resembling a closed venetian blind.
"What you are now watching," said DuBois in the film, "is a replication of
the Elias DuBois theatrical television system. The original image was sent

from an electronic broadcast transmitter erected at Oak Grove Drive, above Pasadena, some fifteen miles from the receiver. Blank thirty-five-millimeter film, coated on one side with a thin layer of metallic silver, has been run at twenty-four-frame speed over a curved brass anvil block. Above the anvil, rotating at high speed, we placed a drum carrying on its edge a series of fine needles, modulated at video frequencies, which etched the film in proportion to the strength of the televised impulse. The film you are now seeing had been televised and etched two and one-half seconds before its original projection. This system has been patented, May 18, 1935, patent number 1,773,216, by Dr. Elias DuBois and is one of a series of such patents held by myself in the fields of motion-picture sound, radio and television broadcast, and an all-purpose radio diathermy treatment which can alleviate ulcers, high blood pressure, diabetes, and certain nonmetastasized tumors." The film rattled on for several more minutes, with DuBois stroking the cat in his arms while taking the viewer on a huckster's tour of his career.

At the end of the film Mike didn't know what to say. He had no idea what he had just seen.

"You noticed the lines?" DuBois asked. "The lines are no good."

"Yes, I noticed that."

"If I can get the machine to produce a hundred-and-fifty-line picture, you wouldn't notice them. That's why I need a hundred thousand dollars."

"Could you explain simply what I have just seen?"

"A picture is broadcast through the air just as if it were a radio broadcast. It is then put on film. They have been able to broadcast images for some years now, but there is no really practical system. What I have just demonstrated could permit you to broadcast motion pictures, sporting events, or plays into theaters anywhere within broadcast range. If you had a relay system of transmitters, you could broadcast all across the country. My system could revolutionize the motion-picture industry. A person could go to the movies, watch the regular feature, then view a sporting event or a vaudeville show originating great distances away."

Mike phoned Thalberg from the projection room and asked him to come over. Fifteen minutes later Thalberg entered, annoyed at the interruption.

He sat through the demonstration with little interest. He squirmed, clicked his gold piece against the arm of the chair, scribbled notes concerning other subjects. When the demonstration was over, he stood. "We'll talk about this later," he told Mike.

"This system will save the movies," said DuBois. "Once television gets into the living room, you people might as well close up shop. You'll need this to draw them out."

"Mr. DuBois, a few years ago I was vacationing in the Austrian Alps," Thalberg said. "People in a little village where I was staying knew that I was an American executive for a large company. They came to me and told me about a genius who lived far up in the mountains. He had invented a miraculous machine. He had worked on it for half a century and now at last it was finished. Would I travel to see the man and take his miracle back to the world? I hiked many miles up into the mountains, where I found an old hermit living in a wooden shack. He took me to his workbench and, glowing with pride, showed me his invention. It was carved entirely out of wood in the most intricate manner, a complex device of cogs and levers and buttons. He pushed various buttons and levers and trembled with excitement about his spectacular invention. I hadn't the heart to discourage him because he really was a genius: this hermit, completely divorced from civilization, in a remote area of the Alps, had, without assistance of any sort, reinvented the typewriter." Thalberg flashed a frosty smile. "As far as I can tell, Dr. DuBois, your device is an elaborate reinvention of motion pictures. I don't think it's anything we're interested in."

He left the room. DuBois stared at the blank screen. "I tried to get them interested in sound film ten years before they came to it. The film business is owned, operated, and watched over by voracious cretins. Television will bury them. People will sit in their living rooms and watch operas and great plays and all the best that the world has to offer. It will bury these cheap hucksters."

He stood up and moved to the projection room and retrieved his demonstration reel. He tucked it under his arm and started out of the room without looking at Mike, nor did he say anything. His mind was fixed on distant things, past failures, old disillusionments.

"Dr. DuBois, I don't have a hundred thousand dollars. But I am interested in your system. Let's discuss this further."

"What else is there to discuss? What do you want to say?"

"I think you're right. I think this invention, this visual radio, will be the medium of the future."

31

Elias DuBois lived in a rented room on Hill Street in downtown Los Angeles. The room was narrow and cramped, filled with books, diagrams, chemicals, electronic gear, tubes, wires, antennae. You could barely move in it, yet it was extraordinarily neat. Everything had its place. On the walls were framed articles and citations of DuBois's achievements.

While DuBois stood at the window and fed the pigeons from a large sack of seed, Mike studied the material on the walls. DuBois turned from the window. "He didn't arrive today," he said, as though to himself.

"Who?"

"A pigeon friend of mine. He's visited me for years. He brings me some of my best ideas." He laughed. "That picture there—do you know who that is?" DuBois indicated a framed picture of three men. The man in the center stood very straight. He wore a homburg and carried a cane. "That's Guglielmo Marconi, the inventor of the wireless. That's me on the right."

"The man on the left?"

"The most despicable human being on this earth. Hubbard Farrell."

In the picture Farrell was young and athletic-looking, with a smiling, open expression. He appeared anything but despicable.

DuBois sat on the edge of the bed. There was a rocking chair in one corner of the room, and Mike sat there.

"We worked together with Marconi in the twenties. I made some important discoveries in regenerative circuits. Hubbard Farrell stole them from me, poached on my patents. Have you heard of Communications Corporation of North America?"

Mike nodded. CCNA was one of the pioneer companies in the field of radio. They manufactured sets, owned broadcast facilities.

"Farrell owns it. Oh, he's very wealthy and powerful now. I've been in court with him for more than ten years on these patent fights. I'll beat him. It might take my whole life, but I'll beat him. He's put a cloud on all of my work. He's bankrupted me. But I'll beat him in the end. That's why this television thing is so important."

"I don't understand . . ."

"I control the underlying patents. Without my regenerative grid, no one can do anything. And that's just one of the key elements I control. CCNA has poured millions into research. They've tried to skirt my patents. It can't be done, though." He stared at Mike. There was something haunted in his look. "It's a race. I have all the knowledge. He has the money. I can beat him. I will beat him."

He spoke with quiet passion, and Mike believed him. He had made inquiries: many considered DuBois to have one of the most original minds in the field of radio electronics, brilliant if a bit unbalanced; he knew his stuff. His great fault was an insane appetite for litigation. He was paranoid, but possibly with reason. The electronic patent game was filled with charlatans, hustlers, thieves. DuBois had either been stolen from or was the one doing the stealing—depending on whom you spoke to.

Mike walked to the window. DuBois's pigeons hovered and wheeled. Mike thought of Yiddle November and the pigeons he had kept. He thought of the old tenement rooftop, of his brother, Harry, and Ben Siegel.

"I think you will do it—beat this Hubbard Farrell," he said at last. "An instinct I have."

He was moved by the pigeons. They seemed to be an omen, an echo of the past, something calling to him to reach out, to dare, to soar. "I have saved some money. Nowhere near a hundred thousand. Perhaps twenty thousand. Can we do anything with that?"

DuBois smiled a faint, sour smile. "I think we can. Young man, you have just made your future."

"I've had the research department give me reams about the man. He has several controlling patents on essential television components . . ."

Mike and Lisa had driven through the canyons above Malibu. They now sat parked overlooking the ocean, watching the sun set. Ever since he had returned from New York, they had spent almost every evening together.

"Then why has he had so much trouble getting financing?"

"He's embroiled himself in a battle with a major corporation. I guess most people feel it's a battle he can't win."

"What do you think?"

Mike grew silent. He stared off at the slate-gray ocean. Beyond it the sun cut a blood-red path into the horizon.

"I believe in him. I'm going to invest with him." He didn't speak for a while.

"I wanted the money for other things. I want to marry you," he said. Since they had been seeing each other, he had never once mentioned marriage, although he had thought about it constantly.

Lisa stared at him, stunned. There was apprehension in her gaze. "It would make me happier than I can tell you to be your wife. But I can't right now."

"When?"

"Everything is so right with my career now. I'm afraid. I don't want to disturb anything."

He didn't try to pressure her. For better or worse, all would work out. There were forces in motion beyond his sway. He thought of DuBois's pigeons, of Yiddle November's. A pigeon, employing a rare, pure instinct, invariably came home to roost, often crossing hundreds of miles to accomplish it. His life would find its way home.

He wanted to marry Lisa, yet there were other considerations. He had discovered that beyond her shyness and insecurity there was great determination, a steely core of ambition. It alarmed him even as he admired it. At first he had been attracted to her because of her helplessness. He discovered she possessed more fortitude than he could ever have imagined. The question for him now was, would her ambition overwhelm everything else in their relationship?

With Mike's investment Elias DuBois rented a loft in a garage in Monrovia, a community just above Pasadena on the edge of the San Gabriel Mountains. The loft was on high ground, something essential, DuBois explained, when working with ultrashort waves: the transmitter had to be placed above the reception area.

DuBois had decided to concentrate on home television rather than the theatrical system he had first demonstrated. "I showed you that system," he explained, "because I figured that's what those movie-folk boobs would be attracted to. Actually, home sets are going to be the battlefield. That's where we'll triumph or be destroyed."

DuBois enjoyed climbing the mountains behind the laboratory. When stumped on a problem, he would take off without equipment of any sort, choose the shortest route up a precipitous slope, and just go at it, clawing his way up, clambering like a mountain goat. Often he would take Mike with him. He was exultant on these excursions, a fearless and indefatigable climber. "We're capturing the high ground!" he would shout, leaping from rock to rock.

As he climbed, he would talk, and the theme was always the same: they were in a race with Hubbard Farrell and CCNA, a desperate war. The future of television hinged on the outcome of this race. Who would triumph— DuBois and his creative genius or Hubbard Farrell and his thieving lawyers? "We have to beat him, Michael. And we can do it. We can!"

They marched up the slope in the silence. At the crest of the mountain DuBois paused. A bluish haze had gathered in the rocks below. A red hawk rose high, then dived into the valley. "This is where we belong," DuBois said. "At the top. Always at the top! We'll beat Farrell. We own the basic patents. There are just a few problems to be resolved."

"How long will it take?"

DuBois hesitated. Obviously he hadn't given it much thought. "Months. Years. Who knows? Could be decades."

The key element, he explained, was the cathode-ray tube. He had worked out the electronics, but the only tubes available were imported from Germany at a cost of five hundred dollars a tube. They lasted only thirty hours, which made them unsuitable for commercial use.

Back at the loft, DuBois gave Mike a lesson in the theory of his system. Using an antiquated cathode-ray tube, he demonstrated: "Think of this as a motion-picture theater in a bottle, the projector at the narrow end. It's like a gun shooting out electrons through a series of magnets, metal lenses, and grids. That's the regenerative part, and I have the patent on it. At the wide end of the tube is a fluorescent screen where the electrons are reconstituted in patterns of light—pictures!" DuBois grinned like a small child who has just performed a dime-store trick. "The problem is developing a tube small enough and powerful enough and cheap enough to do the job. We're going to have to make 'em ourselves!" DuBois laughed. He had a high, whinnying laugh that bordered on the hysterical. "What we're doing is sending and reconstituting dots of light, *seven and a half million variations of intensity every second!* They say no one can do that. Well, I can." He caressed the cathode-ray tube lovingly. "Photoelectric-cell system. Pick up an image, transform it to electrons, transmit 'em through the air. At the receiving end, reverse the process. It's all in this baby!"

"Can we do it on twenty-five thousand dollars?"

"Hell, no!" DuBois's eyes lit up; his face took on a mischievous twinkle.

"We're going to hustle 'em. If we can develop a cheap cathode-ray tube and sell the world on the idea, the big boys will be lining up to buy it. With that we have the financing for the whole system. We own the patents and we have the tubes. They'll stand in line and pay the price we ask."

The work did not go well. Devising a cheap and effective cathode-ray tube was horrendously difficult. As soon as one problem was solved, it gave rise to another. Mike Roth's original investment was soon dissipated. He went to Thalberg and once again tried to interest MGM in DuBois's work. "The man is a charlatan," Thalberg told him. "Everyone knows that."

"I've checked it out. He does own all the essential patents for a feasible television system."

"He owns *disputed* patents, and Hub Farrell and CCNA will whip his ass eventually. And even if he's on the right track, why should we fund something that, if it works, will destroy the motion-picture industry?"

Mike managed to come up with another ten thousand dollars, and the work continued.

Things at the studio went on their rocky way. Thalberg and Mayer fought constantly. Thalberg's heart ailment, exacerbated by Mayer's relentless hectoring, brought him to a point of imminent collapse. Mike interceded on Thalberg's behalf, and Mayer turned on him, accusing him of betraying him. He ranted, he raved, he wept, then hugged Mike to him. "I need you. I have no one—just the sharks in this business, Iggy, Mr. Skunk. Don't disappoint me, Mike, like Iggy did. I need you."

Mike knew Mayer was conning him, but what could he do? He had been seduced into a position he found increasingly distasteful, yet he could not walk away from it. He thought of dreams he had had in the past. Where had they gone? What did his life amount to now?

He had beaten Tony McGrath twice for the heavyweight championship of the world, but he had not really won anything.

32

Mike's relationship with Mayer, his work at the studio, became increasingly difficult for him to live with. He felt useless, an ornament. He was certain that if he and Lisa married, things would improve. He wasn't sure how, but at least the tension of sneaking around behind Mayer's back would be eliminated.

They discussed it. Lisa used her career as an excuse. Yes, she loved him. Yes, she wanted to marry him, but he must be patient. She had done a series of increasingly important roles for MGM. She would be getting leads soon. Mayer himself had promised it.

Mike waited for some success to occur with DuBois. A breakthrough in the television work would enable him to cut free of Mayer and MGM. He would have a company of his own in a revolutionary technology which could affect the whole world. His work with Elias DuBois more and more began to take on significance for his life.

Louis B. Mayer had arranged a special outing to which he invited Mike, Lisa, and Gloria. They would travel up the coast, past Morro Bay to William Randolph Hearst's extraordinary estate, San Simeon, where they would spend the weekend.

Mayer was as excited as a kid. "I have a surprise for you, Mike, a surprise for everyone. This is going to be a great time."

"I think he's going to pop the question," Gloria said to Mike and Lisa later that night. "He's been talking about asking his wife for a divorce, prodding me on what I think of the idea."

"Oh, marry him, Gloria!" Lisa said. "Then you'll practically own MGM!"

"I'll marry him on one condition: you sleep with him for me."

Mike teased her: it wasn't possible she hadn't slept with him yet.

"The God's honest truth. I keep waiting for him to pressure me, trying to figure out how I could turn him down and still keep my job. But he has never touched me. I actually think he won't sleep with me until we're married."

At the last minute before the outing, Mike received an urgent call from Elias DuBois. It was essential that he see him immediately. Mike told Mayer he would come to San Simeon alone the next morning.

DuBois had run out of money again. The work was going well, he insisted. He had erected a transmitter atop the hill behind the laboratory. He was now able to bring in a reasonably acceptable picture. The problem was, as it had always been, the expense of the cathode-ray tubes.

"We're so close. If we have to shut down now, we'll lose maybe years. We can't sacrifice that time. Farrell and CCNA are near to testing their own system. We're in a race with them."

Mike promised he would do what he could. He was growing uneasy, though. DuBois's experiments appeared like a bottomless pit, swallowing up money as fast as Mike provided it.

Was DuBois a fraud and madman, as so many people warned?

Mike planned to drive to San Simeon in midmorning, after first transferring money from his account to the DuBois-Roth account. He was awakened by a phone call. It wasn't light yet. Lisa was on the phone, weeping. "Something has happened."

"What?"

Gloria came on. "There's been a scene with Mayer. You'll have to come and get us. We left the Hearst place. We're ten miles down the coast at a town called Cambria, at a small inn here."

She refused to tell him what the problem was over the phone.

He sped north. The coast highway was wreathed in fog. His mind sifted possibilities. With Louis B. Mayer, the threat of an ugly scene was always present. What could it have been this time?

At the inn Gloria was waiting in the lobby. On the way to the room Mike tried again to find out what had happened. "It's just so insane. Lisa will tell you."

Lisa looked devastated. Her face was pale and streaked with tears. Mike attempted to embrace her, but she pulled away. "We arrived at the estate and everything was fine. Mayer was obviously excited about something. After dinner, Gloria wandered off with some people and Mayer asked me to take a stroll with him. He gave me a little tour of the place and as usual he was tense and uncomfortable with me. Then he asked me to his room. I knew he had planned something special for the weekend and I assumed it had to do with Gloria, that he was going to show me the engagement ring or something like that.

"In his room he poured out a big glass of brandy and gulped it down. I began to feel nervous. He drank down another glass of brandy. He had this frantic look on his face. Suddenly he sank to his knees in front of me. I thought he was having an attack, a convulsion or something. He clutched at me and babbled that he's madly in love with me! Mayer is madly in love with *me!* I didn't know whether to laugh, cry, or throw up. And then he poured out the whole thing: from the first time he saw me he was in love with me! He only showed interest in Gloria because she's my girlfriend. The whole trip to San Simeon was arranged so that he could declare his love for me at last.

"He said he was divorcing his wife. He discussed it with her and she agreed. He had his lawyers draw up a prenuptial agreement which he would sign with me. I would be a rich lady, the power behind MGM. He would be my slave. It was madness. He got up off his knees and tried to embrace me but I pushed him away and told him I couldn't marry him, that I was in love with you."

Lisa began to weep. Mike held her close to him. "What are we going to do?" she cried. "I've never seen anything like it. He was so hurt, so angry. He screamed. He bawled like a baby. He ran to the window and threatened to throw himself out. Then he began to curse me. He swore he would ruin me, he'd ruin you. I ran from the room, found Gloria, and had one of Hearst's people drive us here."

"He's not going to ruin anybody. You know how stupid and melodramatic he gets. It's all an act."

"Don't you understand, it's my career!" Lisa wailed. "He said I'll never work again in Hollywood, and I know it's true."

"I'll patch it up. Don't worry."

At the castle Mike learned that Mayer was swimming in the indoor pool. He entered the pool area, where Mayer was soaking at the shallow end. He spotted Mike and stood up. His bare upper body looked incongruously

youthful and powerful. He screamed to an attendant: "Get that son of a
bitch out of here! Judas bastard!"

There were a dozen guests in the pool. They stared in astonishment as
Mayer moved out of the water, raving, "Get him out of here! I order you!
Get him out!"

Mike tried to calm him, but his voice was drowned out by Mayer's
screams. "I treat you like a son, and you deceive me like this, you ungrateful
bastard!"

"How could any of us know how you felt about Lisa?"

"I loved that girl, and you despoiled her. She's a filthy whore now, and
you're a lying pimp!" Mayer came around the pool toward Mike. "Not even
Iggy treated me like you've treated me, you and that filthy whore."

"Louie, the girl had no idea you loved her."

"That cunt will never work again, I swear on my mother!"

Mike turned from him and began to walk away. Mayer rushed at him,
grabbed him by the shoulder, and spun him around. "I'm going to break
your ass, you bastard!" he yelled. He squared off as though to fight. "Come
on. Fight me, you bastard. Fight!"

He swung at Mike. Mike leaned back, and the punch missed by a foot.
Mayer charged at him, flailing away. Several desperate punches landed with
surprising force.

Mike grabbed him and flung him to one side. Mayer lost his balance and
went into the pool. He swam to the pool's edge and tried to yell, but no
sound came out. When he finally regained his voice, Mike was gone. "I'll
destroy that kike son of a bitch," Mayer screamed. "I'll destroy him!"

No one there ventured to dispute the fact.

33

Tony McGrath had been called to a private meeting with Thomas E.
Dewey, special rackets prosecutor for New York County. There had been
tension lately between Dewey and La Guardia: Dewey had announced he
would be campaigning for district attorney. He was ambitious. His crime-
busting had stolen the headlines from La Guardia.

McGrath was ushered into the private office, where Dewey, a small, lean
man with a brush mustache, sat behind his desk smoking a pipe. His
scrubbed, fastidious appearance belied a basic toughness. "I think we're beginning to get some movement on this Harry Roth thing." He had an incongruously deep voice.

"I'm having a meeting with Bill O'Dwyer later this afternoon."

"Keep your hand in there, Tony. I'm sure if this cracks, the Brooklyn people will try to grab all the credit."

"I'll keep my hand in, don't worry." Tony smiled to himself. Dewey was afraid Brooklyn would grab the spotlight; La Guardia was peeved that Dewey would get it; and Penner and O'Dwyer and the rest of the Brooklyn crowd were fighting tooth and nail to get their share. The battle for publicity was almost as furious as the war on the mob.

"We have three elements that seem to interlock," Dewey said. "The bakers' and garment workers' unions and the Construction Workers Alliance. The same names keep popping up: Lansky, Buchalter, Siegel, and Foster. Foster is the weak link because of his direct connection to the Reles group, so we work our way up the ladder starting with Reles. If we can nail him, we go from there to Foster and on up."

"Well, something's stirring out in Brooklyn. I'm having dinner with Bill-O, so I'll see what the Brooklyn boys have come up with."

"Good," replied Dewey. He smiled, but his eyes were serious. There was a cold watchfulness in the depths of them. Yes, they would work their way up the ladder, Tony knew. But it was the ladder of his own ambition that Dewey was most interested in climbing.

After, Tony met with Bill O'Dwyer at Manny Wolfe's Steakhouse in the shadow of the Third Avenue elevated train tracks. It had begun to rain outside and the rain fell in great sweeping sheets, drenching the avenue. From time to time the elevated train would rumble by, rattling the silver and glassware on the table.

"Nothing so gloomy as Third Avenue on a rainy night, unless it's a jailhouse or an empty ball park," O'Dwyer said. "How's Theresa and the kid?"

"Oh, she has her hands full. The kid's a hell-raiser." Tony's son, Darryl, a blond, chubby three-year-old, occupied most of his wife's energy; he was the center of her existence. Tony was grateful for it because he had little time for home and family these days.

"And Bess?"

Tony shrugged. "I haven't seen her in a long time. She comes to visit the kid when she's certain I'm not around."

Bill-O sipped at his martini. "We've had some activity on this Harry Roth thing. One of Abe Reles's boys. We have him on an extortion rap and he's trying to wriggle off. Abraham Levine—they call him 'Pretty.' He was the go-between when Mike Roth settled Harry's debts. We think it goes from Pretty Levine to Foster and Reles, then Siegel on top."

"What do you want me to do?"

"Your construction company does business with Foster's union. Get to Foster. Let him know Levine is ready to crack. Let's work these boys against each other."

"It could backfire. There could be a lot of people dead."

Bill-O smiled. "There's a lot worse things could happen. If they want to kill each other off, let them do it. It'll save the state a lot of time and money."

"We could lose access to the higher-ups."

"It's our best bet. At any rate, as far as Foster is concerned, it would be to your advantage to see him out of that union. You don't need business with a gangster union. You might want to run for office one of these days."

"No. That's not for me."

"You never can tell," Bill-O said. "I've been considering running for Brooklyn D.A. next year."

Tony looked up, surprised. "You have a fourteen-year term as magistrate. Why would you want to throw that over for the D.A.'s position?"

"I like to be where the action is. My butt is getting calluses sitting on the bench."

Why would Bill-O want to jeopardize what was essentially a lifetime position to do battle for the D.A.'s job? For a moment it made no sense to Tony, then everything became clear. Ambition, of course. The D.A.'s office was a stepping-stone to higher office.

After dinner, he and Bill-O parted. On the way home Tony thought about Bill-O. There had been a change in him these past few years. He was secretive, coolly pragmatic, playing intricate maneuvers whose ultimate aim was known only to him. Tony could not escape the feeling that he was being manipulated by Bill-O.

His wife and son were asleep when he arrived home. He sat on the edge of Darryl's bed and stared at him for a long time. Peculiar how his life had progressed, he thought. Even his family had become distant. He spent so little time at home that he rarely saw them. A gulf had been created between them, as it had in other areas of his life: his relationship to his mother, his brothers, Bill-O.

His days and nights were occupied waging war against a shadow army of killers and thieves. The battle lines were confused; it was hard to tell friend from foe. While he fought to put Jackie Foster in jail, his brothers were doing business with him and the union he controlled. Tony McGrath missed the clear-cut choices of the prizefight ring; he ached at the loss of connection to those around him.

He leaned down and kissed his son. The boy's eyes fluttered open. "Daddy," he said. Tony winked at him. Darryl smiled and closed his eyes. His breathing deepened.

Tony was flooded with love for his son. It was ever-present, even if he didn't always recognize it. Though other areas in his life might be confused, his love for Darryl was powerful and binding. He would do what he could in this life for the boy. He sloughed off his doubts and went to bed.

Tony had his brother Emmett set up a meeting with Jack Foster at the offices of McGrath Construction on Forty-second Street off Times Square.

Foster entered looking prosperous. He had grown a mustache. He sat himself in a leather chair opposite Tony and said admiringly, "Things are going well for you, Champ." On the walls were photographs of projects the company had worked on—the Empire State Building, the West Side Highway, the World's Fair site. "Your brothers do a good job. We enjoy doing business with them." Foster took a cigarette from a gold case and lit up. "What's on your mind, Tony?"

"Pretty Levine. Pretty Levine is talking."

"You know how it goes. Bullshit talks, everybody walks. You have nothing unless there's corroboration."

"He could talk about the murder of Harry Roth."

"Yes?" Foster stared at the end of his cigarette, knocked the ash into a tray on the corner of the desk.

"He implicates Abe Reles. Reles sees they can make a case. He looks to make a deal. Corroboration."

"They would never get past Reles."

"Is that right?"

"It's politics, Tony. Forget that windup doll with the mustache and the little fat man. It's the Democrats own this town, Tammany. You know that better than anybody."

"So?"

"Like I said, they'll never get past Reles. You're talking about important people and big unions. Forget my union, we're small potatoes. We're talking about very important people."

"Abe Reles is ripe to fall. If he falls, you fall."

Jack Foster stood. His face was tight with anger. "This is a waste of time, Tony. We go way back. I thought we'd have a nice chat about the old days. This other stuff is no good to anybody."

"You have a good lawyer?"

"Five of them."

"You better call them."

"Don't impose on my friendship, Tony. One hand washes the other in this business, you know that. I could give you people here a lot of heartache. I could have your brothers back digging ditches."

"They're strong. They'll survive."

"Anything else?"

"I just thought you'd want to know about Pretty Levine."

"Is he really pretty?"

"He's beautiful."

"Give him a kiss for me," Jack Foster said, then left.

Pretty Levine signed a consent order and was moved from the Tombs Prison in Manhattan to the Brooklyn D.A.'s office in Boro Hall. He requested a meeting with Penner, the assistant D.A., and Dewey asked Tony to be present.

Pretty Levine had large feminine eyes, long lashes, a girlish mouth. He

didn't look at McGrath or Penner. "We want Abe Reles," Penner said.
"I can't do that."
"I thought you were concerned about your wife and kid."
"Yes," Pretty Levine said very softly.
"Reles knows you're talking. You'd best tell us something that will get him off the street. Give us a reason to bring him in."
Pretty Levine said nothing, but he looked as though he would weep. Penner left the office. He returned with a young woman who carried a baby in her arms. "Tell them what they want to know," said Pretty Levine's wife. "Tell them, Abraham,"
Pretty buried his face in his hands and sobbed. He turned to Penner, tears streaming down his face. "Abe Reles killed Harry Roth. He did it for Jackie Foster. He told me all about it."
Penner called for a stenographer.
Later, when police went searching for Reles, he had disappeared. No one knew who had tipped him off. Politics, as Jackie Foster would have said, probably played a part. The Democrats were still very strong in the Brooklyn D.A.'s office.

34

Driving along Sunset Boulevard after a day with Elias DuBois at the hillside laboratory, Mike Roth heard the news that Irving Thalberg had died. A cold had developed into pneumonia; his weak heart gave out. Louis B. Mayer had triumphed over him at last.
Since falling out with Mayer, Mike had felt a tremendous sense of liberation. For the first time since his boxing days he had a clear-cut purpose in his life. Though the breakthrough in DuBois's work hadn't occurred, he was certain it would. He immersed himself in the company, forced himself to master the basic technical aspects of television. He knew just how close they were to success.
Shortly after the rift with Mayer, Mike and Lisa Haynes drove down to the desert and were married. Lost, desperate, convinced her career was over, Lisa married Mike more out of panic than love. What could she do? Where could she go?
Mike sensed her disquietude. He knew she had entered the marriage like a frightened child fleeing the dark. Still, he was certain that beyond her anxiety was a very real, rich love. He would be patient. It would work.
She fought to get work as an actress. No one would have her. Mayer had

succeeded in wrecking her career. For a while she involved herself in Mike's work with DuBois, hoping that things would eventually improve for her. They never did. She stopped accompanying Mike to the laboratory.

They purchased a small house on the beach north of Santa Monica. She spent most of her time tending a small garden in a patch of grass alongside the weathered clapboard house. She slept until noon, rose to read movie magazines, putter around the garden, walk the beach.

As Mike entered now, she was seated on the couch, surrounded by movie magazines. She was still in her housecoat, though it was late afternoon. She didn't look at him as he came into the room, but continued to turn the pages of the magazine in her lap, and lipped a cigarette as she read.

More and more it was like this: he came home to find her sullen and uncommunicative. It upset him but he tried to control his anger, to prevent her unhappiness from turning into overt hostility. "What's on for tonight?" he said.

"We're due at Gloria's."

He remembered now, and the thought of the evening filled him with dread. Gloria Wakefield, cashiered from MGM at the same time as Lisa, had married a wealthy doctor specializing in nervous disorders. There was a party at Gloria's Bel-Air mansion that night.

The doctor, whose clients were drawn primarily from the film industry, liked to throw parties. Mike detested these gatherings, with their weaselly agents, actors, producers, hangers-on, hucksters, and starlets all engaged in a daisy chain of furious hustle, sucking up to the more successful while spurning those who exhaled the sour breath of failure. As Leach Cross once told him, it was either kiss ass or kick ass, and it turned Mike Roth's stomach.

In the land of the Chinese, he had not yet become a Chinaman.

It would be a grim time, and Mike had agreed to go only for Lisa's sake. She only came alive when she was part of the movieland game. Like an exiled princess, she desperately awaited the time when she'd be recalled to the arenas of glamour and power.

"Did you hear about Thalberg?" she asked.

"Yes."

"He got him. Mayer got him." Mike didn't answer. "He got us, too."

He walked to the window and stared out at the beach. "Only if we let him," he said.

"Why do you think you're immune to him?" Her voice had a nasty edge to it, and he was sorry he'd let himself be drawn into a discussion of Mayer.

They had been through this so many times before. He had tried to explain that problems occurred only when you *cared,* when you played Mayer's game as Thalberg had, as so many people did. It was a business of terrified, impotent people who would do anything to hang on to their power.

Lisa wouldn't accept this. A slave to her ambition, she knew only that she had been doing well and now it had all been taken away from her. Whatever love existed between them foundered on this obdurate fact.

He had expected to find happiness with Lisa Haynes, but he had been mistaken. With her career destroyed, she would never be happy. Every day he questioned the wisdom of their having married. He never talked about it with her, but it ate away at him. Like an ancient wizard, Mayer had cast a poisonous spell over their relationship.

At the party they went their separate ways. Mike found himself cornered by his host, Doc Canfield, who, it turned out, was a Marxist. He lectured Mike for forty-five minutes on the situation in Spain, the theory of surplus value, and why Bel-Air should organize itself into revolutionary cells. From time to time his wife would pass and he would interrupt his discourse to smack his lips and comment admiringly to Mike on the size of Gloria's mammaries.

Gloria eventually grabbed her husband away to dance.

"Hello, Mike."

He turned and found Ben Siegel, dressed in a sky-blue tuxedo, standing next to him. Ben hadn't changed since the last time Mike saw him. He was smiling, and as Mike stared at him, he thought of his brother and an immense fury swelled within him.

"You don't look happy to see me, Mikey. We don't have a quarrel, do we?" Mike didn't answer. He could feel the anger pounding in his temples. Siegel leaned close to Mike and spoke in a quiet, concerned voice. "If it's about Harry, I want you to know I had nothing to do with that. I was saddened to hear what happened. I liked Harry very much. He was a harmless guy." He continued to smile. "So how's everything with you, Mikey? We hear you're doing big things out here. I'm very happy for you."

"Stay away from me, Ben."

"You're getting touchy these days. I heard what you did with that punching bag, Mickey Cohen. He was furious. He wanted to do you a lot of harm. I talked to people for you, Mike. You don't know what a good friend I am." Ben Siegel chattered on, exuding charm. He was drunk on Hollywood glamour.

"If I run into you again, I'll break your pretty face wide open," said Mike. He turned from Siegel and walked away, his insides on fire with anger.

"I met your wife," Ben Siegel called after him. "A lovely lady."

Mike found Lisa on the patio talking to a man he recognized from MGM, one of the directors in the B-movie unit. She was smiling too hard, and Mike knew she was angling for something from the director. He could tell by the man's tense expression that she could never get it: MGM would never hire her, nor would any of the other studios; not for a long while.

He took her by the arm and drew her away. They drove home in silence. Lisa brooded. As they neared the beach, she said, "What was it?"

"One of the men at the party was responsible for my brother's murder."

"What was he doing there?"

"Who knows? Maybe he wants to be a movie star." He didn't speak the rest of the way back home.

The work with Elias DuBois continued. Hanging over everything they did was the shadow of Hubbard Farrell and CCNA in New York. Mike studied the technical journals and learned that CCNA was close to achieving a practicable television system. "It won't matter," DuBois insisted. "Whatever they do, we'll do it better." He was close to a major breakthrough.

They had almost exhausted their finances. Mike had poured every cent he had into the project. It became an obsession with him. He believed in the work, believed in DuBois. He knew they were near. He was determined that they succeed.

Then they reached the point where either the system worked immediately or they'd have to close up shop. They had run out of money. "We'll test it this Friday, make or break," DuBois said.

Lisa and Mike arrived early at the laboratory. DuBois looked ghastly. He had been driving himself for months now. He had lost weight and his face was hollow, haunted, unshaven; his fingers were stained yellow with nicotine, his hair long and scraggly.

He decided to test the system using a reel of motion-picture film. If the scanning tube produced sufficiently high resolution, DuBois was certain the transmission of live pictures would present no problems.

A few minutes after noon he announced he was ready to broadcast the film strip. An assistant turned on the transmitter. DuBois tuned in the receiving element. A test pattern emerged with thrilling clarity: "DuBois-Roth Television" bracketed by dollar signs.

Lisa and Mike stared at the picture in the darkened laboratory. A tremendous sense of excitement moved within Mike. The pattern was glorious—clean, hard-edged, glowing. The assistant cued the film clip into the circuit. There was a soft popping sound and the picture went black.

The cathode tube had blown.

DuBois leaned back in his chair. He fished for a cigarette in a crumpled pack, lit up, exhaled smoke. "Son of a bitch," he said quietly.

No one spoke for a long time. DuBois puffed on his cigarette. "We have it, I know we do," he said at last. "We're there, Mike. I know where the problem is. In a few days—"

"We're broke," Mike answered.

DuBois walked to the window. A pigeon landed on the ledge. He reached into his pocket, withdrew some seed, and held it out to the bird. He watched the bird with mournful concentration, as though expecting it to provide the answer to all their problems.

Mike took up the phone. He had made a painful decision: he would call Jason Karl. He would ask for a loan.

After he had explained the difficulties, Jason asked, "How close are you?"

"Elias says a matter of days."

"Hub Farrell's group is ready to demonstrate their system at the World's Fair this spring."

"We own the underlying patents, Jay. Our system is light-years ahead of theirs. We'll even have a method for integrating color into the basic system."

"How much do you need?"

"Immediately? Twenty-five thousand dollars. More later."

"I'll have my banker contact you in the morning."

"I hate like hell doing this," said Mike. "I don't deserve anything from you."

"Now, that's plain ridiculous. Why would you say such a silly thing?"

Work resumed the next day.

Several weeks later Mike returned from the laboratory to learn that Ben Siegel had called and spoken with Lisa. She was as excited as a little kid. "He wants to help me with my career. He's talked to Harry Cohn at Columbia for me."

"You can't do it. You can't accept anything from him. If he calls again, hang up."

"But this is my chance," she said. "He's working with the unions and he can get me going again."

"He was responsible for my brother's death. Don't you understand that?"

She began to weep, and he put his arm around her. "You don't need him. There'll be other ways. We're so close on this television thing. Don't you see? If it works, the movie people will come to *us.*"

"My best years will be gone," she sobbed. "Everything will be finished for me."

He held on to her and rocked her against him and knew that unless she were able to resume her career, nothing would ever work out between them.

She never discussed Siegel again. A change came over her. She grew very quiet. She spent more and more time in bed. A wall of silence closed between them.

A week later, Siegel called again. Mike answered the phone. "Don't call here again."

"I'm trying to make it up to you, Mikey. I can get your wife a contract at Columbia."

Mike hung up. Lisa didn't ask him what it was about and he told her nothing. The silence between them grew.

Two months later DuBois brought Mike and Lisa into the laboratory for another demonstration. The test pattern was perfect and the film clip snapped on bright and clear.

Mike looked on, stunned. DuBois began to laugh. The clip was a newsreel of the second McGrath-Roth fight. Mike was against the ropes. McGrath slammed at him. In the film you could see his lips: he was cursing Mike Roth.

Next, DuBois showed some of the work he was doing with color—it wasn't successful yet. The picture was blurred, the color a muddy orange. "It'll get better," DuBois said. "We're on the right path."

Mike spoke with Jason, who said, "If you're going to beat Hub Farrell, you'll have to perfect the color. Everyone here says CCNA's black and white is beautiful."

"The problems are enormous," replied Mike. "But Elias says we can do it."

"Why don't you bring the system to the World's Fair?" Jason asked. "You could go head-on against CCNA. If you beat them, the whole world will know it. It'll be expensive, though. You'd need your own pavilion."

"We need every cent we have to work on the color system."

"Let me think about it. I could line up some investors. Is this guy DuBois reliable?"

Mike hesitated. "Yes," he said, not certain. "Yes, he is."

Over the next weeks plans were formulated to bring the DuBois-Roth television system to the New York World's Fair. The only stumbling block would be the large amounts of money needed to finance the pavilion. Jason told Mike to come to New York; they would plan a way of getting additional backing.

The night before Mike was to leave, Lisa told him she was pregnant.

35

The TWA trimotor airplane bounced through turbulent skies, thick patches of cloud; rain squalls whipped against the skin of the plane and its motors strained in the wind, vibrating loudly. From time to time it would emerge from the storm, and spectacular vistas—rivers, mountains, farmland—would come into view below.

It was Mike's first plane trip and he felt awe and disbelief. What was keeping them up? He stared out at the heavy metal wings, the cumbersome motors, and it seemed miraculous to him that they didn't fall from the sky.

Eventually he settled back and thought of the reason for his trip to New York. Hub Farrell and CCNA had announced that they would hold the first public demonstration of a commercial television system at their World's Fair pavilion. In order to compete, DuBois-Roth would have to be there too. If they wanted to win, they'd have to top CCNA's demonstration. They'd have to come in with a color system.

As usual, money was the problem. Jason Karl had invested a sizable amount of his own money; it had got them this far. To build a pavilion at the fair they would need outside financing.

Jason and Laura were waiting at the airport. Laura looked coolly beautiful, regal and elegant. She had matured, and it only enhanced her loveliness. She looked as though she were fashioned out of marble.

Jason had taken a suite for Mike at the Waldorf. Mike wanted something less grand, but Jason insisted, and he was picking up the bill. Over dinner in the Starlight Room Mike and Jason discussed how they would approach the business of DuBois-Roth television and the World's Fair. "Tony McGrath's company controls construction at the fair," Jason explained. "They could help us enormously on the pavilion. I spoke with John McMahon. He'd like to set up a fight between you and McGrath, an exhibition thing at the fair. The gate would be rich. We'd repay them for financing the pavilion out of the proceeds."

After all these years, McGrath was still pushing for a fight! Mike Roth realized what a boon it would be to have McGrath Construction defer costs. Yet he couldn't go through with it. He couldn't fight McGrath again. They had fought in an arena of hate and murder, and he wouldn't allow himself to sink to that level ever again.

"I can't do it, Jay."

"I understand. We'll find the money somehow. One thing—I was able to get space for a transmitter atop the Empire State Building. Algie Smith helped on that one."

"How is the governor?"

"Not happy. When he broke with the Democrats, he cut himself off from what was most important to him in this life. He had everything—except the presidency. Now he has nothing."

"Dance with me," Laura said to Mike. "I know you hate it, but I insist!"

Mike got up and moved awkwardly about the dance floor with her. They didn't speak for a while. He could feel Laura's body pressing gently against his.

"How have you been?" she asked.

"I'm all right. You?"

"I'm always happy," Laura said. "Maybe that's a great lack in me. I do things, then never look back. Is that terrible of me?"

"Only if you hurt people."

"I try not to hurt Jason, if that's what you mean." He didn't answer. "Did anything ever exist between us?" she said.

"Not really. You thought I was someone else. I was always someone else for you."

"Yes."

He felt her pull back from him. What might have happened between them was buried by time. It would always be there, encrusted in the past, but it would continue to fade and merge with dreams. Time spun masks, scars of the thinnest tissue, dreams parading as reality.

* * *

The next morning he traveled down to the Lower East Side to spend the day with his parents. It saddened Mike to see how they had aged. They spoke of the people who had moved from the neighborhood, the ones who had died. They were concerned about the Jews of Europe. "A terrible thing is happening, Mikey," his father said. "Why won't the world do anything?" His tone was plaintive, confused. Gone was the fire of the earlier years.

His mother questioned him about Lisa. Was she a good housekeeper? Did she cook? Was she pretty? Beneath the delving was pain and reproach: the girl he had married was not Jewish.

Mike told them his wife was pregnant, and they pretended to be happy; their enthusiasm was forced. He had married a gentile and their grandchild would not be a Jew. The line of tradition would be broken.

Their family would exist no more.

In the afternoon Mike took a stroll through the neighborhood. It hadn't changed. Tenement blocks had been torn down and replaced by parks and housing projects, yet the essence of the place remained. The grimness, the despair, remained.

What had become of the dreams—his sketches, his plans!—the passion for a more beautiful life for his family, his neighbors?

He reached the settlement house on Rutgers Square. There were no lights on. He tried the door. It was locked.

The heart of the ghetto was dying.

When Bill O'Dwyer decided to run for district attorney of Brooklyn, he came to Tony to ask for support.

Tony discussed it with La Guardia, who exploded: "It's a lousy Tammany plot. O'Dwyer has a lifetime judge's job. Why's he giving it up to run for D.A.?"

"He's determined to break the Brooklyn mob."

"You're naive," La Guardia said heatedly. "I use my nose in these situations. It smells like garbage. Don't touch it. Already people are whispering in my ear . . ."

"What?"

"I'm not talking about you, Tony. I'm talking about your brothers. Jack Foster's union is giving preferential treatment."

"Do you believe that?"

"I know it's not true," La Guardia said. He was angry, felt betrayed. "Maybe it's best you work for O'Dwyer. We need to put some distance between us. It pains me. I like you, you big Irishman."

"I hate going like this," Tony said.

The mayor made an impatient wave of his hand. "Get out of here," he said.

The break with La Guardia was painful, but there was nothing else he could do. Bill-O had come to him for support—how could he turn him down? Bill-O was family, a good, just man. He owed Bill-O his loyalty.

And so Tony came back to the Democratic party.

The day after Bess McGrath heard her son had returned to the fold, she moved back into the house and John McMahon organized a grand celebration. All the old crowd from the United Irish Club was there. There were speeches, laughter, tears, songs.

Suddenly the room was alive with reminiscenses of Tony's career. Thinking back on the old days, the championship days, brought the glow of those good times back into the house, the times when the world belonged to Tony McGrath and Tammany, when they all rode the tiger, rode the majesty of power, secure in their alliances and friendships, political jobs, family. It was a time when they were all family, and now they were together again.

Bill-O sat at the piano and began to play. Bess came forward, and while Bill-O played "After the Ball," Tony and Bess danced a slow waltz while the crowd sang. "Ah Tony, Tony, it's good to be back," Bess said. "I've missed you. I've missed you so bad."

Tony kissed her on the cheek and the crowd whistled and applauded. Then Bess took Theresa by the hand and pulled her to Tony, and he and his wife danced.

After the ball is over/ After the break of dawn/ After the dancers' leaving/ After the break of dawn/ Many a heart is aching/ If you could read them all/ Many the hearts are aching/ After the ball.

Later, Tony sat with John McMahon. "Will Roth fight me?"

"We're trying to work it out. They need us, but he's stubborn. I don't know, Tony. I just don't know."

Inside, Tony McGrath was seized by a great anguish. Nothing in his life had been truly right since the days of his teens and early twenties, the brawling days of his youth, the days of fights and glory. Nothing in his life had been truly right since Mike Roth had beaten him.

36

Mike Roth agonized, but he couldn't bring himself to fight McGrath again. He was torn. He knew how crucial the pavilion was to DuBois-Roth's future: if they were to challenge CCNA, it had to be built. McGrath Construction could make it possible. Yet something unyielding in the core of him would not permit him to do what he knew he must do: fight Tony McGrath.

Jason Karl conveyed the news to John McMahon, who looked glum.

"Tony is insane on this thing. He won't do anything unless Mike agrees to fight him again."

Jason and Mike went from meeting to meeting, trying to secure financing for the pavilion. All of Jason's usual sources backed off: no one would risk going up against CCNA.

Every day Mike received optimistic reports from Elias DuBois detailing the progress of the work. They were about to come up with a major breakthrough. He swore to Mike that they could challenge CCNA and beat them. It was all bound up in a single demand: Mike Roth would have to fight Tony McGrath again. And this he could not do.

When things looked bleakest, word suddenly came from John McMahon: Tony had changed his mind. McGrath Construction would build the pavilion. They would defer payment.

Why had Tony reconsidered? Mike asked himself. Was he trying to get Mike Roth in his debt? Would he try to use this debt to force him to fight again?

Papers were drawn up, notes signed, and work on the pavilion begun. Mike attempted to contact McGrath to thank him; his calls went unanswered.

Elias DuBois came to New York to set up the exhibit. Despite the glowing reports he had given Mike over the phone, he now seemed less sure of things. Mike pressured him: they were out on a limb. Would they be able to challenge CCNA?

"Trust me," DuBois insisted. "Trust me." He said it without conviction, and suddenly Mike didn't trust him.

He and two assistants started work at the fairground. They stayed there around the clock, living in temporary huts while McGrath Construction labored on the pavilion. Mike tried to see how the work was progressing, but DuBois barred him from the lab area. They argued. DuBois grew more and more uncommunicative, nervous. He lost weight and rarely slept or ate. Mike found him at odd hours of the night wandering the fairgrounds alone.

Mike Roth was seized by concern. Was the man having a breakdown? Was the whole thing a delusion? Did DuBois know deep down that they could never overtake CCNA?

Jason Karl and his friends had invested considerable sums in DuBois-Roth, and the company was heavily in debt to McGrath Construction. The newspapers had begun to play up the competition between DuBois-Roth and CCNA. If they didn't come up with *something,* the humiliation would be immense, the financial loss devastating.

During this time things were becoming increasingly tense between Mike and his wife. He thought about her constantly and discovered that he missed her terribly. He called Lisa every day and tried to get her to come to New York, but she displayed great coolness toward him over the phone: his calls were an annoyance.

The thought of their child filled him with wonder and anxiety. If they were to bring a child into this world, things must improve between them. Instead, they were growing worse, and he was powerless to stem the deterioration. There had been love and promise, but it had begun to rot and die. Was it her ambition? The power of Louis B. Mayer? His inability to recapture the passion and strength of his earlier years?

It was terrible, he realized, to have once been a champion.

"Hubbard Farrell would like to meet with us." Jason Karl phoned Mike in his hotel room. "Dinner tonight."

They discussed Farrell, whom Jason had known for a number of years. A man of considerable brilliance, the son of missionaries, he had a reputation for cunning, energy, ruthlessness. He was a world traveler, explorer, inventor, news correspondent. He also had a talent for marrying well. His first wife left him the fortune that formed the base of his broadcast empire, CCNA. His present wife, Patricia, was the daughter of a founder of Standard Oil. An accomplished journalist in her own right as well as an expert airplane pilot, she was considered the perfect mate for someone as flamboyant and adventurous as Hubbard Farrell.

"He's formidable, Mike," said Jason. "Very bright, completely unprincipled."

"Why should we meet with him?"

"It could be instructional. Since we're jousting with him, we should take this opportunity to size him up. You're a scrapper. I think you might enjoy it."

Jason, Laura, and Mike met at the Ritz-Carlton Hotel and entered the dining room. Farrell and his wife were already there. Near fifty, tall and handsome with gray hair and a hawklike face, Hubbard Farrell possessed a sleek athleticism. He might have been an ex-football player, a prizefighter. His wife was considerably younger, perhaps thirty, small with a freckled face and red hair. If Farrell looked as though he could have been a football star in his youth, Patricia was the all-American girl who had cheered him on.

The dinner went off pleasantly enough. Nothing was said about the purpose of the meeting, although Mike could feel Farrell sizing him up, studying his dress, his manners. The Farrells were superb storytellers and they complemented one another, yet their styles were in severe contrast. Hub Farrell took himself very seriously. His tales had a single underlying point: in a dangerous situation no man was more brave and accomplished than Hubbard Farrell; he was a hero creating and defining his own legend.

His wife minimized it all. She was witty and lighthearted and found their adventures mostly silly. She took delight in puncturing her husband's guise of infallibility; she humanized him, made his pomposity palatable.

Not until coffee arrived did Hub Farrell edge around to what was on his mind. "How are you and my old friend Elias DuBois getting along?"

"Very well," answered Mike.

Farrell waved the waiter over and ordered brandies for everyone. "This ridiculous race we're involved in is wasteful and unnecessary. We're rational men, you and I, Mike, which is more than I can say for poor Elias. Why don't we work out a settlement?" Farrell was smiling now, and his smile was not attractive: it had a little too much dazzle in it, too many teeth.

"What sort of settlement?"

"Look, I'm already involved in enough patent suits with Elias. Let's admit that your company might have something we need and work out a licensing arrangement. We'd make a nice little deal which would let us take over your patents."

"I think you'd have to talk to Elias about that."

"The man is unreasonable."

"He feels somehow that you've used him badly in the past. He thinks you're a crook."

The smile remained fixed on Farrell's face, but the effort it took was enormous. "Look," he said with forced reasonableness, "Elias DuBois is a fraud. To be characterized as a crook by him is really a compliment. He's been slandering me for years. The truth of the matter is, we both did significant work with Marconi. Marconi controlled the major patents. The only things I took with me when I left Marconi were a few of my own minor enhancements of Marconi's work—"

"The regenerative grid?"

"That's one."

"Elias feels the regenerative grid is not minor," said Mike, "and he also claims he's the one who developed it."

"Insane." The effort to smile had done Farrell in. It faded as though a switch had been thrown. "Look, all that's in the hands of the courts. They'll decide."

"Until they do, I don't really see how Elias could do business with you."

Farrell shrugged and stared into his snifter. "And what's all this scuttlebutt about some grand surprise you people are planning for the fair? Some rabbit out of the hat?"

"If I told you, it wouldn't be much of a surprise."

"Surprises can be costly for everyone. I want to be rational about this whole thing." Farrell had dropped the pretense of affability now. His voice had a nasty edge to it. "If you really have something, a major company like ours could help you put it over."

Mike said nothing.

"Is it a color system?"

"You'll find out at the fair."

"It can't be color," Farrell stated. "If he's told you that, he's selling you a bill of goods. Color is at least a decade away."

Mike didn't answer. He noticed Hub Farrell's wife staring at him, and her eyes were smiling. She was enjoying her husband's discomfort.

On the way home to the Waldorf, Jason said, "He can be a dangerous enemy."

"Good," Mike answered. "I need an enemy like that. I need to get the blood pumping again."

"This isn't the prizefight ring."

"Any tough fight has a cleansing effect."

"Farrell was worried," Laura said.

"Yes," Jason agreed. "He must feel DuBois is on to something."

"Does he really have a rabbit in his hat, Mike?" asked Laura.

"My worry is that may be all he has," Mike Roth said. No one laughed.

On the opening day of the World's Fair, Mike arrived alone at Flushing Meadows shortly after dawn. A few groundsmen in white were already at work doing some final tidying up.

He strolled through the main fair area, along tree-lined avenues, past lawns, gardens, fountains. Through the greenery Mike could see the rainbow-colored pavilions of the nations represented at the fair. Beyond, a worker threw a switch and a series of fountains sent geysers of water erupting in the center of a lagoon. Mike moved along a wide, elm-bordered mall, between an immense statue of George Washington and the theme structures of the fair, a seventy-foot obelisk and globe, the Trylon and Perisphere.

He passed the Court of Peace, a vast quadrangle framed with pavilions. Colorful flags of the nations of the Court snapped in the wind. Court of Peace: it was a curiously optimistic concept in this tense month, May 1939.

He came to the Court of Communications. He entered the DuBois-Roth pavilion, a white plaster amphitheater. DuBois and his crew were struggling with last-minute preparations for their exhibit.

A dozen nine-inch circular television screens were arranged in a crescent at the far end of the amphitheater. The sets were on, but there was no picture. The screens were riotous with movement, a crazy herringbone jumble of zigzag lines.

DuBois paced in the center of the amphitheater. His expression looked bleak. He spotted Mike and stopped. His voice was hoarse with cigarettes and fatigue. "He sabotaged us. Farrell did it. He sabotaged us."

"What are you talking about?"

"Look!" DuBois yelled, waving at the television sets. "They got to the transmitter. They wrecked it. Farrell did it, goddam it!" He yanked a cigarette out of a pack, lit up, took several puffs and threw it to one side. "What time do the ceremonies start?"

"Two o'clock," Mike said. It would be the official opening of the fair, and DuBois-Roth and CCNA were to broadcast the ceremonies.

"We can't make it," said DuBois. He didn't look at Mike.

"What are you trying to say, Elias?"

"I told you he was a lying, thieving son of a bitch! He sabotaged us. He knew we had him beat, and so he did this. I'll sue the bastard for his underwear. I'll own his balls!"

All strength and energy drained from Mike Roth. They wouldn't make it. Elias DuBois had courted disaster, and disaster is what he had achieved. "The demonstration is off? Is that what you're telling me?"

"I don't know."

"What about broadcasting film? We don't need the transmitter for that."

"I don't know whether or not we can run film."

"If it's the transmitter . . ."

"That's something else. This has nothing to do with the transmitter."

"What is it, then?" DuBois didn't answer. "Forget about the opening ceremonies," Mike said. "The fair is going to be on for a long time. Are we going to have an exhibit or not?"

DuBois looked like a caged animal. He avoided Mike's gaze. He paced, lighting cigarettes, taking a few puffs, then throwing them to the floor.

"Elias, months ago you guaranteed me we'd have an exhibit. Everything is on the line now. What's the problem? First you tell me it's the transmitter, then you say it's something else. What is it?"

"I can't do my work with you breathing down my neck!" DuBois shouted. "Either you have faith in me or you don't. And if you don't, fine. I'll just pack up and get myself another partner. There are thousands just panting to get in on this thing."

"You assured me we'd be ready today. Now you can't even assure me we'll ever be ready! I've gone with you every step of the way, but you lied to me. You lied!" Mike was yelling now; he'd come as far as he could with DuBois.

DuBois had conned and hustled him. He had used his money and the money of his friends, his reputation, his goodwill. His system was a madman's dream, a shot in the dark. They would have nothing.

Mike turned and hurried from the exhibition area. His worst fears were realized. DuBois had deceived him. He had made grand claims that he could never achieve. Mike had drawn Jason Karl into the project, and everything they owned was now in hock to McGrath Construction. The national press and radio were waiting to break the story: DuBois-Roth television had arrived.

There was nothing. Twelve television sets of crazy-quilt patterns, circuits gone insane. A fiasco.

Mike found a pay phone and tried to call California. He had difficulty in getting through. Why was he calling? To tell his wife their world was collapsing? When the circuit was finally completed, the phone rang and rang. Lisa didn't answer.

At the entrance to the fairgrounds a huge crowd had gathered. President Franklin D. Roosevelt and his family had arrived. They were brought to the enormous Federal Building, where a buffet luncheon for visiting dignitaries was in progress. A thousand guests, including senators and representatives brought from Washington on a special train, were in attendance.

Mike entered the building. He found Jason and Laura at a table not far from Roosevelt and his family. "How does it look?" Jason asked.

"Not good."

"What's the trouble?"

Mike just shook his head.

Hub Farrell and his wife stopped by the table. "We're all waiting for DuBois to pop his rabbit from his hat," Farrell said. He flashed a wolfish grin, baring his teeth. "Everything on the money?"

"A few minor problems," answered Mike.

"Hubbard's system is *smashing*," said Pat Farrell. "Can you believe it? Snow in May! If you squint your eyes very tight and get your nose right up to the screen, the picture almost makes sense! This whole television thing is *silly!*" She laughed. Hub Farrell didn't seem amused, though he continued to smile. Pat Farrell gave a small shrug and rolled her eyes toward the ceiling; then the two of them moved off.

Fifty thousand people participated in the opening ceremonies. Troops with colors flying, bands playing, marched smartly along the grand mall—khaki-clad soldiers, bluejackets from the Atlantic Squadron, snappy-looking marines, Coldstream Guards in their busbies. High above the reviewing stand, Mike could see the CCNA television platform; on a scaffold next to it was the DuBois-Roth camera.

La Guardia and Roosevelt spoke. The CCNA camera area was furious with activity, men rushing back and forth, adjusting lenses, tinkering with cables. The DuBois-Roth cameraman sat on the edge of his scaffold eating his lunch and watching the proceedings through a pair of binoculars. He was not televising the ceremony.

After, Mike walked with Jason and Laura back to the exhibition area. Elias DuBois was nowhere to be seen. The sets were on, but there was no live broadcast: a film strip was running. A small crowd watched the film played on all twelve sets.

It was the newsreel of Mike Roth's second fight with Tony McGrath.

Mike turned and left the pavilion, with Jason and Laura following. "We're beaten, Jay. We missed it. We have no way to broadcast."

They stood outside the pavilion and watched the crowds milling around. There was a line in front of CCNA's exhibit.

"What do we do now?" Jason asked himself as much as Mike.

"We're going to have some fun!" Laura said. "This is a fair, dammit, and there are some pretty miraculous things to see. I want to see them!"

Mike tried to beg off, but she wouldn't hear of it. "Look, this DuBois is a bozo. He's costing us a mint. All right, if that's it, that's it, but I'm not going to let him ruin the World's Fair for me. No sir!"

She dragged them from exhibit to exhibit—to the Crystal Lassies, a huge glass polygon in which a flower of nude female dancers blossomed on a mirrored floor, and to the General Motors Futurama, where they traveled on moving chairs over hundreds of mock-up miles of American landscape past cities, towns, mountains, farmlands. Traffic flowed along fourteen-lane motor highways; factories belched smoke; whole cities glowed. A recorded voice described the future, the year 1970: people would live in villages built around a single factory; the chief source of power would be liquid air; cancer would be cured; houses would be made of disposable plastic; poverty and disease would be eradicated; labor would be handled by robots; people would spend all their time reading, learning, listening to good music, having fun.

Mike took it all in, but little of it registered. 1970! What did that matter now? He could only think of DuBois and their monumental failure.

Later they went to a ceremony at the Academy of Sports, where Joe Louis, the heavyweight champion, and Tony Galento, an immense tub of a fighter who had challenged Louis for his title, were introduced to the gathering by Mayor La Guardia. Mike Jacobs, the promoter for the Twentieth Century Sporting Club, was with Louis. Tony McGrath and his party were all seated at the edge of the exhibition ring where the ceremonies were taking place.

La Guardia was having a grand time. He squared off with Galento, teased Louis, who looked shy and uncomfortable. La Guardia asked him to say a few words and he mumbled a greeting to the crowd.

The mayor called Tony McGrath and Mike Roth to the ring. "We have here in this ring now three of the greatest heavyweight champions the world has ever known—Mike Roth, Tony McGrath, and the Brown Bomber, Mr. Joe Louis. If we could send these three over to Germany to have a talk with Mr. Hitler, I'm sure all the trouble with that lousy bum would be over before it got started. Tony and Mike, you are both young men still in your prime. It would be a great treat for you to reenter the heavyweight division. I think Mr. Louis has been having too easy a time of it with bums like Two Ton Tony Galento."

Everyone laughed, Galento most of all. McGrath stepped to the microphone. "Mr. Mayor, I agree with what you just said. I'd like nothing better than to have a go at it once again with Mike Roth. For five years now I've been trying to get him back in the ring with me. Well, now I have him here, but I can't seem to get him to put on the gloves again."

La Guardia turned the microphone over to Mike Roth. "I think that Mr. McGrath and I are grown men now, beyond the point where it would make sense to beat each other's brains out—"

There were scattered boos from the crowd. "You're afraid of him!" someone yelled out.

"Yeah!" "Fight him, Roth!" "Fight him!"

Mike Jacobs pushed his way to the microphone. "As the representative of the Twentieth Century Sporting Club, I would be more than happy to see McGrath and Roth returned to the heavyweight division. We would sponsor a fight between them, with the winner to fight the current heavyweight champion, Joe Louis—"

The crowd cheered. Roth, La Guardia, and McGrath left the ring. There were a few more short speeches, then Louis boxed an exhibition round with a sparring partner.

It was the first time Mike had seen Louis in action. He was impressive, smooth as glass, swift, with a compact effortless style. He was taking it easy on the other fighter, yet his punches cracked in with telling effect, sharp, ripping blows that staggered the other man. Mike found himself wondering how he would have done against him. He glanced over at Tony McGrath and wondered if he was asking himself the same question.

A terrible awareness now came upon him: he was thirty-three years old. If DuBois-Roth collapsed, what would he do? Could he come back to the ring? Could he fight McGrath again, Joe Louis, even Tony Galento? The world of boxing seemed alien to him now, yet fighting was the only trade he really knew. Would he be forced to go back to it?

The sparring ended and everyone applauded. People moved toward the exit. Jason, Laura, Tony McGrath and his wife stood in a group talking to Mike Jacobs and Louis, while news photographers called out for pictures. Flash bulbs exploded. People shouted. Someone was yelling his name. Someone else waved him over to the crowd. He left the building and crossed the mall to the Court of Communications. Huge floodlights had been set up in front of the Perisphere and Trylon. A crowd had gathered. La Guardia was holding a press conference while newsreel cameras rolled. Next to the newsreel cameras were the television cameras of CCNA and DuBois-Roth.

As he approached the DuBois-Roth exhibit area he met a large crowd of people streaming toward the pavilion. The entrance was jammed with people. He pushed his way through them.

Inside, the place was filled to the back wall. As Mike entered, a roar went up. The crowd was applauding him, calling his name, screaming congratulations.

He reached the center of the amphitheater. DuBois saw him and rushed to meet him. He threw his arms around Mike and embraced him.

Mike gazed up at the semicircle of television sets. The conference with La Guardia danced in front of him, each set carrying a picture of stunning clarity and brilliance.

Mike stared at the sets and he couldn't quite comprehend what he was seeing. He shook his head, stunned. The picture was in color—beautiful, dizzying, overwhelming!

"We have them! We have CCNA!" DuBois screamed. "We've done it in color, Mike. An electronic color system, and it's fully compatible with black and white! We've done it all! We own the world, goddammit, we own the world!" He leaned close to Mike. "The dove I told you about, the dove who gives me the ideas? She finally came back to me. . . ."

37

"Why don't you fly out here tomorrow?"

"I can't. Something has come up with my career . . ."

Mike Roth was on the phone to Lisa from the World's Fair grounds, where a celebration was still in progress in the DuBois-Roth pavilion. Word had spread of DuBois-Roth's spectacular color television system, and the pavilion had been swamped with newspaper folk, politicians, businessmen, entertainers.

Mike Roth shouted through the din to Lisa, "Don't you understand? Elias has done it! We're years ahead of everybody in the industry. Hubbard Farrell and CCNA will have to come begging to us in order to participate—"

"I can't come out there just now."

"We're going to be reorganizing the company. It could be two more weeks—"

"Something has come up for me here."

"What?"

"I'll let you know when I'm certain about it. I don't want to jinx anything."

He hung up feeling depressed. She had received the news of DuBois-Roth's triumph with relative indifference. He couldn't persuade her to come to New York. Nothing seemed to be right in their relationship.

Over the next week Mike and DuBois met with patent lawyers, underwriters, financial consultants. The enthusiasm for the DuBois-Roth color television system was unbounded. They were bombarded with offers of financial backing.

Jason Karl worked with them to set everything up as tightly as possible. It was a tricky time. Things must be done properly. Jason explained: "CCNA has enormous sums invested in black-and-white television technology. There are other companies in the field similarly involved. There's going to be a battle with the Federal Communications Commission to see which system will prevail."

DuBois suddenly became agitated. "Farrell will fix the damn thing! He'll never let us beat him out. CCNA buys and sells those damn government bureaucrats!"

Jason brought a prominent patent attorney with him. "My advice is to come to an accommodation with CCNA," the lawyer said. "Make a licensing agreement with them. It'll be cheaper and better in the long run than a disastrous court battle."

"The son of a bitch has stolen me blind all these years. Now I have him on the hook, and I'll be damned if I'm going to let him squirm off," DuBois insisted.

With fresh financing, the company was restructured. The McGrath Construction loan was retired. Three corporate sections were formed: development, broadcast, and manufacturing. There would be A and B stock. DuBois and Mike would control the A stock, which gave them operating control of the company; DuBois would be president, Mike vice-president. The B stockholders, Jason and his group of investors, would control three subordinate corporation positions as well as three seats on an eight-man board of directors.

In order to battle for licenses and markets, the company would be moved to New York. It was just too distant in California to carry out the fight effectively.

The World's Fair broadcast had been generated under a temporary license. Now they would have to secure a more permanent arrangement with the federal government. They would apply for licenses in Los Angeles, New York, and a Midwestern city—Pittsburgh, Cleveland, or Chicago.

"You have a war on your hands," the patent attorney said. "You're asking CCNA to cave in completely. It's going to be a long, bitter fight."

"Good," DuBois crowed. "The more grief I can cause that arrogant, larcenous bastard Farrell, the better I'll feel."

DuBois and Roth returned to California to prepare for the move east.

Mike's first night home, he and Lisa dined at a seafood restaurant in Ocean Park. The restaurant was on a pier overlooking the water. She was now in her fifth month of pregnancy and it was beginning to show.

She was quiet, subdued, strangely indifferent to her husband's presence. Mike found himself pushing too hard, fighting to generate enthusiasm, trying to reach her. "We'll wait until after the baby is born, then move east," he said. "They won't need me there for another few months. Believe me, it's going to work out fine with your career. Television is going to need actresses. We'll be doing dramatic plays, variety shows."

She toyed with her food. She didn't speak for a while. "I'm not going to New York with you," she said at last.

Mike gazed out the window at the water. He heard her and yet he couldn't *feel* the sense of her words. Things were tense with them, but they *had* to work out. The sun had just gone down, the sky was muddy orange, streaked with gray.

"I'm happy for you, Mike. I just can't give up here."

"Don't you see, it can't work out for you here. If you want a career, believe me, on the East Coast—"

"There's a complication," she said. "While you've been gone, I've been seeing someone."

He stared at her, stunned. He could feel the pier sway with the heave of the ocean. It was as though his world was collapsing. "Who?"

"Ben Siegel. He called when you were gone. He's trying to get me back into MGM."

He fought to keep himself under control. He felt a great emptiness within, a feeling of everything falling away from him. "How does he plan on doing that?"

"Mayer is having union problems. He's helping Mayer."

"Why is he doing this for you?" She didn't answer. "Have you slept with him?" She put her hand to her eyes and covered them.

"Please, Michael, I don't want to hurt you. I tried to figure out a way to work it so it wouldn't happen this way. I should never have married. I didn't want it. You pushed it on me. I didn't want to have a kid. I want my own life . . ."

"Do you know what he is?"

"People tell me things, but I don't believe them. I see a respected man, a powerful man. He loves me and he's going to help me."

"Ben Siegel is a man who kills people. Do you understand that? Kills."

"I know him differently."

"Lisa, our child is inside you. You can't do this . . ." He was pleading and his voice was thin and harsh now and he hated the sound of it, but there was nothing he could do. His anguish poured from him. "You can't do this."

She began to weep. "I care for you deeply, Michael. I didn't want this. Please, just let me go. Move to New York. Become wildly successful. Just let me live my own life."

He stared out at the water. The sky was dark now.

In September a child was born to them, a boy. They named him Matthew. Two weeks later Lisa drove to Nevada, where she filed for divorce.

In the midst of the divorce proceedings, as Mike prepared to leave for New York, the German army invaded Poland.

38

Tony McGrath indulged himself in a little routine when he was working late at the Brooklyn district attorney's office. He would take a break for ten minutes or so and do a couple of fast rounds with the jump rope, fifty push-ups and fifty sit-ups, then shadowbox until he worked up a sweat.

It got the blood circulating, eased the tension.

They were closing in on the Brooklyn mobs. A break was imminent in the Harry Roth murder case. Word came to the office that Abe Reles, on the run for nearly a year, was looking to make a deal.

Bill O'Dwyer won the election as district attorney. He brought in John McMahon as his chief clerk and Tony as special assistant. He continued Tom Dewey's strategy: keep the pressure on the street-level hoods, slap them with any charge you could make stick, sow seeds of discord, work your way up the ladder.

Something would crack. When it did, like a house of cards the mob would collapse. Reles, Foster, Siegel, Lansky, Buchalter—they would all fall.

Tony finished his workout. He washed at a sink in the corner of the office, then returned to his desk and began to work his way through stacks of interrogation transcripts.

A pattern was emerging: Reles and his group had been operating not just in Brooklyn but over the whole United States. The murder of Harry Roth was just one in a staggering epidemic of killings in Jersey, Chicago, Kansas City, Pittsburgh, Los Angeles. It was a brutal, ugly tangle of murder with all lines stretching to Brooklyn, all knots tied in Brooklyn.

Bill-O entered the office. He looked tired but he was smiling. "Get your coat," he said.

"What is it?"

"Reles. He's coming in."

Outside it was a bitter mid-January night. Snow was falling. Two detectives sat in Bill-O's car. At curbside a convoy of cars filled with detectives waited.

In the rear seat of Bill-O's car, Tony leaned back. A great rush of excitement surged through him. His body tingled with it, the same rush he used to experience in the dressing room just before a fight. Reles!

"Walter Winchell is bringing him in, lad," said Bill-O. They sped through the darkened Brooklyn streets followed by an army of detective cars.

"What kind of deal?" Tony asked.

"He cracks the mob open for us. We let him plead guilty to second-degree murder. We ask the court for consideration."

It was the wedge they needed. With Reles's testimony they could work their way right up to the top.

At Van Brunt Street on the Brooklyn waterfront the car slowed. The area was blocked off by police cars. At the end of the street McGrath could see a dark Plymouth with two men in it. They drove to the end of the block and came to a stop opposite the parked car. The driver got out and approached Bill-O's car. Bill-O rolled the window down.

A short, scowling man peered into the car—Walter Winchell. His voice was harsh and nasal. "This man is my responsibility, Bill. Play this one right, you'll be the biggest name in the country. Bigger than Dewey. I'm giving you front page on this, a political home run."

"Politics has nothing to do with it," Bill O'Dwyer said.

Winchell smiled. It was a tight smile by a man unused to smiling. "Don't shit a shitter. Everything is politics. The only boy scouts are camping up at Bear Mountain." He turned and waved. Abe Reles stepped from the parked car.

The two detectives in the front of O'Dwyer's car got out. They looked wary. "Easy," Bill-O said. "Everything's going to be all right."

Running on the lam seemed to have agreed with Reles. He had gained weight, looked plump and relaxed, sported a tan. He was dressed as though planning a night out on the town, blue shirt with matching tie, blue pin-striped suit. He slid into the backseat of the car next to Tony.

Bill-O shook hands with Winchell through the open window. "Thank you, Walt," he said.

"Write a good story," Reles added. "One that'll sell a lot of papers."

"How about 'Kid Twist Reles Gets the Chair'?" Tony said.

"What are you, a comedian now, fucking Irishman!" Reles lisped grinning. He was having a good time.

At the Municipal Building Reles was taken upstairs to the fourth floor by a rear elevator. Bill-O, an assistant D.A. by the name of Fargas, and Tony sat with Reles in an inner office. The front office was filled with detectives. "We won't get down to business until tomorrow, Abe," Bill-O said. "We're arranging things now so that we can keep you safe."

For the next hour people came in and out of the office, conferred with O'Dwyer and Fargas. Sandwiches were brought in. Reles declined to eat. "Walter and I had a terrific dinner at Lindy's," he said.

O'Dwyer and Fargas left Reles and Tony alone in the room together. "Who would have thought they'd make such a *magilla* for a *putz* like Harry Roth?" Reles said.

"Who'd you kill him for?"

"What are you asking me such a dumb question for? It was a job. I did it for the people who pay the bills. When you fought Harry's brother, it was a job, right? My job, your job. Hey, I hope wherever they put me up, they got a good bed. I don't want no bed like rocks. Hey, Tony, how could you have been such a *zhlub* to let Mike Roth beat you like he did?"

"It happened."

"*Schmuck,* you cost me big money."

"You want to play, you got to pay."

"Very funny. Georgie Jessel write your material?"

"You're going to love it in the can, Twist. Especially when they play hide-the-salami with your butt."

"What kind of thing is that to say? Thick-headed mick! I got hard time facing me, and I got to take a *zetz* from you? Punch-drunk Irish ass-hole!"

Tony hit him. He slammed him against the wall, then banged a double hook off his head. Reles's nose split at the bridge and blood poured from the nostrils.

It felt good. After skipping rope, doing push-ups and sit-ups and shadow boxing, it felt good to hit someone.

O'Dwyer and Fargas came back in. "What happened?" asked Bill-O when he saw Reles, who was sitting on the floor holding his suit coat up to his nose.

"We started talking about boxing. Abe brought up one of my fights. He asked me to demonstrate why I lost."

"Dumb fucking Irishman!" yelled Reles. "You can't fight worth shit. You can't kiss Mike Roth's ass!"

"All right, Abe. Take it easy," Bill-O said.

As dawn light filtered into the room, Reles was taken downstairs and a caravan of detective cars escorted him to Coney Island on the oceanfront. There, at the Half Moon Hotel in the east wing of the sixth floor, Reles was placed in protective custody. Even as he arrived, workmen were installing a wall-to-wall steel divider and door at the end of the wing.

A half-dozen uniformed police including a captain were waiting to watch over him.

39

Mike Roth sat at his living-room window and watched the tugs churning through the waters of the Hudson River. Things were going well, and DuBois-Roth was holding its own in the battle with CCNA. The company had attracted a number of first-rate people. It was well-funded. They had the most advanced television system in the world.

They set up manufacturing facilities in an old two-story brick warehouse building in Passaic, New Jersey. Mike took an apartment in a nineteenth-century row house in Ft. Lee, on the palisade across the Hudson from upper Manhattan. After a long day at the factory, he would return to the apartment, sit by the window, and watch the lights winking on across the river, the grand sweep of the George Washington Bridge, the boats plying their way along the river. It reminded him of the times when, as a boy, he would climb onto the roof of his tenement building and look out over the city.

It was only late at night, as he lay in bed trying to sleep, that a feeling of great emptiness seized him. He would think of his son, Matthew, three thousand miles away, of Lisa, his former wife. They were lost to him now. Lisa lived in a large house in Beverly Hills with Ben Siegel as her protector, her lover. She was working once again as an actress.

Ben Siegel! Mike thought of his son being raised in the same house with him, and the anger he felt was enormous. He would lie in bed damp with perspiration, his hands clenched in tight fists, and sleep would not come.

The river was filled with mist now. The lights of Manhattan glowed through the fog. The phone rang, rousing him from his reverie.

It was Bill O'Dwyer. "Abe Reles has been taken into custody," he said. "He's confessed to the murder of your brother. He had two other men with him on the job. He'll be testifying against them."

"What about the other ones, the ones on the top? Ben Siegel? Foster?"

"One thing at a time. I can't promise anything."

"Without them, though—what do you have? Nothing." It was important they get Ben Siegel.

"We're doing our best. Everyone down here is doing his best."

Mike Roth hung up and stared out the window, and all he could think of was how the murderers still walked the earth.

Tony McGrath was not happy at how things were progressing in the Reles matter. True, the killers of Harry Roth were coming to trial, the men who had done the actual work, but those who had planned and ordered it—they were still free. Aside from Lepke Buchalter, who had been nailed by Dewey, all the big boys had managed to escape prosecution.

He pressed the point with O'Dwyer. O'Dwyer was evasive. Things must be taken one at a time. They were dealing with a vast combine of killers. Time and patience. Corroboration. They would reach the top—one of these days.

Reles was spilling reams of incriminating testimony, but he went at it in a maddeningly discursive way. And always the big boys were left out of it.

Assistant D.A. Fargas was given the responsibility for the Reles case. Tony kept after him: Get Jack Foster. Make Reles give him up. If Foster falls, the whole pyramid of killers would come tumbling down.

The work was ugly and frustrating. Jack Foster was just out of reach. Reles would come close to him, then veer away. Tony knew that Foster had engineered Harry Roth's murder. He followed every aspect of the interrogations, worked impossibly long hours, rode herd on Fargas and his aides. Get Jack Foster.

Tony felt fleeting moments of guilt. He was hardly home at all these days. He slept on the couch in his office, neglecting his wife, his son. The few times he did get home, Darryl would shy away from him. He was a stranger there.

And yet he could not give up. He had to break Reles. He had to make a case against Foster.

Reles testified to a ghoulish conspiracy of murder, a corporation of killers who had slaughtered hundreds of men across the United States. A half-dozen of Reles's original Brownsville gang formed the core of these killers. Among them were Pittsburgh Phil Strauss and Marty Goldstein, the ones who had performed the actual murder of Harry Roth.

The killers would go to trial, but a link had not been made to Jack Foster. "When the time is ripe, we'll get to Foster," said Bill-O.

* * *

The trial of Harry's murderers began in early fall. Mike Roth appeared in the courtroom every day. He had little interest in Reles, Strauss, or Goldstein. He was concerned only about Jackie Foster.

Pittsburgh Phil grew a beard, feigned insanity, raved that his brain was being tapped. Goldstein, an overweight clown, joked, insulted the judge, badgered the prosecutor. His exuberance faded when Abe Reles took the stand.

Fargas attempted to tie Jack Foster to the crime. "On whose orders did you carry out the murder of Harry Roth?" Bill-O, sitting in the courtroom with Tony, scowled.

"Some people said, 'This guy Harry Roth, someone ought to hurt this bastard.'"

"Who said this?"

"It was just a general thing."

Bill O'Dwyer leaned close to Tony. "What the hell is Fargas doing out there?" he whispered.

During lunch recess Bill-O lashed out at Fargas. "You're clouding things. Keep to the line of questioning we agreed on."

"It's my fault, Bill," Tony said. "I've been pressuring him to crack Reles on Jack Foster."

"Listen to me, lad," Bill-O said heatedly. "We don't want fireworks. We want to build a case as strong as cement."

In the afternoon Reles described the actual killing: "We take Harry back to my house. I think my wife and her mother are at the movies. Well, they're not, so I send my wife out shopping. My mother-in-law, she goes to sleep. I get an ice pick out of the cupboard and a rope from the cellar and Marty and Phil they go to work on Harry. Harry bites Phil on the hand and Phil goes wild 'cause he thinks he's going to get rabies."

The court adjourned for the day following Reles's testimony. Mike sat in the courtroom for a long time after everyone had gone. He remembered how eager Harry had always been to ingratiate himself with the tough guys of the neighborhood, how much he wanted to be liked. And that was how Harry Roth had died—in the living room of a man he thought was his friend.

Mike had dinner with his parents that night. They didn't talk about the trial. Charlie was very quiet. He stared at his plate and didn't eat much, and Mike knew that he too was thinking about Harry.

Virtually no defense was offered for Pittsburgh Phil Strauss or Marty Goldstein. Ninety minutes after the jury went out, they returned with a verdict of guilty. The judge sentenced the two men to death in the electric chair.

Abe Reles was returned to his room in the Half Moon Hotel.

The war in Europe raged on. Roosevelt defeated Wendell Willkie to gain his third term as President. The situation in the world worsened. Jews seeking to flee Nazi persecution found the havens of the world closed to them.

Work on commercial television was halted: the government needed the technology to prepare for the day when the United States might be forced into the conflict.

On the strength of the publicity generated by the Reles trial—the breaking of what became known as Murder Incorporated—Bill O'Dwyer was chosen by the Democratic party as its candidate for mayor against Fiorello La Guardia.

Tony was troubled. It had been one thing to support O'Dwyer for Brooklyn district attorney, another to back him against the man he felt was the best mayor New York City had ever seen. He couldn't understand why O'Dwyer had chosen to challenge La Guardia.

He loved O'Dwyer, but knew the man lacked any real commitment to ideals. He had none of La Guardia's ferocious passion to salvage the city and its people, to elevate them, redeem them.

Tony met with Bill-O in his office at the Municipal Building in Brooklyn. He had not yet agreed to support him in the election. "What's holding you back?" O'Dwyer said.

"I feel like you're dragging your feet on Jack Foster."

"We haven't a viable case."

"You haven't tried to get one," answered Tony. "I can't understand why we're messing around, why we don't break Reles on this Foster thing. We haven't even tried. I know I can break him. The only thing that would stop him from cracking is if something happened to him . . ."

"What could happen to him? We have him in a fortress."

"Then let me at him!"

"Tony, do you realize what it means if I become mayor? An Irish lad who started out as a longshoreman? I know there are people who doubt that I have it in me, but I can be a great mayor. I can lift up the common people. I can transform this city."

"We have a man who's doing that now, Bill. Why buck a man like La Guardia?"

"You have to grab at your opportunities, boyo. This Reles thing has made me a national figure. The mayor is just another step up the ladder. Perhaps one day . . ." He hesitated, smiled.

"You want to be President?" Tony said. He began to laugh.

"Why not?" said Bill-O, laughing also. "Why not?" They both laughed and laughed at the absurdity of the idea, but Tony sensed that Bill-O had truly considered it.

"Will you let me go after Reles with everything I can? La Guardia's people are going to claim you're a Trojan horse for Tammany. They're starting rumblings already. If we break Reles completely, they'll never be able to say it."

Bill-O puffed for a long time on his cigar. He stared at the wall. "Of course, Tony. Break him on the Jackie Foster thing. But do it gently, lad. It's a delicate area."

Tony traveled down to the Half Moon Hotel. He was taken past the steel door that blocked off the wing where Reles was being kept.

He sat in Reles's room and talked. He pushed hard for Reles to open up on Jackie Foster. "It's the only way you'll ever get out of here."

"If I open up, a lot of big people are going to go under. As soon as you go after Jackie, he'll blow the whistle."

"Tell me about it."

"Thick, fucking mick, don't you know anything? This is all politics. We're talking about going into the highest circles of the Democratic party. We're talking about Washington, people close to the President of the United States!"

"Give me some names."

"Let me think about it."

McGrath went back to Bill-O. "He's going to talk."

"Wait until after the election, lad."

"It's that big?"

Bill-O smiled. "Tony, I don't know what he's going to say. Let's just not open ourselves up to something we can't handle right now."

Bill O'Dwyer lost the election by a slim margin. Tony was right: accusations over the Reles case cost him the election. Fiorello La Guardia became the first mayor in the history of New York City to be elected for a third term.

A week later, Jackie Foster visited a construction site on Neptune Avenue in Coney Island, not far from the Half Moon Hotel. It was not yet light out. He spoke for a short while with the union representative on the job. Two men joined him.

As the sun came up over Jamaica Bay to the east, Foster and the two men walked through the quiet dawn streets to the Half Moon Hotel. They took a rear stairway to the sixth floor. The steel door leading to the wing where Reles was kept was open.

There were no guards.

Foster told the two men to wait for him. He walked down the hallway to Reles's room. "Abe? Abie?"

Reles, asleep in bed, opened his eyes. He stared stunned at Foster standing above him. He couldn't speak or call out.

"They're going to kill you, Abe," Foster said. "Ben Siegel's boys."

"Where are the guards?" Reles could barely get the words out.

"They reached them. There's no one out there. You only have a few minutes. Get dressed."

Reles hurriedly put on a gray suit with a blue-gray sweater underneath. He began to take his topcoat. "Leave that. It'll get in your way."

"What do you mean?"

"They're waiting at the end of the hall, Benny's boys. You'll have to climb out the window. On the floor below, you go into the room, then out the back stairway. I have a car waiting downstairs."

"You're not going to do nothing to me, are you, Jack?" Reles asked, terrified.

"Look for yourself. There's no one guarding the door. How do you think I got in here? They've set it up to kill you. Two of Ben's boys are waiting down the hall. I told them I'd bring you to them. I'm giving you a chance to escape."

They took the sheets off the bed and knotted them together. Then they twisted the cord from the radio around the end of the sheet and tied the wire to the end of the radiator. They pulled hard on the sheets and cord. "Will this support me?" asked Reles.

"It'll hold."

Abe Reles was trembling now. Perspiration poured from him. Why was Jack Foster doing this for him? "Am I awake, Jack? Am I dreaming this? Why is this happening?"

"It's the way I am, Abe. When I'm for someone, I'm loyal to them down the line. If you don't trust me when you get downstairs, just take off."

Reles opened the window, climbed out onto the ledge and lowered himself down the sheet-rope. He reached the fifth-floor window. He got his feet on the ledge. With one hand he began to pull at the window screen.

Jack Foster watched from above. He had a penknife in his hand now. He leaned down and cut the sheet where it was knotted to the radio cord.

Abe Reles plunged to the concrete roof of the hotel's kitchen, forty-two feet below. He landed on his back, breaking his spine.

A furious storm erupted over his death: How had it happened? Who had been responsible?

A month later, it was all forgotten: Japan had invaded Pearl Harbor. The United States was at war.

IV

40

Mike Roth, a major with the Signal Corps, sat in the jeep in the cool predawn and waited. All about, he could sense an immense power, an enormous dark animal, a great metallic army poised to strike.

At morning's first light they would be plunging into battle. The war had been an agony of anticipation for him, and now the moment had arrived: he would be going into the fight.

Next to him in the jeep was Major General Maurice Rose, commander of the Third Armored Division, the man responsible for Mike seeing battle at last. General Rose—large, athletic, with a handsome, somber face—was a legend among members of the invading force. Always in the lead in any attack, he pursued the war with quiet ferocity, total dedication. Mike often wondered what impelled this man. Where did his extraordinary courage come from?

The general checked his watch now, scribbled something in a notebook. "If anything happens," he said, glancing at Mike, "just keep moving forward. Only two kinds of people will hang back—the dead and the dying."

All about them in the dark predawn, a great silence had settled over everything. A blanket of fog had spread in from the ocean, a thick white wall pressing against the night.

It was July in Normandy, on the western section of the Contentin Peninsula, just above St.-Lô. The year was 1944.

The Allied armies had pushed out from their D-day beachheads and were now preparing to strike into the heart of France.

Waiting for the attack to commence, Mike had strangely conflicting emotions. He considered his relationship to General Rose. Though he had been singled out by the general to accompany him into the fight, he didn't feel comfortable with him. He sensed a wariness toward Mike, a veiled hostility. It was unnerving to be moving into battle with a man who didn't particularly like you. He reminded Mike of the woodcutters he had worked with in upstate New York. Mike sensed that the general did not like Jews.

Waiting with General Rose for the attack to begin, he thought of the time leading up to this moment.

At the beginning of 1942, shortly after Pearl Harbor, Jason Karl had approached him. He was working with Henry L. Stimson in the War Department and wanted to know if Mike would accept a commission with the

Signal Corps. He would coordinate electronic development for the armed services, using the resources of DuBois-Roth. The government would provide funding; DuBois would oversee research and development.

He resisted. He was only thirty-six and in good shape. He wanted to see battle. It had to do with the bloodbath of Jews taking place. He wanted to put his body on the line for his people.

"This isn't a prizefight," Jason said. "We're not going to win this thing with you out there throwing punches. DuBois-Roth has valuable technical expertise that the country desperately needs."

Reluctantly he agreed to join the Signal Corps. He came in as a captain, quickly rose to major, spent the next year shuttling between the company's factory in New Jersey and army installations around the country. Development of television was halted. Work went forward at DuBois-Roth on electronic robots, television-guided missiles, precision bomb releases, radar, navigational systems.

On a trip to the West Coast he visited Lisa. She was still attractive, but there was a sadness about her now. Ben Siegel had put her up in a huge house, had helped her with her career. It had not been enough: she would always be a supporting actress, never a star, and this awareness ate away at her.

His son, Matt, a thin, quiet boy, was a beautiful child, but there was no fun in him. He spoke little, never laughed. He had large gray eyes and he would stare at Mike with something like fear in them. It disturbed him, filled him with regret and guilt: how could he have allowed himself to become so separated from his son? How could he have permitted him to remain in a house with Ben Siegel?

He tried to get Lisa to give him custody of the boy. She refused, clinging to Matt with terrifying ferocity. He threatened to bring her into court but didn't. His wife was irrational in the matter; she would have seen the boy torn apart in a brutal legal battle before relinquishing him.

He came away from the visit angered and defeated, so he channeled his frustration into the war. He grew increasingly impatient. He must get into the fight. While he sat in an office or traveled about in an army car hobnobbing with politicians and military brass, people were dying by the thousands.

It became the most important thing in the world to get into battle.

He wrote letters, badgered people, argued with Jason Karl. At last the War Department informed him he could indeed do battle—in the prizefight ring. He was assigned to participate in a series of boxing exhibitions at army bases around the country.

He learned that Tony McGrath was attached to the Air Force as an assistant to Bill O'Dwyer, a colonel now with a special unit investigating procurement fraud. The War Department pressured Mike to put on a series of bouts with McGrath. He refused.

He fought others, though, ranking heavyweights, and he did well. He sparred with Billy Conn, who had almost beaten Joe Louis before the war. He staggered Conn in the second round, then carried him in the third. The exhibition lasted three rounds, and it was more than enough for Mike.

Through the invasion of North Africa, the battle up the boot of Italy, Mike followed the war with increasing frustration. The tide was turning. The Allies were winning. He would never get into it.

In the spring of 1944 he was ordered to report to the commanding officer of the Plant Engineering Agency in Philadelphia. He would touch base with the Signal Corps brass in Washington, then fly overseas without delay to the European war theater. At last the repeated demands he had made to the War Department had paid off. He would be getting into the fight.

He arrived in London at the end of March and was assigned to work on coordinating communications for General Eisenhower at SHAEF, Supreme Headquarters Allied Expeditionary Force. The invasion of France was in the works. A massive radar-jamming operation was being organized, and he was thrust into the thick of it. It was war of a sort, but not battle. He was still on the sidelines.

One evening in early May, as he was having a drink at the Claridge Hotel bar, a woman dressed in khaki outfit and knitted helmet liner pulled over her hair came over to him. She called him by name, but he didn't recognize her. Laughing, she took off the helmet liner. It was Patricia Farrell. "Hub's in Italy with Clark's army, rushing toward Rome. I'm on assignment for *Life* magazine. We've made a deal to meet in Paris. Some way to run a marriage!"

He invited her for a drink and they sat at the bar and toasted television, the war, the impending invasion. Though he hardly knew her, she felt good to be with. She had humor, was a good talker, a better listener. He found himself venting his frustration at not having been able to get into the fight. He realized he was getting drunk, but he didn't care. "I'm a professional at fighting," he said. "I specialize at that sort of thing. And i can't get near this damn war!"

"It's not so much fun, battle," Pat Farrell said.

"I don't care. I want to be there."

Several army brass came into the bar. Pat Farrell waved to an officer she knew, and he joined them. It was General Rose, commander of the Third Armored Division. Mike knew of him, one of the bright, tough tank commanders in Omar Bradley's First Army. He had been raised in the mountains of Colorado and he reminded Mike of a cowboy: he was tall and solidly built. His narrow eyes had a cool, far-off look, as though he were gazing at distant horizons.

"Morry, my friend here is unhappy," Pat Farrell said to the general. "He wants to fight and he has the qualifications. Meet the undefeated heavyweight champion of the world, Mike Roth."

"You're working over at SHAEF, aren't you?"

"I want to get into the war," Mike said, drunk.

The general smiled. He had a lean, leathery face, and his smile was tinged with irony: a prizefighter wanting to do battle, it seemed to say, an Eastern Jewboy. Well, fighting a war was another business. Mike recognized the edge of condescension in the general's attitude and he felt foolish. Drunk and foolish.

After Mike and the general got into a technical discussion of communications problems, Pat Farrell said, "If you gentlemen will excuse me, I'm heading for my digs. I've spent the best years of my marriage chitchatting about electronics. It took a damn war to give me some relief!"

Mike stayed at the bar with General Rose and pleaded his case. He didn't want to be a hero and he didn't want the general to think his passion was empty rhetoric. He wanted the general to know that he was willing to fight and die if need be because Jews were being slaughtered. "They're killing my people," Mike said. "I'm a Jew." His tone was challenging, and he sensed the general stiffen, but he didn't care. "They're killing Jews and I want to help stop them. Do you understand?"

General Rose listened without comment. He stood there stiffly, formally, and Mike sensed the great disdain the man felt for him, but he didn't care. He would fight the man, if need be. He would fight this general if it would help him get into the war.

They parted. Two days later Mike received a call at the hotel from General Rose's adjutant. Inquiries had been made on Mike's behalf; nothing could be done because he was considered indispensable at SHAEF.

The next few weeks Mike spent a good deal of time with Pat Farrell. They drank a lot and talked about their pasts. They revealed more than they might have had there not been liquor and the war. Mike spoke about Tony McGrath, about the pressures to get the two of them into the ring again. "Everybody thinks I'm afraid of him. I'm not afraid."

"Why won't you fight him, then?"

"I have my reasons. I don't want to talk about them."

"And your marriage?" she asked.

He shrugged. "We were just very wrong for each other. I don't feel all that badly about it breaking up. I do feel rotten for my son, though."

"My marriage isn't happy," she said. "It astonishes me that we're still together. I guess it's because I've put so much into it—I just can't cut my losses. The truth of it is, though, Hub Farrell isn't a very nice person. He uses people, he lies. He wants to dominate everyone around him. Every decision he makes in life turns on the question: What does it accomplish for Hubbard Farrell?"

"And you fell in love with him?"

"If I'm really honest, I suppose I did it because of the *drama* of it. It was playacting. We were two people caught in the Spanish Civil War and as *characters* we were a proper fit. I mean, even Ernest Hemingway thought we looked *swell* together. That's how he used to put it: 'You look *swell* together.' I mean, everyone encouraged us to create a legend—it was the thing to do then—so we did. And it wasn't until we came back home from Spain that I realized I didn't much like my co-star." She smiled ruefully. "Who knows—maybe this war will finish it. One of us will get killed, and that will be that. I doubt it'll be Hub. He has an uncanny knack for becoming a hero with little risk to his own skin. When we go into France, I'm sure I'll find myself in the thick of it, and who knows if I'll make it out alive. Hub, though, will come through smelling like a rose, that bastard! And with a chest full of medals, too!"

"I would take it badly if you got killed," Mike heard himself say. She laughed. He was drunk. The room rotated gently about him. Pat Farrell looked extraordinarily lovely, small, pixielike, with a radiance about her that stirred something inside him, made the world seem bright and worthwhile. He leaned across the table and they kissed. She pressed her mouth against his and she kept it open, and he felt as though he were melting into her. "Hey, Roth!" she said, drawing back. "So far I've managed to stay faithful to my husband. When I change my style, I'll look you up." She stood up. She didn't want to leave. "I don't know when I'll see you again, Mike. I'll be going away in the morning."

"The invasion—"

She held her fingers to her lips. "Naughty, naughty." She blew him a kiss and was gone.

He sat there and suddenly he was seized by regret, by a terrible sense of loss. He had let her go. Stupid, stupid! Run after her! he told himself. He didn't move. He was very drunk.

The southern part of England had become one vast military encampment. The greatest amphibious assault in the history of the world was being readied. The Allied armies were poised like a coiled spring to leap the channel into continental Europe.

And Mike Roth would remain in England.

Accompanied by the chief signal officer of the British army, he toured installations at Plymouth, Torquay, Taunton, and Somerset; he visited a floating electronic center aboard the ship *Ancon*, where a thousand men worked at maintaining communications with the invading force.

He returned to the Claridge Hotel and waited. The first of June arrived and the tension around the hotel was palpable. The invasion was at hand.

On the night of June 6 and into the morning hours, wave after wave of bombers pounded the French coast from Pas de Calais to Bordeaux. The day before a fierce storm had raged in the channel. Wind and rain had buffeted London. The rumors hit a pitch of hysteria, then abated with the onset of the storm: an invasion in such abominable weather was out of the question.

Mike Roth was at the Ministry of Information when word came through from SHAEF over the radio, Eisenhower's order of the day: "Soldiers, sailors, and airmen of the Allied Expeditionary Force, you are about to embark on a great crusade, toward which we have striven these many months. The hopes and prayers of liberty-loving people everywhere go with you. In company with our brave allies and brothers in arms on other fronts you will bring about the destruction of the German war machine, elimination of Nazi tyranny over the oppressed peoples of Europe, and security for ourselves in a free world. . . . Good luck, and let us beseech the blessing of the Almighty God upon this great and noble undertaking."

The invasion had begun.

By the beginning of July the Allies had consolidated their hold on Normandy; they had captured Cherbourg, the key port on the Contentin Peninsula. They were now prepared to drive on St.-Lô, the provincial capital.

The second week of July Mike was contacted by the deputy chief of the Army Communication Center. There were grave problems with the Allies' radio installations. V-1 rockets had taken a terrible toll of receiving equipment at Portsmouth. Across the channel, feuding among various factions was creating chaos with transmission.

Mike was sent to Portsmouth first, to assess the damage; he was then flown across the channel in an L-5 liaison plane and arrived in a heavy drizzle. He found the area around Cherbourg a nightmare—a million men in the process of being put ashore, beaches littered with destroyed vehicles, wrecked artillery, blasted pillboxes. Tanks, jeeps, landing carriers, armored trucks, men, clogged the roads in clots that stretched along the coast as far as he could see.

The port of Cherbourg, though captured, was far from operable. A completely new system of roads and debarkation areas was under construction.

For the next days Mike sped from point to point, crisscrossing the bridgehead, through Barneville, St. Sauver, Valognes, Montebourg. He toiled ceaselessly to bring a semblance of order to the Allied communications network. Equipment shipped from England to the French installations in place was finally integrated. Things began to take shape. Messages were sent, received.

He had been in Normandy a week. In that time he had had less than a full night's sleep. It was late in the day. He was stranded on the road to Caretan, stalled in a hopeless tangle of foot soldiers, tanks, jeeps. While his driver left the blocked jeep to see what was holding things up, Mike dozed.

He awoke with a start. Someone was shaking him. "Mind if I hitch a ride?" It was General Rose. "My damn jeep broke an axle."

"Get in!"

The driver returned, and traffic began to move. "You made it to the action," the general said to Mike.

"Is that what they call this?"

"When the generals are thumbing rides, you know things are in a mess," Rose said. He looked tired and angry.

Outside Caretan the convoy came to a halt again. General Rose's headquarters was in a farmhouse not far off. "Come on, you'll have dinner with me," the general said. His manner toward Mike was unchanged, still aloof, vaguely hostile.

After a meal of lumpish stew, Rose brought out brandy and cigars. They had them with coffee as thick as syrup. "I saw Pat Farrell several days ago,"

General Rose said. "She was heading toward St.-Lô. I tried to get her to turn back. All hell is about to break loose down there. She wouldn't listen to me, of course. More guts than brains. How's communications?"

"If the splices hold, we should be all right."

"Why don't you ride with me for a while? We need a communications expert."

During the meal, Mike had noticed the general staring at him. It was not a friendly look. What the hell does he want with me? Mike now thought. "Will we see action?"

"We'll give you a few loose bowels—I guarantee."

He explained that they were about to launch a concerted drive to smash the German forces in the area. The next day, they would be striking at St.-Lô in an attempt to break out of the hedgerow country of the Contentin Peninsula and sweep into the flat wheatfields of the Falaise Plain.

That night Mike Roth stayed at the farmhouse. Lulled by the thud of Allied artillery, he had his first restful sleep in a week.

He was awakened before dawn. General Rose and his officers gathered in the main room of the farmhouse. An aide served coffee, eggs, rolls. General Rose spoke to his men. "In less than an hour we go at it. In the fight, it's going to seem like I'm pushing too hard, going too fast, but I've always gone into battle with the belief that an ounce of sweat is worth a gallon of blood. The harder we hit them, the more men we kill, the fewer of our boys will be killed. And that means no holding on to positions. We hold nothing. Let the enemy do that. We advance constantly, and the only thing we hold is the Kraut, and we hold him by the nose while we kick his butt in!"

He shook hands with his men. Mike followed the general out of the farmhouse. They entered the jeep together. They didn't talk. The attacking force waited. The fight was about to begin.

Mike glanced at the general. He was smiling a thin, ironic smile. Mike could not shake the feeling that the man did not like him. He had brought him along to teach him a lesson. Yes, the cowboy soldier would be teaching the Jewboy prizefighter a lesson in bravery and toughness. And Mike Roth, wondering if he would survive it, was afraid.

41

It started at dawn's first light, wave after wave of fighter planes and bombers, medium bombers, Liberators and Flying Fortresses, a shattering roar rising out of the west, an enormous storm cloud of metal streaking across the morning sky.

The ground beneath the jeep began to quake. The whole countryside trembled. The sound was deafening, two thousand tanks revving up, three thousand planes splintering the skies, the earth swelling up in furious billows of exploding bombs.

Off to the left not more than ten miles away Mike Roth could see spouts of fire erupting in breathtaking leaps as rows of fragmentation bombs carpeted the distance between their position and the town of St.-Lô.

Dust and smoke swirled about them. The rush of wind took their breath away. They were in the eye of a tornado.

The army began to move forward. "We're off with our tails up!" the general shouted in Mike's ear; he sounded gleeful, like a kid at an amusement park. The jeep sped on past Périers and turned in the direction of St.-Lô.

The air was racked by the thunder of tank motors, artillery, bombs; the earth trembled as the tanks clattered along. The turrets of the tanks turned with slow, awesome deliberation; machine guns chattered; there was the constant sharp crack of small-arms fire.

Often General Rose's jeep was ahead of the tanks. Rose, looking unconcerned in the midst of chaos, directed his troops over a two-way radio.

Trees were blasted, dead cows were strewn about the fields, the ground was churned into a cratered waste of broken tanks and trucks and German dead. Mike's eardrums ached from the incessant percussive sound.

With General Rose in the jeep he bucked across the fractured roadway; storms of yellow dust enveloped them, cleared, swirled over them again. Often they could see only a few feet ahead.

As they rounded a bend, General Rose yelled for the driver to stop. Off to one side of the road, a group of perhaps two dozen dazed German soldiers staggered out of a stand of trees. They were pale with shock and fright. Several waved weapons over their heads, unsure whether to fire them or throw them away. One man was bleeding from the side; he attempted to stem the flow, then stared at his hand as though amazed at the redness of his blood.

General Rose grabbed up a light machine gun. He tossed Mike a .45. "Let's go," he said. Mike jumped with him from the jeep, and they advanced on the Germans.

Mike was not afraid. A dizzying sense of excitement came over him. *This is it, this is war,* he thought as they moved forward.

The Germans halted, frozen like deer surprised in a field. They looked at one another, questioning who was the leader, what should they do?

Several men threw their weapons forward. Two appeared undecided. An armored truck had pulled off the road and was moving toward the stunned group of men. A half-dozen American infantrymen approached between Mike, the general, and the Germans.

Suddenly there was a soft popping sound and one of the American soldiers fell. The infantrymen hit the ground. The group of Germans, panicked, shouted shrilly, and held their arms up high.

Two of the soldiers had broken from the group and were running back toward the wood. General Rose fired a burst from his machine gun at them, a soft purring sound, and one of the men went down, his legs cut out from under him.

And now Mike Roth realized he was running. He sprinted past the fallen American soldier, who lay very still. He tucked his .45 into his waistband and, legs pumping furiously, charged after the remaining German soldier, who had shot the infantryman. "No!" General Rose shouted, but Mike kept going.

The German had entered the wood. The American armored truck opened up, blasting into the thin trees. The trees were sliced to kindling as though hit by an immense buzz saw.

Farther on in the wood, Mike could see the German still running. He came on after him, gaining. He heard his own voice inside his head: *What am I doing? What the hell am I doing?*

He entered the wood. Blasted chunks of trees smoldered, burned. He leaped over fallen logs, tangled charred brush. The German had tripped and fallen. He struggled to his feet.

Mike slammed through the brush. Embers from burning twigs flew about him. He felt something slip from his belt and he reached for the .45 and it was not there.

The German, ten feet from him, was up now. He wheeled around, swinging his rifle in front of him. Mike dived headlong at the rifle, knocked it to one side, and drove the German backward.

The German was a man his own age. He had a broad, reddish face, with thick nose and mouth. He said something in German. It sounded like Yiddish, but Mike did not understand it. He hit the German very hard in the face and he kept hitting at him and the man went back into the smoldering brush and Mike was on top of him hitting him over and over as hard as he could.

The German groaned, then did not move. Mike pulled him from the brush. General Rose and two of the infantrymen pushed forward through the wood to Mike, who was struggling to catch his breath. His lungs burned with smoke and heat. He waved toward the unconscious German on the ground. One of the infantrymen leveled his rifle to shoot, then saw the general watching him and lowered it.

On the way back to the jeep, General Rose did not appear pleased. "That wasn't too smart," he said curtly.

"How's the boy who got hit?"

"He's not hurt bad. What the hell got into you?"

Mike didn't say anything. He couldn't explain that he had done what he had done in order to make the general think differently of him. He wanted to show the general just how tough a Jewboy could be. And he realized how important the idea of proving himself was to him: his whole life had been motivated by it. When it was no longer necessary to prove himself, he had lost the fire and purpose in his life.

At midmorning they reached Canisy, a village south of St.-Lô. The village had taken a terrible pounding. The smoke was so thick they could hardly see in front of them; the heat from burning buildings seemed to snuff out the air. A Frenchwoman stood beside the road, silent, stunned, two small children clinging to her; she watched without emotion as the Americans entered, her expression as blasted as the town about her.

In front of a shop facing the town square an American soldier crouched on one knee, rifle in hand. As the jeep passed him, Mike Roth realized he was dead.

The tanks moving through the dusty, smoke-wreathed town raised a deafening clatter on the torn macadam street. All about them were smashed-up and burned-out German armored cars and trucks. Hand grenades, holsters, gun belts, family photographs, mess kits, blankets, pillows, were strewn everywhere—the detritus of the scattering enemy.

Above the town American fighter planes wheeled and circled, peeled off, and dived so close to the rooftops that Mike was certain they were about to strafe their own troops. They passed low, then sent off streams of bombs at a German gun emplacement just beyond the town on the far side of the Vire River. They rose up, circled, then came back again, this time pouring machine-gun fire into the target.

Suddenly the square in front of their jeep was raked by machine-gun fire. Mike, the driver, and General Rose leaped from the jeep and scrambled for shelter in the smoldering ruins of a building facing the square.

At first Mike thought they had been attacked by their own planes; then he saw the plane bank toward the square again and realized it had German markings.

From above, an American plane pounced on it and opened fire. The German plane was hit. It turned on its side, spewing smoke. Just before it crashed across the river Mike saw a parachute open and drift toward a line of trees. The plane exploded in a great orange ball of fire.

"It's beautiful, isn't it!" General Rose shouted. "Who would have ever thought death could be so beautiful!"

It was true. The devastation was grotesque and terrible, and yet it possessed something in it that was powerful and stirring, cleansing. Mike felt purged of all boredom, frustration, and meanness. He was exalted, reborn by the awesome fury of war.

Over the next several weeks Mike traveled with General Rose's Third Armored Division. The British and Canadians broke through at Caen, moving toward Falaise, while the Americans raced around Avranches, south of St.-Lô. The whole German line had given way. Village after village collapsed on the Falaise Plain. In the rolling countryside south of Falaise thousands of broken, bewildered German soldiers, the remnants of some forty divisions, were being crushed, captured, maimed, killed.

The August sun beat down with relentless brilliance, burning the trampled corn a crisp gold color. The heat and dust were terrible. The Allies pressed on, inexorable hunt dogs, their quarry at bay.

Trapped between the Orne and Vire rivers, the Germans broke ranks and fled, were pursued, run down, slaughtered.

There were no drugs for the wounded, no time to bury the dead; their mechanized vehicles had been destroyed and the Germans were using horse-drawn carts to carry supplies and the wounded.

Horses panicked, kicked down fences and hedges, shrieked through the surrounding apple orchards, plunged into the muddy waters of the adjacent rivers. They dragged with them gun carriages, lorries, supplies, men. All became one struggling, shrieking mass. The brown water of the rivers turned red with blood. Men and beasts were trampled, crushed, drowned. Those soldiers who lived made no attempt to fight but huddled beneath their useless artillery or ran blindly into the hedges and trees, staggering about, screaming.

They surrendered by the tens of thousands. The roads were jammed with wreckage, abandoned loot, cases of wine, typewriters, truckloads of food, dying men. The stench was overwhelming. Allied soldiers moved through the chaos herding prisoners together, disarming them, shooting injured horses, trying to lessen the misery about them.

Mike's initial exhilaration in battle had long since vanished, replaced by fatigue and horror and revulsion. The moment of heroism when he had disarmed the German soldier seemed to him now to have been incredibly stupid, an aberration. General Rose never mentioned it, and if Mike had done it to prove something to the general, the point had gone unnoticed.

War, he realized, was survival. He watched Rose. Rose was brave. He never ceased driving his men forward, and more often than not, he was at the head of the attack. But it was bravery with a purpose: you tried to preserve yourself to fight another day. You took bold, productive chances, not foolish ones. You didn't die if you could help it.

Rose's attitude toward him remained peculiarly ambivalent: he kept Mike with him, yet treated him with a coolness that bordered on contempt. Mike had not earned Rose's respect and was certain it was because he was Jewish.

They were pushing on the Seine River now. General Rose informed Mike that orders had come through from SHAEF that he was to enter Paris with the Allies. Radio Central in Paris and the main Radio France station at Ste.-Annise were destroyed: Mike would be in charge of getting them into working order once Paris was captured.

Thirty miles outside of Paris, in Rambouillet, Mike Roth and the general prepared to go their separate ways. The Third Armored Division would skirt the city, moving across the Seine at Mantes to the north. Mike would enter Paris with the Fourth Infantry Division. It was drizzling, a light mist of rain. General Rose drove Mike to the Hotel du Grand Veneur, where a number of journalists, photographers, and radiomen were gathered.

On the way over, Rose did not speak. Even now the coldness, the tension were there between them. They sat in the jeep in front of the hotel. The general seemed preoccupied.

"What is it about me that you don't like?" Mike asked.

"What makes you think I don't like you?"

"Is it because I'm Jewish?"

The general flinched almost imperceptibly. His face grew tight. He stared at Mike for a very long time. Mike did not look away. "Yes," the general said quietly, "but it's not the way you think. I grew up in Denver, Colorado. I've been a professional soldier for twenty-nine years. There are not many Jews in Denver, and there are even fewer in the professional army." He hesitated, and seemed to have difficulty saying what was on his mind. "You see, I'm Jewish also. My father is an Orthodox rabbi. It's not something I've ever talked about. I've been ashamed of it. I've always felt an outsider and wanted more than anything to belong. That's why I joined the army."

Neither man spoke for a very long time. General Rose looked away, struggling to regain his composure.

It was clear to Mike Roth now, the general's discomfort with him, his implacable fury toward the Nazis. He was a man who had lived a lie for twenty-nine years, who was now fighting an enemy intent on destroying his people.

"I wanted you with me for a purpose," said Rose. "And yet I didn't know how to approach you on it."

"What is it you want from me?"

"If I'm killed, I want you to say kaddish, the prayer for the dead, for me. If I die, I want to die as a Jew. Do you understand?"

"Yes."

"They're trying to wipe us from the face of the earth. Promise me you'll say kaddish for me."

"I will. I promise."

"I'm sorry if I made you uncomfortable," the general said. "What you saw was my own shame."

They parted. Mike stood and stared after General Rose's jeep long after it disappeared down the narrow rain-shrouded street.

A steady stream of trucks and tanks rumbled through Rambouillet. A man in a captured Mercedes touring car pulled to the edge of the street. He aimed his camera at Mike, took a picture, then hurried over to him. "Mike Roth, the boxer?"

"Yes."

"Bob Capa. I'm with *Life* magazine. Want a lift to Paris?"

Mike entered the touring car and the two of them joined the convoy. They drove toward Limours and arrived at Longjumeau, fifteen miles from Paris. It continued to rain, and Mike and the photographer were wet, but they paid it no mind.

French troops were moving into position. They were joined by FFI forces, men in civilian clothes wearing tricolor armbands and carrying rifles and submachine guns. The air was charged with tension: Paris was about to be liberated!

People raced up and down the streets. Flags were unfurled—the French flag with the Cross of Lorraine. They flew from every window. Young children ran about waving flags over their heads.

At evening, from a hill just outside town, the Eiffel Tower could be seen in the distance.

The road leading to Paris was jammed with armor and tanks preparing for battle. Men occupied themselves ripping branches from trees to be used as camouflage; guns were wheeled into position.

The rumble of bombardments could be heard like distant thunder. Mike Roth and the photographer slept under a tarpaulin in the touring car. From time to time Mike awakened to see flashes of artillery and geysers of flame erupting in the far countryside.

At dawn everything was covered in a pearl-gray mist. The convoy stirred and prepared to move forward. There was a sudden commotion; vehicles were waved to the side of the road, and through the fog an open jeep appeared. Seated in the back, very straight and handsome, was General Jacques Leclerc, the leader of the Free French fighting forces.

The convoy started off behind him, gathering men as it went—partisans, regular soldiers, Americans, French. The ragtag column picked up speed. The fog dissipated. Road signs came into view: Paris six kilometers, five, four, three.

As the day cleared, the crowd became animated. Shouts of joy started. People pressed in on the column, screaming, grabbing at the soldiers. They surged out to meet the advancing army. From every direction Mike found himself bombarded by flowers; women and men leaned in and grabbed and kissed him. They shouted their thanks in French over and over. Bottles of wine, baskets of fruit, were pressed on him.

They came to the edge of the city, passing through the Porte d'Orléans, moving down a hill toward the Seine. The procession pushed on, gathering force, a river of people, tanks, armor, sweeping now down the Boulevard du Montparnasse, past the Dôme and Rontonde, past the train station. The railroad yard had been smashed; it stood disordered as a haystack in a hurricane, coaches scattered about, miles of track uprooted and snarled, grade crossings and loading platforms obliterated.

People streamed from every doorway. Men and women in wooden shoes clattered along the cobblestones, pushed on through torn-up streets strewn with barricades. From one side to the other, building to building, the street bubbled with humanity, cheering, laughing.

Streetwalkers dressed in tight, colorful costumes rushed the procession. An enormous-chested whore with dyed orange hair bound up in a fantastic headdress of red, white, and blue ostrich feathers, mounted the hood of the Mercedes and began a wild cancan. She lifted her skirt waist-high. She wore nothing underneath. The crowl roared, whistled, and sang.

Suddenly a firefight erupted somewhere up ahead. At the roar of the guns, the crowd scattered. In an instant the street was empty, save for tanks of the Second French Armored Division rumbling into position.

A battle had begun beyond the Esplanade des Invalides at the Ministry of Foreign Affairs. Grenades and fire bombs were flung from windows. Tanks swiveled and fired. The ground trembled violently.

Mike and Capa moved forward slowly in the touring car. They passed a group of collaborators being guarded by members of the FFI. The crowd returned. A woman rushed forward and struck one of the prisoners with a broken bottle; she ground the jagged glass into his face, shouting hysterically. Two FFI men pulled her back.

The man stood dazed, blood streaming down his face. Mike Roth saw the *Life* photographer push his way to the man and snap off a series of shots with his camera.

A young French girl wearing an FFI armband and poilu helmet ran up to Mike; strung around her waist were bloody hand grenades, which, she explained in broken Engish, had been taken from a man who had just been wounded. She was weeping; she grabbed Mike and kissed him, then pushed off and ran back in the direction of where the fighting had been.

Mike and Capa left the Mercedes and moved down a side street. They were carried along by the sweep of the crowd into a small restaurant. Everyone was passing around food and drink, singing, shouting—"The Marseillaise," "Lilli Marlene," "The Star-Spangled Banner."

Outside, an open car moved down the street. Seated high on back of the folded top was a woman with her hair shaved off. A swastika was painted on her skull with black paint and she wore around her neck the sign "Je suis collaboratrice."

The crowd surged forward at her, screaming curses, spitting, pelting her with garbage. She stood motionless, staring straight ahead. Her eyes were empty, devoid of emotion, dead eyes.

"Hey, you!" Mike heard someone call. "Hey! Mike Roth!" He looked up the block. Standing, waving at him from the back of a jeep, was Pat Farrell.

He shouldered his way through the crowd toward her. She helped him into the jeep. She looked at him for a moment, smiling, then leaned forward and kissed him very gently. "Isn't Paris romantic?" she said.

Mike called to Capa. He saw Pat Farrell and waved and continued snapping pictures. "We'll meet at the Scribe," he yelled back. The Scribe Hotel was where journalists entering the city were to be billeted.

Mike drove in the jeep with Pat Farrell through side streets into the heart of Paris. They emerged just beyond the Arc de Triomphe on Avenue Foch. Gunfire broke out in the street and they abandoned the jeep and ran for cover. They were at the Tomb of the Unknown Soldier, guarded by a group of crippled soldiers, several in wheelchairs. The soldiers remained at attention even though gunshots continued to explode about them. Up ahead

Mike could see the Hotel Majestic; it was on fire, smoke pouring from its upper stories.

One of the soldiers pointed to the Arc de Triomphe and motioned for them to follow him. He took them through an entrance in the Arc and led them to the roof.

The city stretched below them. It was dusk. In the Place de la Concorde and the Tuileries Gardens they could see tanks and armored cars burning. The Majestic and Crillon hotels were on fire. The Chamber of Deputies was burning. They could see snipers on rooftops just beneath them, firing onto the street. Men crouched in the street and fired back.

Mike had no idea who was friend, who was foe; he doubted the men doing the shooting knew either. Suddenly the roof where they crouched came under fire; they lay flat while bullets pocked the stone parapet of the Arc.

A German 88 opened up and the Arc de Triomphe trembled with the blast as it took a partial hit. All about them now tanks opened fire. The avenue raged with exploding shellfire. "What do you think, Roth? Have we worn out our welcome?" Pat Farrell said.

"I think that's what they're trying to tell us."

They made their way back down to the street. The men guarding the Tomb of the Unknown Soldier were still standing at attention. One of the men in wheelchairs had been knocked into the street, where he lay in a pool of blood. He was dead.

There was a lull in the firing and they made their way back to the jeep. Both front tires were flat. They drove off, bumping their way to a side street, where they abandoned the vehicle.

At dark they came to the Hotel Scribe, designated headquarters for the American press. Before they even had time to find out about quarters, an American officer rushed forward. "Hurry," he said.

He led them through a courtyard at the rear of the hotel, where the underground radio station, Poste de Radiodiffusion de la Nation Française, was situated. Everything was going full out, typewriters clattering, turntables spinning, shortwave equipment crackling.

An officer Mike had worked with at SHAEF in England was gearing up a transmitter. He looked over at Mike. "What the hell took you so long, Roth?" he said as though it was the most natural thing in the world to fight across the belly of France, enter Paris with the first wave, and end up at the very place he had been expected, without his even knowing he had been expected there.

Later, he lay with Pat Farrell on a bedroll spread out on the carpeted floor of a narrow room in the hotel. They had collapsed there as soon as they entered the room, without even taking off their clothes. "I'm glad I found you," said Mike.

"I'm glad too."

They kissed, then rested back. In a minute Pat Farrell was asleep and Mike could feel himself drifting off. Outside in the street people were singing "The Marseillaise."

In the morning Mike awoke first and showered. Pat joined him in the shower. They returned to the bedroll and made love. It was very good for both of them.

"What are you thinking?" Mike said after.

"What a lousy lover Hubbard Farrell is," she answered.

42

After the fall of Rome to the Allies in June 1944, Bill O'Dwyer was named by Roosevelt to be chief of the Economic Section of the Allied Control Commission. He was given the rank of brigadier general. Tony McGrath, who had spent most of the war in Washington as O'Dwyer's head liaison officer, was made a colonel and accompanied Bill-O to Italy.

Rome was declared an open city and was taken by the Allies with almost no destruction. Mike and Bill-O were given suites at the Excelsior Hotel, which, until recently, had been the headquarters of the German army.

Overnight the Italians, with a chameleonlike instinct for survival, became fierce antifascists. The lobby of the Excelsior was crammed with people fighting to do business with the Allies: politicians, industrialists, workers, partisans, religious leaders. Everyone, it seemed, hated the Nazis and Fascists. No one had ever cooperated with them.

They all had a story to tell, a deal to offer: men in shabby but well-tended suits wearing monocles and smoking cigarettes through holders—Count So-and-so, Prince Such-and-such; women in tight skirts, blouses with padded shoulders, wedge-heel shoes—models, actresses, shop girls, contessas: none admitted to being prostitutes, but their favors were passed around for cigarettes, candy bars, canned food.

Everything was chaotic, desperate. Everyone was on the make for a deal. Neighbor denounced neighbor, friend turned on friend. It was always the other person who could not be trusted. "Impossible," Bill-O complained to Tony after they had been at the job several weeks. "It's like trying to unscramble an egg."

The Allies had differing ideas among themselves as to just what the primary purpose of the Control Commission was. The British were eager to keep a firm grip on the political situation, hoping to minimize the influence of the Communists; the Americans were more concerned with saving the Italians from starvation. Though the Americans were furnishing most of the economic aid, the last word on how it was to be used was given by the British general Sir Henry Maitland Wilson, Allied Theater commander.

Every day was a battle between representatives of the two countries. "Goddammit," Bill-O would scream at General Wilson, "people are starving and you're playing God with their lives!"

General Wilson would stare—a gaze of maddening imperturbability. He spoke in tones of plummy reasonableness: "The combination of your Irish romanticism and American naiveté, though not without charm, is essentially foolish. When this war is over, Italy will either be a partner in democracy or a dagger in the belly of Europe. We do not intend to help fashion a dagger."

And so the battle went on. Tony could not rid himself of the idea that he and Bill-O were pawns in the situation; they were being used. Nothing was what it seemed: it was a hall of mirrors.

One night, sitting at the bar in the Excelsior, he saw an attractive girl enter and look shyly about her. She was not yet twenty, dark, hauntingly lovely. He had seen her around the hotel for nearly a week but she never spoke with anyone. There was an expression of fear, of loss in her eyes that touched him. She reminded him of his dead sister.

He watched her now in the mirror behind the bar. She walked to one end of the room as though looking for someone, then returned to the bar area. She caught sight of him in the mirror and approached him. "Do you mind if I sit here?" she said in heavily accented English, a very soft voice. "You needn't be concerned. I am not a prostitute."

"I didn't think you were," he said. "Would you like something to drink?"

She ordered a Coca-Cola and stared into her glass. "Is something wrong?" Tony said, regretting the question as soon as he had asked it. Of course something was wrong; in this time, in this place, something was always wrong.

"My troubles are no more than anybody else's," she said.

"Do you have family?" he asked.

"I am Jewish. Most of my family and friends were killed just before the Germans retreated. My father was killed."

"I'm sorry."

"So many people killed. So many." She didn't speak for a long moment. She gazed about her as though looking out for someone. "You are staying here in the hotel?"

"Yes."

"I don't like to ask for things," she said. "I know everyone today is asking for things." She groped for the words, embarrassed. "What I would like is very simple. I hope I don't seem too much pushing."

"What?" Tony said.

She couldn't look him in the eye. "You will think it stupid, but I would like to take a bath," she said, blushing. "It has been so long."

"Of course," he said.

He led her through the bar and into the lobby. She gazed at the floor as she walked. He took her upstairs to his suite, a grand place with a view through the hotel's mosquelike cupolas of the Via Veneto sweeping down to Piazza Barberini. He was surprised at how coolly she accepted the surroundings. In the suite her shyness vanished immediately. It was as though she belonged here. She moved to the bathroom without a word.

He heard the water running for her bath. She left the door open. After, she came out of the bathroom completely nude. Her body was that of a young girl, well-formed with small, shapely breasts. She came to the bed and sat on it. She stared at Tony with an objective, almost quizzical look. "What's your name?" she said.

"Tony."

"Me Star—Stella. In English, Star."

"Ah," he said.

"Come over here to me," she said. "Make love to me." She stretched out on the bed, spreading her legs. The unsettling mix of elements, her angelic loveliness, her overt sexuality, aroused Tony and puzzled him. Her initial attitude had not been that of a prostitute, yet she obviously was one—or something very close to it.

They made love. She began to weep. "What is it?" Tony asked.

She shook her head and turned over on her stomach. "Make love to me in the back," she said. "Make love to me there. It is how I like it."

She drew herself up on her knees and spread her buttocks, and Tony moved into her. She moaned, and the moan heightened to a cry. She wept uncontrollably.

Tony rested back, unsatisfied, feeling ugly, brutal.

She got up and dressed. He offered her money, but she wouldn't take it. "Can I buy you dinner?" he said.

She hesitated. "Where?"

"Rosati's or the Strega on the Via Veneto."

"I cannot."

"Why not?"

"There are some people there who do not like Jews."

"That's foolish. You'll be there with me."

She thought for a while. "No," she said at last.

After she left, Tony thought about her for a long time. There had been something so removed about her, so empty: it was as though he had been with a ghost.

Over the next days he and Bill-O struggled to deal with the mountainous problems that had been heaped on them. People came to them and pleaded, fought, argued. They needed food, shelter, medicine. And always raging about them, a storm within a storm, was the bureaucratic infighting between the Americans and the Allied Theater commander.

They could placate; they could promise. But they could accomplish little. The frustration was enormous.

Hub Farrell arrived in Rome. Accredited as a war correspondent, he functioned more as a gadfly, a political hustler, moving between competing bureaucracies. Tony suspected he was working with military intelligence.

One evening a few days after their first encounter, the girl who called herself Stella showed up again at the bar. They went to his room and made love. She would not accept money.

Night after night she came to him, but she would accept nothing from him.

Slowly he found himself being drawn into an involvement with her. He realized he had begun to care for her; he thought about her constantly. Why? How did she touch him so! It had to do with her peculiar combination of innocence and need to be debased. He was excited by her, repulsed, enmeshed in the mystery of her.

He noticed small things. She could never look him in the eye; she would enter and leave the hotel only by a side entrance; from time to time Italian men and women in the bar would stare at her and she would grow nervous and insist they leave.

One night in the bar a heavyset dark woman and an older man sat near them. They gazed at her with undisguised hostility. He felt her tremble against him.

That night she asked if she could stay with him all night, and later she asked if he could help her get to America.

"It would be very difficult. I'll make inquiries. Is that the reason you came to me? Because you want to come to America?"

"No," she said. "I know it is impossible. It is just a dream."

After that night she did not come again to the Excelsior bar and he didn't see her for almost a week. He knew only her first name, had no idea where she lived. He couldn't find her, and even if he could, he doubted that he would try. Still, he was haunted by her in his memory.

After a terribly contentious and difficult day he came to the bar and met a discouraged Bill-O sitting at a table by himself. "It's like trying to hold water in a sieve, lad," said Bill-O. "We're failing here. I want to help, but politics is strangling everything we try."

"It'll soon be over," Tony said. "The whole war."

"When we get back it'll be politics again. Not like this, but politics, nevertheless. The whole world is politics." He smiled and shook his head. "I've been in contact with people back home. They want me to challenge La Guardia again for mayor when I get back. I just don't know what to do."

"Do you want all that again?"

"On my own terms," Bill-O said. "But you can't have it like that. You have to make your peace with them."

"Who?"

"That's the trouble, lad. I don't know. A person never knows."

"What are the chances of getting someone into the States?" Tony said. "Someone from here."

"The girl?" Tony had told Bill-O about Stella.

"It's crazy. I know there's no chance of it and I wouldn't want the responsibility. She just seems so desperate."

"They're all desperate, Tony. It's a desperate situation."

The next day the Excelsior was abuzz with a terrible event that had occurred. One of the drivers who worked for the Allied Control Commission told Tony that a girl had been attacked by a mob, dragged out into the street opposite Rosati's restaurant. A streetcar was stopped and the conductor pulled out. The girl's head was placed on the tracks and the streetcar was run over her, decapitating her. "What was her name?" Tony said, alarmed.

"Celeste Di Porto," the man said.

"What did she do?"

The driver just shook his head; he didn't know, or if he did, he wouldn't say.

That night in the Excelsior bar Tony sat by himself. He stared in the mirror, waiting, hoping Stella would arrive. He couldn't erase the story of Celeste Di Porto from his mind. Was it possible that the woman was Stella?

He found himself praying for her to show up, studying each person who came into the bar. He sat there drinking for a very long time.

It was late and he knew he was getting drunk. He told himself to go to his room, but he couldn't leave. An enormous sense of dread had come over him.

Two people entered the bar, the heavyset woman and older man he had seen a week earlier. They sat at a nearby table, staring at him. The woman had a hint of a smile on her face. "Did you hear what happened?" she said loudly to the man in English. "They killed that whore, Celeste."

Tony approached the table. "Who is Celeste?"

The man offered Tony a chair. He spoke excellent English. "In the days before the Nazis left Rome, they began to round up Jews. Everyone went into hiding. Celeste Di Porto, who was a Jewess herself, walked through the poor neighborhoods of the Jewish section accompanied by members of a Fascist band. Whenever she recognized a Jew, she went and talked to him and moments later the person was taken away to be killed. She did this to many people. Many people died, friends, relatives. She became an Angel of Death. People of the ghetto recognized this and came to her and pleaded for their sons and daughters. She told them they were going to a fine place where they would be well fed, given a nice bed, treated with respect. Her father, a pious old man, knew what was occurring and in his grief went to the Fascists and asked to be killed. They were happy to accommodate him, of course.

"There was a popular man among the Jews, a famous prizefighter before the war. He was known as Bucefalo the Boxer. He stood up for his people, even in the darkest days. He was loved by everyone in the ghetto and respected by the Fascists because of his courage and toughness. On the Via Arenula, Celeste Di Porto betrayed him. It took nine men to subdue him. He was taken to Regina Coeli prison and there he was killed. After the Nazis left, the prison was opened. In cell number 316, scratched on the wall, was the inscription: 'I am Lazzaro Anticoli, known as Bucefalo the Boxer. If I don't see my family again, it is the fault of that traitor Celeste Di Porto. Avenge me!' Today, on the avenue in front of Rosati's, Bucefalo the Boxer was avenged."

"This girl," Tony asked. "Did she have another name?"

The heavyset woman smiled. "Of course," she said. "She called herself Stella. Star." And she laughed without emotion.

"The War Office wants you to go to Paris," Bill-O said to Tony. They were in Bill-O's office with Hubbard Farrell. "They want you to help entertain our people there. Perhaps fight an exhibition or two. Mike Roth is in Paris. You can fly up with Hub tomorrow."

"Will Roth fight me?"

Bill-O shrugged. "You can try. Oh, by the way, I made inquiries. If you're serious, we might be able to do something for that girl you were talking about."

"No," Tony said. "It's not necessary now."

43

On Saturday, August 26, 1944, General Charles de Gaulle made his official entry into Paris. All morning the radio broadcast news of his arrival. Masses of people began to gather in the center of Paris.

Mike Roth and Pat Farrell hurried from the Hotel Scribe to the Champs Elysées. People were pressed along the broad avenue as far as one could see; they hung out the windows, stood on rooftops. Flags of the Free French flew from every building.

Mike was drunk with the excitement of the occasion, with the emotion he felt for Pat Farrell. Everything vibrated with color, seemed spanking new: he gazed on the world as though he had never seen it before. "How do you feel?" he said.

"Terrific."

"I feel terrific too. I feel better than terrific. I feel sensational!"

He lifted her from the ground and swung her around and kissed her. The crowd about them cheered.

She laughed and struggled and he swung her round and round. He lifted her through the crowd, still kissing her. Then he set her down and they ran off down the avenue, giggling like a couple of kids. They moved through the crowd toward the Arc de Triomphe. A band played. People applauded. The world was freshly born to the two of them.

"You know something?" he said. "I think I love you."

"You know something? I think I love you, too."

At the Arc, at exactly three o'clock in the afternoon, a car carrying General de Gaulle moved slowly through the crowd. De Gaulle, towering above the mass of people, got out of the car and pushed his way to the memorial to the Unknown Soldier. He relighted the flame, then, followed by the leaders of the Resistance and General Leclerc, moved with solemn grandeur through the wildly cheering throng.

At the Place de la Concorde, as he paused to enter the automobile which would take him along the Rue de Rivoli, rifle fire erupted from the rooftops of the surrounding buildings. The crowd scattered. Mike and Pat, directly behind De Gaulle's car, crouched low. The chatter and crack of small-arms fire intensified. The general, unperturbed, stared straight ahead; his car moved slowly through the people down the Rue de Rivoli.

The gunfire continued. De Gaulle got out of his car at the square in front of Notre Dame. Tanks of the Second Armored swiveled about, raking the rooftops in the direction of the gunfire. As he entered the cathedral, there was still more gunfire, this time from within the cathedral itself, from the upper galleries. Several people fell wounded.

De Gaulle stood motionless in the center of the cathedral, as though impervious to bullets.

The ceremony was cut short and the crowd dispersed.

Throughout the night as Mike and Pat lay together in their room, distant bursts of gunfire sounded through the city. A mop-up of fugitive Germans and collaborationists was being carried out.

At midnight German bombers raided the city. Near the Jardin des Plantes a huge warehouse for bonded wines was set afire. Mike and Pat stood at the window to their room and watched the central part of the city blaze up and lick at the sky with red tongues of flame.

Pat clung to him. He wondered at her love: would it persist beyond the fire of war?

Several nights later they entered the dining room at the Ritz Hotel. Hub Farrell and Tony McGrath were seated at a table with a man who wore a khaki field jacket and a .45 on his hip. He was a big man and had a broad, flushed face and a mustache. "Hello, Patty," Hub said.

"Patty!" the man in the field jacket bellowed. "Come over here, little lady! Have you been fighting this here rotten war, or have you been playing around?"

"A little bit of both. What are you doing here!"

"I led the damn attack on this town, what do you think?" the man said. He put his arm around Pat's waist and pulled her to him.

The table was covered with empty champagne bottles. All three men were very drunk. "Do you two know each other?" Pat said. "Mike Roth—Ernest Hemingway."

Hemingway looked up but said nothing.

"When did you get here, Hub?" Pat asked her husband.

He stared at her with glazed eyes. "A few days ago."

"Did you know where I was?"

"Yes."

Hemingway sat stiffly, glowering at Mike. He thrust his face belligerently toward him. "When are you going to fight McGrath?" he demanded.

"I have no plans to fight him."

"You're a goddamn coward," Hemingway said, rising. "You're a kike coward. The only way you ever beat this man was because you had the mockie gangsters behind—"

Tony pulled at Hemingway in an attempt to get him back in his chair.

"He's a lousy coward," Hemingway said. "If none of you are man enough to tell him, then I'll tell him. For Christ's sake, Hub, don't you see what's going on? He's been sleeping with your wife!"

Hemingway pushed around the table. He took off his field jacket and tossed it to one side. Tony jumped up and grabbed him, but he yanked away and squared off with Mike. "Come on, let's go. You and me."

"You're drunk," Mike said.

"I'll flatten you, drunk or sober! Come on!" Hemingway swung at Mike, who ducked. Hemingway stumbled and fell over a chair and went sprawling on the floor.

He started to come up, still swinging. He rushed at Mike, his arms pumping furiously. Mike tapped him on the jaw and he went down on the floor, unconscious, as much from drink as the punch.

Farrell came to his wife. He was breathing heavily. "Is it true? Is he sleeping with you?"

"Yes."

Farrell stared at Pat with a murderous glare. Then tears came to his eyes. He sagged against her and bawled like a baby. Pat took him to a side table and talked with him for a long time. He continued to weep and she cradled him in her arms while staring over at Mike.

Several of the hotel's people came forward to attend to Hemingway. He was seated on a chair now. A waiter held an ice pack to his jaw.

"Sit down, Mike," Tony said, drunk. "Let's talk."

"What about?"

"*I want to fight you.* Conn and Louis are due over in a week. They want me
to do an exhibition. *I want to fight you!*"

"No."

"Why not?" There was desperation in his eyes. "We have things to settle.
Please!"

Hemingway had pulled away from the hotel people. He came rushing toward the table. "I'm trying to give all you people the real gen!" he yelled. "I
risked my life in this war to save mockie cowards, and what do they do?
They sleep with my friend's wife!"

Once more Tony McGrath intercepted Hemingway, grabbing him
around the chest and holding him back. Farrell pulled away from his wife
and threw his arms around Hemingway. "You were right, Ernie," he
bawled. "He's been sleeping with her. You gave me the real gen!"

The hotel people pushed Hemingway toward the door. Tony followed
after, tripped, and almost fell. Farrell continued to blubber on about how
Hemingway had given him the real gen.

Lurching, arguing, crying, the three men staggered from the dining
room.

Pat Farrell poured herself a glass of champagne from a bottle on the table.
"And that's the end of that marriage," she said, lifting the glass to Mike in a
toast.

At the beginning of the year 1945, with Germany's defeat imminent,
Mike Roth was assigned back to the States. Pat returned with him. A divorce agreement was reached with Farrell.

She flew to Nevada for the divorce and, immediately after, she and Mike
were married in a civil ceremony. They honeymooned on a ranch in Mon-
tana owned by her family.

They returned to New York and took an apartment on Fifth Avenue, a
grand, spacious place also owned by her family.

In early May Mike picked up the New York *Times* to read that Major
General Maurice Rose, commander of the Third Armored Division, had
been killed in action in Panderborn, Germany.

The article mentioned that Rose believed the best way to drive his Third
Armored Division to victory was to get out in front and lead it; it told of
his many narrow escapes, how his men had always felt he was living on bor-
rowed time. It quoted his eighty-nine-year-old father, Rabbi Samuel Rose:
"It is well that since this had to be, it happened in the week of Passover. As
Jehovah said. 'When I see the sacrifice, the blood, I will pass over you.' He
spoke not only to the Jews but to all people—to the Gentiles, to Americans,
to Germans. And so may Jehovah accept this sacrifice, and see the blood and
pass over all the peoples for their sins, at this Passover time, for my son's
sake."

Mike traveled down to the Lower East Side, to a small synagogue there,
where he said kaddish, the prayer for the dead, for General Maurice Rose.

44

Tony McGrath sat on the porch of his Long Island home and gazed out over the broad, rolling lawn. A curving drive shaded by impressive oaks led down to a high brick wall and iron gate. Scattered over the estate grounds were groves of maple, pine, birch.

It was late afternoon; the sun dipped low in the west toward Sands Point and Manhasset Bay.

On the lawn, Tony's son Darryl, fourteen now in this year 1949, was playing touch football with several boys his age. Tony watched him and he felt an ache within, love for the boy, regret: he had not spent the time he should have with Darryl. There was something lacking between them, a wall of shyness.

The ball spiraled in the direction of the porch. Darryl, tall and muscular, moved with a superb fluidity, the wondrous grace of the natural athlete. He went up for the pass, tipped it with one hand, spun around, gathered it in. "Way to go!" Tony yelled.

Darryl tossed the ball to Tony. He stood and waved his son out for a pass. The boy raced down the lawn, and Tony lofted the ball toward him. It fell short. Darryl retrieved the ball, grinning. "The old soup bone ain't what it used to be, Pop," he yelled.

Tony nodded and laughed. "Nothing's what it used to be."

He sat back in the rattan chair and thought about his life, how it had changed since the end of the war.

Returning to the house on Christopher Street, he had discovered a terrible tension between his wife and his mother. They rarely talked to each other; when they did, it ended in an argument. How had the friction grown up? Where had it come from? Something was not right, yet no one would speak about it.

He had been home nearly two months before he uncovered the secret in the house: his wife drank. She hid it; she denied it; but she had been drinking heavily for a period going back to the beginning of the war. She could not stop. He fought to discover how it had happened, why. He could learn nothing. Her drinking had appeared like a plague, mysterious and incurable.

The year after his return from the service, another child was born, a boy whom they named Sean. A year later they had a girl, Sharon.

Theresa's drinking continued. Tony accused himself; it was his fault. He had neglected her over the years. He had been obsessed with politics, first La Guardia, then O'Dwyer. He had been obsessed with Mike Roth.

O'Dwyer ran for mayor in 1945 and won. Tony helped manage his campaign, and was given the position of chief of staff in his administration.

The war's end also brought a spectacular boom in construction. In New York City, the McGrath company dominated the industry. Though his brothers ran the company's day-to-day affairs, Tony was forced to devote more and more time to the business.

He had ignored his wife and family. A gap grew between him and his children. His wife's drinking grew worse. Tony felt responsible, and yet he could do nothing to ease the situation.

He tried. The move to Long Island was an attempt to make things up to her. If he could get his wife out of the Greenwich Village house, away from his mother, perhaps her condition would improve.

In the beginning she had been excited by the estate: the spacious grounds, trees, magnificent stone house. Gradually her enthusiasm drained away. She missed the old neighborhood, the proximity of her family. The drinking, which had waned, started up again.

Tony had found an immense contentment in the place. In his spare time he would tend the gardens, plant trees, work on the stone wall. It was only his wife's problem and the coolness between him and his children that un-settled things for him, gnawed at him like the ache of an abscessed tooth.

He was forty-three now. He still kept in shape, laboring around the estate grounds, sparring with his son, working out at the New York Athletic Club. Still, he was aware of a decline in his physical powers. The muscles had lost their leanness; his reflexes had slowed. A thickening had occurred. That was it—a thickening.

He thought now: For almost a decade and a half I have lived with a single consuming purpose—to fight Mike Roth again, to regain my heavyweight title. But in recent times the dream had begun to die. Was this middle age this acceptance of things, this death of dreams? He fantasized about getting into the ring again. Watching his son playing football on the lawn, he coveted Darryl's youth, his prowess.

Unless a hero died young, he thought, his later life was fraught with regret, a veneration for what had been. Al Smith, the great hero of his family, had died just before the end of the war, disillusioned, betrayed by friends, a failure in business, a man soured against his own early political beliefs. The last years of his life had been spent staring out the window of his Fifth Avenue apartment or wandering through the Central Park Zoo.

One night just before the war, Bill-O, Tony, and John McMahon had visited the Man in the Derby in his apartment. After dinner Al Smith invited them across the street to the zoo: he had been made an honorary night superintendent, with his own keys to the animal houses. He took them to the tiger cages, where he had a favorite; he called her "The Tammany Tiger."

"Watch this," he said to his friends. He glared at the tiger, then yelled: "Tom Dewey!" The tiger snarled loudly and leaped at the bars.

Al Smith laughed and laughed and the others laughed also, but there had been no real joy in it. The Tammany Tiger, the tiger of the old days, the old ways, was dead. Al Smith was gone. Two years later, Beau James Walker was dead also.

He had been living in an apartment on East End Avenue, not far from the mayor's residence at Gracie Mansion. Bill-O by then was mayor. He heard that Beau James was ill and he and Tony McGrath walked to the apartment and paid him a visit.

Walker greeted them in a silk dressing jacket over matching pajamas, spiffy as ever. His face, though, was the color of paste, with splotches of pink, as though it had been rouged. His blue eyes were watery and without luster. He coughed constantly, a dry, hacking cough. "I can't get rid of this damn cold," he told them. "It's the moisture in the cigarettes I smoke." He showed them racks of cigarette holders he used to filter out the moisture.

"I've come back to the Church, Bill-O," Walker said. "I go to a little church now on Eighty-fourth Street." Above his bed was a religious lithograph. There were shelves along one wall filled with religious books.

They talked about the job of mayor. Walker joked with Bill-O and made him promise he'd do a good job. "I got my eye on you." He laughed a dry, empty laugh—from his window he could see Gracie Mansion. He made Bill-O promise to invite him over one day.

They set a date, but Walker never showed up. He took ill and was rushed to Doctors Hospital, directly across the street from the mayor's residence. He died the very night he was expected at the mansion.

Yes, all the old-timers, the old warriors, had passed from the scene; La Guardia dead, Walker dead, Roosevelt dead. Time was passing, dreams were dying.

Letha, the black housekeeper, moved out onto the porch. "Dinner here tonight, Mr. McGrath?"

"I'll be going into the city. How's Mrs. McGrath today?"

The housekeeper shook her head. "I can't get her to eat. She's thin as a bird. I don't know what to do with that woman."

Theresa's drinking had grown worse lately. She stayed in her housecoat, wandered about in an alcoholic stupor. The staff of the house—a butler, cook, governess for the young children—did all they could to keep her away from liquor. They made constant searches through her closets, drawers, suitcases. Somehow, though, she always managed to obtain it.

A chauffeur-driven limousine pulled up to the gate. Tony waved to the driver and entered the house. His younger children, Sharon, two, and Sean, three were brought to him by their governess. They were both thin, blond. They were shy with him. Was it because of Theresa's difficulties? Was it because he was absent so much of the time? Perhaps he tried too hard with them. Perhaps that was why they were never comfortable with him. "Will you save some dessert for me?" Sean said yes. "All right. I love you both very much. Do you love Daddy?"

They nodded. "Give Daddy a kiss." They kissed him.

Jason Karl waited in the back of the limousine. They drove toward Manhattan. "How's Theresa?"

Tony shook his head. "I don't know what to do, Jay. I'm afraid I might have to hospitalize her. I just don't know."

"Laura's concerned about her. She's fond of her, fond of you both."

The Karls' summer house was less than a mile from Tony's estate, yet he rarely saw Laura. He preferred it that way. Though he and Jason had considerable business together, Tony managed to avoid socializing with them.

When La Guardia had chosen not to stand for reelection, Jason gave his support to O'Dwyer. Bill-O embarked on an ambitious program of urban renewal and appointed Jason Karl as head of the City Planning Commission. Jason's influence with the liberal wing of the Republican party had been instrumental in getting funds for the city from New York Governor Tom Dewey. All in all O'Dwyer had done an admirable job in his first term as mayor: bridges, roads, parks, housing projects, schools, sprang up all over the city.

A disturbing issue, however, cast a pall over his administration: the Abe Reles affair. It loomed large during the campaign for his first term but he managed to quiet it then. Now it had come up again. How and why had Abe Reles been killed? Who was responsible? Why had none of the top gangster bosses been indicted—Ben Siegel, Jack Foster, Meyer Lansky?

"I spoke with Hub Farrell this morning," Jason said as the limousine approached the Triborough Bridge. "His television station here in the city is about to start an editorial campaign calling for a full-scale investigation on Reles again. Why do they keep coming back to this thing? You've been with Bill-O as long as anyone. Is there anything at all in the story?"

"Of course not," Tony said. "Bill-O has his faults. He's no La Guardia. But I was with him throughout the whole Reles business. He's an honest, honest man. Whatever happened to Abe Reles, Bill-O had nothing to do with it. He did his best to keep the man alive."

"He's too lax, Tony. Too much favoritism. Your father-in-law doesn't help him."

John McMahon had gained power in Bill-O's administration. Tony knew his influence was essentially benign, but he operated in the old Tammany way, through cronies and favors. "He's harmless," Tony said. "He buys drinks for a lot of freeloaders. That's about the extent of it."

"It's appearances, Tony. Bill-O has to be aware of appearances. We must all be above suspicion. It affects every one of us."

The limousine moved down off the Triborough Bridge and onto the East River Drive. They left it at Ninety-sixth Street and pulled onto East End Avenue. They came to Carl Schurz Park and Gracie Mansion, the mayor's residence.

A houseboy in white jacket answered the door and took them into the library. Through the window Jason and Tony could see Bill-O walking in the garden behind the house. An attractive dark-haired young woman was with him. "What do you think?" Jason said, indicating the woman.

"He says he's going to marry her."

Bill-O's wife, Catherine, an invalid for many years, had died shortly after the election. Lately he had been seeing a fashion model, a woman half his age. He never spoke to Tony or Jason about her, but Tony was convinced Bill-O was in love.

He was a complex man, Bill O'Dwyer, Tony thought. There were layers of him you couldn't touch. Even relaxing over a drink, swapping stories, reciting poetry, singing Irish songs, Bill-O kept hidden a dark area of himself.

"Welcome, gentlemen!" Bill-O briskly entered the library. "What'll you have, lads?"

The houseboy moved to a liquor cabinet at one end of the library and fixed drinks. "I figured we'd go to the fights tonight at St. Nick's. How does that sound?" Bill-O said as the drinks were being passed around. "Ginks Belloise is fighting."

"I'd rather watch it on the television," Tony said.

"It'll be good for you to get out in a crowd, lad. Working with the boxing commission, you ought to show your face from time to time."

O'Dwyer picked up a dark briar pipe from a table next to his chair: his woman friend had recently converted him from cigars to a pipe. He tamped in some tobacco and lit up, puffing on the pipe for a while. "I called you here tonight to bounce things off you," he said. "I don't know whether I'll be running for a second term. I'm tired, just damn tired. The job's too tough for me."

"The Reles business," Jason said.

"That and other things. I don't have the strength to fight it out all over again."

"Don't let them hound you with a ghost."

"A lady has come into my life. I just can't subject her to that sort of thing. We're all used to the game. She isn't."

"If you drop out, Bill-O, it'll look like you have something to hide," Jason pointed out.

Bill-O puffed for a long time on his pipe. His expression remained thoughtful. "Then there's Farrell and the television campaign," he said. "There's no discussion or balance like in a newspaper. This damn television thing was made for smearing folk."

"I'll talk to Mike Roth," Jason said. "We can have DuBois-Roth defend you."

"Will he do it, Jay?" Bill-O said.

"If we can reassure him—"

"Of course we can reassure him!" Bill-O's eyes flashed anger. "What are you trying to say, Jay?"

"If Mike defends you, he'll be going out on a limb. Hub Farrell's just waiting to bury him."

"There's no problem there," Bill-O said. "But will he go along?"

"I think he will."

"How does he feel about Tony?"

"Tony helped him at the World's Fair. He hasn't forgotten," Jason said. "One thing you should do, though—get rid of John McMahon. He's of the old Tammany ways. Your enemies will club you over the head with him until you're bloody."

"We've been pals a long time, ever since Tony here was a young brawler fighting in the speaks. He's a good soul, Johnny McMahon."

"I love John," Tony said. "But Jason is right—he demeans your administration."

Bill-O sighed. "That's the trouble with this whole damn business. Everything's black or white. For God's sake, Jay, we're human beings, not saints. Johnny may smell of the back room, but he's no grafter or tinhorn. They're trying to crucify me on appearances. That's what makes me want to chuck the whole thing. Reles, for God's sake! As if I had something to do with the death of the key witness in my most important case!" He walked to the window and stared out at the garden. He shook his head. "I should have followed my early inclinations. I wanted to become a teacher. Join the faculty of a university and bury myself in books. I was seduced by America. The damn lady wooed me and won me and I kissed the books good-bye!" He turned to them, smiling. "Well, what do you say, lads? Shall we go see Ginks Belloise fight?"

DuBois-Roth was televising the fights. Their cameras were set on a platform above the ring. Tony looked around for Mike Roth but didn't see him. He did spot Hub Farrell, who waved to him across the arena. "Vicious, slimy bastard," Bill-O said under his breath.

Between the early bouts Bill-O excused himself and walked around to where Farrell was sitting. Tony watched as they talked. Bill-O was turning on the charm full blast—joking, laughing, hugging Farrell around the shoulders. Farrell treated Bill-O with casual disdain, a king suffering a court jester, yet Bill-O plowed on, trying to win him over. Television, though in its infancy, loomed as a powerful force in shaping public opinion. If CCNA Television came out against O'Dwyer, the effect on his campaign could be devastating. Bill-O was doing his best to woo Hub Farrell.

Watching Bill-O at work, Tony thought about how killing the effort must be. It was brutal, demeaning, playing the sycophant's game to a man you loathed. It sickened and saddened Tony: Bill-O should have had the strength to rise above such sleazy horse trading. La Guardia never would have abased himself like that. But then, Bill-O was no Fiorello La Guardia.

Jackie Foster was seated a row behind Farrell. His wife was with him—a lacquered number with platinum hair and mean eyes. Foster looked puffed and prosperous, pounds heavier than when Tony had seen him last. His chubby fingers were jammed with jeweled rings. Soon he'll have to start wearing them on his toes, Tony thought.

Anger stirred inside him. They had let Foster wriggle off the hook in the Reles case, and Reles's death had put an end to any possibility of opening the thing up again. In the last few years Foster's power and his respectability had grown to such a degree that it would be nearly impossible to bring him down now. He moved very carefully these days. He had other people to do the dirty work for him.

The Ginks Belloise fight was over almost before it began. In the first round Belloise hit his opponent with a counter right and dropped him for a nine-count. The man got up, staggered around the ring, and collapsed before Ginks could hit him again. This time he took an eight-count, got to his feet, lurched to the ropes, and went down again. He didn't get up.

Bill-O was jubilant. "Three knockdowns on one punch!" he yelled. "Never saw that before, lad!"

"What did Farrell say?"

Bill-O didn't look at him. "He thinks he can buy me. He doesn't know me very well, does he, Tony? If ever I was to sell out, it sure as hell wouldn't be to some arrogant bastard who can make me look good on television!"

A well-packaged young blond approached Tony; earlier he had seen her talking with Jackie Foster's wife. "How'd you like the fight, Mr. McGrath?" she said.

"Fun."

"Ginks is good." She had a purring Southern accent. "But not as good as you."

"Who told you that, your mother?"

The girl laughed, showing very even teeth, a dainty tongue like a dart. She pressed close to Tony. "I'm very interested in prizefighting. Could you teach me about it?"

"I could probably teach you a few things."

"Yes," she said. "I'm sure you could. Why don't you take me home?"

He took the girl by cab to her place, a shabby hotel on West Forty-sixth Street. She undressed as soon as they entered the room and kept the lights full on. They were bright as spotlights.

She was boundlessly accommodating, a miraculous mechanical doll. In the heat of passion he thought he heard a soft clicking sound. He got up and pulled back the covers on the bed; under the mattress pad he found a cable. It led to a gift-wrapped box on the bureau.

The girl watched him without emotion.

Inside the box, packed in cotton, was a 4X5 camera focused on the bed. "I collect pictures of celebrities," the girl said.

"How much did Jack Foster pay you?"

She lit a cigarette and stared at the smoke. "I did it as a favor. He said give you a good time and get some pictures. Did I give you a good time?"

"If you like making love to an eggbeater," Tony said. The girl shrugged.

Tony smashed the camera against the wall. He took out the film pack and exposed it. The girl looked mildly peeved. "Jackie's going to be mad."

In an election year everyone was looking for an edge, he thought. People were yelling about the Reles thing. Insurance—Jackie Foster needed it. A storm was gathering: a wise man looked to his insurance.

45

Mike Roth was uneasy, although on the surface things were fine. His marriage was happy; the television industry was booming. But he could not shake a sense of apprehension.

A child was born to him and Pat—a girl, lovely and blond, with enormous blue eyes and a smile that lit up any room she was in. They named her Jennifer. She was adored by both of them. Pat, a woman who had thrived on action and competition, discovered a gentler side to her nature. She channeled all her energies into her daughter, lavished attention on her, spent most of her time with her.

One aspect of Mike's uneasiness was his wife's wealth. Though she went out of her way to downplay it, he had difficulty accepting it. They lived by her social standards, traveled in her circles, associating with many of her old friends, pillars of the Eastern establishment who had also been close to her ex-husband.

He sensed they looked down on him, treated him as a washed-up ex-athlete who had latched on to a meal ticket, a fortune-hunting Jew.

And there were problems with Elias DuBois. DuBois-Roth, second only to CCNA, was a major force in the television industry. With stations in New York, Philadelphia, and Los Angeles, they had established the first network in the nation. The manufacturing division in New Jersey turned out sets at a rate of three thousand a month and could barely keep up with demand. As the company grew, DuBois's manic energy threatened to rage out of control. He worked round the clock, pushing development in areas that seemed of only marginal concern to television.

His fertile brain seethed and erupted in bizarre obsessions. He grew secretive, withdrawn, developed an aversion to people and a germ phobia which sent him rushing to wash as soon as anyone touched him. Days would go by when he did little but feed the pigeons from the ledge of his office window, searching for that magical bird, the dove of his genius, which would wing to him once again, carrying answers to the most recondite questions swirling at the heart of creation.

Work continued on his color television system, but DuBois had entangled the company in a massive legal war with CCNA over patent infringements, and even if they won the battle, it could have disastrous financial consequences.

The base of the company's broadcast strength was sports. Mike, using his influence in the boxing world, had lined up a series of spectacular events starting in June 1947 with the Joe Louis-Billy Conn bout—the first prizefight ever televised. They went on to broadcast weekly fights as well as a full schedule of baseball, football, and basketball.

CCNA battled them at every turn. Hub Farrell had never forgiven Mike for having alienated his wife's affections. Vowing to destroy him, he positioned the immense power of his corporation for a savage war on DuBois-Roth. And DuBois's penchant for legal adventurism and bizarre scientific exploration had put DuBois-Roth in a vulnerable position.

Mike also had other very real concerns. His parents were in failing health and he was increasingly estranged from his ex-wife and son.

In the summer of 1947 he was awakened in the middle of the night by a phone call. It was Jack Foster calling from California. Ben Siegel had been gunned down! The murder had occurred at Lisa's house. Matthew, his son, had found the body. Foster was exultant as he conveyed the news to Mike. He had been in Los Angeles when it happened—a tragic coincidence, he insisted.

"Benny's been having his problems, opened a casino in Vegas, got caught short," Foster said. "I came out here to help him. He's been trying to swing a loan from our union's pension fund." He had called, he explained, to assure Mike that his ex-wife and son were unharmed. "But can you imagine? Someone killing Benny? He was such a misunderstood fellow. I liked Benny, that crazy bastard."

It was midmorning when Mike finally reached Lisa. She had been questioned by the police all night and was in a terrible state. "I loved him," she said over and over, weeping bitterly. "He was a wonderful man, kind, considerate. No one knew him the way I did. Why did they do it? He never harmed anyone in this world."

Mike wanted to bring Matt to New York, and suggested that he fly out and pick the boy up. "No!" she screamed hysterically. "He stays with me! I need him here with me!"

Mike tried to reason with her. The boy had been through a horrific experience. It would be a good thing for him to get away from Los Angeles and spend some time with his father.

She wouldn't hear of it.

In the two years following Ben Siegel's death, Mike had sporadic contact with his ex-wife. She would call to tell him about problems she was having with Matt. He began to throw tantrums in school; his teachers couldn't handle him. Once again, Mike tried to persuade her to let Matthew come to him, but she refused. "He's all I have now. Don't try to take him away from me." Her career, marginal when Siegel was alive, collapsed completely after his death. Mike became her sole support, regularly sending her substantial sums.

Just before the mayoral election of 1949, Jason Karl, concerned about the political situation, invited Mike and Pat to dinner. "Hub Farrell is looking to destroy Bill-O," Jason said over cocktails before the meal. "This will be the first election in which television will be a factor. I think DuBois-Roth ought to consider supporting O'Dwyer."

"It's tricky business, Jay," Mike said.

"I know Bill-O is not a perfect candidate. He's certainly in no class with La Guardia. But he cares." Jason spoke with passion. "I'm almost seventy years old, Mike. I had dreams of accomplishing certain things . . ." His voice trailed off. He was embarrassed.

He was a man of the highest standards, but the one opportunity he had to effect change on a grand scale, when the Fusionists wanted him to run for mayor, he had let go by. Mike understood the desperation that came over him. Bill O'Dwyer's administration gave him the opportunity to do *something*. "I know how you feel, Jay—"

"Years ago you and I dreamed of things that could be done on the Lower East Side. Well, I've started some things and I can do more. If O'Dwyer is not elected, I will never be able to realize those things. I care about them, Mike. I care very deeply about them."

"I like Bill-O. I think he's an honest man. But I don't think we in television should become hucksters for politicians."

"What of Hubbard?" Pat said. "Isn't that what he's doing? Shouldn't you at least provide a balance to CCNA?"

Over the next week Mike Roth wrestled with the problem. He and Pat discussed, argued, fought it through. "Hub is ruthless," she said. "You have to battle him on his own terms. If not, he'll bury DuBois-Roth."

With misgivings Mike threw his network into the fray. DuBois-Roth adopted an editorial position supporting the reelection of Bill O'Dwyer. The voters of New York returned him for another term.

CCNA continued the attack. In Washington they lobbied relentlessly before the FCC to keep DuBois-Roth from going forward with its color system. They fought in the courts over patent rights. And, most amazingly, they continued to hammer away at the O'Dwyer administration and the Reles affair even though the election was over.

Later that year Mike's mother entered the hospital. The doctors ran tests and discovered she had acute leukemia.

She stared at herself in a hand mirror. Her face resembled a skull. "I'm dying, Mikele," she said without sadness. "I look like my mother just before she went."

Two weeks later she was dead.

Charlie Roth agreed to leave the Lower East Side and move in with Mike and Patricia. A dramatic change came over him: he ceased to brood, to complain. He was positively lighthearted. It was as though with the death of Florence an enormous weight had been lifted from his soul.

He fussed over Pat, adored Jennifer. He set up a small workshop in one corner of his bedroom and repaired every broken appliance, lamp, gadget in the apartment. He refinished a night table, built a doll's house for Jennifer.

One evening Mike and his father took a long walk through the neighborhood. They strolled along Madison Avenue down to Fifty-seventh Street, then circled back alongside the park. "Your mother's gone," Charlie said, "and I miss her, but I don't feel bad. I feel good." He sighed and shook his head. "I was in love with your mother from the first time I met her until the moment of her death. I'm still in love with her. She was always a beauty to me." He didn't talk for a while. They walked several blocks in silence. "You see, I promised her when I asked her to marry me that I would give her a good life. That I would become rich and successful. She didn't care about that stuff, but I could never forget my promise." He shook his head and laughed at his foolishness. "Now she's gone, and I'm released from my promise!"

One morning Charlie went out alone. He didn't return during the day. When Mike arrived home in the evening, Patricia was concerned. Where was Charlie? Why hadn't he called? Mike went out and drove around the neighborhood. When he came home there was a phone call for him—a police captain on the Lower East Side.

A man had been observed sitting on a bench in Rutgers Square. He sat there most of the day, reading the newspaper, talking with people. At evening time he dozed off. Some time later a passerby tried unsuccessfully to rouse him. The man was dead. It was Charlie Roth.

Clenched in his hand was a snapshot of his wife.

46

In a fury, Tony McGrath drove the distance from his home on Long Island to the mayor's residence. It was evening, and raining out. He shifted the car with angry impatience, weaving in and out of traffic, speeding over water-slick streets through the downpour.

Earlier he had received a disturbing phone call from Jason Karl: a city commission had supported CCNA against DuBois-Roth for the right to televise prizefights from Madison Square Garden. Behind his back his father-in-law had helped fashion the agreement.

At Gracie Mansion he was brought into the library. Bill-O, in a silk dressing gown, an after-dinner brandy resting in his hand, sat in a large leather chair. On the arm of the chair was his new wife: shortly after the election Bill-O had married his woman friend.

Bill-O, smiling, offered Tony a chair. He declined. Bill-O's face was flushed with brandy. "Nothing so gloomy as a rainy night in the city—" Bill-O began.

"—unless it's an empty ball park or a jail."

Bill-O laughed. "He knows all my little wisdoms," he said to his wife.

"Do you want me to leave?" the new Mrs. O'Dwyer said.

"No, no, darling. Anything Tony and I have to say to each other, you certainly can hear. Now, what's put you in a lather?"

"Jason is upset. In the election, Mike Roth and his network went out on a limb for us. Now we tilt our support on the Garden fights to CCNA—"

"Talk to your father-in-law—"

"Hub Farrell crucifies us over Reles, never lets up, and now we side with him against Roth's people."

Bill-O's wife lifted a dark briar from a table next to his chair and handed it to him. She lit the pipe for him. "Why this sudden love and concern for Mike Roth?" Bill-O said.

"We came to Roth for help and he gave it." Tony's voice was strained.

"Let John deal with this, Tony. It's a rotten situation. The Garden people are up to their eyeballs in shady characters. Let's keep clear of it all."

"We're not keeping clear, though, Bill."

"There are a lot of messy situations to be taken care of. John is very good at these things. For garbage, you send the garbage man. Lad, this is politics, not the seminary. There are always little ugly, dirty things buried in corners. Someone has to look after them."

"Why, Bill? Why even take a position?"

"To get Farrell off my back!" Bill-O said heatedly. "He's hounding me with this Reles thing—"

"Bill, the election is over."

"But I can't do anything if I'm forever answering questions about Abe Reles! My God, that was almost ten years ago. So we help out Farrell with the Garden and I get him off my back!"

Tony walked to the window and watched the falling rain. It moved in great sheets across the back lawn. He could see Wards Island to the north, the waters of Hell's Gate, the borough of Queens across the strait. A blood-red sign advertising Pearl-Wick Hampers glowed through the rain. "I thought we would operate differently, Bill."

"We're doing the best we can, lad."

"What do I tell Jason?"

"Tell him to talk to Johnny McMahon," Bill-O said, puffing on his pipe. He patted his wife on the hand. She smiled down at him. He looked tired, a bit drunk, but contented. "It's a helluva job governing this city, Tony. On rainy nights things look worse than they are." Tony started for the door. "Why don't you have a drink before you go, lad?"

"No, thanks."

"He claims it's Johnny McMahon's responsibility," Tony said to Jason Karl in the living room of his apartment.

"He's just passing it off on John. That's how he operates these days."

"He has a new wife. He wants some peace and quiet."

"He should never have stood for mayor, then. We can't do this to Mike Roth."

"Maybe it's for the best," Tony said. "It's a rotten bunch that has taken over the Garden."

"Televised fights from the Garden are a prize plum. If the Garden promoters are rotten, we should be working to get them out of there, not cooperating with them. I don't understand Bill-O at all in this thing." Tony had never seen Jason so upset. He was pale with anger. "It's not like La Guardia, is it, Tony?"

"It started off with hope, but it's all changed."

Laura entered the room. It was the first time Tony had seen her in a long while. She looked lovely, immaculate. No matter how unexpected his visit, she was always impeccable, elegant. She stirred Tony deeply.

His insides twisted with love; he fought to push it away.

"It's the influence of your father-in-law," Jason said. "More and more Bill-O depends on him. And John only knows how to operate in the old way."

"It troubles me, Jay. It troubles me."

In the next week Tony was called in by the state attorney general's office to discuss gangster influence in the promoting of fights at Madison Square Garden. There had been rumors of bribes over television rights. Jack Foster and the Construction Workers Alliance were implicated.

Tony asked his father-in-law out to the estate on Long Island for dinner. Bess and his brothers were also invited.

Theresa, excited at the prospect of an evening with the whole family, scurried about in eager anticipation. An hour before the guests were to arrive, she began to drink. By mealtime her speech was slurred. She sat through dinner stiff as a waxwork doll.

After the meal, the talk turned to politics. It was the kind of conversation Tony despised, old Tammany political-hack talk—who was doing what for whom and at what price. His brothers and father-in-law entered the discussion gleefully.

Tony's son Darryl, now a freshman in high school, joined in. Tony was immeasurably proud of the boy. He was a first-rate athlete—varsity football, baseball, track—and a fine student. He read voraciously and had a passionate interest in world events. Since he was a child he had followed politics avidly and he could discuss the old warriors of Tammany with the same ease he talked of baseball or football heroes.

Now he confronted John McMahon: "Grandpa, how could you have ever associated with the likes of Eddie Ahearn and Boss Flynn?" Darryl enjoyed riling him, and though he did it in a joshing style, there was an edge of seriousness in his probing. He had inherited Tony's distaste for the ancient machinations of Tammany.

"They're good enough to sit at dinner with the President of the United States, they're good enough for me," McMahon said.

"Old Silent Charlie Murphy would turn over in his grave to see the kind of men who have taken over from him," Darryl said.

"What do you know about Silent Charlie?" asked McMahon.

"Everyone said he was more a gentleman than a thief," Darryl said. Tony's brothers laughed loud and long.

"Don't get so high and mighty, youngster," Bess said, "because you're out here on what they call an *estate*. There are plenty of people have a pot and no chicken, and the likes of Ahearn and Flynn is what puts the chicken in there!"

"The Mafia feeds the poor, too," Darryl said.

McMahon, who had tippled a few during the evening, grew red with anger. "Now, wait one second here, young man. You're equating the sons of Tammany with wop killers! Just wait one minute—"

Darryl didn't back off. "I'm saying that because someone is kind to the poor doesn't make him honest."

"You hear that, Tony? Your son is equating me with common gangsters!"

"Nothing common about Ed Flynn and Boss Ahearn," Tony said, enjoying his father-in-law's discomfort. Things had been tense between them for some time now. McMahon's overt power-grabbing in O'Dwyer's administration rankled him; they had not had much to do with each other ever since the election. He had invited him over this evening because he felt it would give pleasure to Theresa as well as provide him the opportunity to get into the Madison Square Garden business.

Darryl and McMahon continued their discussion. Emmett, James, and Willy joined in. His brothers irritated Tony—their smug pragmatism, their cynicism. Somehow they had absorbed all that was crass and superficial in the United Irish Club: everyone had a price, everything was a deal ripe to be cut.

Darryl was giving better than he got, and McMahon steamed. He pushed away from the table. "I can't talk with my own grandson, for Chrissake!" he yelled. "He knows it all. He knows every damn thing in this world. He even knows where all the devils and angels live!"

He stalked out to the porch, and Tony joined him outside. "He's just a boy, Johnny. He's idealistic."

"He has no respect. You spoiled him. You should take a strap to him from time to time." McMahon flung his arms about, gesticulating, lost his balance, and almost fell off the porch. He sat heavily on the top step. Tony sat next to him.

"Why are we getting involved in that Madison Square Garden thing?" Tony said.

"What thing?"

"Supporting CCNA over DuBois-Roth on the television rights?" John McMahon didn't answer. "I had a call from the attorney general," Tony said. "They're concerned about mob influence in the new Garden group—"

"Stay out of it, Tony," McMahon said. "That's no place for you to be butting in."

"I'm on the boxing commission. How am I supposed to stay out of it?"

"This is gutter-level politics here, Tony. You're not supposed to dirty your hands."

"I'm afraid I'm going to have to involve myself in this thing," Tony said. McMahon studied him with narrowed eyes. "During the election when Farrell was savaging us, Mike Roth helped us out, and I won't be part of any plot to freeze his group out of the Garden."

"You're a damn fool, Tony! We need Farrell. You're going to muck about and blow the whole shebang sky-high!"

"As long as I'm working for Bill-O, I want things done in the right way. You understand me, John? Not the old way—the right way."

"There's no old way and there's no new way. There's only *one* way, and that's the way of the world, the way it's been, the way it'll always be!"

"Not with me around," Tony said.

"Tell that to your kid. Don't tell it to me and don't tell it to Bill-O. You got the Reles thing—"

"What happened to Reles was a long time ago."

"It's the appearances, Tony. That's all politics has ever been—appearances. Television screaming, 'Abe Reles, Abe Reles.' Soon the newspapers start up. Next thing you know, the ghost of that little kike is sharing your underwear, and who knows what mess Farrell will go after next. Don't you see that?"

"Only thing I see is you cutting the deck, dealing him a pat hand. I won't permit it."

McMahon stood unsteadily. His face was flushed. "You took too many punches, Tony. Your brain's mush." On wobbly legs he moved back into the house, with Tony following.

Theresa stood in the archway between the living and dining rooms and stared at her father with an empty expression. "Get my hat and coat!" he yelled at her. "Are you coming, Bess?"

"You have to listen to him, Tony," Bess said. "He's been through the political wars with the best of them—"

"The only thing he learned," Tony said, "is how to get his mitt into the till up to the elbow."

A maid brought their coats. Emmett and the boys struggled to get

McMahon out of the house. "The sheenie made mush out of your brain!" Tony's father-in-law roared.

At last they dragged McMahon out of the house. Everyone left. Tony settled into a chair in the living room and sat for a long time. He thought about Bill-O and his father-in-law, his relationship to Mike Roth. Things were going sour for him. He thought back on his time with La Guardia and he felt a sense of loss. There had been real belief and commitment in the La Guardia days. All that was gone now.

He started to doze, but sensed someone standing above him. It was Theresa, in her nightgown. "You finally found him out," she said slowly. "He's a rotten crook, and you found him out."

"He just likes to bend things a bit."

"You don't know." She stood smiling in the center of the room. It was not a pleasant smile. Her face was puffed from alcohol. She looked frail and aged, and Tony felt a stab of regret. Their marriage had been a mistake; she would have done better without him. "I learned things, Tony. When you were away during the war, I learned things."

"What did you learn?" he said wearily. When she drank, she would become obstinate, grab on to some obscure point and hammer away at it as though no one in the world spoke English.

"You were in the army then. You didn't know. Bill-O would drive up from Washington. My father and he would talk for hours about the future. Bill-O said he would like to become President of the United States. They talked about visiting a certain man."

"What man?" Tony said, exasperated.

"Jack Foster."

What was she talking about? "Why would they visit him?"

She smiled knowingly. "My father told me. 'Bill-O knows about Reles,' my father said when he was drunk. He told me, 'Bill-O knows about Reles. Bill-O was in on the whole thing.' "

"What thing?"

"Bill-O was in on the killing."

Tony stared at her, stunned. What was she raving about? Bill O'Dwyer in on the Reles killing? Insane. "Terry, you're drunk—"

"Yes, I'm drunk. Yes!" She sat on the floor and began to weep. "They used you. Bill-O. My father. They were all in on it. I knew it, and there was nothing I could do. I could just drink and drink and drink. That was all I could do. Oh, God."

She sobbed bitterly, and Tony came to her and held her, but she could not stop crying.

Later, in bed, he had difficulty sleeping. Her words burned in his thoughts. *Bill-O knows about Reles. He was in on the whole thing.*

Was it possible? Did Bill-O and John McMahon hold the key to the mystery of Reles's death? It was inconceivable, and yet the idea pricked at his brain like a poisoned needle.

The next day he tried to bring up the Madison Square Garden situation with Bill-O, but the mayor cut him short: "It just doesn't interest me all that much, Tony. Please. We'll talk about it tonight."

Tony called the chairman of the commission involved with the Garden matter. "I want you to hold off on any decision regarding CCNA," he said.

"I was under the impression the mayor—"

"It hasn't been decided yet."

That night Tony attended a party at Gracie Mansion for Miguel Alemán, President of Mexico. It was a gala affair. The broad lawn of the mansion had been festooned for the occasion with Japanese lanterns. Cultural leaders of the city, Broadway show folk, United Nations dignitaries, milled about while red-coated mariachi musicians strolled among them.

Mrs. O'Dwyer, in a long white gown, looked radiant. Bill-O called together the musicians and sang "Some Enchanted Evening" to her in a pleasant baritone. He had never looked so happy, so carefree.

Hubbard Farrell was at the party. Quite late, as the guests were departing, he informed Tony, Bill-O, and Jason Karl that he wanted to talk with them.

They went into the library. Bill-O was still glowing with the magic of the party, his enchanted evening. "What can I do for you, Hub?" he said expansively.

"Today I received a call from the Garden commission. They said the matter of the television rights was being reconsidered."

"I asked them to hold off," Tony said. "Certain things have to be cleared up with the state attorney general's office."

"Wait a minute, Tony," Bill-O said, flustered. "I thought I told you—"

"What does Farrell have over you?" Tony said quietly.

"This is a party here. What are we all getting so serious about?" Bill-O said.

"I have an investment to protect," Hub Farrell said. "I was promised television rights for the Garden."

"Let's discuss this tomorrow," Bill-O said.

"What does he have over you?" Tony demanded.

"Do you really want to know?" Hub Farrell asked. He was staring directly into Tony's eyes. His gaze was empty.

"Yes."

"Abe Reles," Hub Farrell said. "We know all about Abe Reles."

"What do you know?" Tony said.

"How he died. Who killed him. Who set the whole thing up."

"Who?"

"Ask Bill-O," Hub Farrell said. "He knows everything." He moved to the door. "I'm meeting with the Garden commission tomorrow. I expect to have that contract when I come out of there." He turned his gaze once more on Tony. *"Everything,"* he said softly.

He left, and Bill-O turned to Jason and Tony. His face was gray, blasted.

He looked suddenly very old and tired. "I never wanted this job. They forced me."

"Who forced you? Jack Foster? Lansky?" Tony said. Bill-O didn't answer. "What did they force you to do? Did they force you into setting up the death of Reles?"

"Tony . . ." Jason Karl said quietly.

"He owes me an answer. I've put everything on the line for him. He owes me an answer. What did they force you to do, Bill?"

O'Dwyer didn't speak for a long while. "When you shake hands with the devil, it's hard to let go," he said at last.

"Why? Why did you shake hands with the devil?"

"What does it matter? It's all over now. It's all over."

He didn't look at Tony McGrath or Jason Karl.

"Theresa was right. They had you the whole time," Tony said. "You really were the one, the Trojan horse. You belonged to the big boys above the Tammany bosses. You belonged to the killers. You and Johnny."

Bill-O didn't answer.

Tony turned from Jason and O'Dwyer, hurried from the library and rushed from the house. He walked through Carl Schurz Park to the East River. He hurried along the river, heading downtown. An excursion boat plowed its way through the waters. He could hear laughter from the boat. A group of men and women in evening clothes stood on the deck. They waved at Tony.

He began to run. He ran two miles, from Carl Schurz Park to the United Nations. It was like the old days, the boxing days, the days of roadwork and training, getting up for the big fight.

There would be no more big fights. The knowledge pounded in his head, surged with his blood. There would be no more glory, no more cheers.

Bill-O had deceived him. Bill-O!

He never talked to Bill O'Dwyer again, nor did he ever mention him to anyone.

47

In August 1950 William O'Dwyer resigned as mayor of the city of New York after serving seven months and seventeen days of his second term. He was immediately appointed by President Harry Truman as ambassador to Mexico.

A half-year later he returned voluntarily to New York to the United

States Courthouse on Foley Square to testify before the Senate Crime Investigating Committee. The chairman of the committee was Senator Estes Kefauver of Tennessee.

Tony McGrath watched the proceedings on television in his home on Long Island. In the months since O'Dwyer had resigned, Tony had remained secluded at his house. He planted new trees. He worked in the gardens. He did not go out beyond the estate. He saw no one, not even Jason Karl.

He would not speak to his father-in-law. His brothers ran McGrath Construction. Tony took no interest in the business.

Perhaps the most painful aspect of the O'Dwyer scandal was how it undermined his relationship with his son. Darryl refused to believe his father had no knowledge of O'Dwyer's involvement in the murder of Abe Reles. He grew withdrawn, hostile.

Tony struggled to explain to him the circumstances: How secretive Bill-O had been, how adept at compartmentalizing his life. Darryl refused to accept this. "You must have known! You were with him all the time. You were in the army with him!"

"Darryl, I believed in him. I trusted him—"

"Don't lie to me! It's bad enough what happened, but don't lie to me!"

Late at night Tony would sit alone in the living room of the house and go over his relationship with O'Dwyer, searching in his mind for hints of Bill-O's perfidy, accusing himself, seeking areas where he should have been more vigilant. A litany sang in his thoughts, words he had heard in parochial school as a child: *Ye cannot find the depth of the heart of man; neither can ye perceive the things that he thinketh.* It always came down to that. Who could have plumbed the depths of Bill O'Dwyer? Who could have known?

The Kefauver hearings were carried exclusively by CCNA Television. Hub Farrell had the hit show of the season. The Senate committee's morning, matinee, and evening performances exceeded even the baseball World Series in popular interest. Housewives skimped on their chores. Public officials, business executives, secretaries, crowded around available TV receivers in clubs and offices. A nation watched in rapt attention as an unparalleled spectacle of deceit, bribery, and murder involving some of the top elected officials in the land played out before it.

Thirty million people—the largest television audience ever to have viewed any program—watched as ex-Mayor William O'Dwyer was brought in to testify.

He began his testimony with a general statement on his career and his experiences in law enforcement. He looked tan and fit, although his voice was hoarse from a bout of bronchitis. He wore a blue suit and blue tie. He toyed with a pair of shell-rimmed spectacles. He bent and unbent a paper clip.

"In 1917 I became a member of the police department in this city and remained there for seven years. . . ."

Darryl McGrath came into the den, where Tony sat before the television set. He took a straight-backed chair and moved it near the set. His father did not look at him.

On the television set O'Dwyer continued his rambling discourse.

"I think it might be well to get on with our inquiry into organized crime," said Senator Kefauver, the committee chairman, a tall, courtly Southern gentleman.

"I would like to refer to the Reles case, Mr. O'Dwyer," Senator Charles Tobey of New Hampshire said. A man in his seventies, elfin in appearance with a passionate, evangelical style, he resembled a preacher more than a politician. "Is it not a fact that at the time when Reles was being held as a material witness you had a good case of murder in the first degree against certain very high members of what Mr. Reles called Murder Incorporated?"

Tony leaned forward, his hands clenched in front of him.

"Reles didn't refer to Murder Incorporated," said Bill-O. "Other people used that word. He called it 'the combination.' "

"The combination, then," Senator Tobey said. "Who did he say was the president or the chairman of the board of directors of this combination?"

Bill-O toyed with his spectacles. "As far as he knew, there was no chief man in charge. Just a mutual understanding by the underworld of the various cities throughout the United States, and they sat around and agreed to things among themselves."

"Bugs Siegel—was he one of the top men?"

"They put much trust in him."

"And then he had a partner named Lansky. Was he big at that time?"

"He would be on the same level as Siegel, except that it is quite possible that Lansky went in for things on a grander scale."

"For instance?"

"Narcotics."

"And Jack Foster?"

"He performed a function for them."

"He was and is quite involved in the labor movement? The Construction Workers Alliance?"

"Yes."

"Now, isn't it true that you had an indictable case of murder in the first degree against Mr. Siegel, Mr. Lansky, and Mr. Foster?" Senator Tobey said.

"We had a case on which we wished to indict. But there was a principle of law involved. On the unsubstantiated statement of a co-conspirator you can't possibly get a good indictment. Now, you must realize that the higher up we went, the less independent proof we had, and in the case of Foster and Lansky and Ben Siegel this was very difficult, very high up. This was why Reles was so important—"

"But you had an indictable case?"

Tony watched as, on the television set, Bill-O poured himself a glass of water. Tony pressed his fingers to his brow, massaged the area between his eyes. "As long as Reles remained alive, we had an indictable case," Bill-O said.

"And that was why he was locked up in the hotel, the Half Moon, to keep him alive?"

"Yes."

"And are you familiar with the facts of his death?"

"I am."

"And what is your version of it?"

"He tried to escape and was killed in the attempt when he fell."

Theresa entered the room. She stood in front of the set. "He should be wiped from the face of the earth," she said, drunk.

She moved to the set and tried to turn it off. Darryl grabbed his mother's arm and tried to ease her from the room. She pulled away from him.

"I want that man wiped from the face of the earth!" Theresa screamed.

Letha, the housekeeper, came into the den. She took Theresa by the hand and led her from the room. Tony McGrath stared impassively at the television set.

"Now, let me ask you also," Senator Tobey said, "isn't it a fact that the police records on the Reles case, on the case against Lansky, Siegel, and Foster—that the relevant records were removed from the files on that case?"

"Three years later, when I came back from the war, yes, I learned that the files had been removed."

"Under the circumstances, and in view of the great importance of the matter, would you think there would have been any justification for removal?"

"After Reles's death we did not have an indictable case for murder against these men."

"Did you ever visit Brooklyn between 1942 and 1945?"

"Yes."

"And you frequently saw John McMahon; is that right?"

"That's right," Bill-O said.

"Did you ever check up on whether anything had been done about this most important case in your entire career?"

"Yes."

"And did you discover that the files of the Murder Incorporated case had been removed?"

"I learned that in 1945."

"You learned from Police Captain Frank C. Bals that John McMahon, your assistant, ordered the files removed?"

"It didn't exactly happen like that."

"Don't run away from it, sir. Face the facts." Senator Tobey's voice was vibrant with indignation. "We are asking you serious questions and you are quibbling!"

"I resent the suggestion that I am quibbling."

"You're not going to weasel out of this thing," Tobey said. "I will put it as bluntly as possible. There is no statute of limitations in a murder case. That is the law. But the disappearance of witnesses, by death or otherwise, is just as effective in nullifying as the statute of limitations; yes or no?"

"I will agree that if there are no witnesses, you can't prosecute."

"Now, you had a valid case but the main witness went out a window. However it happened, he did go out that window?"

"Yes."

"And the very man responsible for maintaining the life and safety of that individual, Police Captain Frank C. Bals, is not only not disciplined, but is also given responsibility over the whole investigation of the case, what remained of the case."

"You might put it that way."

"Would I be quibbling if I did?"

"You would not be quibbling."

"And this very same man, this brave police officer, whom others have found to be a flat tire, this Captain Frank C. Bals, is eventually elevated by you to the position of deputy police commissioner?"

"The sequence of events—"

"We'll get to sequence of events. Furthermore, all the relevant files in this investigation are removed less than a half-year after Mr. Reles went out the window, are removed by your very close friend and most confidential assistant."

"I would not characterize Mr. McMahon as my most confidential assistant. Close friend, yes."

"Mr. Tony McGrath was your most confidential assistant, isn't that so?"

Tony McGrath slowly tightened his hands; he stared intently at the screen.

"We had a confidential relationship. Yes."

"Did he know about the removal of the files?"

"He knew nothing about that."

"Why not? Surely as your most confidential assistant he would know these things."

"This matter was not in the scope of his duties."

"But he was deeply involved in the Reles case, was he not?"

"Yes."

"But not in the aftermath?"

"No."

Senator Kefauver interrupted the proceedings. "I would like to note here that Mr. McGrath has in no way been directly implicated in this matter of a cover-up, that in testimony by both Mr. McMahon and Captain Bals he was exonerated of any knowledge in these matters. I consider Mr. McGrath a fine citizen and an exemplary champion in the world of prizefighting."

"Mr. McGrath is blameless in this whole matter," Bill-O said.

"Who, then, is to shoulder the blame?" Senator Tobey said. "Mr. Bals? Mr. McMahon? Or you, Mr. Ambassador, as the immediate superior to these men?"

"Well, you are making great leaps here . . ."

"Would it be fair to say that not one of the men, not Siegel, Lansky, or Jack Foster, who through your investigation you learned were the top people in what you have characterized as 'the combination,' not one of these people has in any way suffered for any of their deeds, including the death of Mr. Abe Reles?"

"I would not agree with that. Mr. Siegel has suffered greatly. He has suffered, as you might say, until death—"

"But that was none of your doing, as far we know."

"I resent the implication."

"I meant to imply nothing, only that the death of Mr. Siegel had nothing to do with the inexorable workings of the law of civilized men. Would that be fair to say?"

"Yes."

"Now, let's discuss Mr. Jack Foster. Did you in December of 1942, while you were in the army, travel from Washington to New York City and go with Mr. John McMahon to the apartment of Jack Foster?"

"I sought out Mr. Foster to find out whether he knew of rumors that friends of Foster and possibly Foster himself were interested in Air Corps contracts, construction supplies and such, whether there was any truth in them."

"Did Mr. McMahon go with you?"

"He did."

"Why did he go with you? To carry a bag, or what?"

"Senator, if the question is legitimate, and intended to be other than sarcastic, I will be most happy to answer it."

"The question is legitimate, bearing on the importance of Mr. McMahon in your official life as district attorney."

"He was a friend of mine, and still is."

"And who was at the meeting?" asked Rudolf Halley, the counsel to the committee, a balding man with a nasal voice.

"There was, in addition to Mr. Foster, Mr. McMahon, and myself, I believe, Mr. Kennedy."

"Congressman Michael Kennedy," Halley said, "who was then leader of Tammany Hall?"

"Yes. I believe he was there when I arrived."

"Did Kennedy seem at all surprised that you were taking up army business with Foster?"

"No, I didn't notice any surprise."

"And how did this meeting with Foster end?"

"I told him that the Air Corps didn't want anyone having contracts in Wright Field unless they were legitimate people."

"And what did he say to that?"

"Nothing. He just said, well, that was all right."

"And when you went to see him, you were conscious, of course, that he was a gangster, a suspected killer, weren't you?" Senator Tobey's voice vibrated indignation. O'Dwyer continued to toy with his spectacles.

"Yes," O'Dwyer said.

"You were not embarrassed by any political or ethical implications be- cause this man is a suspected murderer, and you met with him at his apart- ment with a Tammany leader? This doesn't embarrass you?"

"This happened in Manhattan. Nothing embarrasses me that happens in Manhattan."

There was tense laughter in the hearing room.

"Why would Kennedy have been there?"

"I don't know."

"Was there any political talk?"

"None."

"There was no talk about political plans in regard to support by Mr. Fos- ter and his union, talk about the indictment that had conveniently evapo- rated, no talk of quid pro quo?"

"I have no idea of what quid pro quo you're referring to."

"Did you feel there was any tie-up between Kennedy and Foster and Tammany Hall?"

"This is difficult to ascertain. I was in the army at the time and I had to depend upon what I read in the newspapers."

"And then you came back after the war and proclaimed your determina- tion to rid Tammany Hall of its grip on New York politics; is that right?"

"Yes. I organized a nonpartisan coalition with Tony McGrath, Jason Karl, people of that sort who had participated in the La Guardia adminis- tration to make certain that this city had a clean democratic organization."

"The years previous to your election, the army years—did Jack Foster visit you in Washington?"

"Yes."

"Did anyone know of these visits?"

"John McMahon."

"McGrath?"

"No."

"Even though he was your assistant in your army procurement work, he did not know of these meetings? Why not?"

"He had very emotional feelings about Jack Foster."

"Because of the Reles matter?"

"His general involvement with Lansky and Siegel and so forth, the in- dictment we had been trying to obtain . . ."

"And yet you continued to meet with Mr. Foster for several years after the case had been conveniently squashed?"

"We met several times—his union was involved in government contracts, and in connection with that—"

"And you kept right on meeting with him right through until after the election in 1945?"

"I met him several times, yes."

"Did you ask him to help in your campaign?"

"That was his idea."

"He was tied in with Lansky and Siegel?"

"As I understood it, yes." Bill-O said.

"And Foster had the reputation," Senator Tobey continued, "as the lord high executioner of the combination, didn't he?"

"Well, I didn't know the facts ..." Bill-O said.

"You had the indictment."

"We never made the indictment."

"There were a number of phone calls in the year 1945, through your election, between you and Jack Foster, you and the Construction Workers Alliance ... "

"We were looking for union support."

"Did you talk with Lansky? Siegel?"

"Not to my recollection."

"But you might have?"

"I doubt it."

"Now, when you take help from a man like Foster, let alone Lansky and Siegel, they usually expect something back—that is what they tell me. Is that right?"

"They might. They never ... Jack Foster never mentioned to me any help that he expected."

"He had already received help," Senator Tobey said.

"I don't know what you mean."

"Reles had gone out the window. The indictment, the files on Foster's involvement with Reles, his involvement with Murder Incorporated, 'the combination,' whatever you want to call it, had gone out the window. Frank Bals, your good friend John McMahon who removed the files, they had been rewarded. Isn't it true that Jack Foster had received all the help he could reasonably expect, and isn't it true that the support you received from his union was quid pro quo?"

Darryl stood up, trembling. "You knew! You knew!" He yelled at his father. "Don't lie to me! Don't tell me you didn't know!" Tears streamed down his face.

"I knew none of this!" Tony said. "I swear to you, Darryl. I knew none of this!"

"Liar!" Darryl said. He rushed sobbing from the room.

On the television screen Bill O'Dwyer was leaning forward, shaking with anger. "I reject entirely the implication you have just drawn!"

"Be that as it may," Senator Tobey said, his voice rising, "we'll permit the American people, through this miraculous medium of television through Hubbard Farrell and the Communications Corporation of North America, to draw their own conclusions. And let me just say with the poet John Greenleaf Whittier, 'But solution there is none, Save in the rule of Christ alone.'" The senator's voice choked with emotion. "When the hearts of men are touched, they take their inspiration from the Master of men, and then we will have a righteous and a new America, and we will have in this nation a nation in which dwelleth righteousness, and before God it is high time!"

Bill O'Dwyer smiled a thin, uncomfortable smile. The winners at the hearing had been God and Hubbard Farrell.

Tony McGrath snapped off the set.

48

Mike Roth had not been sleeping well. A recurring dream haunted his nights. He was in Yankee Stadium, boxing. He was blinded by the lights. He could not make out his opponent, though he was fairly certain it was Tony McGrath. In a brutal fight, he was being beaten badly. He was knocked down. He shielded his eyes from the lights and realized he was staring up at Hubbard Farrell.

In 1955 things went poorly for DuBois-Roth. CCNA attacked the company relentlessly in pretrial hearings on DuBois's assertion of patent infringement. It was apparent that even should DuBois-Roth win, the victory would be moot; the legal fees would break them.

They were on the edge of disaster.

All advice to DuBois to settle out of court and grant CCNA a licensing agreement had been refused. DuBois would not even consider the idea.

He rose at three A.M., read the transcripts of the previous day's hearings, jotted down questions to be pursued; at ten he would appear at the DuBois-Roth offices on Madison Avenue for a council of war with Mike, Jason, and the lawyers. The sessions usually continued until four in the afternoon. After, there would be a rehash lasting until eight or nine in the evening.

DuBois insisted on handling everything himself; he followed each legal twist and turn, worried over every detail. Nights and weekends were spent poring over stacks of documents. He argued with everyone, fired lawyers, abused secretaries. He never seemed to sleep. When he was not involved with the patent hearings, he was badgering his research crews as they toiled to make sense out of the manic fire-storm exploding from his fevered brain.

It was obvious to everyone that Elias DuBois was near a breakdown, yet no one could persuade him to relent, to settle.

Hub Farrell and his attorneys moved in for the kill.

Mike rose, shaved, then joined his wife and daughter in the glass-walled breakfast nook of their apartment overlooking Central Park. The dream he had the night before had put him in a sour mood. Without thinking, he picked up the New York *Times* and began to read. "Daddy, you're being rude," Jenny said. She banged her spoon against the side of her cereal bowl.

"Don't play games with your oatmeal," he said.

Pat warned, "Don't start with her."

"Don't start with me," Jenny mimicked.

"Quiet, peanut," Mike said.

"I'm not a peanut. Patricia, will you tell your husband your daughter is not a peanut."

"She's not a peanut, Mike."

He glanced at the sports page. Darryl McGrath, Tony's elder son, was playing football at Princeton. Tailback in a single-wing formation, he was being considered for All-American. Mike read about him and thought of all the years that had passed. Tony McGrath's son at Princeton! It seemed to him that only the day before McGrath and he were duking it out down by the Fulton Street docks! His life was whizzing by, moving with such rapidity that he could barely grab hold of it. Where was it leading?

He turned to the financial page. CCNA was in Washington meeting with the Federal Communications Commission. Angrily he folded the paper and put it away.

"What?" Pat said.

"While we're up to our ass in lawyers on the patent-infringement thing, Farrell is beating our brains in down in D.C."

"Daddy, your language!" Jenny said.

"You can't let DuBois do this."

"What do you suggest I do? He won't sell. The company is his life. He won't listen to anybody . . ."

"Force him out. You and Jason could do it. Force him out!"

Lately, his wife displayed a ruthlessness in these discussions that cut through to him. A fierce, hard look came over her, and something grew very tight inside him. She was accusing him, blaming him. She married him, in part, because he was a champion, a winner. Now it looked as though her ex-husband was the true winner. She was disappointed in him.

Tension between them festered. Discussion became argument. The fabric of the marriage began to tear.

"It's war," Pat said. "You can't win with DuBois." She wanted Mike to win, of course. Yet she constantly threw it up to him that he couldn't win.

"I'm not going to jettison DuBois. What Farrell is doing to him is wrong. I have to fight for him." His stomach was tight with anger. The dream of the night before stayed with him: blinding lights, an opponent he couldn't see, a knockdown, Hub Farrell standing over him, gloating.

"Elias DuBois is certifiably insane."

"All right, then, I'm fighting for myself!" He stood up, pushing away his breakfast. "That smooth, conning, son-of-a bitch ex-husband of yours has got to realize I won't back off."

"Daddy, watch your language," Jenny said.

"Finish your oatmeal!" She stuck out her tongue at him. He slapped her. "Michael!" Patricia yelled.

Tears came to Jennifer's eyes; her lower lip began to tremble. Mike grabbed her and hugged her to him. "I'm sorry, sweetheart. Forgive me." He held her to him for a very long time, brushed her tears from her face. "Do you forgive me?"

She nodded her head.

He left the apartment and walked down Fifth Avenue. It was a bright, early-fall day. At the corner of Sixty-fifth Street, Jason waited in his limousine. "Let's walk, Jay," Mike said. The two of them strolled down Fifth Avenue, walking to the DuBois-Roth offices.

In the five years since Bill O'Dwyer had left the mayor's office, Jason had aged considerably. In the past he always looked younger than his years. Now, at seventy-plus, he looked his age. The O'Dwyer affair had taken its toll.

"What do we do with him today?" Jason said as they turned east on Fifty-ninth Street. For months now it was their morning conversation: what to do about DuBois.

"I don't know, Jay. I just don't know."

"If we could only compromise. Work out a licensing arrangement with Farrell . . ."

"He won't permit it, Jay. Either he prevails or he'll bury the company."

"We're going to need outside financial help, you know. We could approach McGrath."

"I can't bring myself to go to him," Mike said. "Not again."

"Very likely it's too late now anyway."

"How's he doing these days?"

"He's isolated himself from everything and everybody."

They walked in silence for a while. "Why don't you bury things with McGrath?"

"I wish I could. I just can't."

At the office, DuBois was waiting for them. He stood very stiffly; his eyes were narrow and bright, piercing, as though a red flame burned behind them. "I want to get rid of the lawyers."

"Elias, we can't start with new lawyers—not again," Mike said.

"They're sabotaging us. Farrell's gotten to them."

"It's too late to start again," Jason said. "CCNA has gone before the Federal Communications Commission. We might beat them in court, but the FCC will lock us out. I implore you. Let's settle now while we can!"

"It's not honorable," DuBois said quietly. "What Hubbard Farrell has done to me is sinful. The verdict of history will be that a crime has been committed against me and against the art of television."

The lawyers arrived, two dry, proper men who served DuBois's cause with patience if not enthusiasm. They discussed the day's interrogatory hearing. Things were not going well. If CCNA received approval from the

Federal Communications Commission on its own color system, DuBois-Roth would be effectively frozen out of the market. It was probably too late even to swing a deal with Farrell.

"We will win," DuBois said. "We're in the right and we will win because of that. The Federal Communications Commission will acknowledge that we are right. *All the patents underlying everything Hubbard Farrell has done have been stolen from me!*"

They were off again. For the next hour Elias DuBois railed against the courts, the government, CCNA. Mike Roth watched him and felt an immense sadness, not so much because he obviously was cracking, but because there was truth in what he said.

At last his fury was spent. He gazed at the wall. "It's time," one of the lawyers said.

They left the office and traveled together downtown to Broad Street, to the offices of Hubbard Farrell's attorneys. On the drive, DuBois was listless. He stared out the window without talking.

With the CCNA lawyers, ground previously covered was gone over again. A new team was at work for the defendants, a stratagem to drag things out in Farrell's war of attrition. CCNA's lawyer began the session: "What is your occupation?"

"I am an executive in charge of research and development with a television company," DuBois said.

"Do you have any other occupation?"

"I occasionally make inventions." DuBois's voice was weary. "You know, of course, this whole thing touches on material of record in the Patent Office going back some forty years?"

"What has been the basic direction of your inventions?" Farrell's lawyer was a heavyset man in his late fifties, dressed in a gray pinstripe suit with a vest. He had narrow eyes and a serious mien. He appeared bored by DuBois, affronted by the necessity of going through a pretrial interrogatory.

DuBois barely listened to the CCNA lawyer. He stared out the window watching the flocks of pigeons that roosted on the ledge. "I'm sorry," he said, when he realized the lawyer was waiting for his answer. "I've gone over this so many times . . ."

"Yes, but it's necessary, you see . . ."

"The basic work that I have done for over forty years has been to discover new principles and apply them to the production of original results in the art of radio and television. I have succeeded three times in doing things that could not be done. Three times Hubbard Farrell has attempted to usurp my work."

"But the regenerative-circuit patent was long ago decided in the courts against you," Farrell's lawyer said.

"Courts deal with facts. Fact is not necessarily truth, though it can be arranged to give the appearance of truth."

The interrogation droned on. DuBois stared out at the pigeons.

Toward the end of the day Hubbard Farrell arrived. He appeared buoyant, glowing. The lawyer for CCNA completed his questioning and DuBois's attorneys requested the opportunity to ask some questions of Farrell.

Farrell avoided looking at Mike and DuBois. He glanced often at his gold wristwatch: a man with more important things to attend to. The lawyer asked Farrell to discuss his background in electronics and particularly to touch on his relationship over the years with DuBois. Farrell spoke of how he had gone to work for the Marconi Company as an office boy, how he had met and admired DuBois, who was then an important associate of Marconi's. "We were quite friendly in those days," Farrell said, speaking as though DuBois were not in the room. "He was witty and imaginative, though prone to exaggeration."

"Did you learn from him?"

"I learned a good deal from him, although I fear his reach sometimes went beyond his grasp."

"What do you mean by that?"

"I have never regarded myself as a genius. I always knew my limitations. DuBois never accepted his. He invented, but sometimes his inventions were in the nature of dreams rather than actualities."

"Haven't you claimed, though, to have made significant contributions to the television art?"

"Not for myself. I always relied on advisers. I've had as many advisers as a dog has fleas. Many of the elements that DuBois has claimed as inventions, many of the patents he applied for down through the years, were actually built on the work of others or skirted the work of others."

"Are you denying the contributions DuBois has made to the art?"

Farrell looked impatient. "It's possible that a court in certain circumstances might feel that some contributions claimed by DuBois were in the nature of inventions, but on the whole I am confident that my company has done more to develop the state of the art in television than anybody in the country, including Elias DuBois."

DuBois, who had been staring out the window, suddenly snapped to attention. He glared at Farrell.

"Mr. Farrell," the lawyer said, "in 1941 the Franklin Institute of Pennsylvania awarded Elias DuBois the Franklin Medal, one of this country's highest awards for achievement in electronics, for his work in regenerative circuits. In giving the award, it was noted, and I quote, 'This invention alone would entitle Elias DuBois to a place with the greatest inventors and benefactors in the radio and television art.' In 1942 he was given the highest award by the American Institute of Electrical Engineers, the Edison Award."

Hubbard Farrell smiled. "As you well know, the question of the regenerative circuit was fought out in the courts over a period of years and decided against DuBois."

"According to the citation accompanying the Edison Award, DuBois was praised in these terms: 'The regenerative circuit was the keystone in the development of radio and television and though in eighteen years of litigation lay courts handed down decisions based on errors of fact and judgment contrary to scientific truth, depriving Mr. DuBois of legal possession of his invention, it is undeniable that his genius was the guiding light behind this discovery.' "

"Yes, I am aware of the award. Nevertheless, the legal judgment stands. We have never denied DuBois's eminence, only the legality of his claims."

Hubbard Farrell completed his interrogatory. He sat back, a half-smile on his face.

DuBois was permitted to make a statement. His voice was so soft everyone had to strain forward to hear him. "I belong to a generation which learned the meaning of volts and amperes during a time of giants—Edison, Pupin, Marconi. These men were my mentors." He spoke with enormous fatigue and continued to stare out the window. Pigeons rose and fluttered in his gaze. "When I look back at my life in science, I am seized with an almost inexpressible sense of loss. In the beginning I believed that only the discovery was important. I knew nothing of the greed and mendacity of men. I have made certain contributions, and some people have taken note of these. However . . ." His voice trailed off. He stared at the pigeons.

Farrell glanced at his watch, fidgeted. He signaled to his lawyer, who said, "Perhaps we should cut this session short. Mr. DuBois seems fatigued."

"Yes, I am tired today," DuBois said.

Farrell scribbled a note and passed it to his lawyer. The lawyer read it, then stared at Farrell, who nodded his head, a hint of a smile playing at his lips. "All of this is rather academic," the lawyer said. "At an investment of nearly twenty million dollars, the Communications Corporation of North America has developed a color system which we are convinced does not infringe on the patents of Mr. DuBois. We have petitioned the Federal Communications Commission for approval of our system. I have just learned that earlier today the FCC has approved our color system for commercial development and rejected that of DuBois-Roth as being incompatible with present broadcast standards."

Mike Roth looked on dumbfounded. Farrell had entered the office in possession of the news. He allowed DuBois to be raked over yet again, then sprang the news on him. It was a crushing development. DuBois's work on color television was swept away. CCNA would prevail.

DuBois showed no emotion. He walked to the window and gazed out. Farrell left the office without a word.

On the drive back uptown, Mike, Jason, and DuBois did not speak. DuBois's face was ashen. He had been defeated. CCNA had effectively appropriated his ideas, skirted his patents, and won the prize.

DuBois asked to be left off at the Madison Avenue offices. "Why don't you go home and get some sleep?" Jason said.

"Yes. As soon as I check some things in the files."

DuBois entered the building. Jason and Mike crossed Madison Avenue and entered a café on the corner of Forty-sixth Street. It was early evening now. They sat at a small table by the window and had a drink. Neither spoke for a long time. "It's over, Mike," Jason said after a while.

"Yes."

"Hub Farrell just had too much power behind him. Poor Elias."

Mike smiled a bitter smile and sipped at his drink. "The poor son of a bitch. The poor, poor son of a bitch."

Elias DuBois removed some papers from a file. He began to read over them, but could not concentrate. Outside the office window a single bird of pure white alighted on the ledge. It fluttered, cooed softly.

DuBois moved to the window and opened it. Seventeen stories below, cars and people appeared unreal, toys, tiny and inconsequential. All of it seemed inconsequential. At this moment the only thing of importance was this dove, the dove of his past, the dove of his genius.

He reached his hand out to the bird. If he could hold it in his palm, whisper to it, explain his situation, the bird would give him an answer. The dove knew it all, knew past and future, knew the secrets of the universe.

Slowly, slowly he reached for the dove. It squatted on the ledge, puffed its chest out, stared at him with a look of eerie cognizance.

Elias DuBois's hand trembled, inches from the dove. He moved to touch it. He was so close, so close.

As he moved his hand a last delicate distance, the dove backed off. DuBois grabbed at it but the bird rose out of his grasp, soared gracefully from the ledge. It swooped down, then fluttered up, disappearing into the shadows of the surrounding buildings.

At that moment the flight of the dove was the most exquisite disappointment of DuBois's life, painful, exhilarating. *"He wants me to follow,"* DuBois said aloud in a tone of wonder.

He climbed out onto the ledge and searched the sky for the white dove. He saw something far, far above him dip, then rise beyond the building tops.

Elias DuBois stretched out, yearned to reach the dove. He hurtled himself after it, leaped into vast emptiness, flung himself beyond dimensions of law and fact, mundane science, and into a universe of purity unimaginable, where motes of light, particles of energy, danced in awesome coloration, embracing him as though a lover, because he was truth. He was the dove.

Down below, Jason and Mike saw a dark form spread-eagle against the building facade opposite them and plummet toward the street.

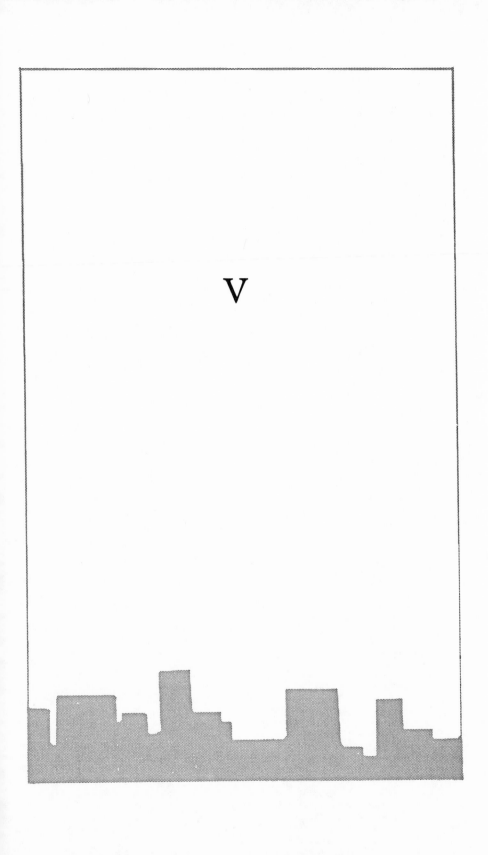

V

49

In the spring of 1959 New York City Mayor Robert F. Wagner was the main speaker at a dinner for reform Democrats at the Commodore Hotel. Darryl McGrath, who had published several articles in a scholarly journal on shifts of power within the Democratic party, was contacted by people working for Senator John F. Kennedy. Kennedy, pushing to gain the presidential nomination, was seeking out bright young people with fresh ideas.

At the dinner Darryl found himself seated at a table filled with youthful Kennedy supporters, Ivy league types who drank a lot, laughed, made farting sounds with their lips, and exchanged wisecracks.

New York Mayor Wagner, a short, serious man with a colorless style, droned on in a speech of numbing banality. Darryl remembered stories of Al Smith and Jimmy Walker he'd heard as a child and found himself thinking how dreary the modern political scene was. Earlier someone at the table had commented: "Poor Bob Wagner—doesn't have anything except the votes on election day." Darryl found the remark apt and depressing.

Wagner finished his speech. The people in the banquet room began to mill about, and Senator Kennedy, tanned and extraordinarily handsome, moved through the room shaking hands.

Someone introduced him to Darryl. He flashed his brilliant smile and said, "I've had it in for you. You're the man who humiliated my alma mater in '56." Princeton had devastated Harvard that year; Darryl scored three touchdowns and passed for another. "How's your dad?"

"Fine."

"He's one of my heroes," said Kennedy.

He seemed genuinely pleased to meet Darryl, and though his aides were eager to keep him moving around the room, Kennedy was in no hurry. "My boys tell me you've turned out some first-rate material. Scholar-athlete. That's good."

"Not much of a scholar. As an athlete, well . . ." Darryl shrugged.

"How do you enjoy playing the pro game?"

"It's a job," Darryl said. After leaving Princeton he was offered a professional contract with Cleveland. With his political-science major he had planned to enter graduate school, but was unable to resist the challenge of pro football. He was in his third year now, good and getting better, and was operating as first-string quarterback this season.

"Think you'll stick with it?" Kennedy said.

"As long as I'm healthy."

"How do you like the political game?"

"I have all I can handle with football right now."

"Can you spare me some good tough Irishmen to block downfield for me?" Kennedy asked. His eyes had a nice twinkle to them. Darryl liked him.

"I thought you had all those up in Boston."

Kennedy laughed. "We have a few, we have a few." He patted Darryl on the shoulder. "When you see your Grandma Bess, give her love from Jack Kennedy!" Then he moved off through the crowd, winking and chatting as he went.

"Handsome son of a bitch, isn't he?" someone behind Darryl said. He turned. An attractive woman in her fifties stood there with a drink in her hand.

"Yes."

"You're nice-looking too," the woman said, the hint of a smile playing at the corners of her mouth. She was looking at him in a mock-sultry way and Darryl couldn't decide whether or not she was serious. "You don't remember me? I'm Laura Karl, Jason's wife," she said, laughing.

Darryl hadn't seen Jason since leaving Princeton and he had met Laura only once or twice when he was a child.

"Let me buy you a drink," she said.

He followed her to the bar at the far end of the room. "I knew it was you the minute I saw you," she said. "You look so much like Tony. What'll you have? Your father was partial to gin."

"I prefer Scotch."

"With all the money Joe Kennedy's got, you'd think he'd at least spring for the drinks," she said. Drinks were priced at ten dollars a shot: the money went to Kennedy's campaign.

"How's your father?" Laura said after they had seated themselves at a round table near the bar.

"I don't see him these days."

"You're still on the outs. That's sad."

"He's very proud."

"Your mother? How's she?"

"In and out of clinics. She'll beat the sauce for a while, but she always goes back."

"The kids, Sean and Sharon—they must be . . . how old?"

"They're getting into their teens."

Laura Karl sipped at her drink. She smiled. Darryl didn't speak for a while, then said hesitantly, "I was just thinking—you're a very attractive lady."

"Why, thank you, sir!" She laughed. It was a throaty laugh, seductive. "You remind me so much of your father! I've known him since we were kids. Your grandmother—she practically ran the neighborhood. She and

Johnny McMahon and Eddie Ahearn and all the other Irish elves and lepre-
chauns!" She shook her head slowly, smiling. "How is Bess?"

"Feisty as ever. She's nearly eighty and she's down at the United Irish
Club every day playing poker."

"You're a football player, and I remember Jason telling me you were
somehow involved in politics."

"In an academic sense only."

"It's a heartbreaking game. Jason tried so hard to accomplish things. In
the end, what did he have to show for it? Your father, also."

"He's like a wounded animal now," said Darryl. "He has such immense
pride . . ."

"I know. He's carried on that silly feud with Mike Roth for twenty-five
years now. Both of them are proud, honest, generous men and so alike they
could be brothers." She drained her drink. "Can I buy you another?"

"This one's on me." Darryl brought the drinks to the table. "How is
Jason?"

"He won't touch politics with a ten-foot pole. I pestered him to come
here tonight, but he arranged to be out of town on business. He wanted me
with him, but I said, 'Jay, John Kennedy is good-looking enough to be a
movie star and he's going to become President of the United States and I'm
going over there to the Commodore and see if I can have an affair with him.
Before I die, I want to be able to say I bedded a President!'" She laughed
the same throaty, vaguely sexual laugh. "Jack Kennedy shook my hand and
winked. I guess that's as close as this old lady is going to get with him."

The orchestra struck up a fox-trot. "Shall we?" Laura said.

"All right."

"You feel familiar," she said on the dance floor, and nestled in close to
him. Her body felt soft, youthful to Darryl, and he marveled at it. She was
his mother's age, yet he found her as attractive as though she were in her
twenties. "I'll bet you're devastating with women," she teased.

"I'm better at football."

"Are you a good lover?"

"I said I'm better at football."

"Ah, athletes." She looked up at him, smiling. "Excuse the foolishness of
a sexy old broad."

"Not old," Darryl said. "Sexy, certainly." They laughed.

"I like you," she said.

"I like you, too."

"Let's get out of here," Laura said when the number was over. "I can only
take so much of politics and politicians. It's an allergy I've developed. Now
that Jack Kennedy has left, all these people suddenly look very avaricious
and somewhat foolish."

They left the hotel. Darryl hailed a cab. "Where to?" he asked once they
had settled into the backseat.

"How about a nightcap at my place?" She gazed at him with a look humorous, inviting. "That is, if you trust yourself with me. I told you Jason is out of town."

"I think I can trust you," Darryl said, laughing.

The living room of the apartment was done in blue and white. The furniture was delicate antique. She fixed Darryl a drink, then excused herself. She returned in a quilted housecoat and sat in a chair opposite him. "What are your plans for the future?" she asked.

"I've thought about getting into active politics, maybe running for office after my football days are over. I've *thought* about it, but I don't think I have the stomach for it."

"It takes a strong stomach," said Laura.

He finished his drink. She took his glass, moved to the bar, and poured him another. "In the immediate future I'm considering a change," he said. "Some people have contacted me. They're forming a rival league to the National Football League. They'd like me to come over as both player and management."

Laura returned and sat next to him on the couch. "That would be a challenge," she said.

"They'd really like to have someone like my father, someone with money and a national name in sports. He won't talk with them."

"How about Mike Roth?" she suggested. "He's out of the television business now. I'm sure he might be interested."

"Mike Roth," said Darryl. "Yes."

"I could talk to Jason. The three of you could get together."

"He's exactly what they're looking for," Darryl said. "Yes." They didn't talk for a while. Laura shifted on the couch, leaned close to him. He could feel her staring at him. She radiated sexuality. He could hear her breath quickening. His heart was racing.

She was not a young woman, and yet she was beautiful. Since they had first talked at the Commodore Darryl had been aware of the seduction she was carrying on. It was obviously sexual and yet it was more: there was a charm about her, a quality of intelligence and warmth that Darryl found immensely appealing. He wanted her not just because of her beauty but because of some inner fineness that touched him deeply.

She leaned back, smiling. "You remind me so much of your father," she said. "When I was young, I was very much in love with him, as he was with me. Did he ever tell you that?"

"No."

"I don't think I ever got over it. Isn't that stupid?"

He took her in his arms and kissed her. She was soft against him, inexpressibly lovely. Their bodies seemed to flow together, and Darryl felt as though he were being carried along by some swift, delicate stream, ˙ ˙zying, blissful. He was drunk, not so much with liquor as with the loveliness of Laura Karl.

She permitted her housecoat to fall open. She was naked beneath it. He lowered his lips to her breasts and marveled at how soft, how youthful, how perfect they were.

And then she took his face and drew it up to look in his eyes. She shook her head, smiled wistfully, and hugged him to her. "Oh, Darryl, I'm so stupid! I brought you up here to make love to you, but it was foolish. I really wanted your father. I wanted him as both of us were thirty years ago. And of course that can never be." She kissed him gently. "I would go through with it, I would make love to you, but it really wouldn't be you, and that's quite silly, isn't it?"

"It's not silly, I think it's perfect. I understand, and I love you for it," he said, and he meant not a passionate love, but a love for the quality she possessed, the honesty, the fineness.

"We would both feel rotten after. This way we can still like each other."

"Yes," he said.

"That's the miserable thing about this life. You'd like to take Time and turn it on its ear. And that's the one thing you never can do."

"I think you're a magnificent lady! My father has exceptional taste!"

"Oh, he loved someone much different from this old gal," said Laura. "I've done so many ridiculous things since then." And suddenly she was crying.

"What is it?" asked Darryl.

She smiled through the tears. "I feel so happy to have met you again. My long-lost love, my sweet Tony!" She dried her tears. "I know, I know. But for a moment there . . . oh, what a sweet moment!" She shook her head and looked at him directly. "Hello, young Darryl McGrath."

50

Mike Roth nicked himself shaving, and as he tried to stop the bleeding he paused, gazed at his reflection, and saw the face of a stranger. Staring at his face in the mirror, he realized he was aging. He felt a sense of wonderment: one day you're a young man and in the blink of an eye you've become middle-aged.

Over the years he had put on weight. He was active, played handball several times a week, went sailing in the summer, skied in the winter. Nevertheless, a bulking up, a thickening had occurred.

As he stared into the mirror observing the stranger he had become, he found himself considering his life as though it, too, belonged to someone else.

It was a pleasant life, financially secure, lived by a man who commanded respect for his past accomplishments and his present position. And yet it was a life essentially without direction. Mike was fifty-three years old; for all intents and purposes, he was retired, his best days behind him.

He entered the living room of the apartment. Pat was seated at the window, reading. His fourteen-year-old daughter, Jenny, a redhead like her mother, though tall and willowy, rushed to him. "Hi, cutie," he said, hugging her.

"Where you going?"

"Dinner at the Princeton Club."

"Can I come?"

"Women are not welcome there," Pat said.

"Why not?"

"Men feel they need a haven from us, dear," Pat said.

"That's really rotten," Jenny said. "Why do you need a haven, Daddy?"

"You're my haven," said Mike.

"Slick, Roth, slick," Patricia said. "Let me look at you."

Mike stood in front of her for inspection, feeling, as he always did at these times, foolish. Over the course of his marriage Mike found himself adapting to styles of behavior that went against his grain: he became a fashion plate to please his wife, joined the right clubs, weekended on Long Island, suffered interminable boring luncheons and banquets, talked endless business deals with men he would have preferred not to have been in the same room with.

Things had deteriorated between him and Pat. Ever since the battle between CCNA and DuBois-Roth there had been a quiet, corrosive tension in the marriage. The truth of it was that Pat had never fully forgiven him for having lost out to Hubbard Farrell.

His daughter had become the true center and focus of his life.

"You look nice," Pat said, her appraisal completed.

"He looks like an undertaker," Jenny said.

"Better than looking like the corpse."

"Not much," Jenny cracked.

"No one likes a wiseacre." He kissed her, then his wife, and departed feeling vaguely empty, defeated. Yes, his life had not worked out precisely as he would have liked it. And yet whose life ever did?

His meeting at the Princeton Club was for eight o'clock. He arrived ten minutes early. The maître d' treated him with elaborate courtesy, addressing him by name. He was seated at a table in the wood-paneled dining area and he ordered a martini.

Several people in the dining area nodded and smiled at him. Though this recognition had been his for nearly thirty years, he had never really felt comfortable with it. Undefeated heavyweight champion of the world. It was like a chronic ailment: it would follow him to the grave.

Jason Karl arrived, looking gaunt. He leaned heavily on a cane. A young man helped him into the dining room—Darryl McGrath. Mike, who had seen him only in newspaper photos or in full uniform on a football field, would nevertheless have recognized him immediately: he was a slightly taller, blonder replica of his father. He moved with the same grace and controlled energy, had the same handsome, rugged look.

"How are you feeling, Jay?" Mike said as they reached the table.

"The only thing to be said about getting older," Jason said, easing into a chair, "is that it's better than the alternative—although I'm really not certain." He introduced Darryl to Mike.

"I'm a fan," Darryl said. "My father would never mention you, so naturally I went out of my way to learn all about you. You were a helluva fighter."

"Your father was no pantywaist either," Mike said.

"I'm sorry about the bad blood between the two of you."

"I suppose it's natural that two men who spent so much effort trying to beat each other's brains out shouldn't be bosom buddies."

"Why is it that you got along so badly?" Darryl asked. "He would never tell me anything about it. No one seems to know."

"I'm not so sure I know too much about it either," said Mike. "It all happened a long time ago. Shall we order?"

Over dinner they engaged in small talk, sports, the political scene. At last Darryl got to the point of the meeting. "I've had an offer from a group of men interested in setting up a league to rival the National Football League. They wanted my father to head up the New York team. He wouldn't talk to them. Jason thought you might be interested."

"How would you fit in?"

"I would play with the team, eventually shift over to management."

"It would be a murderous job trying to muscle in on the National Football League."

"Television would be the key," Darryl said. "With sufficient television revenues you'd have a margin to make it go."

"Mike, you have the connections and expertise in that area," Jason said. "You're a significant sports figure. You'd give the league a certain solidity."

Mike remained quiet for a while, turning the idea over in his mind. It didn't appeal to him. The chances of success would be slim. He remembered the other past attempts to establish rival leagues in baseball and football. They had all failed ignominiously.

"You'd have to go up against Hub Farrell again," said Jason.

"How so?"

"He's firmly behind the National Football League on this thing," Darryl said. "He's determined to keep the television networks in line. If they don't give the new league television exposure, it wouldn't have a chance."

And now a certain excitement began to stir in Mike. He would have to go up against Hub Farrell again! "That might be interesting," he said. "It could be a fight."

"I thought that might have some appeal for you," Jason said, smiling.

"Yes." Suddenly he was alive inside. A great energy and passion rose up within him. He had a debt to repay Hubbard Farrell, and he would have another chance at it.

In his mind's eye he saw the dark form of Elias DuBois plunging to the earth.

"Tell your people to count me in," Mike said to Darryl.

"Good," Darryl McGrath said. "I think we might have some fun."

"I agree. I always questioned the value of fighting, even when I was doing it for a living. I was wrong. There's great value in a worthwhile fight. Yes."

He felt better, more alive, than he had in a long, long time.

51

Mike Roth drove through the foothills of the San Gabriel Mountains. The city of Los Angeles sprawled to the south, a vast patchwork of bungalows, freeways, gas stations, supermarkets, drive-in movies, hamburger stands, used-car lots. To the west he could see the ocean; to the east, the desert. Over it all, a dark, angry streak in the sky, hung a pall of smog.

It was more than twenty years since he had been here, and the change in the city filled him with dismay. When he was here before, the place had the feel of a small town. Now it was a bloated monstrosity.

He tried to shake his depression. It's the clutter, he told himself, the smog. But he knew that it was something deeper.

He would be seeing his ex-wife and son.

Over the years he had tried to stay in touch with Matthew, but his son was cold and hostile over the phone. Eventually Mike lost all desire to have anything to do with either the boy or Lisa. And yet he suffered remorse. Of course his son had been cold to him. He had deserted the boy, hadn't he? The mitigating circumstances, Lisa's involvement with Ben Siegel, her refusal to permit Mike even limited custody of his son—how could the kid have understood it? Who knew what his mother had told him?

Young Matthew was a problem child; he had difficulty in school, truancy, expulsions. As an adult he had bounced from job to job. Recently he was in more serious trouble: he had served a short prison term. Now he was out.

And Mike, who was in California on business, would be visiting both Lisa and Matthew.

He would try to help the boy, but he had misgivings. How would Matthew react to him?

His position in professional football had brought him to Los Angeles: the

previous year he was made president of the New York franchise in the new
league rivaling the National Football League. The team was called the
Tartars and it was made up of rejects from the other league, with a few
established players who had been lured away. Darryl McGrath was the quarterback on the team.

The new league was struggling. They could only succeed by gaining television coverage and revenues. But the networks, led by Hubbard Farrell and
CCNA, would not deal with them.

Mike was on his way to Monrovia, where DuBois-Roth television had
once been located. There he would meet with the chairman of the board of
Western Television, the group that had purchased the broadcast facilities of
DuBois-Roth.

Wilfred Lowry, the head of Western Television, had a strong dislike for
Farrell, who had crossed him somewhere along the way. Mike had a double-
edged strategy: he would attempt to get Lowry and his regional syndicate to
break ranks with the networks. And he would fight to outflank the new
league in the college draft by signing a bona fide star.

The area in Monrovia where the laboratory had once been was almost
unrecognizable. What used to be wooded hills dotted with an occasional
frame shack was now terraced with concrete and stucco, offices, studios,
parking facilities. The sign at the gate proclaimed: WESTERN TELEVISION.

Wilfred Lowry's office was large and sunny, affording a magnificent view
of downtown Los Angeles. It was done up in bright plastic, oranges and
yellows. Lowry, a chubby man of middle age, wore colors to match the office decor, canary-yellow slacks, Hawaiian shirt with a pattern of tropical
fruit.

"What kind of deal can we make?" he said, offering Mike a low-slung
canvas chair of modern Danish design. "I want to give Hub Farrell heartburn."

"I think we can do that."

"I'm listening."

"Who's the premier college football player in the United States?"

"Duane Gurley, USC," Lowry said without hesitation. Gurley, a handsome, articulate black man, had broken every collegiate running record in
the book. He was drafted by the New York Giants in the NFL, and though
the Tartars had picked him in the AFL, no one gave them the slightest
chance of landing him.

"What if I sign him?"

Wilfred Lowry smiled and shook his head. "That would be a helluva
coup."

"Would Western Television enter into a contract with our league?"

"How are you going to get Gurley? Hub Farrell's working with the
Giants on this thing. They're offering Gurley a television contract in addition to his regular player's contract."

"They're offering it, but it won't go through," Mike said. "There's not a
Negro working in any major capacity in the television today. The networks

are scared to death of the Southern markets. Farrell will never risk it."

"What do you want from me?"

"If I get Gurley, would you be willing to risk your Southern markets?"

"Match Farrell's offer, you mean?"

"And deliver on it."

Wilfred Lowry puffed on his cigar, thinking; his baby face grew serious. He leaned back. A twinkle came into his eyes. "That would really stick it to old Hub, wouldn't it? I might just do that. Not out of any principles, you understand. And not for profit. Just to stick it to Hub Farrell. But you have to land Gurley. The Giants have him locked away someplace out in the desert."

The competition between the two leagues for college stars had been fierce, with all manner of farcical skullduggery employed to outwit the other side. Players were spirited away in the middle of the night, sequestered in remote hideaways, bombarded with round-the-clock negotiations.

"I have a rabbit up my sleeve," Mike said. "I think I can get Duane Gurley."

Wilfred Lowry moved to Mike and shook him vigorously by the hand. He was positively beaming. "Pull that off, boy, and you got position. And that's all this life is—position. With Duane Gurley, we got us a deal!"

Mike left Western Television and drove from the foothills down into the San Fernando Valley. He had spoken with Lisa that morning, and she had given him an address in North Hollywood.

The house was a run-down frame with a sagging porch and weedy lawn. The bell didn't work. He knocked at the screen door and he could hear someone moving around inside.

A woman opened the door, and it was Lisa; for an instant Mike did not recognize her. She wore a loose-fitting cotton dress that hung like a tent on her. She was immensely fat. Her eyes were narrow and swollen, her breathing labored as she led him into the house.

The place was a mess. She had made some attempt to straighten things up, but hadn't succeeded. There was a vacuum cleaner in the middle of the living room and a can of spray wax on an end table.

Lisa moved to a sagging settee and sank into it. There was a plate of salted peanuts and a bottle of beer on the table next to the settee. The floor was littered with movie magazines.

The sight of his ex-wife shocked and dismayed him. He had always pictured her essentially the way he had left her—petite, attractive, aging certainly, but in a gentle way. He had no idea she had changed so drastically.

"Things have been tough," she said, lighting a cigarette. She inhaled and coughed, a hacking smoker's cough. "I haven't been well. Metabolic problems. Thyroid. Causes this rheumatoid condition." She held up her hands; they were swollen, whether from rheumatism or fat, Mike could not tell. "My knees, the same way. They just swell up on me." She ran her hand through her hair; it was a dirty blond, black at the roots. "After Ben was killed, I just fell apart."

"I can understand that."

"Really? How? You never knew Ben," she said. She spoke the words in a breathy, noncommittal way, showing no emotion.

"I knew him well."

"You thought you knew him. Did you ever lie in bed with him? Make love to him? Devote yourself to him? No? Well, you never knew him. He was a marvelous man, full of kindness and humor."

Kindness? Bugsy, the killer? "I never saw that in him."

"That man knew how to live," she said, and for the first time there was emotion in her voice; she spat the words at him as though it were an accusation: Mike's life was an empty lie; Ben Siegel's, the real thing. "He had unlimited charm. And he took very good care of me. After he was gone, I was lost. My career just never worked out . . ." She shrugged, stared at the end of her cigarette. "Oh, there were a few things. Did you see me in that flick with Tony Curtis? That desert thing?"

"No."

"I had a chance with that one. My son was giving me heartaches at the time, though . . ."

"I wanted Matthew with me."

"Why should he have gone with you?" she said, as though it were the most unlikely thing imaginable.

"Had I known your situation . . ."

"We have a good relationship, Matt and I. I need him. He's always loved me. Whenever he gets in a jam, he comes back to Mom. And he's doing fine now. Sells ovenware. Some fellow he met in prison. They buy the stuff wholesale and sell it door to door, or in parking lots. He makes a nice living."

"What was he in jail for?"

"Passing bad paper. It was just a phase. I'm worried about him now, though. He's so desperate. He feels like such a loser. I tell him, 'Matty, you're a good-looking boy, personable. When people get to know you, they like you. You just have to give them a chance.' I want to help him, but I'm tired," Lisa said. "Ben still has friends around. I could make some calls for him, but I'm tired."

Mike didn't ask her who Ben's friends were or how often she had gone to them. He could imagine it, though: labor racketeers, fringe movie people, gangsters, gamblers. He could see them helping her out with a few bucks from time to time, setting up minor roles for her in films, offering her hat-check jobs in clubs around town.

"I'll try to do something for Matthew, if you like," he said.

"What could you do for him?" Again, she asked the question as though it were unimaginable that he could ever do something for their son. He was not Ben Siegel.

"I could talk to a few people. I might be able to get him a job in television."

She laughed quietly to herself. "Office boy? Go-fer? I told you, Matty is doing very well for himself. He's making some good money. You can't expect him to go backwards. Not at his age."

"What do you want me to do for him, then?"

"Pay the kid a visit. You're his father. Show him you care."

"All right," he said, resigned.

"Do you care? Do you care about anybody?"

"I cared about you a great deal once," he said.

She smiled grimly. "Did you? That's not the way I remember it."

"You were the one who wanted out of the marriage."

She remained quiet for a very long time. "What's the use of rehashing all this?" she said. "We've always had very different ideas on what life is really all about."

"Yes."

"Matty's living in a rooming house downtown. If you want to see him, the address is on an envelope on the table there."

There were bills scattered over the top of a scarred table. Propped against an empty vase was a Mother's Day card from Matthew. The handwriting was curiously childish, the letters large, sloppy.

Mike copied the address. He removed two hundred-dollar bills from his wallet and placed them next to the vase. Lisa watched him; he expected her to berate him for the gesture, but she said nothing.

He wanted to tell her how sorry he was that things had not gone better for her; he wanted to apologize. Her gaze, though, was unkind. The words wouldn't come. "Is there anything I can do for you?"

"No," she said. "Nothing I can think of."

It was nearly 2:30 when he left the house and sped toward the airport in Burbank. He had to meet someone who was flying down from Las Vegas. It was the rabbit up his sleeve, the gambit that was essential to convincing Duane Gurley to sign with the New York Tartars.

He waited as the plane taxied to the gate. A large, balding black man moved down the loading stairs. He was dressed in a baggy tan suit with a tan sport shirt. He smiled shyly as he reached Mike and they shook hands.

One of the ground crew hurried over to them. He had a pencil and paper in his hand and he pressed it on the black man for his autograph. "You're the greatest fighter of all time," the man said. The black man winked at Mike. He signed the paper: Joe Louis.

52

They drove northeast out toward the desert. "I spoke to his dad," Louis said. "They're keeping him in a motel outside a place called Barstow. You know where that is?"

"It's in the desert," Mike said.

"His pappy tol' me they drivin' the boy batty. They got him holed up in this place, no phone in the room, no nothing. He sneaked out and called the old man from a gas station. He says if the Brown Bomber comes to talk with him, he'll listen."

"How many men are baby-sitting him?"

"Four."

They drove eighty miles an hour through the San Bernardino Mountains until they reached Barstow in the Mojave Desert.

It was late afternoon and a strong wind was blowing. It was high desert country. As the sun slipped behind the Tehachapi Mountains in the west, the day turned cold.

Louis and Mike checked into a truck-stop motel on the edge of town. The place where Gurley was being kept was well out on the highway, miles from anything.

"How we going to lure him away from his baby-sitters?" Louis asked.

"You'll see," Mike said, smiling.

They ate at the motel, then Mike left Louis in the car and went into a tavern next to the motel. He spoke with the man behind the bar. The man made a phone call. Mike returned to the car with a shopping bag full of liquor.

A half-hour later a '53 Chevy coated with desert dust chugged to a halt next to their car. Four ladies in fake-fur wraps and slinky cocktail dresses got out.

Three were in their late teens; one was pushing forty: a mother and her daughters. The teenagers were presentable; the mother, with leathery skin and stained teeth, less so.

Mike brought the mother to the car. She grew surly when she spotted Louis. "We don't do colored," she said.

"You're not doing him."

"Anything to do with colored is bad news. It'll cost you extra."

Mike agreed to her price, then outlined what was expected of her and her daughters. She stared at Louis. "Don't I know you?" she asked.

"He used to drive a truck between Baker and San Bernardino," Mike said.

"Oh, sure. That's it. I was sure I knew him. I never forget a jig's face."

The girls followed their car to the motel where Duane Gurley was being kept. It was stucco, surrounded by Joshua trees, and looked as though its only patrons were prairie dogs and coyotes. The wind was kicking up a storm by this time, and the place was almost completely obliterated by blowing sand.

Mike pulled up to a shut-down one-pump gas station not far from the motel. He turned off the car lights and he and Joe Louis waited while the four women entered the motel.

Louis chuckled. "Never thought I'd see the day I'd be sitting out in the middle of nowhere waiting for four white chippies to make a score. But, hell, sitting on my rear up in Vegas ain't so much fun neither."

Nothing stirred at the motel entrance. Mike grew uneasy. The ploy was to pass off the girls as a gift from Hub Farrell. When the party started, one of the girls would slip Gurley a note to come out to the car.

"Why'd you never fight McGrath that third time?" Louis said to Mike. "I heard lots o' stories. I figure you must know the true one."

"He did some things in the ring that got to me, that's all. Personal things. I figured he never deserved another fight with me."

"You never did lose a fight, did you?"

"No, but both McGrath fights sure felt like losses. He whipped me something terrible."

"I know what you mean," Louis said. "Sometimes a win takes more out of you than a loss. I learned more from my loss to Maxie Schmeling than any fight I ever had. Before that fight I was cocky, figured he couldn't whip the lazy side of me. When he beat me, I learned to take no man for granted."

There was activity at the front of the motel. A door opened. The sound of laughter and music drifted on the desert wind. A man jogged toward them. Mike opened the car door and Duane Gurley climbed in.

He was larger than either Mike or Louis, but so beautifully proportioned you didn't notice his size. He was very dark and handsome and there was something gentle, princely about him, a quiet intelligence in his expression.

Mike Roth started up the car and they sped through the night. The wind snapped against the car in jolting waves, causing it to buck and shudder.

"Joe Louis," Gurley said softly as though uttering a prayer. He shook his head in disbelief: Joe Louis had traveled into this godforsaken no-man's-land to talk with him!

"This is Mike Roth," Louis said. "You ever hear of him?"

"Sure have," Duane Gurley said.

"Hear me, Duane, this is a man you must listen to. This is a man you can trust."

All the way back to Los Angeles, Gurley listened. They drove to his home and talked some more with his father. By the next afternoon the deal was set. The New York Tartars had signed the most exciting football player in the country. Mike Roth's team would break into the television market. The new league was established.

* * *

Before he left Los Angeles, Mike visited his son. Matthew lived in a narrow rented room in a Mexican section on the edge of downtown.

He was a tall boy, strongly built. He wore his sandy-colored hair unfashionably long and had a mustache. Despite his size, there was something weak and pampered about him, a softness in the eyes and mouth. He tried to conceal this vaguely feminine quality with an affected toughness.

He invited Mike into his room, but didn't seem particularly happy to see him. To Mike there was no sense of being with a son. The man opposite him was a stranger. "Your mother says you're doing well now."

"Is that what she calls it?"

The rooming house was near the Santa Monica Freeway. Through the open window Mike could see cars whizzing by.

"Aren't you?"

"I could be doing better."

"I'd like to help you if I can."

"What for?" Mike didn't speak. "I don't like you very much," Matthew said.

"Why not?"

"You're supposed to be so tough, but you don't impress me that way. Ben was tough. He was *really* tough. Guys like you play by the rules of the world. Weak people do that—Ben never did."

"That's punk talk," Mike said quietly.

"Maybe that's what I am."

"It's nothing to be proud of."

Matthew stared at him. "I don't like your type either."

"All right. We'll just leave it like that."

"You know what I think of you?" Matthew spit at Mike's feet. "That's what I think of you. Now, get out of here. I don't want to ever see you again. I don't want to ever hear from you again."

Mike stared at his son. He could see nothing of himself in him. He searched for a hint of some connection. There was none. He wanted to say something which in some magical way would erase the bitterness of years. No words would come.

He left.

53

Tony McGrath was increasingly isolated in the world. O'Dwyer's betrayal caused him to close off certain doors in his life, doors to politics and politicians, doors to his past, his family.

He ran McGrath Construction through his brothers, rarely visiting the offices in midtown Manhattan. He spent most of his time at his estate. He knew that he was cutting himself off from the mainstream of life, yet he couldn't bring himself to change. His wife's drinking weighed on him, as did the rift between him and Darryl. Even his relationships with the two younger children were strained.

Sean was tall, athletic-looking, extremely bright, yet he had little interest in sports or schoolwork. He was fascinated by things mechanical and spent most of his time working on hot-rod cars. He was a quiet, unresponsive boy.

Sharon, a year younger, was more extroverted, but still things were not right between her and Tony. They did not talk easily. It was his fault, he knew. She was sixteen years old and had begun to date. He saw in her behavior a shadow of his dead sister, Rose Ann. Physically she resembled her, and a whole tangle of complex emotions was aroused in him because of it.

He worried about her constantly, argued over the boys she saw, set up strict rules for her to follow. Of course she resented his overprotectiveness, and they fought. A gulf widened between them.

His relationship with Darryl continued to be painful. Since the addition of Duane Gurley to the New York Tartars, the fortunes of the American Football League had skyrocketed. His son and Mike Roth became increasingly close. With Gurley, they were the Three Musketeers of professional football—the club president and his two star players. They were seen together constantly, interviewed on television, quoted in the newspapers.

Sportswriters were quick to point up the irony of Darryl playing football for his father's longtime rival. Someone asked about this in an interview. "Mike Roth is an exceptional person," Darryl had said. "I don't know why there should be a problem between them." Tony felt as though Mike had replaced him in his son's affection; he felt a sense of betrayal.

Darryl, more and more involved in politics, became close to the people around John Kennedy. In 1960 he campaigned for Kennedy in the presidential race. Joseph P. Kennedy had attempted to secure Tony's support for his son in the election, but Tony would have none of it. He had washed his hands of politics.

One afternoon he received a call from Darryl. They hadn't spoken in months, and it was a tense conversation. "I want you to meet Jack Kennedy," Darryl said.

"I'm not interested."

"Just talk with him," Darryl pleaded with his father. Tony recognized how difficult it had been for his son to make the call and he agreed to meet with Kennedy.

Jack Kennedy arrived at the house the next evening. His brother Bobby was with him. They all sat on the porch and talked.

At first Tony was uncomfortable with the smoothness of the Kennedys, their self-assurance. Their charm and intelligence reminded him of Bill O'Dwyer. Both quoted poetry, as Bill-O used to do. They were a little too slick. He missed the rough edges, the openness of the old politicos—Al Smith, La Guardia.

Gradually, though, he warmed to Jack. Tall, graceful, courtly, Jack Kennedy spoke in a simple, direct way, as though they had been friends for a long time. Bobby, compact, abrasive, appeared abstracted, eager to move on to other, more important matters.

"One of the reasons I'm here," Jack said, "is because you were my hero when I was a kid. You were the best."

"No. Not the best."

"You were better than Roth," said Kennedy.

"He beat me twice."

"You had both fights won. If you had fought him a third time, you would have beat him."

"We'll never know that," Tony McGrath said. "Why else are you here?"

"You knew Al Smith and La Guardia. I want to learn about them. I want to know what made them great."

"That's not so easy," Tony said. How could he characterize the Man in the Derby and the Little Flower? How do you define their kind of greatness, a greatness of spirit more than anything else?

Kennedy watched him with serious interest. Bobby sat a distance away from them, digging at the porch railing with his fingernail. "They genuinely cared for people," Tony finally said. "Passionately cared. They felt that nothing else mattered—not fame, politics, pragmatic considerations—except that the little guy got a fair shake."

"Yes," Jack Kennedy said. "That's what's important." He nodded his head slowly. "We're nothing without them, and they always get a screwing. If I become President of the United States, I'm going to try to change that. Not only for the people of the United States, but for the whole world."

Tony smiled. "The whole world? That's a pretty big place."

"I know."

"Start small, the people closest to you," Tony said. "The neighborhood, the ward, and so on, expanding. The whole world's one poor slob trying to feed his family. That's the way they thought. That's the way they worked."

"That's the way I intend to work."

"Is that a promise?" Tony said, amused at Kennedy's ambition, his far-reaching concern. The world!

"Not a politician's promise. My promise."

After the Kennedy boys left, Tony sat on the porch and thought for a long time about Kennedy. He believed him and liked him. He might not have greatness now, but he would strive for it, and there was reason to believe he might achieve it.

Tony called his brother Emmett and instructed him to contribute to Kennedy's campaign.

From time to time after becoming President, Kennedy would call Tony. The calls would always come at odd hours, late at night or early in the morning. There didn't seem to be any particular purpose. He just wanted to chat. They would discuss sports, women, the world in general. The tone was light, bantering. Once Tony questioned why the President, with his impossibly busy schedule, would take time to call him. "I told you once—you're my hero. I speak to you and I feel like I'm reaching out to Al Smith and La Guardia. If I ever do anything to shame those men, don't answer my calls."

In November 1963 Tony made one of his infrequent trips to the offices of McGrath Construction. A new contract was coming up with the Construction Workers Alliance. Building was booming on the Upper East Side of Manhattan, and Tony's brothers were worried that Jackie Foster's union would make things difficult for them. They wanted to make a deal with him. "He wants a payoff," Emmett said.

"No payoffs!" Tony said angrily.

"If we're going to be competitive, we need to cut a deal with him," Emmett insisted.

"Negotiate with him aboveboard. If you get in bed with him, he'll plow you into the mattress."

During a break in the meeting Tony called Theresa. He could tell by her slurred speech that she had been drinking. The radio was turned up so loud he could barely hear her. He yelled for her to turn it down; she began to rage at him, ticking off a long list of his derelictions.

She had only recently returned from a stay at Payne Whitney Clinic, the alcohol-rehabilitation ward, and now she was on the booze again. The situation was maddening. Her affliction was a cancer: no medicine could defeat it; there was no cure.

In the midst of their argument he heard over the radio in the background something about an assassination attempt. "What did the radio say?"

"What?"

"The radio!" he shouted.

"You're not going to shut me up mister! Are you listening to me or the radio! I demand to be listened to! No one listens to me. . . ."

She began to weep on the other end of the line. He hung up and went to the outer office and asked the staff if anyone had heard the news. "Something about an assassination attempt," Tony said. "I think he said the President."

He went back to Emmett's office and poured himself a cup of coffee. A short while later a secretary rushed in from the front office. "It just came over the radio. President Kennedy's been shot. They've rushed him to the hospital . . ."

Twenty minutes later a bulletin came over the television: John F. Kennedy was dead.

Tony sat at the desk for a long time. He thought about Jack Kennedy sitting with him on the porch. He saw his smile, the seriousness, the concern in his eyes. And he remembered Kennedy's promise to try to change things for the little people of the world. *My promise, not a politician's promise,* he had said. Now he was dead.

Tony got up and moved to the outer office. Everyone sat in shock.

He left the building and walked up Sixth Avenue. He had no idea where he was going.

People gathered in clusters on the corners, black men and Puerto Ricans, street hustlers, salesmen, messenger boys. A few held transistor radios up to their ears. They stood pale and stricken, but he saw no weeping.

Eventually he came to Central Park and he walked until he reached the zoo. He entered the tiger house, where he had stood so many years before with Al Smith, Bill-O, and John McMahon.

The place was empty of people. The cats dozed. He stood before one of the cages. A large tiger raised its head and gazed at him, and suddenly he was certain it was the same cat that had been Al Smith's favorite. "Jack Kennedy is dead," he said to the tiger. The animal stared at him. "Jack Kennedy is dead." The animal continued to stare at him with a look that was human, aware. He understands, Tony thought. He's the Tammany Tiger, old friend of Al Smith's, and he understands. "Jack Kennedy is dead," he said softly, remembering how the tiger would roar when Al Smith mentioned Dewey.

This time the tiger did not roar.

54

The assassination of John Kennedy had a profound effect on Darryl McGrath. Until that day he had flirted with the idea of a political career, but after Kennedy's death, trying for political office seemed an obligation.

He had grown close to the Kennedy family. Before the President's death, the Kennedys had him up to Hyannis Port for weekends of games and drink and laughter. The whole clan engaged in rough-and-tumble touch football. They went at it with a passion. Darryl would head one team, made up of wives and kids, while the other team usually included the Kennedy brothers, Jack, Bobby, and Ted. If there was a single person around capable of catching the ball, Darryl would pass his side to victory.

The Kennedys ribbed him about running for office. He had all the qualifications, Jack said to him one day. "You're Irish and you know how to pass. A politician must know how to pass—pass the law, pass the hat, and pass the buck!"

Another day Jack Kennedy asked him to accompany him on a walk down the beach. As they strolled along, Darryl was thinking: I am walking now with the President of the United States and he is talking with me about *football!* He is asking my opinion about *football,* what I feel about the Tartars' chances for the coming season, how I think the new league will do!

They walked for a while in silence. "I'd like to see you run for office," Kennedy said. "Politics is in your blood, you've studied it, you've lived with it. And you have values and beliefs. The country needs people like you."

Kennedy spoke quietly, sincerely, and Darryl was moved. He felt embarrassed and somehow unworthy of Kennedy's trust. "My father never got over what happened to him in politics," he said. "It scarred him. I suppose it's scarred me, too."

Kennedy smiled. "In politics people get seduced without even realizing it. Political success is a whore posing as a lady. You might suspect what she really is, but once you get into bed with her, you discover a thousand reasons why it's the best place in the world to be. The reality is, you're being screwed in more ways than one." Kennedy laughed, bent down, and picked up a pebble from the beach. He flung it into the ocean.

Both men stood at the ocean's edge throwing pebbles into the water. They began to compete to see who could throw the farthest. Kennedy tried hard, but Darryl beat him every time. He shook his head, laughing. "You have the knack, the flick of the wrist."

They walked back down the beach toward the house. A damp wind gusted in off the ocean. The air was fresh and clean, the day bright. I am walking with the President of the United States, Darryl thought. I have just been throwing pebbles with him, and I have beaten him!

"You could go into this political thing with your eyes open," Kennedy said. "You'd recognize her for the whore she can become. You'd know how to handle her."

And now Kennedy was dead and Darryl felt an obligation to try to live up to the expectations Kennedy had had of him. He discussed the matter with Mike Roth. He would enter the primaries. If he won, he would announce his retirement from football. "You don't need me here anymore," Darryl said. "All you need is someone who can hand the ball off to Duane and get out of the way."

"I envy you," Mike Roth said. "Boxing wasn't enough for me, yet I was never able to find anything else. I've spent my whole life trying to find something more."

In May Darryl entered the primary fight for congressman from the Seventeenth Congressional District, the fashionable Upper East Side. The incumbent was an old-line Tammany hack, supported by the party regulars. The Kennedy people pushed hard for McGrath.

Darryl had a fight on his hands. McGrath Construction had become an issue in the primary battle. A strip of tenements on the Upper East Side had been torn down and replaced by high-rise apartments. Much of the work had been tied up by McGrath Construction through sweetheart deals engineered by the politicos in the area.

If Darryl was to stand a chance in the primary, he would have to attack McGrath Construction. He would have to attack his own family.

He went to Mike Roth for advice. They had dinner at Mike's apartment. Duane Gurley was there, as well as Pat and Jenny, and after the meal they all played Scrabble in the living room while Mike and Darryl remained in the dining room to discuss Darryl's future. "Are you prepared to go against your family?" Mike asked.

"I'm worried about my grandmother. She's an old lady. It could kill her, having her grandson go up against her sons."

"And the allegations—are they true?"

"I don't know. I don't know what to believe. I always knew my uncles would bend the rules to suit themselves, but my father . . . I just don't know."

"What don't you know?" Mike Roth said.

"Whether or not my father's an honest man," Darryl McGrath said quietly. "Until the O'Dwyer thing, as far as I was concerned he could do no wrong. Now I just don't know."

"If you're going after McGrath Construction, you must discuss it with your grandmother—and your father and uncles. It's a tough, tough matter to go after your own relatives."

"Even if what they've done is wrong?"

"You must be sure it's wrong," Mike said.

Darryl struggled with the problem. He found himself trapped by family loyalty, political pressure, his own sense of right and wrong. At a political gathering for reform elements in the Democratic party, he decided to tackle the thing head-on. He was scheduled to address the group. He threw away his prepared speech.

His mouth was dry as he began to talk. His voice came out unnaturally high and thin. He spoke about his beliefs, what he would attempt to accomplish should he win the nomination and the election. Then he brought up McGrath Construction. The room grew very quiet. "There have been rumors about my family, the influence of their business in the Seventeenth Congressional District. I honestly do not know to what extent if any they have committed wrongdoing. But I pledge here and now to make public any information pertaining to corruption or sweetheart deals that I can find on McGrath Construction. And if it appears that the information would be in any way damaging to myself or the party, I would withdraw my candidacy."

After, he was approached by a balding and somewhat paunchy man who had been drinking. There was a weary sadness about him. "That was very courageous," the man said.

"It was the only thing I could do." Darryl didn't want to discuss it; he tried to excuse himself.

"You don't remember me. I knew you when you were a kid."

Darryl studied the man. He looked anxious, uncomfortable, and suddenly Darryl recognized him. It was Bill O'Dwyer.

"I thought you were still in Mexico," Darryl said.

"I've been back for quite a while now. My wife and I divorced and..."
Bill-O had trouble looking Darryl in the eye. His voice was very soft, almost
inaudible. "I'd like to explain some things to you," he said. "Why don't we
go to my place."

Darryl had always expected that if he ran into O'Dwyer he would be
overwhelmed by anger. Instead, he felt a curious pity. In front of him now
was a shy, lost old man.

His apartment was on East Fifty-seventh Street, a neat, comfortable place,
obviously a bachelor's quarters. There were stacks of records next to a hi-fi
set and a copy of a paperback book, *Four Great Tragedies by William Shakespeare,* on a table next to the couch. Bill-O settled himself on the couch. "I
hope this isn't uncomfortable for you," he said. "I've reached a point in my
life, though, where I don't care what people think about me anymore. You
want to touch people. You want to say hello and good-bye to them."

"I'm not uncomfortable."

Bill-O looked over at Darryl. "You could have a great political future.
But you must be your own man, lad. You must." He drained his drink. "I
treated your dad badly," he said, "and a day never goes by that I don't remember it."

He sat lost in thought for a while. "There were so many things I wanted
to explain to your father. But he had his problems and I had mine. He never
got over the Roth fights. He fought them again and again in his mind. If I
could have just talked to him and explained it all to him ... It just got out
of hand. Too many people you're responsible to. It's a murderous job."

Bill-O walked unsteadily to the bar and started to pour himself another
drink, then thought better of it. He put down his glass. "They'll drag you
through the mud, lad. They'll bring up all that garbage, the Reles stuff.
They'll try to link it all to your father. And there never was a more honest
or dedicated man. He believed in me and I let him down, and for that I'll
suffer till the end of my days."

"He never knew, then?"

"He never knew a thing."

"I'm glad you told me that. I wasn't sure."

"It was me and Johnny McMahon and your uncles. But not your father.
Never your father. The Murder Incorporated thing—he hadn't a hint. It
was the gangster union boys. They ran the show, the whole political thing.
They had me from the first judgeship I landed. They had me in their
pocket."

He stood up and moved into an alcove off the living room. There was a
large trunk there, and he opened it. He took out a photograph and showed
it to Darryl. It was a picture of a very young policeman holding a night-
stick. "This was in 1917," O'Dwyer said. "I was pounding a beat at Bush
Terminal. Police Shield 6406. I'll never forget that number."

He took a black robe out of the trunk and put it on. It was a magistrate's
robe. He admired himself in a mirror on the back of the hall door. "Not

bad," he said, smiling and touching the sleeves. "Not bad at all." He leaned down and picked up another police shield from the trunk; in gold embossed on blue were the words "Police Department, City of New York."

"This was given to me by the department after I became mayor." He stared at the badge for a moment, put it on the table, and slipped off the robe. "Oh, the old days," he said softly.

Darryl left him a short while later. They said they would get together again, but they never did. One day, in the fall of the year, Darryl picked up the New York *Times* to read that ex-Mayor William O'Dwyer had died of a heart attack at the age of seventy-four.

Darryl went to the funeral. His father did not attend.

55

As the Democratic primary battle approached, Darryl invited the family to the house on Christopher Street. Tony and Theresa drove in from the Island with the kids. Emmett, James, and Will came with their children, more than a dozen among them. The brothers' wives, three dumpy neighborhood Irish girls, overdressed and over-made-up, sulked. Given to airs, they carried imagined slights against each other and everyone else in the room. In truth, they all thought they were too good for any of this.

Theresa's mother and father were there. Following the O'Dwyer scandal, Johnny McMahon had withdrawn from the construction business. He tried his hand again at running his own tavern, but couldn't make a go of it. He had become an outcast in Tammany circles. It was one thing to have your hand in the till, but to get caught with it there under the bright glare of television was unforgivable. The pols of the United Irish Club were still cordial toward him, but they shied away from his place of business, and it went under.

He was broke. He mortgaged his house to finance his business, and he lost that. Theresa funneled money to him from time to time. The money, of course, came from Tony, who would have nothing to do with his father-in-law, but, feigning ignorance, permitted his wife to contribute to his support. The McGrath brothers also sent him money from time to time. John McMahon and his wife moved into a tenement flat on Hudson Street. After nearly seventy years in America, he found himself sunk to the very level he had known as a child newly arrived in this country.

Dinner was over and everyone came together in the living room. It was the first family get-together in years, and it was strangely subdued. Tony hadn't wanted to come and had only bowed to great pressure from his mother. He spoke little all evening. There was some small talk between him and Darryl, but it was forced and uncomfortable. Large, brooding, Tony was a formidable figure to the younger members of the family, his body grown massive with the years, a great shock of graying hair, eyes angry, piercing.

He hated this night, hated his situation. He was comfortable nowhere these days. His estate was a prison to him, but it was a prison he knew, and he preferred to be there. The old faces and memories of bygone times stirred pain deep within him—pain of deception, pain of disappointed dreams, pain of ancient losses.

"I've brought the family here," Darryl began, "because of a decision I must make. I'm considering running for Congress from the Seventeenth District. I face a murderous fight. Ugly things about our family will be brought up, ugly things about McGrath Construction."

His uncles stirred. Their wives looked uncomfortable. Tony raised his chin as though he were about to speak, but he said nothing. John McMahon, standing at the opposite end of the room, gazed nervously over at Tony, who didn't return his look. They had not talked since they arrived. McMahon, political being to his core, valued compromise and conciliation and was willing, even eager, to make things up with his son-in-law. Tony, however, had made it clear he was not there to make peace.

"I want all of you to know," Darryl said, "that despite the fact that you are family, if I enter the congressional race I will have to bring out and attack any wrongdoing you've been guilty of." Darryl paused and took a breath. He was not having an easy time of it.

He turned to Bess. "Grandma, I've brought everyone here because of you. You are the heart and soul of this family. You have baptized us all in the water of politics."

Bess stared at her grandson without blinking, watched him alertly, her lips pursed, her expression serious. She sat so motionless she might have been molded in concrete, with only a slight, shallow rise and fall of her narrow chest as she breathed.

"Grandma, I don't want to hurt you. I'm asking you what I should do. If you feel that I would be a traitor to the family by my political actions, I will give the whole thing up."

He waited for her to answer.

She flicked her tongue over her dry lips. Her voice, when she spoke, was strong and clear. "It's as a Democrat you'll be running?"

"Yes."

"And you have the support of a good segment of the party?"

"Yes. Kennedy people."

She nodded her head slowly. "And has anyone in this family done such terrible things as to cause you worry in this campaign?"

"I don't know. I'll have to find out the truth. If it's there, the bad things, I'll have to come out against them."

"Yes," she said quietly. "We have grown rich, people tell me. The people of the neighborhood sometimes treat me as though I was a queen. I used to think it was because of Tony, because of his boxing. But that's way in the past and I realize it's because of Emmett and James and Willy, because of the construction company. I've always been proud of you boys, but I've been proud because I assumed you built what you have built by your own sweat and energy and ambition. Even when I heard terrible things, those things on television and in the papers, I always assumed you were being attacked because of envy of your accomplishments. I raised you all to be honest. To care for people, for working people, for our good, honest Democratic men and women. The Hall has had its share of thieves, and goodness knows I've been around long enough to know a number of them pretty well. But I never believed my own sons could be tarred with the brush of dishonesty. I ask you all now, does Darryl have anything to worry about?" The brothers didn't speak. "Emmett?" Bess asked.

"The construction game has always had its rotten side. We've been more honest than most," he said, squirming.

"I'm not talking about the little white lies, the penny-ante stuff," Bess said. "The saints are only in heaven. You know what I mean. I'm talking about the real crooked business. Is there any way that this beautiful, glorious boy could be dragged into the mud because of anything you've done?"

"I don't think he should get involved," Will said. "It's an ugly game, politics. There are people who could use it as an excuse to get at us."

"Can they drag us through the mud? Can they disgrace him?" Bess repeated, her voice hard now.

"Ugly things could be brought up," said James.

"What kind of ugly things?" The brothers looked away. "Do it, then, Darryl!" Bess shouted. "You do it! Turn a light on them! If they've been wallowing in the mud, you be the one to show it to the world. If they're filthy, you be the one. They deserve it! I didn't bring them into this world to become cheap, corrupt thieves!"

Tony suddenly burst out, his face white with fury. "Do what you have to do, Darryl. Shame us all. If we deserve it, then do it! But for God's sake, let me alone. Don't invite me to these things. Don't force me to look at all of this! I never would have believed my family, my brothers, could be accused of these things, let alone do them. But I hear it in their voices now, the ugly sound of guilt and deception. If they've done things, they've deceived me too! Tear them to shreds! Redeem us all, Darryl. But please, in the name of God, leave me alone!"

He hurried across the room and went out the door into the night.

No one spoke. Bess continued to stare straight ahead. She tapped one finger against the back of the opposite hand resting in her lap. Then she held out her arms to Darryl. He moved forward and embraced her.

* * *

After rushing from the house, Tony continued down Christopher Street toward the docks. He entered a workmen's bar in the shadow of the West Side Highway. He took a table in the corner and began to drink. He thought about his son, his brothers, Bill-O, Mike Roth, Rose Ann.

I live too much in the past, he said to himself. And yet he yearned for the old times, the old ways.

He realized he was getting drunk. A young girl in a cotton dress entered with two longshoremen. She was pretty, in a fresh, small-town way, and through a haze of alcohol it seemed as though he was seeing his dead sister.

She noticed him staring at her and approached him. "Hello," she said.

"Hello."

"Are you having a good time?"

"Are you?"

She shrugged. One of the men she entered with came to the table. He was a large man with a wide, brutal face. He grabbed her by the arm and yanked her to one side. She moved to the other man. "What are you staring at?" the man with the brutal face said to Tony.

"You."

"I don't like people staring at me." Tony shrugged. He continued to stare at the man. "Did you hear me?" the man asked.

"I heard you."

"You and me are going to go outside, old-timer."

"All right," Tony said. He stood unsteadily. He kept his eyes on the man and his friend.

"Don't!" the girl called out. The man swung at her and she fell back against the jukebox, fighting tears.

Outside, the two men stood relaxed, waiting for Tony. "I don't think you want to do this," said Tony.

"Really?" The man swung at Tony. Before he could complete the swing, McGrath had hit him twice, a cracking combination. The man sagged against a parked car, blood spouting from his nose.

His friend started forward and Tony smashed a rapid flurry of punches at him. His fists were a blur and the man fell under them, hit the wall of the building, and slid to the ground.

The girl stood in the doorway of the bar. She stared at Tony in panic. He started toward her. She moved off down the street, backing away, her eyes wide with fear.

"Rose Ann!" he called to her. She began to run. "Rose Ann!" The street was wreathed in fog off the Hudson River. Her figure was a shadow now disappearing into the fog. "Rose Ann!" he called again.

He could hear only the sound of her footsteps running away though the fog.

56

"They're using the old Jimmy Walker trick," Bess McGrath said to Darryl as they sat together in the card room of the United Irish Club. "The Talker had a favorite ploy: invent the most outrageous accusations. By the time the poor slob gets through denying them, the people have forgotten what the charges originally were—they only remember the fellow done something wrong!"

After a rough-and-tumble primary fight, Darryl McGrath won the Democratic-party nomination. The O'Dwyer affair had been resurrected; his opponent had somehow linked O'Dwyer, Abe Reles, and the fortunes of McGrath Construction in one ugly, pervasive conspiracy, and though the Democratic party rejected the idea, Darryl's Republican opponent picked it up and continued to hammer away at it.

Bess became her grandson's political mentor. She had been at the game a long, long time, and the style of play had not changed all that much. Darryl was astounded at her savvy, her political intelligence.

He met her several times a week at the United Irish Club and together they went over strategy. His opponent was on the attack, hitting relentlessly at the theme of McGrath-family corruption. He monopolized television time, kept the story in the newspapers. He was beating Tony badly.

"The only way to counter these things," Bess advised, "is to fight back with facts, with truth. Don't explain, don't complain. Just hit back with the truth. Expose the man for the miserable, small-minded liar he is!"

The truth in the case of McGrath Construction was complex, all shades of gray. The company operated as all the large outfits did, making deals where it had to. Darryl didn't back off the charge. He criticized the system and his uncles' participation in it. And though his father had not taken part in the daily affairs of the company, he was guilty for what he had failed to do, and Darryl was forced to condemn him for it.

It was painful, tearing, and even Bess argued with him over this point. "You must defend your father!" she insisted. "He's done nothing wrong. It's ugly for a son to attack his own father. It's ugly and unfair and it will lose you votes!"

"I'm not attacking him. I defend him where I can. But the truth is, as long as he was collecting money from the company, he was responsible for seeing how it was run. That's the truth, Grandma. He's a good man, and I tell people that whenever and wherever I can. But he has been badly used by his brothers, and it's his fault as much as theirs."

Bess knew her grandson was right: Tony must take responsibility for his brothers' actions. The Republicans would attempt to make Tony's behavior seem worse than it actually was. Darryl had no choice but to insist on the truth of the situation and hope that the truth would prevail.

Save for his grandmother, he was completely isolated in his family. His father would not talk with him. His uncles, openly hostile, bombarded him through intermediaries in an attempt to get him to tone down his attacks on them. John McMahon, his grandfather, cursed him as a Judas wherever he could.

His own supporters were losing faith in his campaign. He was always on the defensive, and his possibilities for election appeared increasingly slim.

More and more he began to depend on those closest to him for aid: Bess, Duane Gurley, Mike Roth. They were a tight circle in an ever-more-hostile political landscape.

Duane Gurley organized a group of athletes to campaign for him. They addressed community groups, booster clubs, canvassed the district, passed out leaflets, carried on the wearying foot-soldier work in the campaign. Jenny Roth, just out of high school, not even old enough to vote, worked with Duane and his group.

Over the weeks of the campaign, Darryl began to notice a shift in the relationship between Duane and Jenny Roth, and he grew troubled. Always close, they were now almost inseparable. Once she was fond of Duane in a little-girl, hero-worship way; now she related to him as a woman. Something more complex, more emotional, was growing up between them.

Duane picked up Darryl's uneasiness and late one evening when they were alone he broached the subject. "Something's on your mind," he said.

"Jenny."

"Yeah?"

"I think she feels for you . . . she feels in a way more than just pals."

"I think she likes me, yes. And I like her too. So?"

"She's a kid, for Chrissake."

"Hey, wait a minute, Darryl. Are you afraid I'm looking to *mess* with her or something? Are you afraid I'm going to *seduce* her?"

"No, no."

"What is it, then? She's a fine girl and she likes me and I like her too. Now, is it the color thing? Is that what you're talking about?"

"I don't know what I'm talking about."

"I go along with that."

"I just don't want any kind of stupid situation arising. I don't want her to get hurt."

"Do you think I would hurt her?"

"No."

"Then what's this all about? If it were one of the other guys, the white guys, who had become close to her, would you be going on about this with him?"

"Yes. If I thought they were going to go beyond just a friend thing. Yes."

"Come on, Darryl. You know that isn't true."

"All right, all right. I'm stupid. I shouldn't have said anything. Forget it ever came up."

Duane looked at Darryl for a long time. "All right," he said at last.

The campaign continued, grew more heated. Darryl's political situation did not improve. Late one afternoon as Darryl, Duane, and Jenny were working at his campaign headquarters on East Seventy-second Street, word came in of trouble in the district.

A group of black boys attending summer school on East Seventy-sixth Street had been lounging around the sidewalk in front of an apartment house opposite the school. There was an argument with the superintendent of the building. The disturbance attracted an off-duty policeman. A scuffle ensued, and the cop had shot one of the boys to death.

Now gangs of black youths from uptown were pouring into the neighborhood. Several white youths had been beaten. A full-scale riot was in the making, fueled by the angry rhetoric of black militant groups.

Duane and Darryl left the campaign headquarters and rushed to the area, only four blocks away. They encountered opposing forces of angry blacks and whites. Darryl spoke with the whites and attempted to quiet them down, while Duane engaged the blacks. The presence of two well-known athletes had its effect: the showdown was defused.

Later, however, word came of a further flare-up, this time in Harlem. Crowds had begun massing in the streets. Arms were being distributed by the militants.

Duane and Darryl prepared to take off for the scene of the trouble. Jenny pleaded to stay with them, but they insisted she remain downtown.

She watched them drive off, then hurried to First Avenue, where she boarded a bus heading for Harlem.

Mike and Patricia sat in front of the television set, watching the evening news. The screen was filled with live action of the riots on 125th Street. A heavyset man in a dashiki stood on a milk crate haranguing a crowd. The street was jammed with black, angry faces. "My God!" Patricia said. "Look!" Two men were moving through the crowd toward the man in the dashiki: Duane Gurley and Darryl McGrath.

They could be seen joking with people in the mob, trying to lighten things up. The television camera bobbed through the crowd. It came in very close on Darryl and stayed with him. A reporter tried to question him about his political campaign.

There was a commotion at the edge of the gathering. The camera swung around to cover it. A young white girl was trying to get through the crowd. "It's Jenny!" Patricia shouted.

And then all hell broke loose.

It happened so fast Duane and Darryl couldn't be sure what touched it off. One minute they had things under control; the next, the air was split by screams, exploding fire bombs, gunshots. Trash, bricks, garbage-can covers rained down from the rooftops above. Store windows were shattered, cars overturned. Police sirens wailed.

Engulfed by people, Jenny screamed and Duane heard her and charged through the crowd after her. Darryl tried to follow, but someone hit him and he fell to the ground. He struggled to get up. Two men were beating on him with lengths of board. He fought his way past them.

Down the block, he saw Duane rush into a mob of people. He had Jenny by the hand and was pulling her through the crowd. Darryl started after them, but they disappeared into the swirling mob.

He heard a terrific roar and suddenly the tenements on either side of the street erupted in flame, great plumes billowing into the sky.

Darryl spotted a group of helmeted riot police and raced for them. A police lieutenant leaped from a patrol car to take command. Behind him was Mike Roth.

"Where's Jenny?" he yelled to Darryl.

"Down there!" Darryl waved toward Lenox Avenue.

"Jesus," the police lieutenant said. The block raged with fire.

Darryl and Mike entered the police car. Siren howling, it moved through the mob. All about them, Harlem went up in flames.

Duane held Jenny to him. She couldn't stop trembling. "I'm sorry," she said over and over again. "I was worried for you. I had to be here with you."

They had taken refuge in a deserted building, the bottom two floors of which had been savaged. They had made their way up the dark stairway to the third floor and waited in an empty apartment.

They heard footsteps, yells, gunshots, echoing through the building. Police cars roared up and down the streets, sirens shrieking. Jenny couldn't stop trembling.

"We're safe here, Jen," Duane said. "I'm not going to let anything happen to you."

Her terror subsided. She relaxed in his arms. She lifted her face to him and he kissed her. They kissed for a very long time. "I love you, Duane."

"I love you, too. Oh, Jen. I love you."

At that moment they heard a quiet, crackling sound. It grew louder. A gray curl of smoke licked up from under the door.

The building was on fire.

"This is crazy, fellas. This is crazy," the cop driving the car said to Mike and Darryl. They had entered an inferno of fire-ravaged streets.

"Keep going!" Mike yelled.

People surged in on the car, pounding it with clubs, smashing at the windows. The cop speeded up, and they careered through the throng, sending people scurrying out of the way.

And now they were in front of a burning building. Two people stood at an upper window screaming for help.

"Jenny! Jenny!" Mike yelled, and then he was out of the car and rushing toward the building, with Darryl right behind him.

Inside, heat and smoke formed a thick wall. Mike crouched low and started up the stairs. "Mike, no!" Darryl called from behind him.

But he had already pushed his way into the wall of smoke. Keeping low, he made his way upward. The second floor was relatively clear. He could see sheets of flame dancing up the walls of the stairwell. He continued forward.

He reached the third floor. It, too, was relatively clear, though above he could see the upper floors blistering with fire.

"Jenny!" Mike called out. "Jen!" His lungs were raw with heat and smoke. The roar of the fire above was deafening. Chunks of flaming debris plummeted down the stairwell.

"Jen! Jen!" Mike screamed.

A door at the end of the hallway opened and now Jenny and Duane were rushing toward him. Mike took his daughter by the hand and they moved back toward the stairs. Now there was an immense roar and the whole building shuddered and seemed to be collapsing around them.

Jenny stumbled and fell. Duane took her up in his arms. The three of them moved down the stairs. Splinters of fire rained down all about them. They hurtled through a hail of fiery debris.

At the ground floor, Darryl waited. They ran into the night. Behind them the tenement exploded in a furious storm of fire.

57

The Harlem riots and those that followed in the Bedford-Stuyvesant section of Brooklyn in the summer of 1964 thrust Darryl McGrath into a position of prominence on the New York political scene. Millions saw him on television in the midst of chaos fighting for calm and reason. Though barbarism had prevailed, he became a hero.

The attacks by his opponent on his father's involvement with the O'Dwyer administration and McGrath Construction were effectively neutralized. He won the election by a resounding margin.

The night of his triumph, a grand party was thrown at the United Irish

Club. People came from all over the city, from Long Island, New Jersey, Pennsylvania, the old-timers who had moved from the neighborhood, the sons and daughters of the old-timers and *their* sons and daughters. Darryl McGrath, one of their own, grandson of Bessie McGrath, who herself had been a confidante of Al Smith and Jimmy Walker, who had known and argued politics with the great Tammany bosses, Silent Charlie Murphy, Eddie Ahearn, Boss Curry, had been elected to Congress! No matter that all Darryl McGrath stood for was a repudiation of Tammany's ancient scoundrel pragmatism: he was one of their own, from a line that extended back to the beginning of the century.

John McMahon was there, and Darryl's uncles, and, so it seemed, every Irishman who had ever shaken hands with his father or tipped his hat to his grandmother. His father did not appear. Theresa had reentered the hospital and he now spent all his time there. Her condition was grave, her whole system on the verge of collapse.

Darryl learned from his brother and sister that even in the hospital his parents argued constantly. Theresa was deeply troubled over the breach between Darryl and Tony: she begged him to make it up with his son.

Darryl wanted to go to his father, thrash it all out, apologize if need be. But he knew that it would not work. The desire for reconciliation would have to come from his father; Tony would have to be ready for it.

At the victory celebration Bess sat in the center of the main room in the clubhouse. She held a champagne glass in her right hand, sipped at it slowly, allowed it to be refilled, participated in every toast.

She had worked unflaggingly on Darryl's campaign and she was worn out. Though she looked tired, frail, her eyes burned with fierce pride. "Darryl, Darryl," she said, hugging him, "I've never been so happy in my life. When your father became heavyweight champion of the world, that was something—but this! Congress! And you did it on your own, clean, no deals. You did what you had to do!"

Toward midnight she stood and addressed the crowd. "I've been a member of the United Irish Club for the better part of sixty years," she said, her voice thin yet vibrant. "And there have been times when I've hated the things it was doing, but still the club has been part of my heart and soul. I want to tell you something, though, and I mean this to every crook and cheap hack among you—a new day has arrived at last! A day of doing things the right way, with honesty and dignity and respect for the real value of people, and with determination to do things for the people who need them most. And to do them aboveboard and in the right way."

John McMahon and her sons applauded, and she shook a finger at them, spilling some of her champagne. "Yes, you clap for me, but I'm telling you, straighten up and fly right! No more of the old ways, you hear me?"

"No more of the old ways, Bessie, no more," McMahon said, swaying and smiling, drunk.

Mike Roth arrived late. "Can we talk?" he said to Darryl when the crowd had thinned out and Emmett had at last persuaded Bess to let him take her home.

They went outside into the alley behind the club. The night air was sharp. They stood in the cold. "What's the matter?" Darryl asked.

"Jenny. She and Duane have been . . . together." He struggled with the words. He was embarrassed. "She and her mother had a fight over it . . ."

"Where is Jenny now?"

"Up at school. Sarah Lawrence in Bronxville, Pat's alma mater. He's been visiting her up there."

"Has she slept with him?"

"I don't know. It's possible she has."

"Is that what's bothering you?"

"Yes, it does bother me."

"Because he's black?"

"I'm ashamed," Mike said. "How my wife feels—there's nothing I can do about that. I'm ashamed of the way I feel. It's tearing me apart. Yes, it bothers me because he's black. I fight with Pat over it and I defend Duane and Jenny, but inside . . . inside . . ." He shook his head. "I hate myself for what I feel in my heart."

"We all like to feel we're so open and understanding," Darryl said, "and yet old hates remain, don't they?"

They didn't talk for a long while. Finally, they walked back up the alley to the United Irish Club.

When they got there, the celebration had ended. The club was locked up tight.

"What do you want me to do?" Darryl said.

"Nothing. I guess in some stupid way I expected you to bail me out, to tell me that Duane was wrong and that you would talk to him. But of course, he isn't wrong. I'm wrong."

Darryl drove Mike home in his car, with Mike staring out at the deserted Manhattan streets as they sped uptown. "It's a tough one, Mike. I felt the same way when I found out they were seeing each other. And he's my best friend."

"It's terrible that we're so ugly inside."

"Yes. Yes, it is."

Mike grew quiet. He knew that if he continued to hold bitterness and resentment toward Duane, then his whole life had been a lie; his breach with Darryl's father had been a lie; everything had been a lie.

The day after Darryl's victory celebration, Bess was rushed to St. Vincent's Hospital. It was thought at first that she was suffering from simple exhaustion, but her condition deteriorated. Old age had simply overwhelmed her.

A priest was brought in to administer last rites. The family was called to her side.

She lapsed into a coma. Late in the night she rallied. She saw the family seated there and asked them to leave her alone with Tony and Darryl. "I'm so proud of you both. You've achieved so much, so much good, so much for the little people, the poor and miserable in this world. Remember, Tony, how I used to work the neighborhood, how I tried to help those people of the ward? I didn't accomplish very much, but I tried. And you two—you've done so much and you'll do more yet. Please, make it up between you. I've never understood what's torn you apart. I suppose it's the same stupidity and stubbornness that you inherited from me. I'm responsible. But there's no time, no time for that foolishness."

Bess closed her eyes and hummed a soft melody: "Will You Love Me in December As You Do in May?"

"The Talker did one fine thing in his life," she said. "He wrote that tune, that lovely, lovely tune."

She continued to smile. She did not breathe. She was dead.

Tony embraced the frail, lifeless form of his mother. He held her for a long time. Then he stood. Darryl put his arm around his father. Tony leaned against his son and began to sob.

58

"I won't have my daughter carrying on with a black man! I just won't have it!" Patricia Roth was on the edge of hysteria. In the past week she who had always appeared so imperturbable was shaken by violent storms of emotion.

A month before, Jenny had visited them. A fight erupted between her and her mother. Patricia said some ugly things about Duane Gurley.

Jenny had rushed from the apartment and returned to school. Since then she had not once contacted them. Mike called her. She was cool toward him.

Jenny's involvement with Duane dominated Mike's existence with his wife. He woke with the problem, left the apartment with it raging, returned at night to fight it, still unresolved.

He stared hard at his own hatred: *This man is not fit for my daughter because of the color of his skin.* The feeling was inside him and he loathed himself for it. He fought it. He vowed: I will not let my life be dictated by anything so inconsequential as gradations of skin color.

And so the argument went on between him and his wife. What had been a thin crack in their relationship widened into a raw, ugly wound. Like a cancer, the relationship began to feed on itself. Bitterness poured out.

"It's because you're Jewish that you're so damn open on this thing," she said.

"Still you married me. You married a Jew!"

"I married you *in spite of* your being a Jew. I married you because you were a man of accomplishment when I met you and I was certain you would accomplish even more."

"And was it such a horrible mistake?"

"You were a champion when I met you. Champions are a special breed. Champions know how to win."

"And they can also be stupid and vicious—"

"They prevail," Patricia said, and in that moment he suddenly felt an intense dislike for her, for her smugness, for the arrogance of the remark.

"By that yardstick, you should have remained with Hub Farrell."

"I think of that. Hub Farrell would have never accepted his daughter carrying on with a black man!"

"What would he have done?"

"He'd have crushed the man," she said in a quiet, even voice. She lit a cigarette and drew on it with angry inhalations. Her face was tight with anger. "This isn't going to work any longer. The gulf is too wide."

"What does that mean?"

"I don't know how to explain it," she said, suddenly apologetic. "I don't know why this should be. We just don't like each other very much anymore. I think we should divorce."

It didn't come as a surprise to him, and he didn't feel bad about it. He left the apartment, got into his car, and drove up the West Side Highway to the Saw Mill River Parkway. It had been snowing out. He sped along, ignoring patches of ice on the roadway; he was only vaguely aware of where he was going.

His marriage was over. He had seen it coming for a long time, and yet now that it had arrived, he was shaken by it. The woman he married had become a stranger to him over the years. Time, the great eroder, wore away their hearts.

It was dark when he reached Bronxville. He phoned Jenny at her dorm.

"Where are you?"

"In Bronxville. Can we have dinner?"

There was a pause. "All right."

They met at a place not far from the college, a restaurant of quiet elegance overlooking the Bronx River and the parkway.

He could still feel the tension lingering in Jenny from her fight with her mother a month earlier. She sat opposite him looking very much like Patricia, erect, taut, very determined.

She had matured. Six months before, at the time of the Harlem riots, she was a teenager. Now she was a woman. She looked at him with a cool, appraising eye: it was Patricia evaluating him. Did he measure up?

"I'm sure you've noticed that there have been increased strains between your mother and me. Your relationship with Duane—"

"Don't shift the blame to me. I won't accept it."

"I'm not trying to shift anything. I'm trying to explain how the complications in your life have accented complications in my own life. No matter what you think, I have never disapproved of your involvement with Duane—"

"You have never *disapproved?* Well, thank you very much."

"I love you, Jen, and I care a great deal for Duane. There are certain things in your mother's background, however, that make it very difficult for her to accept—"

"I don't want to hear this," Jenny said. "This conversation turns my stomach."

"Jen, I'm trying to show you honestly how things are between us—between you, me, your mother. I'm not a perfect human being. Inside I'm often ugly and stupid, and I admit it. But I'm trying."

"Why have you come here?"

"Things have not been going well with your mother and me. We're getting a divorce."

"My relationship with Duane? How does that enter into it?"

"I'd be lying if I said it hadn't any effect. Your mother feels very strongly about you and Duane . . ."

"And you? How do you feel?"

"I told you. I like Duane very much—"

"You're so smug," she said. "Why don't you admit it? You hate the fact that I'm in love with a black man."

"You're being unfair," Mike said. "I've admitted that I'm not free of stupidity and bigotry, but I've fought it in myself—"

"Bravo," Jenny said.

The waiter arrived with their food. Jenny stared at her plate. Suddenly she threw her napkin onto the table and pushed her chair away. She rose. "I can't stand this hypocrisy," she said. "The reason you came here was to show me how heroic you are. You will *accept* my involvement with Duane. You have sacrificed your marriage for it. Well, I am very sorry, but I'm not all that impressed."

She turned quickly and left the restaurant.

Mike sat at the table for a long time, feeling a terrible emptiness, a profound sense of failure. He thought of his life, how far short of his expectations it had fallen. He had done only one thing well: years before, he had been adept at beating men senseless. He had once thought of himself as a hero. He knew now that it had been a sham, all of it.

An attractive woman was sitting alone at a table nearby. She was in her thirties, stylish, intelligent-looking rather than beautiful. She watched Mike and he felt foolish, exposed under her stare. He prepared to leave.

The woman smiled at him

"I'm sorry if we disturbed you."

"Not at all," she said. "The young lady is very theatrical. I like good the-ater. She's too young for you, though."

"She's my daughter," Mike said.

"Ah," the woman said. "I had invented a more interesting involvement. Older man and his young mistress."

Mike laughed uncomfortably. "No. Nothing like that."

"Why don't you join me?" the woman said. "Or am I being too forward?"

"No, no . . ."

"You look so lost, unhappy."

"Relationships with our children can be very difficult."

"My name is Carol Breakstone."

"Mike Roth." He sat at her table. She was having an after-dinner brandy. Mike ordered one also.

"Your daughter is a student at the college?"

"Yes. Are you at the college?"

"I teach in the theater department—stage design."

They talked easily, as though they had known each other a long time. She told him of her past, how she had arrived in New York from Ohio to pur-sue a career as a designer and married a stage director. It didn't work out. "He had a reputation as a genius," she said. "It wasn't until after we were married that I discovered his so-called genius was really just overbearing ar-rogance, an arrogance which concealed an appalling lack of talent. The the-ater world caught on to him at about the same time I did, and he spent most of his days in the unemployment line or hanging out at Cromwell's."

"Cromwell's?"

"The drugstore in Rockefeller Center where out-of-work theater people gather. After the marriage collapsed, a friend who heads the theater depart-ment up here invited me to teach design. Now, what about you?"

He smiled, toyed with his brandy. "Not much to tell. Two bad marriages. Two wives who dislike me. Two children who I'm afraid share that feel-ing."

"You seem likable enough," Carol said.

"I don't think I've been happy with myself, with my life, and that's made other people unhappy."

"What's wrong with your life?"

"I had certain expectations, unreal expectations. I didn't fulfill them. I'm probably damn lucky. I've done much better than I ever should have done. And yet there's this lingering sense of dissatisfaction."

"What is it you do? Your occupation."

He laughed. "Busywork, mostly. You know what busywork is?"

"Sure. When you were a kid and the teacher gave you an assignment to keep you out of trouble."

"That's it. That's my life."

"That's everyone's life, isn't it? We're here for a damned short time, and most people realize that and so they want to keep occupied and make a big deal out of everything they do. No one wants the world to say, 'Hey, Joe Smith—he doesn't count.' So we're all busy-busy. Sitting in our little puddles, stirring things up all the time."

"Yep," Mike said.

"It's human, isn't it?"

He smiled. "Very human."

They finished their brandy. "Can I drive you home?" Mike said.

"I live just around the corner."

"I'll walk you home, then."

"All right."

They left the restaurant and crossed a stone bridge over the river. She lived in a red-brick apartment building a short walk from the river. "I've enjoyed this," Mike said at the entrance to the building. "Talking to you."

"I've enjoyed it, too."

"Do you ever get into Manhattan?"

"Fairly often."

"Perhaps we could get together..."

"Do you like plays?"

He hesitated. "I might feel foolish."

"Why?"

"I'm twice your age."

"I won't tell if you won't."

"All right. I think taking in a play with you would be very nice."

"And dinner," she said.

"And dinner."

Mike returned to Manhattan and checked into the Delmonico Hotel on Park Avenue. The next morning he called his lawyer. "I already know," the lawyer said. "I spoke with Pat. She wants it nice and clean."

"Fine. Work it out however she wants it."

After, he phoned Carol Breakstone. They made plans to meet late Saturday afternoon.

Early Friday he received a call from Duane Gurley asking to see him. They met for lunch at Delmonico's. Duane looked tense. "This isn't easy for me," he said. "This isn't easy at all."

"What?"

"I want to marry Jenny."

A terrible sinking sensation opened inside Mike, the old ugly racial thing. His daughter marrying a black man! In the past, whenever he thought fleetingly about the possibility, he always pushed it out of his consciousness. Now it came down on him hard. He was stunned, but fought to conceal it. "Does she know?"

"Yes. I told her right from the beginning I was serious. I love her, Mike. I love her."

Mike struggled to behave reasonably; inside, he was crumbling. And disgust at his own meanness, his lack of grace, swelled within him.

"I'm nervous about you," Duane said. "And I'm nervous about Jenny. She says she loves me, but I'm afraid it might just be rebelliousness."

They didn't speak for a while. Duane toyed with his lunch. "How do you feel about it?" he asked Mike.

"It isn't easy for me, Duane. It has nothing to do with you. I like you very much. I should feel proud that you want to marry my daughter . . ." He struggled with the words. "But the color thing cuts deep. It's ugly, the way I feel, but it's there."

Mike knew that he had hurt Duane, but he could do nothing else: he had to reveal what was in his heart. "I'm wrong in this ugliness inside me," Mike said. "I hate it. I'm fighting it."

"If *you* feel this way," Duane said, shaken, "what hope is there for any of us?"

"I'm not accepting it. That's where the hope is. You have every right to marry my daughter. Do it. Do it with my blessing. Forgive the ignorance in me. It'll go away. It'll die. And that's the hope." And he took Duane around his shoulders and hugged him.

On Saturday afternoon Carol Breakstone drove down from Bronxville. She and Mike met at the Museum of Modern Art. "I did some detective work," Carol said. "I found out who you are. Boxing champion, television executive, president of a football club . . ."

"Busywork," Mike said.

They strolled through the museum and paused at an exhibit of early-twentieth-century American painters—Kane, Bellows, Hopper—raw, muscular evocations of an earlier era, working folk, prizefighters, scenes of tenements and factories. "I come from there," Mike said. "That's my life."

They were before George Bellows' work—prizefighters thrusting at each other in combat, teeming tenements—and it seemed as though Mike's past was in front of him now. He thought of the days when he would climb to the roof of his building and feed Yiddle November's pigeons and gaze out over the city and sketch the skyline and try to redream the world around him.

He was losing his past, he thought. His youth, his early dreams, were fast receding into shadow.

When they left the museum, it was dark outside. The air was crisp with winter. Flurries of snow fell.

They had dinner at a small French restaurant on Fifty-sixth Street. "I like being with you," said Mike.

"I like being with you." She reached out and took his hand and he was suddenly embarrassed that she was so young and that people were looking at them. Yet at the same time he felt glorious: there was something warm between them, something honest and true.

Carol had made arrangements for them to see a play Off Broadway. It was at a church on Second Avenue on the Lower East Side. A friend of hers had done the stage set. After, they drove through his old neighborhood and Mike pointed out the tenement in which he had been raised. They came to Rutgers Square. The settlement house was still there, but it was dark. There was a sign on the front of the building: CAUTION—KEEP OUT. DEMOLITION SITE.

It was finally coming down, the old settlement house. What would replace it? Mike wondered. The area was filled now with block after block of public housing—gray, prisonlike buildings that were an improvement over the old tenements but in their bleakness could only serve to further wither the spirit.

He thought of the dreams he and Jason Karl had had for the area.

They sat in Carol's car for a while staring at the darkened building. He put his arm around her. Should he try to kiss her? he thought. She was so young. Would she object? Would he make a fool of himself?

And then he was kissing her tenderly, delicately, and he felt his dreams of the past awaken, come alive within him, but it was also his past he held in his arms, and there was a great surge within him of possibility, and he was flooded with eagerness! There were important things for him to do in the world. He was young and strong and ready to do battle once more. He felt something like love, but much more: he felt resurrection.

Over the next several months Mike and Carol spent every weekend together. They visited museums, art galleries, the theater. They went for long walks, talked deep into the night. His feeling for her was not one of great passion, but rather of enormous respect. She was bright and sensitive and possessed a tremendous exuberance, and he felt alive when he was with her and eager to accomplish things.

They did not make love for a long time, and when it happened, it was immensely satisfying, not wildly passionate, but rich with emotion, with honest concern for each other.

He began to sketch again and when spring came they drove out into the country, to upstate New York or Connecticut. They would pack a picnic basket and spread a blanket on the ground and spend their time drawing the trees, rivers, mountains. At other times they sat alongside the East River and sketched the bridges and skylines of the city as Mike had done in his youth. "What do you want out of life?" she asked him one day as they strolled beside the river.

"I want to create something lasting," he said. He struggled to define it for her, to discover it for himself. It was elusive. He knew the need but couldn't give it words. "I feel it inside, but I don't know what it'll be."

"You'll find it."

"Yes," he said, and held her tightly and turned her to him and kissed her.

He would find something to fulfill, to unify his life. It would be something outside of football, of that he was certain. The challenge of the game no longer moved him. He would sell his interest in the team.

And then his life would become ... What? He could not imagine it. He knew, though, that it would be extraordinary.

In June that year Jason Karl suffered a massive cerebral hemorrhage. He lingered for a week, then died.

His funeral was an impressive affair. The mayor was there, the governor of New York, the leaders of the major political parties. Tony McGrath attended, stolid and grave, with his son Darryl at his side.

Laura Karl, beautiful in her grief, magnificent in her dignity, stood beside the coffin without tears, transformed. She had traveled a great, moving distance from the days of her youth and poor-girl aspirations to this time of regal widowhood.

As the rabbi said the final prayer and the coffin was lowered into the earth, Mike thought back on the dreams and commitments he had shared with Jason. Most of them had remained unfulfilled. He owed a debt to the memory of Jason Karl, a debt to his past. And now, as the remains of his dear friend entered the grave, he vowed to repay that debt.

59

It was a muggy day. People suffered in formal clothes, fanned themselves, perspired. Summer flies buzzed the air.

The area where Rutgers Square Settlement House had been was now an empty, rock-strewn lot. The old settlement house had been torn down; a public housing project dedicated to Jason Karl would be erected on the site.

Tony McGrath and his wife were expected at the ground-breaking ceremonies, but Theresa had been drinking heavily again. There was a fight, and Tony went off without her.

A small group of politicians, reporters, and friends was present for the ground-breaking. It was accomplished in a perfunctory way, everyone eager to escape the steaming heat. Mike Roth, accompanied by a young lady, said a few simple words. A photographer pushed Tony toward Mike, and they shook hands while the photographer snapped pictures.

Laura approached Tony. "How have you been?" she said.

"Fine." They had not spoken since Jason's funeral.

"How's Theresa?"

"Not too well."

They stood without talking for a long while. She stared at him, and the old deep feelings moved within him, within both of them.

They stood gazing at each other and they saw the days of their youth in one another. An echo of their love rustled across an immense gulf of years. "I get lonely," Laura said, "and I think of the old times. I think of you. Call me sometime. Please." He didn't answer, and Laura suddenly became embarrassed. "There's my car. Please call me."

Tony stared after her as she crossed to the waiting car.

A swirl of dust stirred in the vacant lot. Memory danced in the rubble of the old settlement house.

He returned home to discover that Theresa had been taken to Payne Whitney again. She was uncontrollable and the doctor had ordered her back into the hospital.

Tony went to the hospital. Theresa was heavily sedated and stared at Tony with drug-glazed eyes, her face a pale mask. "It doesn't help," she said. "Nothing helps." Over and over she said it, as though Tony weren't in the room.

Sean and Sharon took him from the room and they traveled down in the elevator together and neither of his children spoke. He thought: They blame me for their mother's condition.

That night Tony sat up in bed with a start. What was it? He had been dreaming of Theresa. She was crying out to him: Help me, please help me.

He realized the phone was ringing; he had been awakened by it.

Before anyone spoke, he knew what the call was about.

"Your wife, Mr. McGrath. She's dead," the voice at the other end said, and Tony held the phone there and he didn't talk and was barely aware of the man speaking. There had been an overdose of medication. No one was certain how it occurred. It was entirely possible that she herself had . . .

Dead.

After he hung up he sat on the edge of the bed, staring at the phone. He sat there for a long time thinking of his wife, of the simple love she had held for him, of his dereliction toward her.

"What have I done?" he said aloud. "What have I done to all those around me?"

The funeral was a simple affair. Laura Karl was there and accompanied him back to the house and remained after everyone had left. They sat across from each other in the great living room. They didn't talk for a long time.

At last she moved to him. He took her in his arms. He kissed her, a tender kiss of youth.

The sound of their past whispered about them in the quiet air.

60

Mike Roth met with Darryl McGrath in the offices of the Tartar Football Organization at Columbus Circle. "I'm looking to sell my interest in the team," Mike said.

Darryl looked at him, amazed. "Why?"

"I can't tell you now. Quietly, if you can, talk to people about buying me out. I'm going to need a lot of money."

A remarkable idea had been growing within Mike, an idea begun the day he viewed the empty lot where the Rutgers Square Settlement House had been.

He discussed it with no one, not even Carol Breakstone.

He worked at it all his waking hours, spent long stretches in the library, conferred by phone with people all over the state, consulted with architects and engineers. He filled sketchbook after sketchbook with drawings.

He couldn't contain his enthusiasm. He went to bed at night, the details of his plan dancing in his head, and woke after a few hours brimming with energy, eager to get back to work on it.

Nothing in his whole life had ever fired him up like this.

On a late fall weekend he bundled Carol into the car and announced they were taking a small trip. He refused to tell her anything about it, not the reason, nor the destination.

They drove across the Queensboro Bridge to the Long Island Expressway and headed east. They left the expressway and drove through an area of woodland and farms. The countryside was riotous with colors of autumn, golds and reds and oranges.

Turning onto a narrow country lane, they drove alongside a potato farm. The land was flat and desolate. They came to a vacant section of rocky acreage. Mike brought the car to a halt. He got out.

He had several large parcel maps with him and he spread them out on the ground and anchored them with rocks. He began to pace the land, carrying a sketchpad with him. Carol trailed after him. "This is fun," she said without enthusiasm. "Next weekend maybe we can go walking through the Jersey marshes. What are we doing here?"

He didn't answer. He climbed a large rock outcropping, and shielding his eyes from the sun, studied a portion of the land. He made further sketches; then he and Carol returned to the car.

Mike took a blanket out of the trunk and they spread it on a lone grassy patch among the rocks. They had brought a picnic basket with them—wine, cheese, salami. Mike poured out two paper cups of wine and held his cup in a toast. "To this," he said, indicating the surrounding land. "What do you see when you look out there?"

"Rocks. A *lot* of rocks."

"There ... a farm there. Another. That belongs to a hunt club," Mike said, indicating various sections of the acreage.

"Terrific."

"We're at the tag end of more than a dozen parcels, good for just about nothing, unless someone could get all of them."

"All the tag ends?"

"Right. We're between three major expressways, a half-hour from midtown Manhattan. An area ideally suited for ... what?"

"I give up," Carol said.

Mike opened one of the sketchpads. He showed her a series of drawings—precise, detailed renderings of buildings, malls, fields. "A football stadium. Baseball field. Hockey, basketball, prizefight arena. Children's play area. Little League field ..."

"I don't understand."

"I'm going to build it."

"What?"

He held up a sketch of the whole project. The name was lettered at the top of the page: RUTGERS SQUARE. "A recreational complex the like of which no one has ever seen. A sports city."

"It would cost millions!"

"I'm selling my share in the football team. That will give me the seed money, the money for the land. The rest I'll get from private and public sources. I've already purchased options on a half-dozen parcels, about forty percent of the total. It will be the largest sports complex in the world, a combination of Madison Square Garden, Yankee Stadium, and Central Park. It won't just be a place to come and watch a ball game or a boxing match. It will be a place where people can actually participate. It will be one grand, lovely playground for everyone!"

Carol studied the drawings. "It's good, it's really good. It's extraordinary! If you can make it work ..."

"I'll make it work," Mike said.

The land, as it stood, was of little use to anyone, jagged bits of a jigsaw puzzle. Gradually Mike began piecing together the puzzle. Everything had to be accomplished with the utmost secrecy. If word about what he was attempting leaked out and someone grabbed a key section, the whole thing would be undone.

By spring he had bought up most of the necessary parcels. Several were still in negotiation. With the help of Darryl McGrath he sold his holdings in the football team at a substantial profit and invested all the money he had in the world in the project.

One night as he was preparing for bed he received a call from Jenny. "Duane and I drove to Maryland. We're married!"

Duane came on the phone and they laughed together and talked about the past football season and what the future would be and what it was like to be a son-in-law and father-in-law. Mike forced himself to sound happy, but inside he felt a terrible ache of disappointment and he hated himself for it. Then Jenny tried to get the phone away from Duane and Mike could hear the two of them tussling and clowning on the other end of the line. Jenny won out.

"Mother acted like a perfect ass at first, but I think she's beginning to come around. She whined to me, 'Why didn't you let me give you a big wedding?' She wanted to call up the newspapers. 'Duane is a star,' she said. Oh, Dad, I'm so happy!"

"I'm happy, too," Mike said, though it was a lie.

"Are you really happy for me, Dad? Are you?"

"Yes," he said. "Yes ... I really am."

"When are you and Carol going to get married?"

"I'm thinking about it," Mike said.

"Marriage is great, Dad. You really should try it!"

After he hung up, Mike rested back on the bed and thought about his daughter and Duane, his reaction to their marriage, the bitter ache of disappointment he felt. What was he upset about?

It had something to do with the pain he was sure his daughter would experience, the social pressures, the insults, the confusion, the terrible problems that would follow if they had children.

He felt a sense of hopelessness and loss and anger. He was angry at himself for being so narrow, so fearful. He liked and respected Duane Gurley immensely. His daughter could not have chosen a finer man. To have his reaction to their marriage tainted, demeaned by irrational hate and fear, was something that he could not accept in himself.

And now, suddenly, he let go, gave up his wretched, petty concerns, and a feeling of great peace came over him. His disappointment fled, replaced by an intense optimism. The future would be fine. His daughter and her husband would be fine.

He could see his life before him, opening up, blossoming like a wondrous flower.

Laura Karl and Tony McGrath sat on the front porch of his house. It was the end of summer. The weather was cool. The lawn was dark, the moon shielded by clouds. Wind stirred the trees. The heavy-leafed boughs whispered in the tart night air.

He held Laura close to him. "Are you happy?"

She rested her head against his shoulder. "Oh, yes," she said. "I've never been so happy."

They didn't speak for a while. The treetops danced in the wind. "How would you like to marry me?" he said.

"I'd like nothing better."

And so, two weeks later, in Patchogue, Long Island, a justice of the peace married Laura and Tony.

61

Over the years Jack Foster had witnessed an erosion of his power; he could not quite identify how or when it had happened. The men he had once worked for had diversified, had become increasingly more respectable—the ones who remained alive. Of the top men of the old group, only Meyer Lansky still wielded power. Ben Siegel was dead. Lepke, Longy Zwillman, Farvel Kovalick—all dead.

Over the years, more and more, Foster had come to rely on the Italians for his backing; lately they had begun to put distance between them and him.

He still had influence in the Construction Workers Alliance, but it was influence without muscle. The Italians had the real power now. His reputation as a mad-dog killer of the thirties made him faintly ridiculous, an embarrassment.

His wife, a heavyset, overpainted blond who was a prominent call girl when he first met her, treated him with disdain. Their marriage was ornamental. They had no children; they had not slept together in years.

They owned a large home in Fort Lee, New Jersey, and the whole thrust of Foster's life was toward maintaining appearances. He dressed like a banker. He drove a Lincoln Continental. His title with the union was "chief executive officer." He joined as many community organizations as possible.

Over the years he followed the careers of Mike Roth and Tony McGrath obsessively; each mention of their names in the media cut him to his soul. In his view they had arrived. He was still the pariah, the bastard outcast.

He was crazed by the possibility—more and more he had come to believe it—that he was related by blood to both of them. "Don't you see the resemblance?" he would say to his wife when either Mike or Tony appeared on television or in a news photo. "I have Jewish eyes, Mikey's eyes. Tony and I, we have the same mouth."

A contractor had recently informed him of an unusual amount of business activity on Mike's part. He was acquiring land on Long Island. He was planning something big. What?

Foster struggled to discover the reason for Roth's sudden interest in real estate. He could learn nothing. He had taken options on certain parcels of

relatively worthless land. No one knew precisely where the land was, nor
what the purpose in acquiring it was.

He was consumed with a passion to find out what Mike Roth was up to.
He slept poorly. He began to have stomach problems. He had little appetite,
yet he ate too much. He grew sloppy fat.

In the spring of the year an opportunity presented itself.

The Italians called him to a meeting. There were problems in California
with a union fund, an electrical workers' local. Someone had embezzled
money. When the leadership attempted to recover it, the man threatened to
disclose certain mob connections.

He had to be dealt with.

"You take care of it," the Italians said. They were men in their thirties,
slick, bright, arrogant. They were a different breed. Some had been to college. They associated with celebrities, judges, legitimate business people.
They did not *ask* Foster to take care of it: they ordered him.

That was the way they related to him these days. In years past when he
was dealing with their fathers and uncles, he was treated with the deference
due a man who was an intimate of Lansky, Buchalter, Siegel. Now he was
treated like a run-of-the-mill punk. He was ordered to do things.

Foster explained to the Italians that he was no longer involved in that
sort of thing; for decades murder had been out of his realm. They smiled.
He didn't have to personally pull the trigger. He only had the responsibility
to see that it was carried out.

They were bored with his posturing. They wanted performance to justify
the trappings of power he possessed.

He considered their demand and concluded that he would rather wipe
out these men, the men who now treated him so shabbily, than some rene-
gade union thug. The world, however, had changed, and no one was more
aware of it than Jack Foster. He had no muscle to back him up, no mob, no
gunmen. Functioning as a lone wolf, he might blow away two or three of
them, but they would track him down and eventually destroy him.

Deeper, he had ceased to think of himself as a murderer. In his youth he
killed to establish himself; it was an avenue for making his way in the
world. Now, at retirement age, when he preferred to rest on his laurels, he
found himself being shoved out onto the cold bricks again.

He couldn't fight it. He had to maintain his position in the world. In the
structure of his priorities, his wife and her minks, the house overlooking the
Hudson, the vacation home in Miami, his status with the union—all took
precedence over the serious reservations he had about returning to the occupation of journeyman slaughterer.

He promised to do the job and asked for the details. They told him he
must kill Matthew Roth.

He received the news with elation. Roth's son had crossed the line between the good guys and the bad. Upright Michael Roth with a son worthy
of a mob wipe-out!

They were brothers after all. The same twisted strain ran through all of them. Michael, his son, Jack Foster—they all carried the selfsame blackness, evil, in the blood.

He worked quickly and with diligence, made inquiries, fashioned plans. Arriving home, he began to pack. His wife entered the bedroom. "Where are you going?" she said.

"Out of town on business. It's nothing I can talk about. I'll be gone a few weeks."

He had been told Matt Roth was in Vegas, at the Sands Hotel. A gun dealer had provided him with a precision weapon, a German Heckler and Koch 9mm pistol: in normal mode it could be operated as a blowback pistol, in full automatic as a three-round-burst machine gun. He visited a shooting range in Hackensack and practiced with it. It was a long time since he had fired a gun, and it took most of an afternoon before he felt comfortable with it.

The next day he flew to Las Vegas. He arrived at the Sands Hotel but didn't check in. He asked the hotel operator for Matthew Roth's room and was informed there was no one by that name registered.

The Italians had given him a photograph of Matthew, nothing more. He expected it would take several days to locate him, a day more to figure out where and how to kill him. But in one of those sweet strokes of fortune, sweeter yet because it occurred in a gambling house, he walked right into Matthew on his first stroll through the casino.

He was at a center dice table playing for high stakes. He was not winning. Whatever money he had siphoned from the union fund, Foster mused, was fast disappearing down the tubes.

Foster hung around the table and watched. From time to time he made a small bet. He was surprised by his reaction to Matthew Roth. He liked the boy on sight, and that troubled him. It would make his job harder, killing someone he liked.

He reminded him so much of Mikey, a young, blond version of him; Matt reminded Foster of himself. They were related, of course. No matter how people ridiculed the idea, he knew. Mike Roth's father was his own. A thousand men were his father.

You are my twin, Jack Foster thought, gazing at Matthew, and he was moved by the idea.

He left the dice tables and sat at the circular bar above the gambling area and watched. It was almost dawn when Matthew stopped gambling. He walked through the casino to the elevators and Foster followed after him. He entered the elevator just behind him and pushed the button to a floor several levels above the one Matthew had pressed.

They were alone as the elevator moved upward. Foster kept his hand on the Heckler and Koch pistol in the pocket of his gabardine coat. He considered shooting Matthew in the elevator, but decided against it. Too messy, too much risk. No, he must take him out away from a place so public.

At the eighth floor the elevator door opened and Matthew stepped out. Just before the door closed, Foster moved out after him.

The hallway was empty. Foster walked quickly up behind Matthew and pushed the barrel-tip of the pistol into his side. "Be very quiet."

Matthew didn't seem surprised. He looked almost relieved. He had been waiting for his killer to come to him. "Anyone in your room?" Foster asked.

"No. No one."

Matt opened the door to his room and Foster moved in behind him.

The television set was on. Foster shut it off. He motioned for Matt to sit on the bed. "You've done a dumb thing," Foster said, holding the pistol on Matt. "How could you be so dumb?" Matthew shrugged. "When did you last see your father?"

"A couple of years ago."

"Your father is a fine man. You should be very close to him."

"I don't like him."

Jack Foster appeared offended. "Why not?"

"I liked Ben. Did you know Ben?"

"Benny Siegel?"

"Yes."

"I knew him."

"He stayed with me. My father left. I liked Ben."

"Ben was scum," Foster said. "Ben was nothing compared to your father, and you're talking to a man who knows."

"I don't believe that."

Foster shrugged. "We're related, did you know that?"

"What do you mean?"

Jack Foster smiled. "That's a long story." He shifted the gun in his hand. "You know why I've been sent here?"

"Why?" Matt said, but he knew.

"To kill you."

Matt shifted his weight on the bed. He suddenly looked very small. "Please, don't," he said in a pathetic voice. Foster had heard it many times in the past, the pleas, the rationalizations, the groveling. It had never meant anything to him, but that was in the old days when he was a different person. The days when he was a killer.

An idea had been growing inside Foster's head since he had first seen Matthew in the casino, an idea which played back and forth in his mind while he waited to get him alone. Now the idea made perfect sense to him—it was a way of reentering the life of Matthew's father, it was a way for Jack Foster to finally come into his own and get what he deserved in this world. It was a way of asserting brotherhood with Mike Roth. It was a way of saving his son.

"I want to give you a chance," he said, and he was surprised to hear his own words. "If I don't kill you, will you do what I want you to?"

"I'll do anything."

"You'll come back to New York with me. You'll see your father again."
Foster was amazed at his own voice. He would not kill the boy, and it astonished him. "You'll beg your father for a job."

"Yes."

"You'll have to do more." Foster was smiling now. He gloried in the
boldness of his idea. "Your father is involved in an important business deal.
I want to know everything about that deal. If you do what I tell you, everything will be perfect—for both of us. If not, I'll have to kill you."

Matthew stared at Foster for a very long time and did not say a word.

Foster laughed. He exulted in the audacity of what he would be attempting, exulted in the risk he was bringing once more to his life. He would
turn the tables on the Italians; he would capture a piece of Mike Roth's life;
he would save his son. He embraced his own audacity as one embraces a
long-lost lover.

"All right," Matthew said.

"You won't regret it." Foster smiled. "I like you. To me you look like a
good kid."

62

In the offices of the Rutgers Square Development Company on Madison
Avenue Mike Roth, president of the company, was on the phone. "He
wants me to give him a job. It's just so puzzling. Why?" Mike was discussing his son with Carol Breakstone. That morning Matthew had called his
father to say he was in New York and wanted to see him. He wanted to
work for him.

All about Mike architects, engineers, designers worked. The financing for
the sports complex had been obtained along with most of the land. The details of the operation were kept secret. Only Mike and Carol knew them.

"You owe it to him to give him a chance," Carol said.

"He's always resented me. Why is he suddenly coming to me looking for
work?"

"You're his father, Michael. He's gone through a lot. He sounds like he's
at the end of his rope."

"I feel uncomfortable about the whole thing."

"You have to do something for him."

After hanging up, Mike sat at his desk thinking about Carol and his relationship with her. She had become not only his lover but also his closest

friend, collaborator, and partner. He owed much of the success thus far of the Rutgers Square Sports City to her.

She was a miracle in his life.

He thought about his son. Matthew was suddenly entering his life. He remembered their last encounter—the anger, the hate he felt from his son. How could he deal with him now?

His secretary's voice came over the intercom: "Matthew Roth to see you."

A vague apprehension came over Mike as he waited. The door opened and Matthew entered. Momentarily Mike thought there had been some mistake: his son had changed drastically since he had last seen him. He was dressed in a conservative business suit. He had slimmed down, shaved his mustache, and his hair was short. Gone was the punk swagger he had when Mike saw him in Los Angeles. His manner was shy.

They shook hands. Mike wanted to embrace him but couldn't bring himself to do it. Matthew's handshake was without force; the palm of his hand was damp. He didn't look his father in the eye.

He sat opposite Mike. His voice was so soft Mike had to strain to hear him. "I've had a tough time these last couple of years. I've done some very stupid things. I want to apologize for how I behaved when you last visited me."

Mike forced himself to sound enthusiastic. "You don't have to apologize. I'm happy you've come to me."

"I don't expect an important job. Anything, really. I want to prove myself." Mike noticed his son's fingernails; they had been gnawed to the cuticles. "I want to succeed at something, anything."

"We'll start you in the surveying department," Mike said.

"What is it the company does?"

"Land development. Come on. I'll show you around." He led Matthew down the hallway.

"They'll show you the ropes," he said after introducing Matthew to the head of the surveying department. "At the end of the day I'll see you back in my office. You'll have dinner with me and my fiancée. Are you set with money? A place to live?"

"I'm fine. I found a room over on West Fifty-second Street. Nothing fancy, but it's comfortable."

"If you need anything . . ."

"No, no. Everything's fine."

They shook hands and Mike returned to his office. He felt uneasy. There was something unnerving about the boy, some grave lack in him, a softness. He hadn't once looked Mike in the eye.

They dined at Tavern-on-the-Green in Central Park. Matthew's shyness was oppressive, and nothing Mike or Carol did seemed to help.

The conversation went by fits and starts, with Matthew saying little.

"You're in for a really exciting time," Carol said after a long stretch of silence. "Has Mike told you what his plans are?"

"No. Not really."

"Let him get acquainted with the place first," said Mike. "He has plenty of time to find out what we're trying to do."

"I'm really interested. It seems like a big operation."

"Tell him, Mike," urged Carol.

"He'll learn about it soon enough."

"He's very secretive." Carol laughed.

"I can understand that," Matthew said.

Later, as they lay in bed together, Carol said, "He needs you, Mike. You have to bring him into your life. He seems so lost, pathetic . . ."

"There's something wrong. I've never felt so uncomfortable with anybody in my life."

"You have to realize how difficult this is for him. You yourself admitted you're practically strangers. There's been so much anger between the two of you . . ."

"From him. In the past I've tried to reach him."

"Have you really tried that hard? Mike, you have to make an effort with him."

"Yes. You're right," Mike said, not entirely convinced. Something was drastically out of joint in his relationship with his son, but he couldn't identify it. Beneath Matthew's passive manner he sensed a great sinkhole of hostility. Or was it his imagination, an expression of his own resentment?

Over the next months the first phase of the project neared completion. All the parcels of land, save one, had been secured.

Matthew had developed into an admirable worker. He had no life other than his job. Word of his dedication came to Mike from various department heads. He put in impossibly long hours. There seemed to be no aspect of the business that he wasn't interested in.

Two or three times a week Mike took his son to dinner with Carol. Matthew was invariably polite, yet it was an effort to spend time with him. He didn't speak easily and he had a disconcerting habit of never looking his father in the eye.

"I'm proud of you," Mike said to him one evening as they were having dinner at Manny Wolfe's on Third Avenue. "I get reports. You're doing a first-rate job."

"It's very exciting work. I only wish I knew more about what was going on."

"You have no idea?"

"Only bits and pieces. It has to do with land acquisition. Sports."

"We'll be building a sports complex."

"More than a sports complex," said Carol. "There'll be shops, park areas, restaurants, theaters . . ."

"It sounds wonderful," Matthew said. "Where will it be?"

"We still have one more parcel to acquire."

"Mike, tell him. He's been working so hard."

Mike didn't want to talk about it. He didn't trust the boy. "The Beth-page section? The one you're working on?"

"Yes?"

"That's it."

Matthew nodded his head and smiled. "You're missing a parcel, though. The Donnelly land."

"You've really been keeping tabs on this," said Mike.

"It's my job."

"The Donnelly parcel is the key element. Without it, nothing works. That's why I haven't wanted to talk about it. Obviously, Matt, you mustn't say anything about this to anyone."

"Of course not."

"Very soon we'll own that parcel. We're on the verge of closing the deal now."

"That's marvelous!" Matthew said. He appeared genuinely excited. He's truly happy for me, Mike thought. He wants me to succeed.

Why, then, did Mike continue to feel uneasy?

The Italians were upset with Jack Foster. He had committed to do a job and had not followed through. "The boy is really sorry," he explained to them. "He promises he'll repay every cent."

That wasn't good enough, the Italians said. Matthew Roth had made threats in the past. He knew too much about certain people. He was a knife blade at their throats. He must be taken care of. "Do it now," they said to Foster with great emphasis.

Afterward Foster brooded. He was so close. Matthew promised that the information he needed would be forthcoming. Soon. Very soon. Once he had it, Foster would be in a position to dictate terms to Mike Roth. He would make himself a partner. They would be equals. He deserved to have what Mike Roth had. He was a brother. He would demand it. He would have it. Equality.

Then he would eliminate Matthew and satisfy the Italians.

He visited Matthew at his rented room in a tenement west of Ninth Avenue. "What do you have for me?" he said.

"The key." Matthew spread out a map on the bed. "They'll be building here in Bethpage. They need this." He pointed to a rectangle on the map.

"Donnelly?" Foster said.

"Yes."

"That's good. That's very good. I know the man. Our union has worked projects with him. What's Mike offering?"

"A million and a half."

"Generous. That land's worthless."

"It's in the center," Matthew said. "Nothing can happen without it."

"Yes." Foster was smiling. "This is all good. We can do business with Mr. Donnelly. Yes. This is very good." He stood. "I think we can pull it off. Your father and I are going to be partners on this one. And after, you know what I have planned for you? You'll be my man in the driver's seat! Your father will eat crow out of your hand. You have my marker on it."

"What about that other problem?"

"The money you took? The people you tried to shake down? It's under control. You're a very lucky boy. I love your father. I'd do anything for his son. The best thing that ever happened to you was meeting up with Jack Foster."

63

"I thought we had worked this all out in principle."

"Other elements have entered the picture, Mike. It's not as simple as I first thought."

Mike Roth and Bob Donnelly were having lunch at Voisin Restaurant on Park Avenue. Candles glowed on the surrounding tables. Red-jacketed waiters fussed. The captain prepared an elaborate dish over a flaming brazier.

Donnelly, a large man with bushy eyebrows and florid face, concentrated on his food. He was indifferent to Mike's problem. They had worked out a deal, and now it had fallen through.

"If it's a matter of price," Mike said, "I'm sure we can arrive at something that's satisfactory."

"It's not price. The land has recently become attractive to people to whom I have certain obligations."

"Who?"

"I'm not at liberty to say."

How had the land suddenly become attractive? Who had discovered its importance? How had they found out about it? Or was this only a bargaining ploy Donnelly was adopting?

"And if I substantially raise my offer?"

"There are other considerations. Someone else is interested. They're putting pressure on me. They're in a position to do so."

"Bob, I have to get that piece of land!"

Donnelly shrugged, went back to his crab salad. He wasn't bargaining.

Mike's mind raced. What could he do? It served no purpose to show his desperation. And yet, if he couldn't convince Donnelly to sell, all that he had worked on, all that he had invested, would be lost. He would be wiped out.

They finished their lunch. A waiter brought coffee. "How is Tony McGrath these days?" Donnelly said after a while.

"From what I hear, fine."

"His wife died and he's remarried?"

"Yes."

"Strange, how he just retreated from everything," Donnelly said. "You never fought him that third time. I'm sure you get this question wherever you go, but why? Why didn't you fight him? Were you afraid of him?"

"No, no. It wasn't that. There were other considerations."

"God, I respect that man. I was just a kid when you two fought, but being Irish and all, he was my hero. It was a devastating thing to me when you beat him."

"Is it McGrath who's after the land?"

Donnelly broke into a broad smile. "Heavens, no," he said. "No, not at all." He lit a cigar, puffed on it thoughtfully.

"When are you supposed to close the deal with these other people?"

"They're drawing up the papers now."

"Do me a favor. Don't close it until I get back to you."

"I don't see what good that would do."

"Please."

Donnelly studied the hairs on the back of his hand. He tapped the ash off his cigar. "I'll give you forty-eight hours. I don't understand the purpose, though. Nothing will change."

Mike Roth returned to his office, and the full weight of his predicament came down on him: his world was collapsing. He would lose everything.

Someone had discovered the essential element in the deal and had made a move to take it over, and the plan would succeed. Whoever it was had the clout. He had forty-eight hours to prevent it.

He paced his office, trying to force his mind to come to terms with his predicament. Who had learned of Donnelly's land?

Forty-eight hours. In that time he must find out who his rival was and neutralize his offer. Donnelly had held out no hope. It had become *attractive to people to whom he had certain obligations.* What obligations?

He spent the afternoon in a storm of activity. He contacted everyone he knew, trying to gain information about Donnelly's affairs, trying to discover who was working against him. He learned nothing of value.

By the end of the day he was drained, desperate. Where could he turn? He tried to phone Darryl McGrath in Washington but was unable to reach him.

He left the office, stopping by the cubicle where his son worked. Matthew was sitting by the window, staring out. "Do you want to have dinner with us tonight?" Mike asked.

"No. I have some work to do," Matthew said. Mike sat in a chair by the window. "What's the matter?"

"I received some bad news today. The project's not going to work out. Somebody got to Donnelly."

Matthew stared at his father with an impassive look. "Who?"

"I don't know. Someone with a lot of influence with Donnelly. You've done a good job, Matt. I'm very proud of you. It's a shame we won't complete this thing."

"Isn't there anything you can do?"

"I have forty-eight hours. I've been trying to scare up help wherever I can. The hell of it is, I don't even know who or what I'm up against." He walked to the door. "I just don't know what I'm going to do now."

Matthew stared at him as though to offer help, reassurance, but no words came. He smiled a strange, tense smile, then turned back to the window.

Later that evening Darryl McGrath returned Mike's call. Mike told him what had occurred with Donnelly. "Is it possible your father or your uncles are involved?"

"I doubt it. But let me see what I can find out."

A half-hour later he called back. "They don't know anything about it. More—they can't imagine anyone having that sort of power over Donnelly. Donnelly's not exactly a shrinking violet. How much time do you have?"

"Till Wednesday morning—to find out who I'm up against, get to them, and somehow stop them."

"I don't know how I can help you, but I'll try."

Mike didn't sleep that night. He sat in the living room. It started to rain and he watched the shadow play of raindrops on the window streak the wall and stream down in dark skeletal rivulets.

In the morning he phoned his ex-wife, Patricia. It was a difficult call for him to make, but he had no choice. He told her what had happened and asked for her help. She offered to find out what she could about Hub Farrell.

After lunch she called back to tell him that she had spoken to Farrell and nothing in what he said led her to believe he knew anything about Mike's plans.

They spoke about Jenny and Duane and there was a lightness in Pat's voice that hadn't been there for a long time. He realized that now that they were no longer married they could relate to one another as friends again. "I hope it all works out, Mike. I really do. You deserve the best." Then she said, "What do you think went wrong between us?"

"You wanted a heavyweight champion of the world, and that was long behind me."

"Yes," she said. "Yes."

In midafternoon, desperately weary, he collapsed on the couch in his office and closed his eyes. He tried to think. What could he do? He had exhausted every lead. His mind seemed incapable of putting together the simplest idea. He was at the end.

He was aware of someone standing over him. He looked up. It was Matthew.

Matthew moved away and sat in a chair opposite the couch. Something was troubling him. He tried to speak, but no words came out. He cleared his throat, ran his tongue over his lips. "When I was a kid . . . why did you never visit me?" he said at last. His voice was very soft.

"Your mother wouldn't permit it."

"You could have forced her."

"I tried. I really tried."

"She never talked about you. She wouldn't keep any pictures of you around the house. I used to go to the library and read about you in old boxing books and newspapers."

"I wanted to bring you to New York," Mike said. "Your mother fought me on it. There was nothing I could do."

"You weren't there. You were never there." Matthew's face had grown very pale; his lips trembled. "I used to dream about you. I used to invent stories about you to tell my friends. I acted out all your fights for them as if I had seen them. They wouldn't believe me. They would beat me up. I couldn't fight. I couldn't fight because no one had taught me how."

Mike Roth wanted to say something but couldn't find the words.

"You weren't there. Ben Siegel came to us. And he held me. I loved Ben Siegel. He was there."

Why is he telling me this? Mike Roth wondered. What does he expect of me now?

"Do you love me?" Matthew asked.

A queasiness spread within Mike Roth. Over the years he had barely known his son. Matthew had come to him as a grown man, a stranger really, and he still didn't know him. He stared at the tall blond man in front of him and struggled to feel love for him. He felt nothing. "Of course I love you, Matt," he said, filled with shame.

"I don't think so. I don't think you love anybody."

"If you've come here to attack me, Matthew, this isn't the time—"

"When is the time? When do you have time for anything or anyone other than yourself?" Matthew was trembling now, and his eyes were bright with rage.

"Matthew, please . . ."

"I have to know whether or not you love me!"

Mike Roth didn't speak for a very long time. Finally he said, "You've earned my respect."

"I don't want your respect," Matt said. "I don't deserve your respect. I want your love." He was staring at Mike, his face twisted with agony. He began to sob. "I was the one," he said. "I betrayed you. I gave the information to Jack Foster."

64

The sun was setting behind the Manhattan skyline as Darryl McGrath and Mike Roth hurried from the airline terminal to Mike's car and drove east, heading out to Long Island.

"How much time do you have?"

"I spoke to Donnelly earlier. He's closing the deal at noon."

Headlights of freeway cars swooped in on them, flared through the windshield, swept on by in a blur. "Why, after all these years, have you never made up with him?" Darryl asked. They were talking of his father, whom they were driving out to see. Mike, in a last desperate attempt, was looking to Tony McGrath for help.

"Things were never *finished* between us," Mike said. "I can't explain it, but we each knew it. Something had been set in motion and it was never completed."

"I don't know whether he'll do anything for you," Darryl said. "He only told me he would talk with you."

They left behind the jumble of apartment houses, suburban tract homes, and shopping malls of Queens and headed for the North Shore of Long Island. Soon they drove through the gates to Tony McGrath's estate, moved along the curved drive to the stately colonial house. Two people stood in darkness on the porch; it wasn't until Mike was at the top of the steps that he recognized Tony and Laura. The dim light momentarily washed away the years and they looked miraculously youthful, handsome. As they led him into the living room, the past fled and he saw them as they truly were. They had aged, of course, but well. Tony was bulky, his hair white, the skin of his face ruddy and lined. Laura, too, was gray now, but still lovely; her eyes were youthful, her skin smooth. There was a softness in her manner, a sweetness, and Mike Roth could tell she was happy.

Tony offered Mike a chair then seated himself on the couch next to Laura. She held his hand. His narrow blue eyes rested on Mike, and Mike recognized a glint of something hard and unforgiving in them.

"I don't like coming to you like this," Mike said.

Tony held up his hand to quiet him. It was large, thick-boned, and Mike recalled the devastating power it had once possessed. "I know."

"I don't know how much Darryl told you . . ."

"He told me enough."

"Everything I have in the world is in this development, and Jack Foster will take it away in a few hours."

"Why do you feel I can help you?"

"Donnelly worships you. Foster has a hold on him, but he worships you. I think he would sell to you if you approached him."

"That would make us partners."

"Yes."

Tony didn't speak for a time. His gaze was turned inward. He is thinking of the past, of his sister, of our fights, Mike knew. He is thinking I owe him something. And suddenly he regretted coming here. It could never work between them.

"You owed me a last fight," said Tony. "I lost. You owed me a chance to win."

"I didn't come out of those fights feeling I had won anything. We both lost. All these years I have felt that."

"It was never resolved. You could have resolved it."

"I couldn't. Because of what you said, what you did. You know all this. I didn't come here to dig it up again. I came here prepared to beg for your help. Now I can't do it."

"You have a sick pride," Tony said softly.

"And you? What about you?"

Tony formed a tent with his hands at his lips. He sat that way, lost in thought. "I will contact Donnelly," he said. "I will get the parcel. You and I will be partners in this development you've worked so hard to put together." He looked directly at Mike. "But I'm not doing it for you. I'm not doing it because I have forgiven you or because I feel I owe you anything. I owe you *nothing*. I am doing it because I will not permit Jack Foster to win over you. I will not permit that. Not him. That's why I'm doing it."

He rose and left the room without speaking another word to Mike.

Laura came forward and held Mike's hand and stared into his eyes. "There's no one else as important to him in this world as you," she said. "That's his tragedy. That's the tragedy of you both."

"Why haven't you done what you were supposed to do?" the leader of the Italians said to Jack Foster in a quiet, cultivated voice. He was a handsome man in his thirties, impeccably groomed.

A deal had been consummated between Tony McGrath and Donnelly. Jack Foster had been frozen out.

"I will do it," Foster said.

"Don't make us turn it over to someone else. If you can't do this for us, you can do nothing for us. And if you can do nothing for us, there's no reason for you to exist."

In the past Jack Foster would have become angry, but he was beyond anger now. He had tried to elevate himself and failed. Now he would do what he had to do. "I'll take care of the boy."

He picked up Matthew at his rooming house and drove through the Lincoln Tunnel into New Jersey. He drove until he reached a broad, desolate stretch of wasteland. It was night. The area was deserted.

Matthew sat next to him, slumped in his seat. His face was ashen, but he didn't look afraid. He stared out at the night with a resigned look.

Foster pulled the car to a stop. They were on a flat marshy plain. Tall swamp grass and cat-o'-nine-tails waved in the damp breeze. "I don't want to do this," Foster said. The Heckler and Koch 9mm pistol was in his hand now; he reached under the seat and brought up the gun's twelve-inch shoulder stock and attached it; he activated the toggle lever which shunted the pistol to automatic. He displayed it to Matthew as though it were an object of general interest. "Nice piece," he said. "You see, you have a blowback pistol, then, with the stock in place here, you flick this switch and now it's a machine gun."

Matthew nodded his head.

"Why did you tell him?" Foster asked.

"I love him."

"I love him too. And I love you. You're my brother, you're my son. We're all relatives. Your father, Tony McGrath, you, me—we're all part of one great pool of blood. Don't you see that?" He pressed the pistol against the center of Matthew's chest. Matthew looked unconcerned. He stared out at the marshland. "Why aren't you afraid?" Foster said.

Matthew didn't answer.

Jack Foster's hand was shaking, which had never in his life happened before. He tried to steady the gun stock against his shoulder, using his left hand to prop the gun up.

He could not pull the trigger.

"Get out!" Foster yelled. Matthew stared at him. "Get out!"

Matthew opened the door and stepped onto the spongy earth. The night smelled of the sea, of oil, of decay. "Walk!" Foster screamed.

Matthew moved slowly through the reeds. His shoes sank into the muck of the swamp and he could feel the cold ooze on his ankles. Mosquitoes swarmed about his face. He pushed through the reeds, the cat-o'-nine-tails.

Foster leveled the machine pistol on Matthew Roth's back, but he could not pull the trigger. I am lost, he said to himself.

For three days Foster didn't sleep. He drove on the freeways of Brooklyn, Long Island, New Jersey. He called his home, then the union headquarters. He learned that people were looking for him, watching his house. He could tell by the tenseness in the voices of those he talked to that they knew he was now a marked man.

Where could he go? Europe? South America? The young Italians were remorseless. They would track him to the ends of the earth.

He was lost.

Night and day blended together; it was all one. He drove the grim streets as though in a bad dream.

Toward evening of the third day after he had failed to kill Matthew, he traveled to the Lower East Side. He walked the Bowery. So many years had gone by since he had last been there. He looked at the streets in wonder.

It was a wasteland of rotting tenements, wholesale appliance stores, pawn shops, flophouses. Winos sprawled on the sidewalks, huddled in doorways.

Where were the elevated trains, the dime-a-dance joints, the music halls?

He carried with him an address someone had given him many years before, a tenement near Fifth Street. The address had remained in his wallet all this time, a magical talisman, a key to his past.

He parked his car in front of the tenement and walked up four flights. The stairway stank of rotting garbage, cat urine. He knocked at a door.

Someone peered out through the peephole in the door. The door opened and he stepped into a half-dark room.

A red candle burned before a crucifix on the wall. By its flickering light he made out a woman standing in the center of the room. She was gray, withered. "Jackie, it's you," she said, her voice like thick sand, moist, gritty. "Yes."

"It's you." The woman stared at him and her eyes were wide and lustrous, eyes of death, eyes of emptiness.

"I was thinking of some people," he said. "Yiddle November and Little Augie and Johnny Eggs."

"Ah, the old ones. The good old ones. I knew them all. Fine, fine men. I knew them by the thousands. They always had a good word for me. They were gentlemen. And how have you been, Jackie, little Jackie?"

"I've missed you, Mother."

"Oh, Jack, I've missed you too. I sit by the window and stare out at the street looking for you. Come to bed, Jackie. Come to bed."

She led him through the kitchen into a rear room. There was a single bed in the corner. He took her in his arms and they lay together on the mattress.

In the morning Foster arose. He had a great deal of money in his coat-pocket, thick stacks of bills, thousands and thousands of dollars.

His mother slept, a wraith, thin, fleshless: she seemed no more than the pattern on the sheet, an imprint there without form or substance.

He placed the money on the bed next to her and left. He spent the day wandering the Lower East Side. At evening those who worked for the young Italians found him. They drove him to the Jersey marshes and in the very spot where Matthew Roth had stumbled through the reeds they plunged ice picks and daggers into him, garroted him, shot his eyes out. One of the killers pinned a note to his shirt: "Let's talk of graves, of worms, and epitaphs. Nothing can we call our own but death."

Yes, the killers were educated these days. No lessons could Jack Foster teach them.

65

On the opening day of the Rutgers Square Sports City, Tony McGrath and Mike Roth arrived early.

They walked together through acres of parkland, tennis courts, swimming pools, stadiums. Grass, concrete, glass, ponds, trees, filled the landscape. Where once there had been rocks and weeds, clusters of buildings now stood—apartment houses, a hotel, theaters, a shopping mall.

The area was quiet now. In a short while people would arrive, friends and loved ones, the press, television, politicians.

Tony had not wanted to appear on this opening day. He didn't want to sit on the podium with Mike. He had not worked to save the project for Mike, but to thwart Jack Foster. He had no wish to have anything more to do with Mike, with his sports complex. Darryl and Laura had pleaded with him, and grudgingly he consented to show up for the opening ceremonies.

Mike called him that morning and suggested they meet early and talk. McGrath, who had never once visited the complex while it was under construction, agreed to meet him there.

They walked in silence through the grounds, and the tension between the two men was great.

They came to the boxing-arena building. They moved down a long hallway and through a door onto the main floor of the arena. The place was dark save for the glow of the red exit lights. Mike opened a panel box and threw a switch.

The boxing ring at the center of the arena was suddenly bathed in white light.

They walked down the aisle and climbed into the ring. They stood at the edge of the apron and gazed out at the empty arena. Row upon row of upholstered seats spread upward from the ring.

The two men paced the ring without talking. Dressed in formal clothes, they moved over the canvas gracefully, elegantly, men who, though in their seventh decade, still maintained a sense of youthful athleticism.

Tony turned and faced Mike. "You owed me another fight," he said quietly.

"No. You tried to kill me."

"You were responsible for my sister's death."

They stood facing each other now from opposite ends of the ring.

"You tried to blind me," Mike said.

"You owed me a chance!" Tony shouted, and the accumulated rage of years was enormous. "I could have beaten you. You owed me a chance!"

"I owed you nothing. You called me kike. You tried to kill me."

"You had no right to do what you did to my sister."

"I loved your sister. I did nothing to her."

"You owed me that fight!'

"You tried to kill me!"

They stood opposite each other, shouting across the expanse of the ring, their voices echoing through the empty arena, across the expanse of years. Because you did this, I did that. You did this, so . . .

McGrath trembled with anger. He ripped off his jacket. He stood in the center of the ring, perspiring. His breath came in short gasps. "Come on," he said. "We have to do this." Mike didn't move. "Fight me!" McGrath screamed.

Mike took off his jacket and laid it over the top strand of the ring rope.

The two men began to circle each other. The arena was quiet save for the sound of their breathing and the scrape of their shoe soles across the canvas.

Tony threw a punch. Mike blocked it, danced back. Tony rushed forward and the two men began to chop at each other in short, hard hits. They stood toe to toe smashing at each other.

And now the years melted away. They were twenty-five again, fighting for the heavyweight championship of the world, slamming at each other, punching away with all their strength, the anger of years. They leaned against the ropes and grabbed at each other, lashed out, slipped as their shoes failed to hold, gasped for breath, tore in on one another.

They held back nothing, dug away in ferocious assault. Great welts formed on their faces; their knuckles were raw and bloody; they continued to hit at each other.

They clinched and wrestled along the ropes and then they slipped and fell to the canvas and rolled over, tearing at each other with bare hands. They continued to punch and claw on the floor of the boxing ring.

Mike tried to rise, but Tony pulled him down and they clutched at each other's throats, trying to get a hold there. Neither had the strength and at last they relaxed and lay in each other's arms, gasping for breath.

They could fight no more. Their clothes were torn, their faces smeared with blood. They could not talk.

And now people began to arrive for the ceremony: Mike's family—Carol, Jenny, Matthew, Duane. Tony's—Laura, Darryl, Sean, and Sharon.

Slowly the two men rose. Struggling for air, they stood in the center of the ring, bloody, embarrassed.

They looked out at the people coming down the aisle, and held on to each other, fighting for breath, taking in deep, sweet gasps of air.

The place was filling up. People streamed into the hall. And now they began to applaud. The applause grew, resounded through the arena.

And the two men embraced. They held tightly to each other as the applause grew louder.

"We can rest now," Tony said. "After all this time."

"Yes. We can rest now."

And though the arena rang with applause, there was silence, peace, in the ring where the two men stood.